EMANCIPATING JAMES

by

JOAN VASSAR

PROLOGUE

Upper Canada
April 1861

THE MORNING SUN climbed through the window, illuminating the gaudy room. A purple settee sat to the right and next to it a matching high-back chair. James opened his eyes slowly, trying to get his bearings. He had a banging headache, the effects of too much drink. As he looked to the mirrored ceiling, two women lay sleeping on either side of him. Studying his reflection, he did not recognize himself. It wasn't the scar that ran from the right side of his mouth to his ear that left him unable to reconcile himself with the image above. It was the anger, made prevalent by an emotional ache that would not subside. Even submerging his pain in the softness of a woman did no good, and so he suffered in silence.

As he slid from the bed, the women readjusted, hugging each other in his absence. Turning his back on them, he quietly dressed in black britches, a white shirt, and black boots. James then reached into his pocket and counted out the coin to pay for services rendered. He stepped from the room into the dim hall and headed toward his horse tethered on the side of Miss Cherry's House of Comfort. James had come alone, with no one to watch his back. He had become reckless in his approach to life. While he cared about his family, he did not care if he lived or died.

Mounting his horse, he nudged the beast forward—his destination Fort Independence. The early morning sun was bright in his eyes as he moved onto the path headed for home. A breeze blew, and the sound of leaves moving on the wind was the backdrop to an uneventful morning. His horse fell into a slow trot, and James let him have his head…until he spooked. The animal sidestepped, and James' hand went instinctively to his gun. A lone rider appeared on the path in front of him, and with the sun in his eyes, visibility was zero. Something shiny caught his attention, and without hesitation James pulled his gun from the holster, letting off two shots. The rider dropped from his saddle, and his horse trotted off.

James scanned the area—there appeared to be no one else about. Swinging down from his horse, he slowly approached the body as it lay crumpled on the ground. His victim, who lay face down, appeared small of frame. Next to the body lay a canteen with a metal spout. "Shit," James hissed under his breath.

He flipped the body slowly, and the man's hat fell off, revealing one thick braid with a faded pink ribbon on the end; it was a woman–a woman he knew. James' heart began pounding in his ears as he frantically tried to assess her wounds. "Fannie! Fannie! Can you hear me?"

Fannie opened her eyes and whimpered weakly, but did not speak. James tore her shirt open and saw the clean-through wound in her shoulder. It was the second wound—a gut wound—that concerned him. She was bleeding profusely. When he applied pressure, she moaned. Her eyes crossed, and she passed out.

"Fannie, baby, stay with me! *Please*, Fannie, stay with me!" James pleaded.

❋ ❋ ❋

Back at the fort, James' horse appeared with no rider. Elbert was standing in the barracks and Black was seated in his study when the first alarm sounded. At the second alarm, Sunday appeared in the doorway of the kitchen as Black headed for the front door. Before stepping onto the porch, he turned to his wife and said, "Get the shotgun from our bedroom and lock up."

Sunday nodded, and handed the baby to Big Mama, moving to do as her husband instructed. As Black stepped onto the porch, the eighteen gathered at the bottom of the steps—minus James. Elbert broke the silence.

"James' horse came home without a rider."

No other words were spoken. Black descended the steps, and the men headed for the stables. When they were mounted up, Black and Elbert took the lead as the posse exited the gate. The men fanned out and began their search, starting at Miss Cherry's House of Comfort. They rode hard toward the pussy parlor—their intent was to back into the problem. They would recreate James' steps to get a handle on the matter. When they turned onto the path, a lone figure appeared ahead of them.

Black, Elbert, Tim, and Simon moved forward with caution as their men covered them. James looked up when Black and Elbert came into view. He was covered in blood.

"I thought I saw a gun. I cain't move my hands, she bleeding so bad." James' voice was distraught.

The men were so relieved that James wasn't hurt, it took a moment for Black and Elbert to register what he was saying. Shultz swung down from his horse and began issuing orders.

"Frank! Lou! Bring the wagon, and hurry!"

The doctor knelt beside James to get a closer look at Fannie and from what he could see, it did not look good. Lifting her eyelids, he checked her pupils; they were not responding to light.

James looked to him for help, and Shultz reassuringly said, "Keep holding the wound. The men will be back soon, and we can move her to the fort."

Elbert whispered to Black, "It's the woman from the Mickerson plantation."

After some time, Frank and Lou came rattling down the path in the wagon. Black, Elbert, Simon, and Tim, following the doctor's instruction, helped move James and the woman onto a stretcher. And though James' arms were tired, he continued to apply pressure to the wound. The men lifted them, sliding the stretcher into the back of the wagon. When they were settled, Elbert, Black, and Shultz climbed onto the wagon with James. Elbert and Black watched his back, and the doctor talked him through, to keep him calm. Black made eye contact with Shultz, and the doctor shook his head. When the wagon lurched forward, Fannie moaned involuntarily.

❀ ❀ ❀

Fort Independence

James stared down at Fannie. How had she come to be on the path? He watched as Shultz and Black worked on her. The doctor cleaned the stomach wound and then covered it. She was still unresponsive, and James caught the look that passed between Black and Shultz. Elbert brought water and promptly exited onto the porch of the cabin where Shultz saw his patients. When Fannie was settled, Black turned to James, offering him the painful truth.

"It don't look good—most men don't survive this type of injury."

"I'm afraid Black is right," Shultz said.

James knew Black was right. It was why he always aimed for the stomach. He nodded because he could not speak. His emotions threatened to unman him, so he remained quiet. He stared past Black to Fannie's small form as she lay on the bed. He was afraid. Black, sensing his need for a moment of privacy said, "Me and Shultz will be outside."

Again, James nodded as he watched them exit the cabin. He stood alone in the center of the room and took in his surroundings. To the left of the door in front of the window was a brown desk with a matching chair. At the back of the cabin, two wooden chairs sat against the far wall to the left of the fireplace. A cupboard with all types of medical supplies, behind glass double doors stood next to the fireplace, and in the middle of the room sat a small round table. On the opposite side of the cabin were two cots like the ones from the barracks. Moving one of the chairs next to the bed where Fannie lay, James sat with his head down as he held her hand.

About an hour had passed when Shultz stepped through the doorway, followed by a woman from the fort.

"I have sent the men home," Shultz said. "This here is Miss Abigail. She will help me tend the young miss. We need to try to keep down infection. Why don't you go clean yourself up? We will call you if anything changes."

James did not acknowledge the woman, but to Shultz, he said, "No."

The doctor nodded; he would not argue. He understood James' plight. James stepped back so Shultz could examine Fannie. Touching her forehead, her skin was hot. It was as he feared—fever had set in. Turning to Abigail, Shultz said, "I am going to clean the wound again, and then I will need you to bathe her skin with a cool cloth. Let's hope we can break the fever."

A large black pot hung over the fireplace. Abigail transferred water from the pot to a basin. She retrieved a cloth from the cupboard and helped the doctor get set up. James hovered in the background, anxious and concerned. Abigail looked at him. "The doctor has extra shirts. Go clean up so you will be ready to help me when the doctor finishes."

James was about to refuse when she said, "Ya wanna help fight sickness too, don't ya?" He just stared at her, and Abigail took advantage of his quietness. "Go 'round back to the pump. I'll brang a towel and clean shirt to ya."

James nodded and headed for the door. Shultz sighed. When he heard the cabin door close behind him, he said, "Thank you, Miss Abby. I'm going to need you more for him than her."

Abby reached out and tenderly touched the doctor's shoulder. She gathered a towel and a clean shirt for James, before heading around back. Pausing on the porch for a moment, she soaked in the bright sun as it sat high in the sky. It was just after noon, and though the day was beautiful, she was sad. She thought of the young woman lying in the bed and then of how ungrateful she had been of late. At thirty-seven, Abby had no man and no children. Oh, there was a time when she had wanted those things, but now... It was life as a slave that turned her from thoughts of having a family. And then there was the obvious—she was too old. Since she had been at the fort, one or two men had shown interest in her, but she had not reciprocated. After all she had been through, she just wasn't ready. Now, seeing the life drain from the young woman made her acutely aware of her failures as a woman.

Shaking off her melancholy, Abby stepped from the porch and headed around to the back of the cabin. When she came around the corner she stopped short. A shirtless James was leaning over, holding on to the edge of the trough by the pump. He was crying.

Unsure of how to proceed, she moved back against the house and stood still, allowing him the privacy he needed. She remained motionless for a time, and when she thought he was ready, she made a little more noise to warn him of her approach. Abby could hear the scraping sound of the pump as he worked it. When he turned to look at her, her heart squeezed, for his pain was tangible.

Still, she was not ready for an exchange with him—his masculinity was overpowering.

James stood before her, wet. She handed him the towel, and he looked away, attempting to hide his pain. Abby tried for casual conversation. "I'll take the shirt ya had on and burn it. Leave it on the fence to dry. I'll be back for it."

James stopped drying his face and hair, giving her his full attention. Unable to stop herself, she took inventory of him. He kept his jet-black hair cut close. Still, it was curly when wet. His eyes, red from crying, were otherwise a piercing green and shaded by long lashes. He had high cheekbones, a pointy nose, and full lips. The right side of his face was badly scarred, yet it seemed to enhance him. He was clean-shaven with a thick neck, broad shoulders, and a small amount of hair on his well-defined chest. His stomach was carved into eight bricks with a light dust of black hair that traveled down into his trousers. Abby had never known a man could be so beautiful. When she looked up into his face, she became dizzy with embarrassment.

"Thank you," he said, responding to her direction about the soiled shirt. He took the clean white shirt from her and put it on. Leaving the shirt unbuttoned, he rolled up the sleeves and looked away. Moments passed as Abby watched him wrestle with his hurt. She reached out and touched his arm, hoping to offer him what little comfort she could, given the circumstances.

James stared over her head. His voice was deep and rusty to the female ear—his speech broken when he said, "I shot her."

Dr. Shultz had told her he didn't think the young woman would make it, but for James' sake, she hoped the doctor was wrong. She knew the hurt of being unable to forgive one's self. Some hurts, Abby knew, didn't go away. She chose her words with compassion.

"Come help wit' her care. Let's stick to what we can do."

James threw the wet towel over the fence and followed Abby

back to the cabin. He hung in the background as Shultz asked her for fresh water. The doctor nodded at something she said, and Abigail turned to him. "Come sit wit' her."

Shultz stepped to the side, allowing James to sit. Abby brought fresh water and a cloth. She whispered to James, "We have to try and break the fever. Bathe her skin wit' the cool water."

James didn't speak; he was thankful for something to do. Fannie lay still as death, and she appeared even younger than he remembered. He regretted not forcing her to come with him, but he had gotten hurt himself, and life had become unmanageable. He submerged the cloth and wrung it out. When he applied the cool compress, he felt the blazing heat from her skin. Staring down at her beautiful face, he pleaded silently for her not to die.

Fannie was very dark of skin with chiseled cheekbones and full lips. Her hair, though matted, was braided in one thick braid, and he reached out to touch the faded ribbon on the end. She was naked save for a sheet that modestly covered her, leaving only her shoulders bare. He bathed her neck and shoulders along with her face, but it did no good. Fannie remained hot, and his worry mounted.

As the day pressed on and night fell, the three managed a routine. Shultz checked, cleaned, and re-bandaged the wound while James and Abigail sat with Fannie, bathing her. James emptied the bucket, bringing fresh water when needed, giving himself a chance to breathe while at the pump. When the hour grew late, the doctor suggested that Abby go home and get some rest. She was about to refuse when Shultz said, "After you have rested, the two of us will rest. We can offer 'round-the-clock care if we sleep in shifts."

Abby nodded, and Shultz stood to walk her to her cabin, but James said, "I will take Miss Abigail home."

The doctor gave him a thoughtful look. "Surely. It will give you a chance to stretch."

Grabbing her shawl from a hook on the wall, Abigail stood to the side as James opened the door. Once on the porch, he allowed her to lead the way. They walked in silence, each in their own thoughts, the night air and regret enveloping them. Taking the path behind the doctor's place, they walked for a time until they came upon a small, dark cabin. Abigail stepped up on the porch. "I'm fine. Go on back. I will come at first light."

James gave her a quick nod and, without a word, turned and left. He walked with purpose back to Shultz' makeshift hospital. When he rounded the side of the cabin, Black and Elbert were waiting for him. Black broke the silence. "How you holding up?"

It was dark out, and with the half-moon it was the same as no light. But the men did everything at night. This much-needed conversation would be no different. James' sadness was visible even in the dark. "Shultz sent the girl that helps him home. He don't expect Fannie to make it through the night. When he thinks someone got a chance, he locks down the house to fight infection. He ain't doin' that, so I know what's comin'."

Elbert had never heard James so emotional, and he felt sorrow for his brother. Still, he was at a loss as to what to say. Black continued, "We will be back in the morning."

The silence stretched out between them, and James' voice was thick when he said, "Just us three—no one else."

"Yeah, Elbert and I will take care of the rest," Black answered.

James climbed the two steps and entered the cabin. When the door closed, Black said, "I will get with Paul."

"I'll get the shovels and meet you in the cemetery," Elbert replied.

❊ ❊ ❊

Inside the cabin, Shultz moved to the side so James could sit. James reached for Fannie's hand—the fever had not subsided. Her breathing had become labored, and it was terrible to watch. He put his head down, looking away as tears spilled down his face. Behind him, he heard the door creak on its hinges and then shut with a click. He continued to cry, so great was the pain.

They sat for hours—him, his pain, and Fannie, as they waited on the inevitable. James leaned in and kissed her softly on the lips. "I'm sorry. I am so sorry I hurt you, honey," he whispered.

The small cabin was dimly lit from the one lantern that sat in the middle of the table. James marked the passage of time by the first rays of light seeping through the window. He was vigilant, staying with Fannie every step of the way as she made it to the new day. He heard wagon wheels stop in front of the cabin, and he knew his brothers had come to see about him. James turned his attention away from the door, refocusing on Fannie. As if on cue, she breathed in sharply, exhaling roughly. It was that simple, and life for her was done. James was out of his head with grief, and he was sure he would wake from this awful nightmare. But no relief came, and his sadness paralyzed him.

Behind him, he heard the door open as the hinges squeaked. He knew it was Shultz. "She's gone."

"Black and Elbert are outside. Give me a moment," Shultz replied.

Leaning in, James kissed Fannie one last time, then stood and headed for the door. When he stepped onto the porch into the sunlight, he saw Elbert leaning against the side of the wagon. Black sat on the wagon bed next to a pine box. James didn't speak as he walked to the edge of the top step and gazed out past the wagon. They stood quietly for a moment, until James stepped from the porch to help Black and Elbert bring the pine box into the cabin.

The doctor had swaddled Fannie in a white sheet, leaving only her lovely face showing. The men stood in the background, allowing him a moment. Abruptly, James reached down, lifting her, and turning back for the coffin, he placed Fannie gently inside.

Black came forward, nailing the box shut, and the sound of the hammer signified finality. The three of them carried her out to the wagon. Elbert drove while Black sat shotgun. James sat in the back with his hand on the coffin, and the people of Fort Independence stood about as the wagon rode by on its way to the cemetery.

1

Upper Canada
April 1861

IT WAS A dreary day as Black, Elbert, and James stood at the back door of the barracks. Both the front and back doors were open to allow a cross breeze. Outside, the rain fell in a steady downpour. Elbert broke the silence, directing his words to James. "How do you suppose she found you?"

James stared out at the rain, trying to reel in his feelings. "I wish I knew. I wanted her, but I ain't make no promises. I was already off course in the first place–noticing her in the middle of the plan. It was in my head to go back for her, but the Hunter plantation was first on my list."

Black chimed in. "I sent several messages, we will have the answer soon enough."

"Wit' or witout the answer, I need to retrace our steps in the South. Ain't no other way that I can see," James returned.

"We all have to go back," Black said.

"I cain't ask the men to go back. They just gettin' settled.

Morgan ain't even had her baby. It wouldn't be right to ask that of Simon," James responded.

Elbert's tone was calm. "We ride out together—not apart. Black blames himself for Otis' death, but we all have fault. The lesson here is to watch each other's back. I made things worse by riding off alone, causing all this shit. You will not go alone."

Still standing at the back door, the three had transitioned to an intimate circle. They were all dressed in black with their sleeves rolled up, guns holstered at their upper left sides. The tension was tangible, for they all had the same worry—keeping the women and children safe. James folded his arms over his chest and regarded Elbert before conceding. "We ride out together."

Black felt the strain ease at James' words. "Simon will remain and run the fort. When we get word, we will know how to proceed. In the meantime, we will tighten security here by locking the place down."

James nodded, but offered nothing else. There were so many unanswered questions, yet when he tried to think through a scenario, Fannie's face appeared before him. Sadly, the only image he could conjure up was one of her in the throes of death. Five days had passed since they buried her, and he had not slept. His thoughts were the loudest at night, and his heartache was comparable to no other pain he had ever felt.

"Little Otis is asking for you. You could come to dinner, so he can see you." Elbert said.

James looked up at the mention of little Otis. "I will be there for dinner. If it's all right wit' you, I will stay at Black's for a few days with the boy. Mama and Sunday will help me."

"Anna will be happy to have you," Elbert replied.

The barracks had begun a shift change, and the men turned their attention to security. Black did not return to his study. Instead, he remained at the barracks, instructing Philip, Simon, Elbert and Tim on how they would move forward in light of recent events. The men had moved down the center aisle coming to stand between the neatly made beds that lined the walls. Outside, the rain turned to a light drizzle and then stopped. James made his way to the back door and stepped out to be alone.

In close proximity to the barracks were three large brown buildings and a corral. The structures were set up for easy access, giving way to a military life. The bathhouse was to the left of the barracks and on the right, were the stables with an attached corral. Next to the stables was the mess hall, a place that also doubled as a laundry. A huge oak tree stood between the mess hall and the bathhouse, completing the circle. As James stood behind the barracks, he could hear the men interacting with one another from all directions. But he was removed; life it appeared had gone on without Fannie–without him.

❧ ❧ ❧

It was nearly dusk when dinner was over, and James stepped onto the porch of Elbert's cabin. In the background, he listened to his son's laughter as Anna got him ready to leave for Black's house. Elbert came out to stand with him, and together they waited for the carriage. The rain had started again, accompanied by thunder. It was James who broke the silence as both men stared off in the distance.

"I hates closin' my eyes. I sees the whole damn thing over and over."

"Yeah," Elbert responded.

A carriage turned onto the path and moved toward them. The driver wore a black slicker and a large brim hat. When the carriage drew closer, the driver, Anthony yelled, "Hold on!"

Elbert opened the cabin door. "Hurry, the carriage is here," he said to his wife and little Otis.

Anthony hopped down with an umbrella and bounded up onto the porch. "Evenin' James–Elbert."

"Anthony," both men responded.

Just then the door swung open and little Otis announced, "I ready, Papa."

James smiled as Otis turned to Elbert and said, "Up, Mama."

When Elbert picked him up, the boy hugged him and kissed his cheek. Anthony coughed, then smiled, but said nothing about Elbert being called mama. Otis quickly wiggled down from Elbert's arms. "Hi, Mista Anfaney."

"How is you, little one?" Anthony asked, before raising his umbrella and taking Otis by the hand.

James was about to follow when Elbert spoke for his ears only. "I would walk through fire with you and for you. We will see to this matter together."

James turned and, without a word, shook Elbert's hand, then headed for the carriage. Once inside, Otis climbed into his lap and they were off. In just a few minutes, the carriage came to a stop in front of Black's house. Anthony opened the door while holding the umbrella. He covered James and little Otis until they were on the porch, and shook James' hand before heading for the stables. Otis pushed at the door, and when it opened, he went racing down the hall yelling, "Big Ma-ma!"

As James stood in the foyer, he could hear the women speaking in the kitchen. At the sight of Otis, the women *oooed* and *ahh-hed*. Otis, being the ham he was, strutted about until Big Mama offered him some cake. James sighed before moving down the hall toward the kitchen and polite conversation. He expected to see the regulars seated at the table. Big Mama, Iris, Sunday and Miss Cora sat with a woman he did not recognize. He smiled before greeting the room at large.

The women responded with smiles and an undertone of concern. It was the woman he did not know that took him by surprise. "Good evenin', Mista James. I came to look in on ya."

He narrowed his eyes and stared at her. He did not recognize her, but her voice, he remembered. Still, he couldn't place from where he would have heard her speak. The window curtain was pulled back and the last rays of light were fading, yet coupled with the lanterns, the kitchen was well lit. James assessed her while begging his memory to produce something. She was dark of skin, and her complexion appeared as though she had lain in the sun all day. The woman had large brown eyes, a button nose and full lips, though her top lip was fatter than her bottom. Her hair was braided in two large cornrows to the back of her head. She wore a gray, short-sleeved dress with a decorative white lace collar. He did not know her.

Big Mama took mercy on him. "It's a good surprise to see Miss Abigail this evenin'."

James stared at the woman. In his mind's eye, he could see her standing next to Shultz, discussing Fannie. It was all coming back to him. "Evenin', Miss Abigail."

Abby sensed James' discomfort, and she was suddenly sorry she came. She was about to make her escape when Black stepped into the kitchen, holding his beautiful baby daughter. She was a little chocolate doll, wearing a yellow dress with a yellow ribbon on the end of her tiny plait. The baby was happy to see little Otis; she squealed and wiggled with delight in Black's arms. Smiling at the women seated around the table, Black set his daughter down on her feet. Slowly, Natalie stepped toward Otis, and he hugged her.

"Good to see you, Miss Abigail," Black said.

"Mista Black," she returned.

Sunday, alleviating the awkwardness of the moment, said, "Can y'all help me get the chilren ready for bed?"

The women stood and began moving down the hall toward the bedrooms. Though no one asked Black for his help, he followed the women anyway. When the kitchen was cleared out, Abby and

James continued to stare at each other. Pushing back in her seat, Abigail stood.

"I came to see 'bout ya. I ain't mean to meddle."

James leaned against the double sink. He had not shaved, and his scar was more prevalent since no hair grew on the damaged flesh. His hair, though cut very close, was beginning to curl on top. Abigail looked in his eyes and saw a weariness that seemed to come from his very soul. She knew that feeling—it was why she had come. Now, she felt forward in seeking him out. Stepping from behind the table, she was about to head for the front door. James found his manners, and his voice was thick with emotion. "Feels like time ain't moving. I'm stuck in the moment she drawed her last breath. Feels like I stopped breathing too, but I'm still here."

Abigail understood his plight and responded with the painful truth. "It ain't gonna never go away, but you will get where you can manage–if you allow yoself. You stuck cause it's still fresh."

James nodded.

Abigail stepped closer to him. "I have found it's a lot harder to forgive yoself than it is to forgive others."

Her words hit the mark, causing his emotions to get the better of him. Tears ran down his face and he turned away. He wiped his eyes with his sleeves and asked, "How can I ever forgive myself?"

"The way to forgiveness is slow—it cain't be rushed. I reckon it has to be the goal. If it ain't, ya livin' in hell."

James stared out the kitchen window. Abby knew it was his attempt to regain control of the situation. He cleared his throat, yet when he spoke, his voice was rusty. "Looks like the rain stopped. I'll walk ya to yo' cabin."

She was about to protest. Abby did not want to inconvenience him, but when he looked back at her, his eyes stopped her words. She nodded.

"Please allow me to tell Sunday and Mama I'm stepping out. They has my son."

Again, she nodded, and James crossed the kitchen and disappeared down the hall. Abigail moved to stand in front of the sink; she was looking out the window when she heard footsteps. She looked up just as Black stepped into the kitchen. He smiled as he went to retrieve the pink blanket hanging over the back of one of the chairs. Black had always been a large, intimidating man. He was well over six feet, bald and very dark of skin. Yet, in contrast to his threatening appearance, he had been nothing but kind to her. She smiled back at him, and for a moment they were transported back in time. It had been five years since Black and his men had appeared in the dark woods of North Carolina. She had been quietly hysterical–her husband had been killed. With Black's help, she had pushed on to freedom.

Black, sensing her thoughts, asked, "How you been, Miss Abby?"

"I been good, Mista Black. I cain't complain."

James re-entered the kitchen and stood quietly behind Black. Turning his attention to James, Black said, "I'll be in my study." He looked back at Abigail. "I'm glad to hear all is well with you. Good evening to you."

"Same to you, Mista Black."

"After you," James said, and they headed down the hall to the front door. Their way was lit by a lantern that sat on top of a small, but elegant table in the middle of the hall. Beautiful pictures lined the opposite wall, depicting the difficult lives of colored folk. Yet, each canvas offered a type of dignity that was visible to the observer. At the door, Abigail stepped to the side and James pulled the door open. She reached for her brown-colored shawl hanging on a peg; James reached into the small bin for an umbrella, and when they stepped outside, the weather had cleared. Out in front of them hung a quarter moon; the evening breeze was pleasant to the skin.

They moved down the steps and onto the path leading to Abby's house. The balmy weather and silence enveloped them as they made their way. Three paths back and to the left for a half mile brought them to her door. It was so dark, they moved by memory rather than sight. Abigail stepped inside, lighting a lantern, and when she returned his back was to her. He stood with one shoulder leaned against the post at the top of the stairs—still as a statue.

Abby left the door cracked, allowing the light from the cabin to spill into the space between them. He seemed to suddenly remember her presence and spoke abruptly. "I can't help but think this happened to right a wrong done by me elsewhere."

"Ahhh. You usin' difficult thinkin' to figure a plain matter."

He turned to face her, the scarred side of his face illuminated–the other side in the shadows. The lighting and vicious scar lent to his intimidating appearance. He stood for a moment and even in this setting, she could see that he had focused in on her. Abby worried that she had been too forward. She had been told a time or two that she needed to watch her mouth. It had done her no good—she hadn't comprehended the advice.

His tone was sharp. "What is plain about this matter?"

"You shot her, but you ain't know it was her. Any other thought ain't workin' toward forgiving yoself."

He shifted, moving directly into the light and making his whole face visible. There was pain and anger in his voice. "You a woman–you ain't done nothin' bad enough that you cain't forgive yoself."

"I don't think regret is measured by whether ya got a stick and stones," she shot back, looking him straight in the eyes.

Being with Otis somehow lightened James' emotional load. Still, the pain lingered in the background. Over the next few days, James divided his time between the barracks and Black's house. He worked during the day, and at night, he spent time with his son. In the mornings, he delayed going to the barracks, so he could have breakfast with Big Mama and Otis. Black would join them, making Otis feel that much more special. They would laugh because, though Otis was speaking a bunch, every other word he said wasn't decipherable. "What did he say?" Black would ask James.

James would shrug his shoulders. "Damn if I know."

"Stop cussing in front a the child. He say he done eatin'," Big Mama translated.

"Thop cussin," Otis repeated before babbling something about the baby.

Sliding from his chair, the boy took off running down the hall to find Sunday and the baby. Black laughed. "Why you don't know what yo' child is saying?"

James shook his head and smiled. "The worse is Elbert understands him."

Big Mama sat to the table in a peach day dress, with her gray hair pulled back into one French braid. Black and James came forward and kissed her before moving into their day. Both men were smiling and enjoying family. Times like this made all they went through as men worth it. As James headed to the barracks, he realized he could not make it without his family. It was not lost on him that they might be better off without him. These were feelings he could not shake. If not for Otis, he might have chosen a different remedy for his situation.

Elbert and James left the barracks after a hard day's work and headed to Black's house. Both men were tired and hungry as they moved up the path. It was hand-off day–the day Elbert would take Otis home with him. As they approached, they could see Black standing on the porch. His stance appeared tense, causing them to pick up the pace.

When Elbert and James entered the study, Black was seated with one hip on the edge of his desk, his arms folded over his chest.

"Did you get word about Fannie?" James asked.

"There is no word about Fannie. It appears war has broken out in South Carolina; Fort Sumter has been taken by the South. Frederick's letter says the slave states want to separate from the Union," Black answered.

"Fannie ain't the only reason I have to go back. I exposed us and ya both know it. Otis ain't got no mama because of my actions." James' voice was tight with pain and anger.

"The boy don't have a mama because of the colored overseer. But he got us now, and we will see him through," Elbert spoke up.

"I called a meeting with the eighteen in the morning. We will meet in the barracks at ten," Black said.

The men stood in silence for a time before James said, "I done caused the death of two women. I can't undo my actions. The whole matter makes me feel like a dog chasing his tail. When you both had issues to deal with–it was another man's face ya saw. You were both clear on your enemy, but when I look for my enemy, it be me I see."

"No one blames you for attempting to stop the molestation of a colored woman and her child. Everything we do here is in defense of our women and children. If you are not clear on the enemy, we are," Black answered with affirmation.

"We will go back," Elbert said. "How Fannie got here is not relevant now. You need to set grief aside to see this matter through. Emotion has no place here–if we're to come home in one piece."

James' face turned red, and Black thought he would jump on Elbert. Instead, he turned abruptly and walked over to the window. "Damn you, Elbert! Surely *you* can understand my position."

"We do understand. Me not tending my emotions is what got Otis killed," Black offered truthfully, revealing his own hurt and regret.

"Tilly killed Otis," James replied.

"Yes," Black argued, "because I was not there to tell him not to part with his gun–even Otis did not manage emotions well. It's how Tilly got the better of him. We will not proceed like men who can't learn from past mistakes."

Relentlessly, Elbert pushed him, "Take a woman and let this one go."

James lunged for Elbert, but Black stepped in his way. James' eyes locked with Black's; his fists clenched at his sides. After a moment of palpable tension, James stepped aside and headed for the door.

❉ ❉ ❉

When the door slammed in James' wake, Black turned to Elbert and admonished, "He is going to kill us both if you don't stop."

Elbert smiled. "He needs to hear the truth–we can't ride out with him like this. If something happens, we need to know he can handle himself for his sake and ours. 'Sides, he wouldn't kill me— I'm his son's mama."

Black stared at Elbert for a moment before throwing back his head, laughing.

❉ ❉ ❉

James stormed out of the house past the women and children. He needed to be alone, and he knew just the place. Once inside the cemetery, he headed for Fannie's grave. It still had no marker, but he knew where he had left her last. His agitation was so great, he was drowning in his emotions. Off in the distance a large storm cloud loomed, turning the world prematurely dark. It began to rain as he stood at Fannie's resting place, thinking, hurting, and wishing for peace within his person. Night fell, before discomfort took hold of him.

He was soaked to the bone when he finally turned to leave the graveyard. He wandered aimlessly. The rain continued to fall in a steady downpour. Elbert had been right. He didn't even have enough sense to come in out of the rain.

James walked for half an hour before he found himself at her front door. He stepped up on the porch and stood under the narrow shelter of the roof's overhang. He did not knock on the door. Instead, he wallowed in pity for himself and Fannie. And when he could no longer think about her, he turned his mind to little Otis' mama. He could still see her holding onto the boy, and then she was dead. He was so filled with sorrow that his anger at being shot himself did not prevail.

James knew he could not let Jeremiah live. A colored man with no sense of self was a hindrance to himself and his kind. He sighed. Black had been right as well—he needed to get his shit together, so that he could manage life. As it stood, life was managing him. James ached to his core, but he had his son—and Jeremiah to think about.

❊ ❊ ❊

Abigail heard footsteps on the porch; she stood and put on her wrap. She had to remind herself that she was safe at Fort Independence. Abby retold herself that no one would come and take what she did not offer. As she placed her hand on the knob, she thought of her husband. Pushing back the painful memory, she twisted the knob and pulled the door open. A gust of wind took her breath away, and she let out an involuntary squeak. James, who had been standing with his back to the door, turned to face her.

"Mista James?" She blinked with surprise. "You all right? Come in for ya catch yo' death."

James remained motionless, and Abby stepped into the cold air, took him by the hand and pulled him into the cabin. She pushed the door closed and locked it.

"Come over by the fire."

James approached the fireplace with reluctance.

"Let me help you," she said.

Abby disappeared behind a curtain at the back of the cabin and returned with a folded sheet. Stoking the fire first, she looked over her shoulder. "Take those clothes off. I'll hang them by the fire; you can cover with the sheet."

Abby went behind the curtain again, and when she returned, James had stripped naked and placed his gun on the table. Wrapping the sheet about his waist, he accepted the towel she handed him. He dried his face and hair, but he still seemed out of it. Stepping to the cupboard, she poured him a glass of whiskey.

"Ya hungry?"

"No."

"Come sit." She pointed to a chair by the fire.

He threw back the whiskey before he sat down. Abby sorted his clothes, hanging his shirt and pants on a chair to dry. Moving another chair from the table, she hung his long underwear and socks. When she completed the task, she turned her attention to him. James sat before the fire, elbows on his knees, cradling his head in his hands.

"Sorry, I woke you," he whispered.

"I wasn't 'sleep."

He nodded, but continued staring at the fire. The light danced off his bright skin in hues of orange and gold. His dark hair and eyebrows outlined his features. He was clean-shaven, though his hair was a little long on top. He looked at her, his voice breaking. "I don't know what to do."

She decided to push him no further. Reaching out her hand to him, she offered a quiet comfort. He need not speak or explain himself—she was offering him emotional sanctuary. When he reached for her hand, she could feel his desperation. He stood with the sheet still about his waist and followed her just beyond the curtain.

In the back room was a large bed with a colorful quilt. A lantern lit the small space from the nightstand to the left of the bed. To the right of the bed was a window with matching brown curtains–like the ones dividing the front of the house from the back. Farther to the right was a dresser with three large drawers and next to it a chamber pot. In the deep left corner of the room was a large tin tub with a yellow cloth draped over the side.

"Come lay down. Don't think on nothin'; 'llow yoself to rest."

At her words, exhaustion kicked in and he found he needed sleep. She released his hand and pulled back the cover for him to get in. James became panicked that she would leave him, so he said, "After you."

Abby looked at him, hesitating for a moment before removing her wrap, revealing her powder blue shift. When she was settled on the left side of the bed, James let the sheet fall from his waist and climbed in next to her. Abby had not expected his open nakedness and closed her eyes against the embarrassment. When he got comfortable, he pulled her close. She breathed in sharply at the contact. She had not slept with a man since Harold died.

"I needed this," James whispered.

At his words, Abby relaxed and snuggled close to him. James' body shut down, and he fell immediately to sleep. Until that very moment, Abby had not realized how much she had missed this type of intimacy. She had been prepared to wither away into old age, alone. But now….

✿ ✿ ✿

James' inner clock woke him, and he guessed it to be about

four-thirty am. He felt the warmth of her body next to his, still he was disoriented. He stared around the room and then down at her, before reconciling the last few hours. He closed his eyes again, listening to the sounds about him–peace. Abby began to stir. James knew the exact moment she opened her eyes, though his own eyes were closed. He could feel that she too was disoriented.

She began to shake in his arms, and he asked, "You want me step out and give you a moment."

"Yes," she whispered.

Pulling back the cover, he stood and headed for the curtain. He did not bother with the sheet as he moved through the front part of the house. He opened the front door and stepped out into the morning chill. The earth was wet beneath his feet as he found a tree on the side of the house and relieved himself. Though the rain had stopped, he suspected there would be more to come judging by the smell in the air. He stood for a moment, allowing the cool air to caress his hot skin. He turned back for the house, stepped in a puddle and cursed.

Back inside, he stoked the hot embers of the dying fire before drying himself with the towel she had given him. He looked around the room. It was simple in its functionality. A table with two chairs sat to the right of the fireplace. Two more chairs sat in front of the fire, with his clothing draped over them. Across the room was a small, cast iron potbelly stove and next to it, the cupboard. A lantern on the table was turned down low and he reached for it, snuffing out the wick completely.

The front room was cast in complete darkness, save for the light that peeked through the curtain at the back of the cabin. He approached the curtain and pushed it aside. Abby was reaching for her wrap that lay at the foot of the bed.

James was not ready to end the peace he was feeling. It had been a week of no sleep, with pain as a constant. His voice was rusty, heavy and anxious. "My clothes ain't dry."

"So ya *checked* to see if yo' clothes was dry?"

"No," he admitted.

❊ ❊ ❊

Abby looked away from his nakedness, unsure where to put her eyes. Still, she had the full image of him burned into her memory. His arms and chest were well defined; the muscles in his stomach appeared carved from stone. Between his powerful thighs and nestled in curly black hair–hung his maleness. And though he was relaxed, she was sure, he was unusually large. Yes, it had been a long time since she had encountered such intimacy, and she had never come across such masculinity. Abby reached for the lantern, casting the back room into darkness.

There was silence before she felt the bed dip under his weight. After he got comfortable, he reached for her and pulled her close. She didn't resist him, and when they were snuggled close, he was again pulled into a deep sleep. Abby, who had not slept well in years, followed suit and for both, their rest was dreamless.

❊ ❊ ❊

Later that morning, Abby awoke to birds chirping. James did not stir. She eased herself from the bed and went to her chest. After retrieving a change of clothing, she headed for the front room. She cleaned herself in the basin by the fire, though she was nervous to remove her clothing for fear he would wake and see her. Once dressed, she moved as quietly as possible about her day. She cooked breakfast, ironed his clothes, and began folding towels for the doctor's office.

Several hours passed before she peeked through the curtain. James lay on his back, emitting a faint snore. The clock on the wall read half past eleven when there came a knock on her door. She opened it to find Black and Elbert, with looks of concern on their faces, standing on her porch. The chill had lessened in the air. Both men were dressed in black with their sleeves rolled up.

Black spoke first. "Miss Abby, sorry to bother you. We were supposed to meet with James, but he never showed. As you know, things have been tough for him lately. We were hoping you may have seen him. The men at the gate say he never left the fort. We been looking for him for the last hour."

"Mista James came late last night. He is sleeping and ain't stirred since he laid down. Would you like me to wake him?"

Black and Elbert let out mutual sighs of relief.

"No, don't wake him," Black told her.

Abby nodded. The three of them stood quietly for a time before Black said, "Tell him to come to me when he wakes."

"I sure will, Mista Black," Abby replied before closing the door.

Elbert and Black headed back to the chores that awaited them. Once they had traveled down the path some ways, Elbert spoke up.

"Miss Abby is a fine-looking woman… real fine."

"Yeah," Black responded.

It was after midday when James finally woke. She wasn't in bed with him. He sat up and looked around the room. There was a pitcher with a matching yellow basin on the nightstand. His neatly folded clothes were on a chair near the opposite wall. He swung his legs over the side of the bed and stood. He poured water from the pitcher into the basin, washed his face and wiped his body down before putting on his long underwear and trousers. He drew back the curtain and looked about—Abby was gone.

On the table sat a plate of food covered with a green checkered cloth. Next to the plate was a folded piece of paper. James picked it up and unfolded it.

Mr. James

I have gone to help Dr. Shultz. I won't be back til after dark. Please eat something and rest as long as you need. Mr. Black came by while you was resting. He wants to see you.

Abigail

James was disappointed. He sighed before returning to the bedroom. Donning his shirt and boots, he made for the front door. Stepping out into the dreary afternoon, he shut the door softly behind himself. Though it wasn't raining, the day was dark, cloudy, and wet. He walked back three paths, taking the long way to Black's house. James was evading the conversation that was sure to come.

He arrived at the house far too quickly for his taste and wanting to avoid the inevitable, he paused for some time before he went inside. As he stared off in the distance, his thoughts wandered to Fannie and his failures as a man. Entering the hall, he could hear the women moving about and laughing. When he appeared in the doorway of the kitchen, Iris looked up from the wooden bowl of potatoes she was peeling. Mama, who was at the stove stirring a pot, also turned to stare at him.

"Ya hungry, baby?" Mama asked.

"No, Mama. I ain't hungry." He offered her a reassuring smile.

Mama wiped her hands on her yellow apron and moved forward, hugging him. And though Iris was watching, he allowed himself to be loved on by his mama. When she stepped back, he smiled down at her, allowing her a small glimpse of his pain before shutting himself off again. He cleared his throat. "Imma go talk wit' Black."

Mama gave him a sympathetic nod as he turned to go back down the hall.

James continued on to Black's office, and the door was open. Stepping into the study, he found Black seated behind his desk, reading over some paperwork. His brother looked up but did not smile. When he placed the paperwork on the desk, James noticed his niece sleeping in Black's right arm. She was dressed in an orange outfit with a white blanket haphazardly wrapped about her.

"Miss Abby told me you wanted to see me."

Black leaned back in his chair and stared at James. The little girl stirred but did not open her eyes. When he finally spoke, his words were clear and measured. "Every man has borders and just beyond those borders is a man's patience. In this house live my wife, daughter and our mother. Your child lives here as well, and they will not be troubled because you grapple with your emotions. In this house, your brothers will speak freely and honestly with you. You will control your anger, or it will be managed for you."

James stared at Black. The picture of him seated, holding the baby, warred with the image of the gun holstered to his upper left side, along with the unmistakable threat being issued. He folded his arms over his chest and regarded Black carefully. "I meant no disrespect to the family. I mean no disrespect to you, Black. It will not happen again."

Black stared at him, continuing in silence to further hammer home his displeasure. Finally, he said, "You missed the meeting."

James cleared his throat before admitting, "I ain't been resting. My body shut down, and I was forced to sleep."

Black nodded. "I will not call another meeting. You need time—I have been there."

James walked over to the window and though his anger was dissipating, he still felt choked by it. He jammed his hands in his pocket, as he got up the nerve to ask Black, "From where did you get Miss Abby?"

Black paused a moment before he answered. "About five years ago, the men and I were riding through North Carolina. We found a colored man hanging from a tree. When we cut him down to bury him, we found his woman hiding in the brush. We brought her to the fort, and Miss Abby has been here ever since. She was heavy with child–the baby didn't make it. I think the husband told her to stay quiet to save her and the child. I'm sure she saw it all. Shultz was the first and only friend she made before you. The men have attempted to get know her. I'm sure at least two of the men want more from her."

James didn't know what to say, so he turned back to window. He had hoped for a different story.

Black continued. "Miss Abby has always been kind."

James' voice was thick with hurt. "I wanted Fannie so damn bad. I regret leavin' her. I has little Otis to think of, and I ain't got the patience or the hand it takes for a younger woman."

Shit, Black understood, and he did something he rarely did; he opened up. "I have dealt on both ends of the spectrum. Coupling with an older woman can be healing when a man feels broken."

A lump formed in James' throat. When he spoke, his voice was hoarse. "I'll be at the barracks. You ain't got to worry—I'll make it right wit' Elbert."

Black nodded, and James walked out.

❃ ❃ ❃

As James headed to the barracks, he didn't miss that Black never gave the names of the men interested in Abby. Though he attempted to shut off the ache, his brain was saturated by his grief and inadequacies. He did have one new thought-provoking feeling–curiosity. He wanted to know more about Miss Abby, and most importantly, he wanted to know which men of Fort Independence wanted more from her. Yet, his remorse about Fannie brought him to an emotional, grinding halt.

2

The Hunter Plantation
Horry, South Carolina
April 1861

E.J. STOOD WHEN the door to his study opened and in stepped Jeremiah. Both men were exhausted from the business of overseeing the reconstruction of the plantation. It had been slow going as they had no real workforce. Many of the male slaves had escaped, leaving behind the elderly and the sick. They did not have the resources to track the slaves who had run, and now with the war, the task of tracking one's property was made impossible.

"There are too many similarities to the uprising that took place on the Turner plantation," E.J. said.

Walking over to the window, Jeremiah looked out at the burned cabins and the half-scorched fields. He sighed. "I shot one in the face, and when he fell... they regrouped with no issue. We couldn't get a count; they were too organized for a band of runaways."

"So, you killed one?"

"When we arrived from the neighboring plantation with

assistance, we gathered the dead. I saw no unfamiliar faces. If their man died, they did not leave him behind. This speaks to their ability—I ain't seen the like." Jeremiah answered.

"You sound worried. Do you want to pursue this angle or not? We still have the issue of war, which is happening regardless of our plight." E.J.'s annoyance was evident.

Jeremiah turned from the window and glared at his brother. "So, you blame me for this occurrence?"

"This is not an issue of blame–this is wartime. We must spend funds we don't have to replace the workforce. The real issue is, I may not be on hand. Eventually, I will be required to enlist."

Jeremiah studied E.J.'s body language. Edward Jr. was six feet tall, thin, yet physically fit; his white skin was paler than usual. He had a full head of black hair, large, dark eyes, with a small nose and mouth. It was not their norm to fight, but something was off. "Your anger says different."

"You said that you could manage in my absence, yet I am almost a pauper at this moment."

"Ahhh, you are your papa's son. So, you would dare judge me for having the sense to see a matter for the trouble it is. You are used to dealing with angry slaves, but the man is broken, and he is still a slave. The conditioning in his head is owned from the outside, but these slaves…these men will not bow down to your whiteness. They need to be handled with the respect due an enemy." Jeremiah said, his speech pressured from trying to contain his attitude.

E.J. stared at Jeremiah, assessing him. His large eyes were black as coal, just like his skin. He had keen features with high cheekbones, a sharp nose, and thick lips. His black hair was cut low, though still wild, and he had grown a mustache, making him look more like their papa. Jeremiah stood before him dressed in brown britches, a white shirt, and black boots of high quality. He was cleaned up to attend a slave sale, where they would replenish their workforce. E.J. smiled, because his brother had taken a menacing step forward. Jeremiah was attempting to explain the difference between a slave and a nigger that didn't see himself as a slave. Oh, E.J. knew the like and he sarcastically, responded, "So you are saying there are slaves who do not know they are slaves."

The air around the men was charged. E.J., white and privileged–Jeremiah a slave that did not know he was a slave. They glared at each other for some time before Jeremiah said, "I will bring the carriage around front, *Master,* and wait on you."

Turning on his heels, Jeremiah stormed from the study, slamming the door in his wake. E.J. stared after him, shaking his head. They had gone back to their stations in life, and though they were angry with each other, there was no mistaking they loved one another. They would hatch a plan and seek out those responsible for their papa's death. For above all else, they were brothers.

Charleston, South Carolina

It was a day's ride from the plantation to the old slave mart. E.J. and Jeremiah were met by a hansom cab when they stepped from the five-fifteen train. The weather was mild and overcast, but no rain had fallen by the time they arrived at the hotel. The establishment was called "Home," and while the place was clean, it was far from upscale. Just the same, the dwelling boasted of an upscale clientele.

Home and institutions like it were in larger cities where the foot traffic was higher for the purposes of making a dollar. E.J. stepped into the lobby of the inn followed by Jeremiah, who carried the bags with the help of a stable boy. At the front desk, E.J. inquired about a room.

"I am looking for the basics for two nights."

"We have a room on the second floor. Your nigger will have to stay in the stables," an older woman behind the counter said.

E.J. took in her orange wig and heavy makeup. "Thank you for your hospitality. Please have fresh water brought to the room."

In the presence of white folks, Jeremiah appeared mute, speaking only when spoken too. He stood behind his brother, offering intense eye contact to the white woman glaring at him. When the woman was no longer of interest to him, he turned his mind to his surroundings. The lobby was a cream color and spread out like a warehouse. A brown carpet ran from wall to wall and up the grand staircase. In the middle of the lobby stood a white fountain that was minus water, yet offered a tart smell. On the far wall to the right of the desk was a cream-colored couch, with brown trim. The grand staircase separated the large room, and at the top of the steps several doors lined the hall in either direction. Tables covered with white cloths were scattered from the foot of the stairs to the rear of the lobby.

Lanterns and candles aided in illuminating the place; still, the lighting was poor. Jeremiah was positive the stables would be an upgrade. His brother had just completed his transaction when the woman behind the counter said, "Room two-twelve to the left, at the top of the stairs."

The men stared at each other for a few seconds before they moved in opposite directions.

A light rain was coming down when Jeremiah walked out onto the boardwalk from the lobby. He located the stables around back. An older white man wielding a shotgun stood in front of the door, taking shelter under the roof's overhang. He wore a tan hat and matching overcoat to ward off the evening chill. The man's eyebrows pressed together at the sight of Jeremiah, whose brown hat and matching brown overcoat were of a higher quality than his own.

"Hunter plantation," Jeremiah said.

The white man raised his eyebrows before he stepped to the side, allowing Jeremiah entry. The Hunter plantation had been a cut above the rest–until now. Edward Hunter Sr. was known far and wide before his death. Since his passing there had been word of an uprising. If someone from the Hunter plantation was present at a slave sale, there must be some merit to the rumor.

Jeremiah stepped around the armed guard and into the dimly lit structure. There were several small windows with no coverings that did nothing to mitigate the darkness. Hanging at the front of two stalls were lanterns offering minimal relief to the dismal atmosphere. His eyes adjusted to the gloom, and he began to evaluate his environment. He stood at the head of the aisle and peered down the center. From the stalls on either side of the dirt floor, chained men stepped into view. The men were dressed in threadbare trousers and sweat-stained shirts–some wore no shoes. At the far end of the barn, several women of childbearing age stood staring at him. He counted eight women chained together at the wrist and to ensure immobility, chained yet again to a beam at the end of a stall. The women were garbed in tattered old dresses, and two wore rags tied about their heads. The barn smelled of unwashed bodies and urine. As he stepped into an empty stall, Jeremiah noted there were no horses.

Removing his coat, he threw it over a pile of hay. Seating himself on the ground, he lay back and threw his hat over his face. He listened to the whispers of the slaves speaking with each other. One male slave told a female slave not to trust him, when she said, "He ain't chained, surely he will help us."

Another male slave said, "I knows the type. He ain't finna help us."

Once she was convinced not to speak to him by the other slaves, their whispers became low murmurs. Jeremiah was unable to make out anymore of the conversation, so he began to doze. He was tired from traveling as his brother's manservant. Once on the train, he had been led to a sweat box with the other manservants and maids. The reaction to him had been the same–distrust and absolutely no conversation. He preferred it that way; it made his job as an overseer easier to manage.

Shortly before dawn, he was awakened by a commotion just outside the barn. There was screaming off in the distance, and to Jeremiah it signaled that the auction had begun. He was about to place his hat back over his face and go back to sleep when the thunder of the massive barn door sliding open got his attention. Placing his hat on his head, Jeremiah leaned forward and locked his arms around his bent knees. Several white men holding lanterns stepped forward as the chained men were led by force from the barn.

A male slave at the end of the chained line began to buck as he yelled, "I ain't gon be separate from my family! I's damn tired–Imma be dead dis day."

The slave attempted to rile the others chained to him, but to no avail. The overseers running the Old Slave Mart addressed the troublemaker with swift precision, clubbing him over the head and dropping him to the ground. A scuffle ensued as the crackers pinned the slave to the ground. Several of the overseers stood about, holding their lanterns to ensure there was enough light by which to whoop his ass. Once subdued, an overseer stated smugly, "Take 'im to the morgue."

Jeremiah never moved from where he sat on the floor of the stall. He watched unflinchingly as they dragged the body past him, leaving a trail of blood. At the barn door, a slaver holding a shotgun yelled, "You niggers move along peaceably. We losing coin standing about."

The male slaves filed out first and then the women. Just as the last female moved past the stall, an overseer noticed Jeremiah. "Why ain't you chained, boy?"

Pushing his hat back slowly, Jeremiah stared up at the overseer.

"This one is mine."

The overseer spun in the direction of the barn door. He took a couple of steps into the lantern light, his bearing confrontational. E.J. stood his ground and smiled. Jeremiah was on his feet—the guns at his hips and the piece holstered to his upper left side now visible. He moved in behind the overseer and offered no words.

The overseer looked over his shoulder at Jeremiah and sneered. "So you's broadminded when it comes to niggers?"

The slaves had been moved on down the path to the auction block. Two more white men stood near the doorway holding lanterns, but they did not appear aggressive. The man standing face-to-face with E.J. was angry. The noise of the previous commotion had moved down the path as well, so E.J. did not have to raise his voice. His southern drawl was slow and deliberate as he addressed his antagonist. "Broadminded? Oh, I wouldn't say I'm progressive, Mr....?"

"Sneed—the name is Sneed," the slaver provided nastily.

E.J. nodded. "As I was saying, Mr. Sneed, I am not what you would call progressive. But you may be correct in your assumption that Jeremiah here belongs on a leash."

Jeremiah smiled before pulling the guns from his hips. Cocking the gun in his left hand, he placed the barrel flush against the back of Mr. Sneed's head. The gun in his right hand he aimed at a lantern holder, who was sweating from the exchange. E.J. pulled his gun and aimed it at the other lantern holder. His speech was slow and steady.

"Jeremiah is trained to protect my person, and though he can be more like a rabid dog, he does follow direction well."

A prolonged silence allowed the severity of the situation to sink in. Finally, EJ continued, "I don't want no trouble, Mr. Sneed. Are we of the same mind?"

Mr. Sneed nodded. His eyes were glassy, and his brow wet

with perspiration. Looking past the slaver's ear to his brother, E.J. commanded. "Down, boy."

Jeremiah, taking direction from his brother, un-cocked and re-holstered his guns.

E.J. smiled as he slipped his gun back into the holster. His tone was pleasant. "Looks like the weather will hold up for the auction. You gentleman have a good day."

Without a backward glance, Mr. Sneed and the lantern hold-ers moved swiftly through the stable yard.

E.J. and Jeremiah stared at each other and smiled.

❊ ❊ ❊

The auction house was an open building with a stage and podium at the front of a large room. On either side of the stage were steps used to parade men, women and children of color. The crowd of purchasers was thick, as they stood about examining the mer-chandise. Even though the sun had risen, the atmosphere was still damp and muggy. The odor kept polite company with handker-chiefs over their noses to ward off the foul smell. Still, the auc-tion raged on. The brothers had been at it for hours, but they had done well.

E.J. stood in front of the stage with Jeremiah at his back. Together they had chosen seventy-five men and fifty women. Lastly, they had chosen five children around the ages of six-to-eight summers. They were about to call it quits when onto the stage walked seven slaves. There were six bruising males with mat-ted hair—barefoot and shirtless. They wore nothing but tattered brown britches. Their skin tones ranged from jet black to the mas-ter is my papa–light skinned. Standing in the center of the males stood one female, her gray dress pulled down about her waist. She had caramel skin, large bright eyes and full lips.

Jeremiah stepped in a little closer to get a better look, and he could see that she was far from clean. Her hair was matted, and on her right cheek was a black mark. He couldn't tell if the mark was dirt or a bruise. She was way too slender. Her rib cage was showing, yet she had full, firm breasts. Still, in his assessment, Jeremiah thought her not worth the coin. He was about to turn away, when their eyes clashed. As he returned her stare, she offered no expression at all. But he could feel something coming from her, and he was sure it was disdain.

Jeremiah leaned in whispering to his brother; his eyes never straying from the woman. "Purchase her, and let us be done here."

They stayed in Charleston an extra day to sort out the transportation of their new purchases. E.J. procured the use of three rail cars on a six o'clock freight train headed for Horry. There were no featured comforts, but Jeremiah was used to this type of travel. E.J. hired four more overseers for the trip home to ensure there would be no runners. Though they journeyed by train, progress was as slow as if they had walked. Early the next morning, they arrived at the train station just outside of town. E.J. rode out ahead to get matters situated.

It was not yet noon when E.J. returned with wagons and more manpower. Two hours later, one hundred and thirty-one slaves arrived at their new home, the Hunter plantation. E.J. knew he needed more of a workforce, but this was a start. He and Jeremiah had picked the best the auction had to offer. They would have to track other sales to get the labor force they needed.

E.J. rode his black horse right up to the front steps of the main house. Swinging down from the saddle, he threw the reins to a stable boy and mounted the steps. Jeremiah followed suit and the two men paused at the top of the stairs, watching as the overseers broke the slaves down into several groups. Out in front of them were collapsed cabins and burned fields. E.J. had avoided this view because it was too painful. When his father ran the plantation, it had been prosperous, growing more than just cotton. But under his rule, there had been one fail after another. Gone were the rolling green hills of the gardens. Gone was the singing that echoed from the fields, signifying that life was bountiful.

The sun bore down upon them. It was unusually hot for a spring day. As he watched the commotion in front of him, E.J. was pleased—they were moving in the right direction. The male slaves were ushered to the barn to get them settled and broken to the rules. The female slaves and children stood quietly, waiting for direction. Two old and faithful slaves, Sonny and Ella, came out of the house and stood behind E.J. and Jeremiah. Neither of the brothers could recall a time when these two were not part of the plantation. Ella was a stout, dark-skinned woman, not much above five feet in height. She wore a brown dress with a white apron and a white rag tied about her head. She was about sixty summers or more, with a deceivingly kind smile, dark brown eyes and a round face. When she laughed, her laughter revealed two missing teeth.

Sonny, Ella's younger brother, worked as a butler and was a little more polished than she. He was also taller, about five-ten, with thick wooly hair that was cut low. His eyes were dark brown, and his skin was black as a berry. When he smiled, he had straight, white, even teeth–though he did not smile much. He wore a white shirt with black trousers and vest. At his waist hung every key to the mansion, causing him to sometimes be referred to as "the key man." Sonny had an outwardly soft demeanor, but inside he was fuming. He had been angry since the day he crossed the threshold of manhood, though he managed his rage well.

The smell of foul bodies could no longer be ignored. Ella moved down the steps, directing the women and children to the bathhouse at the back of the plantation. "Follow me. I's gon sho' you how it's done 'round here!"

E.J. turned and walked into the house, leaving Jeremiah

standing on the porch with Sonny. As Sonny awaited direction, Jeremiah stared off, organizing and re-organizing his thoughts. The older slave did not like him, and Jeremiah could feel it. He had spoken with his brother about selling Sonny, but E.J. wouldn't hear of it. Sonny spoke only when spoken to, and though Jeremiah could feel the contempt rolling off him, the older slave was cautiously respectful. Sonny was also clear that the black cracker saw through his façade and did not like him either. With the non-verbal understanding between them in full effect, they stood in silence until Jeremiah finally spoke.

"The female in the gray dress at the end of the line—set her up in my cabin. Give her three dresses and make certain Ella combs her hair."

Sonny nodded, and Jeremiah walked into the house without a backward glance.

❈ ❈ ❈

Callie stood at the back of the line waiting for her turn to bathe. She was still in shock from the events of the last few months. Life for her had always been at the Parsons plantation in Alabama. It had been a good life, until her mistress had taught her to read and write. She had been warned that she could only read what her mistress approved. At first, Callie had applied her new skills in the Parson family library out of defiance. Later, a thirst to know more had engulfed her, causing her to read anything and everything she could find. When the veil of ignorance that cloaked her mind had been lifted, she was left yearning to be free. Secretly, she cursed her mistress for opening her eyes while still leaving her chained to a barbaric existence.

Mistress Parsons had taken ill and died suddenly, leaving everything to a nephew from up north. Walter Parsons came and liquidated all assets on the estate. Families of loyal slaves had been broken down and sold to the highest bidder. Now, here she was, separated from her papa and brother, unsure of what the future held. She was afraid, and in her fear, she remained silent in hopes of being left alone.

"What's yo' name, gal?" Ella asked.

Callie stared at the older woman, who had introduced herself to the gathering of female slaves. Still, she said nothing. "You dere, gal! What be yo' name?"

When she could see that the woman wasn't going to relent, she said, "My name is Callie."

The older man from the porch appeared, and Callie was immediately forgotten. Ella spoke, directing the situation. "You gals get yoselves cleaned up. Don't be heavy handed wit' the soap—it's alls we gots."

Callie surveyed what was supposed to serve as a bathhouse. It was an open structure with five large tin tubs. She watched as water was thrown on the naked women. In the background, the white overseers looked on, leaving no room for dignity. She looked away from the scene before her to find the two older slaves staring at her. Ella began walking toward her, and Callie shook with dread.

"Ya needs to follow Sonny," Ella said.

Sonny did not speak or acknowledge her in any way as he stepped past them. Callie followed him as he led her through some collapsed cabins in the opposite direction of the makeshift bathhouse. The expansive Hunter plantation lay in ruins from what she could see. She had heard of this plantation from travelers and other slaves, but she had not thought it would be so bleak a place. Large trees lined the pathways, as did poorly crafted cabins. The man in front of her walked at a brisk pace, and she almost had to run to keep up. Finally, they came to a stop in front of a cabin of better quality, though it was still quite simple and rustic.

Standing on the makeshift porch was a brown-skinned woman with a scar just over her left eye. As she limped to the edge of the porch, her tan, coarsely-spun dress clung to her thin frame. She smiled, and her face appeared soft, though her features were hard. She looked to be forty summers. She had small eyes with a big nose and very large lips. "I be Eva, and yo' name is?"

"Callie."

Sonny began rolling up his sleeves and turning to Callie, he said, "Strip down here sos'n we can burn dem clothes."

Callie stood, staring at him. He looked irritated that she had not done what he said. Sonny was about to give her the proper set down. One he would give any slave that was making his life as a slave harder. Eva cut him off. "If'n you goes and brangs the water 'round, I could help her from here."

Sonny glared at Eva. "He ain't finna be patient wit' her and ya knows it. She prolly be dead by nightfall."

Eva looked appalled that Sonny would say such a thing in front of the girl. But, Callie surprised them both when she said solemnly, "I'm not looking to survive. I *hope* to be dead by nightfall."

❋ ❋ ❋

Eva stepped from the cabin closing the door awkwardly behind her, leaving Callie to stare about. In the corner of the one room was a fireplace and to the left was a large bed with a brown blanket. At the foot of the bed was a black chest with the top propped open revealing folded clothes. A small, round table with two matching chairs sat to her right. The lighting was dim as evening approached. The windows on either side of the door were covered with the same tan material as her dress–makeshift curtains. The door at the rear of the cabin was barred shut. The place was crude, but clean.

She was told to wait inside the cabin for further instructions. She was tired, but did not move from where she stood in the center of the room. Her skin still stung from the coarse brown soap she was given to bathe with. Eva had braided her hair in two large cornrows and helped her dress. She had to admit, even with her skin stinging, she felt better now that she was clean. Her racing mind came to a sudden halt when she heard footsteps on the porch.

Jeremiah pushed the door to his cabin open to find her standing in the center of the room. She locked eyes with him, but did not speak. Her eyes widened ever so slightly at the sight of him, but other than that tiny display, she offered no other reaction. Closing the door behind him, he crossed the room to the table. He turned the lantern up and seated himself in one of the chairs. She turned facing him, while backing up a safe distance. He broke the silence.

"I am Jeremiah. They tell me yo' name is Callie."

She continued to stare at him, offering nothing. He leaned back and sighed. He was not in the mood, so he offered a warning. "I ain't a patient man."

Callie stood rigid, her silence meant to provoke him.

"You will serve me in all things," he said.

When she still didn't answer, he stood abruptly causing his chair to scrape the floor. He waited for her to step back out of fear, but she didn't. He walked up on her threateningly, and when he was close enough, he leaned down and whispered, "Do you know who I am?"

She stared straight ahead, ignoring his very presence. He backed away and glared at her. The predator within him had kicked in and he circled her. His movements were meant to intimidate, but she didn't react. He felt his temper boiling out of control as he watched her blatant disregard for his authority, so he disengaged. Turning, he headed for the door in an attempt to calm himself, but just as he placed his hand on the doorknob, she spoke. Jeremiah noted that her voice was throaty and her southern drawl–educated.

"I know precisely who you are," she sneered.

Her scorn enveloped him as he stood at the door with his back to her. Slowly, he turned facing her, but he did not move toward her. Instead, he thought through whether to break her neck swiftly or slowly. Brazenly, she stepped a little closer to where he stood. "You are a slave who believes he is not. You need a mirror, so that you *might* see that your skin is the same as those you help to oppress. Oh, I am clear on who you are. It is you who is confused about who you are. You are the problem, not the solution."

At her words, something snapped inside him, and he stepped to her quickly grabbing her by the neck. As he began to squeeze, she smiled, still offering no fear. Boldly, she held eye contact with him while gasping for air. As he stood with his hands about her throat, Jeremiah involuntarily evaluated her. She had a smooth, caramel, complexion with pouty lips. She was a small thing, about five feet–two inches, and her eyes welcomed death. Suddenly, he released her, and she fell to the floor. Her breaths coming in harsh bursts. There was no mistaking her disappointment.

Callie scrambled back against the wall and stared at him. He was a very dark-skinned man with dark explosive eyes and a shock of blue–black hair. His anger was obvious, and she could see that her words hit their mark. He walked over to where she sat on the floor and snatched her to her feet, slamming her against the wall. He pressed his body against hers, and in her ear, he whispered between clinched teeth, "You will not be free of me so easily, Callie, and you will tend me in all things."

"I won't," she whispered back, and to her shame, hot tears spilled from her eyes.

Still crowding her personal space, he stepped back slightly and released her neck. His hands were fisted at his sides. Jeremiah realized he had never felt such emotion about anything other than the death of his papa. He was furious, and something more–he was aroused. When his emotions balanced out and he felt in control of himself again, he said, calmly, threateningly, "Callie, you *will* tend me."

Turning on his heels, he quit the cabin, slamming the door in his wake.

3

Canada, May 1861

IT WAS ELBERT'S turn with their son, and James was working through a shift change at the barracks. The hour was late when Black appeared at the front of the barracks. He wore a look of concern, causing James to drop what he was doing and move toward him. "What is it?"

"Mama, Sunday, Miss Cora and Shultz just went to help Morgan. The baby is coming," Black said.

James smiled and nodded. There had been nothing to smile about in weeks, and the news made him feel lighter. Black always worried when the women neared their time. "Who has Natalie?"

"She is with Iris," Black replied, looking around anxiously.

"Simon?"

"Is with Morgan."

Turning to Philip, James yelled, "Steppin' out!"

"Sho' thang," Philip yelled back.

When they stepped into the evening air, the weather was warm. They made their way down the two paths toward Simon's cabin, their footsteps careful and deliberate under a moonless sky. Simon's cabin came into view, and light poured forth from every window. The twelve, minus Simon and Morgan, waited on news of the baby. Gilbert stepped to Black, handing him the whiskey bottle. While the men stood about talking, there were times when Morgan could be heard screaming her head off. At those moments, the men quieted.

It was dawn when Shultz finally stepped onto the porch and announced that Miss Morgan had a baby girl. "Mother and daughter are doing fine. Simon looks like he'll be all right too." The doctor chuckled.

When the men dispersed, heading back to the barracks, James, Black, and Elbert remained to wait on the women. Big Mama and Miss Cora looked exhausted when they finally appeared on the porch. Black and Elbert moved forward, helping them down the steps.

"Sunday gon stay a little longer to help Morgan," Big Mama said. "They has a beautiful little one."

Black nodded as they headed for home. Once they arrived at the house, Black went to check on his daughter. James and Elbert kept on to the barracks to begin their day. As they walked, Elbert asked "How ya feeling?"

James stopped, looking off toward the front gate. He sighed. "I don't sleep much. I sees Fannie's face when I close my eyes. When I ain't thinking on Fannie, our son's mama comes to my head. I cain't catch a rest from my own damn thoughts."

"Are ya spending time with Miss Abby?"

"Seeing you and Black don't make me not miss Otis." James responded, irritation in his voice.

Elbert reached out and put his hand on James' shoulder. "I'm sure it don't, but knowing me and Black is watching yo' back makes shit a little easier. You and Black being there for me–helped me. It is the same for Black. All ya been through ain't going to just go away, but as men—as brothers—we will continue to watch each others' backs. I'm not saying to forget Fannie, because you won't; but you have to *give* yourself a break. Miss Abby is a fine-looking woman. Spend time with her and let yourself breathe."

James stared at Elbert. He was interested in Miss Abigail, but guilt was eating at him. It didn't seem right to just move on. Elbert must have read his thoughts because he said, "You can't do nothing else but move on; you have the boy to think about."

"Yeah."

They resumed walking toward the barracks. "I been avoiding Miss Abby; ain't see her in about a week or more."

"You could fix that. Just go slow," Elbert replied.

At the front door of the barracks, they changed the subject. But up in James' head, he admitted that he had slept well in Miss Abby's bed.

❀ ❀ ❀

The days were happening slowly, and James could almost hear the passage of time. He did not sleep and neither did he seek out Miss Abigail. At midnight one evening, the off-duty men gathered at the front of the barracks. They were headed to Miss Cherry's. Jake and Lou attempted to coerce him into coming with them. James laughed off the invitation, telling them he would have his son in the morning. "Babies and hangovers ain't partial to one another."

When the men finally left the barracks, James went out back to be alone. He had lied. Elbert and Anna were keeping little Otis a few extra days. He had been stopping by their cabin for dinner and to help with any chores. The thought of Miss Cherry's after the Fannie incident made his dick go limp. He could still see her approaching that fateful morning, and then the vision turned into her lifeless form. It was all too much, and it seemed he could not move forward. His thoughts became so heavy that he pushed off the wall and began walking.

He wandered about on the starlit night until he came upon her cabin. He wanted rest from his pain, and he wanted her company. But it was late and inconsiderate of him to be there. He eased himself down gently and sat on the steps. Behind him, the lantern light spilled onto the porch. He reached into his back pocket and pulled out his flask. The liquid burned through him, and he began to relax. Gazing out in front of him, he listened to the sounds of the night. After a time, he gathered himself to leave. He reached to put the flask in his back pocket and dropped it, making a loud, clanking sound. The curtain in the left window moved, and then the front door abruptly opened.

"Shit!" James hissed.

"Mista James, you all right?"

He stepped onto the porch to face her, and it occurred to him that she too kept strange hours. "I was out walking, and then I dropped my flask," he answered awkwardly, holding up the flask as proof.

Abby smiled, "Won't ya come on in?"

He stared down at her, realizing that Abby was a small woman in stature, standing about five feet–four inches. She smelled of lavender as though she had just stepped from a bath, and he felt the weight of his intrusion. Abby was dressed in a cream-colored night wrap that stopped just about her bare feet. James felt uncomfortable about needing her company so desperately, yet between little Otis' mama and Fannie, he couldn't breathe. She opened the door wider for him to enter, but he just stood there–frozen. Stepping toward him, she reached out and took his hand, leading him into the house.

"Come sit."

He squeezed her hand, and she stopped moving to look up at him. "I just…sorry to come here so late. I keep strange hours 'cause of the barracks."

She squeezed his hand in return. "I don't mind, Mista James. I don't sleep good neither."

James' mind wandered back to the discussion he had with

Black about how she came to be there. He now understood why she couldn't sleep. She pulled him toward the table and he sat.

"You hungry?"

"No," he answered.

She nodded before seating herself across from him. He had never been nervous with a woman, but at this very moment, he could barely organize his thoughts. Guilt over Fannie had entered the cabin with him, threatening the respite he sought. Pulling his flask from his back pocket again, he attempted to separate himself from his feelings. He took a long swallow from the flask and then offered the drink to Abby.

Abby shook her head. "I don't manage strong drink good."

James nodded before placing the flask between them on the table. He focused his eyes on it, so he wouldn't have to look at her.

"Ya looks tired, like you ain't slept none."

James looked up at her and smiled. "I'm all right."

"Ya needs sleep that ain't forced."

"Yeah." James shifted in his chair. He didn't want to talk about himself, and Abby must have sensed as much.

"Miss Morgan got her a beautiful little one."

James smiled. "I ain't seen her yet. Ain't seen Simon either."

"I went with the doctor to check on Miss Morgan and the baby–they well. Mr. Simon is awful proud."

James chuckled, and the awkwardness receded as they found comfortable conversation. He didn't do much talking, but Abby talked about the weather and going to town with Shultz for supplies. Every now and again, James would offer some funny story about little Otis, and she would laugh. An hour had passed before the conversation lulled. Abby stretched and then stood, pushing her chair back from the table. She smiled at him as she pulled her wrap tighter about her. It looked as though she was about to say something, and at once, he felt panicked.

Fearing she was about to ask him to leave, he blurted out, "I wanna rest wit' you in yo' bed."

❊ ❊ ❊

Abby stared at him. She had been about to offer him some coffee, but now the unavoidable vision of him standing naked in her bedroom came to mind. His green eyes were intense as he waited for her answer, and she had to look away to think. When she finally got up the nerve to look at him again, he whispered brokenly, "Please."

She couldn't make verbal her thoughts, so she nodded. Abruptly, he stood, and the chair scraped the floor with his action. This time it was James who held out his hand and Abby who accepted. Reaching back to the table, he turned the lantern wick all the way down, casting the front room in complete darkness. At the back of the cabin, a soft light illuminated from between the seams of the curtain. He led the way. When they were about to enter the back room, she hesitated, causing James to stop and look back at her. She looked down at the floor.

"What is it? Is you wantin' me to go?"

From the small amount of light emanating through the curtain, Abby could see the anxiety in his features. "No, Mista James," she whispered. "I don't mind ya being here, it's just…"

James leaned down and pressed his mouth against her ear. His voice was masculine, gritty and deep. "My name is just James… say it."

"James," she responded, her voice trembling.

He kept his cheek against her temple. "May I call you Abby?"

The sound of her name on his lips seduced her. She could only nod her assent.

"What's troublin' you, Abby?"

"I thanks Imma little too old for ya, Mista James…I mean James."

He smiled. "How old are you, Abby?"

"Be thirty-eight summers on the nineteenth of July. How old is you? Ya don't look as though ya even made thirty summers."

He smirked. "Big Mama tells me I'm 'bout thirty-one."

Abby breathed in sharply at his response. She was about to say something else when he cut her off. "I feels good wit' you, Abby. I can just be me. I ain't carin' 'bout nothin' else. I ain't had rest since I was here last."

Again, she nodded, and standing to his full height, James pulled the curtain back and led her over the threshold. He did not speak for a time. Instead, he placed his gun on the nightstand to the left of the bed and undressed. She stood at the foot of the bed folding her wrap, ignoring him in his various stages of undress. When his movements stopped, she glanced up to find him standing in his red long underwear, staring at her.

"Come," he said, with a smile. "I ain't gonna ravish ya."

She smiled weakly as she watched him pull the covers back. Abby climbed into the bed and when she was comfortable, he reached over to the nightstand and outed the light. She then heard a rustling sound and knew he was removing his underwear. The bed dipped under his weight, and he lay back, pulling her close to him. Abby placed her head on his chest, and when all was still, James spoke into the silence.

"Ya know, Abby, you don't look like ya made thirty summers neither."

❋ ❋ ❋

They whispered to each other for a while until Abby asked a question and James didn't respond—he had fallen asleep. She lay awake thinking about the exchange between them. What she had been trying to say was that she was too old for him. She was about to encourage him to find someone more his age to be comfortable with, but it had come out all wrong. What alarmed her most was that she wanted him around. When he didn't come back after sleeping with her that first night, she had felt a twinge of disappointment. It was then that she reminded herself that she did not want a man in her life—not after what happened to Harold.

Abby hashed and rehashed the exchange between them until her brain finally grew tired. She was about to doze off when James unexpectedly sat straight up in the bed.

"Fannie! Fannie!" he cried out. His was panting and thrashing about, dazed and unaware of his surroundings. Abby sat up and began rubbing his back, soothing him.

"James, James, wake up. You here wit' me. You all right," she reassured him.

Slowly, she could see he was becoming alert, still he said nothing. James finally lay back against the pillows, his body was tense. Abby lay on her side to face him. She leaned up on one elbow and touched his cheek. He was sweating, and she could feel the ache radiating from him.

"I'm here," she whispered.

James turned and kissed the palm of her hand. He was quiet for a moment before he responded, his voice ragged and hoarse. "I could see her standin' before me in the front room. She had a hole in her middle and she was askin' why I killed her."

"Ain't nobody here but me and you," Abigail said softly.

"I know it was a accident, but she was just so damn young. She ain't do no livin' and 'cause of me she never will."

James slid down in the bed and pulled her to him. He placed his face between her breasts and grew quiet. She could feel him trembling as she stroked his back. She was silent, wanting to give him the space he needed to calm down. Abby felt his body relax and thought he had found sleep again. She tried backing away from him to get comfortable, but he tightened his grip on her.

"I ain't 'sleep."

Without thinking, Abby kissed his forehead, allowing her lips to linger. They lay snuggled against one another, and James realized that intimacy with a woman was not always sexual. Abby had created a place so emotionally safe–he laid his very soul bare to her.

"I seen Fannie when I was on a mission wit' my brothers. She was fine-looking, and I wanted her for myself. When we left the plantation she was on, she refused to come wit' us. Her mama was sick, and she ain't wanna leave her mama that way. I ain't make no promises to come back for her, but I mourned leaving her. I prolly would have gone back for her–later. I had more pressin' issues to address. Then she showed up here."

He stopped talking as if working through his thoughts. Abby was quiet and to her shame, jealous. Still, she listened patiently as James went on. "At the next plantation, I seen a woman tryna keep hold of her baby. An overseer was tryin' to take the child from her. I tried helpin' her, but instead got myself shot in the face and her killed. Me and Elbert took little Otis as our own youngun since he ain't got no mama 'cause of me."

His voice was angry, tight, and defeated, but Abby never stopped touching him or trying to soothe him.

"I ain't never felt as safe as I do right now wit' you," she told him. "Even my Harold never made me feel safe, and wit' us being slaves, he couldn't—though he tried. You gonna hafta try and forgive yoself. Circumstances was against ya, but you has a chance to live. Ain't nothin' else you can do."

James offered no response, and Abby thought her words might have hit their mark.

"Do you like resting time wit' me, Abby?"

"Yes," she whispered.

Her answer alleviated the tension in the room, and they could both feel it. For Abby, it was freeing to admit she wanted to feel intimacy with him. For James, who felt mentally enslaved by sadness–emotional freedom lay with her.

❀ ❀ ❀

It was just before sunrise when the people of Fort Independence woke to find the men from the barracks moving about with purpose. Anthony and Luke walked between the cabins with a message from Black, himself, that all would be well. Among the elderly and children, there was fear and unease, yet everyone followed the directions given. The instructions were simple—carry on about your day; the men were handling the matter. As Black stood at the study window contemplating his next move, he watched the men step into their practiced positions.

He had not left the house for two reasons. First, he knew his wife would seek him out. Second, he wanted a better visual on the situation. He would let the morning progress, and most importantly, he would leave his unwanted guest stewing outside the gate. The ambassador did not like him, and Black did not like the ambassador. He was thinking through the issue when Sunday appeared in the doorway. The look of concern on her face made his heart squeeze. Big Mama stood behind her, holding the baby.

Black reached out his hand, and she came to him. He smiled at Big Mama. Little Natalie was asleep in her arms. As Mama seated herself on the gold couch, he saw that she too was anxious. Black sighed. "Outside the gate is a posse of white men. The leader wishes to speak with me."

"Does ya know 'im?" Sunday asked.

"I have had dealings with Ambassador Bainesworth. I do not like him."

"Ya has this issue handled, right?" Mama asked.

"It depends on what he will ask. He only comes when he wants something. He reports to England's queen, who to my way of thinking loosely governs Canada. He is a dangerous man, but he does not try me. I'm sure he understands I would kill him, but the crown would just send someone else. The ambassador attempts to intimidate me with subtle threats from the queen who, I am sure," Black let out a chuckle, "does not know me."

Sunday, in her confusion, had only one question. "Will ya brang him inside the gate?"

"No," Black said without hesitation.

Sunday nodded, but her look of concern remained. Black leaned down and whispered, "I love you, Sunday. Do not worry. All will be well."

He kissed Sunday's cheek, and when he stood, he winked at Mama. "Go about your day. If there is an issue, you two will be the first to know."

Sunday looked as though she wanted to continue the conversation, but smiled instead. Black turned his attention to the door where James and Elbert stood waiting. It was the indicator that meant it was time for him to be Black, the leader of Fort Independence. Mama stood and both men came to her kissing her on the cheek. Sunday's facial expression caused James to step forward and hug her. Elbert followed suit. She nodded, and with that, she and Big Mama stepped from the study to give the men privacy.

As soon as James closed the door, Elbert turned to Black. "What the hell is going on? There is a group of hostile-looking white men waiting at the gate. Their count is about fifty."

"Fifty is the number we could *see*," James added.

"Canada is governed by England," Black began, "and the leader of this posse works for the queen. As men, we do not like each other, but there is a respect. He attempts to intimidate, and I remain unimpressed. The ambassador comes only when he wants something. Herschel knows him better, as he does all the recording of paperwork and paying of the taxes for me."

"What is our next move, then?" James asked.

"I will step outside the gate to speak with him. The men who exited the fort from the back will come around to the front and seal off their exit as I listen to what he has to say. He has, in the past, come uninvited, but never with so many men. If need be, we will kill them and go on about our day." Black's words were spoken with cool nonchalance.

After about an hour, the three men left the study, heading for the front door. The early morning sun shone brilliantly as Black stepped onto the porch. At the bottom of the stairs stood Simon, Shultz and Tim along with other men; they waited patiently for direction from Black. Staring toward the gate, Black exhaled before moving down the steps. At the bottom, he faced Simon and smiled.

"I haven't seen you. How is Morgan and the little one?"

Simon's smile was broad with pride. "They's good. I loves my girls, and Morgan is great at mothering."

Black shook Simon's hand and clapped him on the back. He leaned in whispering something only Simon could hear. When Black stepped back, Simon stared at him, nodded and walked away. Focusing on the front of the fort, Black and the men began moving toward the problem. The women and children stood in the pathways watching as the men headed to the gate. Once at the entrance, Elbert and James looked to Black. Elbert broke the silence. "Both of us will come with you."

Black shook his head. "No, let's stick to the plan."

After giving the final word on the matter, Black walked through the gate to face the unwelcomed guests. He stood for a moment looking about until he heard the gate close and lock behind him. Elbert had been right, out in front of him, in the small circle of trees, stood about fifty white men. The sun was behind him allowing him to gauge the situation. The men before him stood between their horses; some broke off from the group to cover the man walking toward him. Black, who was dressed for his name, clasped his hands behind his back before leisurely moving forward.

Ambassador Bainesworth was dressed in brown trousers, a coarse brown shirt and black boots; on his head was a dusty brown hat that was pulled down over his eyes. When the two men finally stood face-to-face, the ambassador pushed his hat back just a bit to meet Black's stare.

Black evaluated the man standing before him. He was slightly shorter, standing about six-one, and he had aged since the last time Black had seen him. Bainesworth was pale of skin, with brown hair and brown eyes. The ambassador looked to be about forty summers. Despite his thin frame, he would still be a worthy opponent. Black looked past the ambassador and surveyed his entourage. *It appears the queen's man runs with a rough bunch.*

"Black, it's good to see you," the ambassador said in that refined English accent that Black found difficult to understand at times.

"Ambassador."

The men had started with a simple greeting; still, the tension could be felt by both. Black let the exchange hang, offering nothing, leaving the burden of conversation to the other man. Bainesworth understood the message and explained his position. "It would seem we are in a bit of a quandary, my friend."

"Oh? How so?" Black inquired.

"War has broken out in the States and this could prove problematic for her majesty."

Black's silence applied even more pressure for the other man to get to the damn point. And without further delay, Bainesworth stated a little too aggressively, "You are hereby ordered, by myself and the queen, to work with the crown on a matter of high importance."

The word "ordered" did not go over well with Black. More to the point, Black was tired of having to show this man the lines not to cross. He was positive that England's queen had not ordered him to do anything. What looked closer to the truth was the ambassador had been commanded by the queen to handle a matter and he was trying to pawn it off on him.

Black still did not speak, instead, he stepped a tad to the left of his adversary. The small action was a signal to Simon, who lay with a rifle at the ready. Patiently, he waited for Black's gesture and when it came–Simon did not so much as breathe. Watching his prey through the site of his rifle, he took the shot, knocking the hat from the ambassador's head. And when the shot rang out, everyone ducked except Black, who continued to stand leisurely with his hands clasped behind his back.

At the sound of the single shot, the fort's men emerged from the trees closing off the exit to the ambassador and his men. Bainesworth turned looking about, and when he faced Black again, his speech warred with his rough appearance. "I commend your show of strength, my good man. However, I can assure you it isn't needed for this circumstance."

Black stepped up to the man before him, standing nose to nose. The eye contact offered by Black was so intense the ambassador looked away, seeking a mental escape. Only seconds passed, but it must have felt like hours to the now intimidated representative of the crown. It had been a rough two years for Black and his family; he would not stand for being ordered about–by anyone. As he thought of his wife and mama, along with the elderly and the children, his temper threatened to boil over. When finally, he spoke, his speech was tight, though his outward presence was calm.

"You have come aggressively to my home with a band of armed men. You have spoken to me as if I were a damned slave. I should kill you today and wait for your replacement."

Bainesworth blanched as he attempted to clarify the situation. "We are all subject to the Queen of England. I meant no disrespect. I have come on a matter that concerns the crown. The armed men are for my protection. Travel has become hazardous to one's health."

Black glared at the ambassador. In his mind's eye, he could see Sunday's fear. He did not take kindly to anyone who caused her stress. He stepped back, spun on his heels and walked away. They could not move forward in this discussion because he wanted to slit Bainesworth's throat. They also could not move forward because his unwanted guest *had* attempted to coerce, and he was sure of it. Clasping his hands behind his back once more, Black moved toward the gate and Sunday.

"Black, please accept my apologies! The crown needs your assistance!" Bainesworth called out.

"Ambassador, we will try this again later once I have calmed down." Black responded, as he strode away.

Bainesworth opened his mouth to ask a question and thinking better of it, snapped his lips shut. The things he did for England, he thought on a sigh. Dealing with angry savages and damn near getting his brain's blown out. Still, he would wait. He needed the darkie's help.

※ ※ ※

Inside the gate, Black spoke with Elbert, James, Simon, Shultz and Tim. "Meet me in my study in two hours."

There was no further discussion as Black turned and headed for home. James, Tim, Simon and Elbert would continue to manage the situation. The fort men would remain in position outside the gate until the matter could be resolved. Shultz, who had decided to continue seeing patients, walked back through the pathways with Black in silence. Miss Olive, the elderly woman they had stolen from the Bridges plantation, was seated in a rocking chair on her porch as they approached. She had a blanket over her lap to cover the fact that she only had one leg. She wore a gray dress, and her hair was freshly plaited. Giddy and Sadie sat on the top step in front of her, and all three, appeared anxiety ridden.

Black paused in front of the cabin and smiled. "Miss Olive, you are looking well."

"Mista Black, how you? I feels well."

Her smile was weak and her voice shaky. Stepping between the children, he mounted the porch and leaned in to kiss Miss Olive's cheek. She reached up and touched his bald head.

"You think I would bring you all this way and not keep you safe?" he whispered to her.

"They says it's some overseers up at the gate," the old woman replied.

"Things are being handled, and you are not to worry," Black instructed.

Miss Olive nodded, and Black kissed her cheek once more. He turned his attention to the children. Giddy wore brown trousers, a white shirt, and black boots; his hair had been cut low. Little Miss Sadie wore a gray dress like Miss Olive's and her hair was braided in two fat plaits, pinned neatly to the top of her head.

"No learning today?" Black asked.

"No, not today Mista Black," Sadie answered, and her eyes watered.

"I think my mama has biscuits. Would you like that?" Black asked.

"Yes, sah, Mista Black," both children answered at once.

He turned back to Miss Olive. "The children will bring you some biscuits back from my mama."

Miss Olive nodded as Sadie jumped up, taking Black's hand. Shultz just stood in the background awed by Black's ability to be hardened one moment and soft the next. They continued on until they reached Black's house. The children raced up the steps and into the house. Black turned to Shultz. "I will see you in my study in a few."

"Yeah," the doctor said before walking away.

Taking the porch steps two at a time, Black entered the hall and called out, "Mama!"

Big Mama appeared in the kitchen doorway with a smile on her face. "The chilren is here in the kitchen. They's havin' biscuits and gravy."

"Miss Olive would like some biscuits too." Black stepped past Big Mama and entered the kitchen.

Big Mama nodded.

"This is so good, Big Mama. Thank ya," said Sadie.

"Sho' is," Giddy chimed in.

As the children devoured the biscuits, Black looked at Big Mama. "Sunday?"

"She in yo' study."

Black nodded and went down the hall. When he entered the study, Sunday was seated behind his desk, holding his daughter. She stood and came around the desk as Natalie reached out for him. Taking his daughter in his arms, he led Sunday back behind the desk, seated himself in his chair and pulled her into his lap. Natalie, in her yellow dress, was climbing all over them, babbling and cooing. Black chuckled and looked at his wife.

"Everything is all right," he reassured her.

"What is this man wantin' from ya?"

"He has not yet said what it is he wants, and I am too concerned for you to care."

He knew Sunday understood what he was saying. His worry for her was making him unable to concentrate.

"Imma do betta, Nat," she whispered.

"You're not doing bad. I just don't want you to be upset."

The baby whimpered, and Black lifted her above his head, causing her to dribble on him. He kissed her, dribble and all, while she laughed. He placed her on his shoulder and patted her back, but she continued to fuss.

"She thanks you's tryna make her nap, and she ain't wantin' to sleep." Sunday giggled. Big Mama, along with Sadie and Giddy, appeared in the doorway. Sadie came forward and took the baby from Black's arms. Natalie stopped crying. Mama ushered the children from the room and closed the door behind them.

"You trust me to keep you, Mama and our daughter safe, don't you?"

"Of course, I does. I don't want ya hurt, Nat. I cain't take that again," Sunday cupped his face in her hands and kissed him. "Surely ya understands that, right?"

As he and his wife spoke softly with one another, Black calmed down. He began thinking through his next encounter with the ambassador. He was in control, and the queen's man knew it. First, he would hear Bainesworth out—then, they would negotiate.

❊ ❊ ❊

It was just after midday when the eighteen filed into his study. Sunday and Mama brought in extra chairs. Still, some of the men stood and others sat on the floor. When everyone was settled, Black communicated the matter as he saw it.

"Living in Upper Canada as we do makes us subject to English law. By us being colored men, I don't suppose it matters to us really, other than to say we ain't slaves. Herschel records my paperwork with the government, which made them curious about me. When it was discovered that Herschel worked for an ex-slave, Ambassador Bainesworth was dispatched with all urgency to control me. Needless to say, he was disappointed. He is a dangerous man, but not in the way you would think. He is treacherous because he is controlled by greed. He has not tried me until today. He claims to have a request from the queen, herself." Black chuckled.

"So, he here to ask somethin' of ya?" Simon asked.

"It would seem so, but I let my anger get the better of me.

The ambassador was unable to make his request known." Black answered.

"Will you consider his request?" The doctor asked.

"I don't believe England's queen has requested anything of *me*, but yes, I will consider his request. We have the women and children to think of. Seeing their fear today troubled me. I will do what I can to keep mayhem from our doorstep. Gaining an ally is certainly better than gaining an enemy. But if what he asks is unreasonable, I will kill him and hope the next ambassador takes heed."

"Will we be bringin' him in the gate?" James asked, as he stood at the back of the room with his arms folded across his chest.

"Over the years, I have had several encounters with Bainesworth. I have never let him in the gate. We are stronger now. They will make camp outside the fort, and I will go back out to speak with him. He seemed desperate, so the upper hand is ours. Speaking of not wanting trouble on our doorstep—James is worried about the unresolved issue left from the Hunter plantation. The situation is made harder by the war," Black said to the room at large.

"I'm in," Elbert said.

The rest of the men followed suit, committing to riding out together again. When the ripple in the room quieted, Tim asked, "What is our next move?"

Black stood in front of his desk with his arms folded over his chest and his feet spread apart. "The next move," he replied matter-of-factly, "is to hear his request."

❀ ❀ ❀

As the men spoke, James' blood began thrumming through his body, and it was the first time in weeks he felt life coursing through him, rather than death. He remained silent as the men spoke, barely able to contain his glee. In his mind, he explored the many ways he would put the black cracker down.

❀ ❀ ❀

The eighteen walked unhurriedly down to the entrance of the fort. Black was now calm–they would hear the ambassador out. It was around two o'clock in the afternoon when the men stepped through the gate. Out in front of them, their visitors had set up camp as they awaited an audience with Black. The men they left outside the fort to watch over the situation began a changing of the guard and they would do so all night.

Bainesworth was speaking with one of his men when he noticed the frightening group approaching. He had observed the shift change and knew that he had come to the right place. They were impressive and could get the job done; he just needed not to offend Black during this exchange. His safety depended greatly on his ability to keep his foot from his mouth.

When he and Black were face-to-face, the ambassador asked, "Shall we try again, my good man?"

Black nodded and the men at his back remained still. Bainesworth felt the burn of the hot seat and moved swiftly to the point, attempting to speak from an angle he thought would be of interest to the men before him. But, the men offered nothing.

"As you all may or may not know, war has broken out between the states, and this concerns her majesty greatly. We wish to remain neutral so that we might keep control of this region. Our war efforts are engaged elsewhere, and we are spread too thin to be of any real consequence should this war spill over into Canada."

The ambassador stopped talking, and Black and the men continued to glare at him. His own men hung back so as not to appear even the slightest bit aggressive. Bainesworth couldn't tell if Black or his men understood what he was saying, but he contin-ued, "It has been brought to our attention that a plot to kill the

Union president is being hatched right here in Canada. Montreal to be exact. This is where you all come in. We wish to get word of this conspiracy to President Lincoln. Once he is informed, we can back away. The task is really quite simple, if planned accordingly."

Black narrowed his eyes. "Isn't warning the Union president the same as choosing sides?"

"We do not want the death of a president on our hands. More significantly, we do not wish to be part of this war," Bainesworth reiterated.

Black smiled, showing his beautiful white teeth. "And who will the queen send into the south with the same message of neutrality?"

The ambassador's face reddened, as he cleared his throat. "We still trade with the Confederacy and the Union. Great Britain is doing her very best to stay impartial."

"How do you suppose I–a colored man–would meet and speak with a white man of Mr. Lincoln's standing? Why would he listen to me? What aid is the queen offering should I decide to do her bidding?" Black asked, his tone mocking.

"Great Britain has every confidence you can handle this matter without her assistance. You men are impressive. This task is a trifle compared to what you are used to dealing with, I'm sure." Bainesworth replied.

"So, no help from the queen," Elbert added, causing the other men standing about to laugh.

The ambassador opened his mouth to say something in defense of the queen, but thought better of it. When the men quieted, Black took control of the situation. "Where can you be reached for further conversation, Ambassador?"

The stress of being sent away without an answer caused Bainesworth to whine. "What will be most advantageous for you? I can remain camped outside the gate until you come to a conclusion."

Black thought of Miss Olive, who worried that these men were overseers come to take her away. He did not like the strain Bainesworth and his men were producing. His response was to the point. "I will meet you in town at week's end with my answer. I want you and your men to be gone from here before nightfall."

"Shall we meet at the inn in three days to discuss this matter further?" The ambassador asked.

The ambassador was trying to apply pressure to get what he wanted. But, Black was being problematic. "Four days would be best."

Bainesworth nodded, and Black turned, walking away. The eighteen followed suit. There were no more words. Black dismissed both the ambassador and his men.

4

Hunter Plantation
May 1861

E.J. WAS DETERMINED to get his plantation back up and running. He had traveled to Alabama and purchased twenty more male slaves and fifteen female slaves. Jeremiah stayed behind, overseeing the day-to-day operations. In just a few short weeks his land had been cleared and, while not back to the Hunter plantation that he knew, progress was being made. Before the tragic deaths of his parents, he had been about to ask for the hand of Miss Suzanne Wells, daughter of the wealthy Adrian Wells. Marrying Suzanne would have brought E.J. great fortune. But his plantation being molested by runaway slaves left Adrian Wells feeling less than confident in his potential son-in-law's ability to lead. All communication between the Wells plantation and the Hunter plantation had ceased. This would not have been an issue for E.J., except that he was particularly fond of Suzanne, and the thought of her in the arms of another man drove him mad.

Shortly after he and his brother brought the first slaves home, E.J. headed to Georgia to call on Suzanne. It was an impolite and unannounced appointment, but it paid off. Tonight, Suzanne, along with her mother, father and sister were visiting the Hunter plantation. E.J. suspected it was so her father could assess his worth. He would be patient, but if her father didn't come to his senses, he would kill Adrian Wells. Suzanne was aware of his feelings for her, and she wanted him just as badly, he was certain. Still, she had begged him to go easy on her papa. Out of his passionate desire to please her, E.J. had resolved to control himself—but his patience was running dangerously low.

He stood on the balcony just off his room, looking out over the plantation in deep thought. The sun was just starting to set as he watched the activities that were restoring both his manhood and his livelihood. He could hear the slaves singing as they worked the fields until the last bit of natural light was gone. He could also see the overseers moving about on horseback, enforcing peace of mind. On the west side of the plantation, the green rolling lawns were restored with beautiful flower beds that were riotous in color. He stood shirtless in the warm, still air, his arms folded over his chest. He had failed once, but he would not fail again.

Behind him Nettie was readying his bath. He had finally moved into his father's rooms, accepting that his papa was gone. He turned and entered the room, pausing just inside the French doors. E.J. let out a long sigh. On the left of the room stood a massive bed with large, intricately carved black wooden posts that traveled to the ceiling. Across from the bed on the opposite wall was a fireplace that was swept clean. On the right side of the room stood a huge matching dresser and farther to the right was a privacy screen with a chamber pot behind it. A great porcelain tub sat between the bed and the fireplace. In front of a window to the left was a desk. His father would sit there for hours handling matters for the plantation.

"Is ya ready for yo' bath, Masta?" Nettie asked softly.

E.J. focused on the sweet, chocolate-skinned woman standing

naked next to the tub. Nettie had small, slanted eyes, a button nose and thick, juicy lips. She wore her hair in two big cornrows to the back of her head. She had perky breasts, a flat stomach and shapely legs. Nettie had been among the slave women he brought home from the old slave mart. There was no need to train her; she tended him well in all things.

He removed his boots and pants and stepped into the tub, followed by Nettie who climbed in after him. As she washed his face and chest, E.J. relaxed. Nettie afforded him the sexual patience he needed to deal with Suzanne and her damn father.

Nettie slid down firmly onto his hard shaft, splashing water over the sides of the tub. As she found a rhythm, pleasure seized his brain—but not before he made the decision to never sell her.

※ ※ ※

Jeremiah had not been back to his cabin since he installed Callie in it. Truthfully, she scared him, for he could not be sure he wouldn't kill her by mistake. She did not fear him like most people he encountered; in fact, she tried to enrage him. She provoked anger and strong sexual feelings he had never before experienced. In his sexual endeavors, there were many female slaves that bowed down to him and the pleasure he gave. He was also no stranger to the forbidden fruit, having had his fill of white women as well. There was no need to take a woman against her will; the action and violence of force made him flaccid. Still, he did not tolerate high-handed women, and the women who shared his bed knew this about him. He kept his emotions to himself; love was not on his agenda. Jeremiah had enough on his hands maintaining his position as the black cracker.

He continued to hide in his small room at the main house, which gave him access to see her daily. Callie was now working in the kitchen with Ella, and she also cleaned his brother's house. At night, she went back to his cabin. When he encountered her in the halls of his brother's home, she did not speak to him, and for now he allowed it. She cleaned all the rooms in the main house except his. The action made him smile, but he would not admit such a thing to her. He was shaken to the core by this little woman who showed no fear in his presence.

❀ ❀ ❀

Dinner was promptly at seven in the formal dining room. The table was long with a dozen matching straight-backed chairs. The solid cherry wood was polished to perfection, and before each chair was a white linen napkin wrapped about the proper utensils. Candles were lit for the evening. The cream-colored curtains remained tied back by decorative brown stays. The room was impressive, but had not been used in years. When Suzanne was finally his wife, E.J. knew all that would change, and his home would once again feel lived in.

The guests included Suzanne, her younger sister Maryam, her mother and father. Also seated at the table was Norman Shoemaker and Jeffrey Sizemore. Norman worked for the Hunter plantation for about five years. He was an older white man of about fifty summers with blue eyes and a fat nose. The bushy mustache that covered his mouth matched his salt-and-pepper hair. He had a quiet demeanor, but he was all about business. Jeffrey was a newcomer to the planation with a lot of new ways of doing things— Jeremiah did not like him. Sizemore looked to be about thirty summers. He was blond with blues eyes and a clean-shaven face. The group sat to one end of the table for the purpose of conversation. E.J. was smiling for the first time since his parents died, having Suzanne in his home seemed to brighten the place.

She sat between her mother and father, beaming at him. Suzanne had brown hair and blue eyes, a small pointed nose, and a heart-shaped mouth with beautiful white teeth. Her blue dress, with its decorative lace collar, matched her expressive eyes. On her left sat her mother, an older version of herself. Julia Wells was a beautiful woman and soft-spoken like her daughter. Both women were taller than average, standing around five-eight. Adrian Wells, on the other hand, was a short, fat man, with a comb-over. Everything about him was round—his face, his stomach. Still, he was commanding. He had cold blue eyes, a plump nose and an untrustworthy smile. Next to him sat Maryam, who was a combination of her mother and father. She was tall, fat and rather awkward with brown hair and brown eyes. Suzanne was twenty-two summers, and Maryam was not quite twenty.

"I see you've managed to get the plantation back on its feet," Adrian Wells said to E.J.

"Yes, sir. It's been slow going, but we are making progress," E.J. responded.

In an effort to aid E.J., Norman chimed in. "The Hunter plantation will be better than it's ever been. We've already replenished the workforce."

"Will you show me around in the morning, Edward?" Suzanne asked.

Looking to her parents, he waited for their approval. When her father nodded, E.J. responded, "I would be happy to show you around, my dear."

Suzanne offered a seductive smile, and E.J. was again thankful for Nettie. Just then, Ella and Callie stepped into the dining room to serve dinner. The menu consisted of roasted chicken, mashed potatoes and green beans, along with melt-in-your-mouth biscuits. The conversation flowed, and E.J. breathed a sigh of relief that all was going well.

"When will we leave for Virginia?" Suzanne asked.

"I am at the disposal of my guests. Whenever everyone is rested, we can move on to Virginia." E.J. responded.

"I think it's a bad idea to move the capital to Virginia. It makes no sense," Wells said.

When E.J. heard the capital of the Confederacy was moving from Alabama to Virginia, his thoughts were the same as his future father-in-law.

"I agree, but Jeff Davis seems to have a plan, though I'm not certain what it is," E.J. replied.

He would be traveling with the Wells family to Virginia to meet with elected officials about the war efforts. While there, he intended to return to the Turner plantation. E.J. hoped to find someone who knew what happened to his papa. The thought of his father caused his mood to change.

"Is something wrong, Edward?" Julia Wells asked.

"There are three lovely women seated at my table. What could be wrong?" E.J. answered.

The conversation began to flow again. Jeffrey discussed new techniques in slave-handling with Wells. While it wasn't polite dinner conversation, it was a necessary evil to maintain control, especially now, with the war. Ella and Callie cleared the table and were back in no time serving coffee with a moist chocolate cake. When the new slave woman, Callie, stepped between him and Sizemore, E.J. saw him subtly reach out and grab her rear. The slave woman jumped abruptly, but continued on like nothing had happened. He knew his brother had seen it as well.

❀ ❀ ❀

Jeremiah walked the house remaining in the shadows when guests were in residence. He was ever watchful, and in the event of an incident, he was on hand to resolve it with the proper amount of violence. He had been standing behind where his brother was seated, though in the dark corridor. He saw Sizemore touch Callie. It had not been discussed between them, but Jeremiah knew his brother was aware. It had not gone unnoticed that Callie lived in his cabin. He remained calm, not allowing his presence to be known.

When dinner ended, E.J. and company–apart from one guest retired to the sitting room. Sizemore had excused himself, leaving the group. Ella and Callie continued to clean until the hour grew late. The atmosphere was now quiet, and the guests had moved on to their beds. Jeremiah watched from a distance as Callie stepped from the back of the house into the cool night air. The moon was full, and stars covered the sky. Her pace was unhurried, as she strolled toward her destination. The wind blew, and he could smell rain on the breeze. The sounds of the night insects were amplified, masking his presence. She was almost to his cabin, and he was about to turn away when he noticed Sizemore.

Jeremiah observed that her strides quickened, an indication she realized she was being followed. Sizemore's voice floated on the darkness. "Callie, girl, I come to taste ya this evenin'."

As Jeremiah closed in on the situation, he could hear the slurring of the overseer's words. The man was drunk, and his steps faltered as he staggered toward her. Callie tried to run, but Sizemore grabbed her arm and slammed her against the side of the cabin. She tried to fight him, but even unsteady from drink, he was stronger.

"Hush now, girl–hush," the overseer crooned.

Jeremiah heard the hasty sounds of cloth ripping and Callie sobbing. As Sizemore stepped back to fumble with his own clothing, Jeremiah stepped up behind him. In one fluid motion, he cocked his gun, placing the barrel to the overseer's temple. Before his victim could turn back toward him, Jeremiah pulled the trigger. There was a flash of blinding light, accompanied by a loud booming sound. Sizemore fell forward, briefly pinning Callie against the cabin before sliding to the ground. Everything grew still, and from the eerie silence, Jeremiah ordered, "Go on to the cabin."

Callie did not hesitate and without a word, she ran for the front of the cabin, slamming the door behind her.

❀ ❀ ❀

Under the cover of darkness, Jeremiah dragged the dead overseer to a place where there was always an open hole–the slave cemetery. The full moon provided just enough light for a man to face himself and his jealousy. So high were his emotions, he began pacing. The idea of Callie being touched by a next man had driven him to fatal acts. His temper extended to her as well, for she had introduced him to his more vicious self. After he shoved Sizemore into the hole, he removed his blood-stained clothing and boots, dropping them into the grave with his victim. When he was done covering the body, Jeremiah leaned the shovel against a tree. Throwing his gun harness over his shoulder, he walked back to his cabin in the suit God gave him.

He washed up at the pump located behind the cabin. The chilled water was just what he needed to cool his blazing temper. When he entered the cabin by the front door, Callie was seated on the bed with her legs drawn up in front of her. She looked up at him, her gaze blank and unfocused. In the bright lantern light, he saw her fear but no tears.

Jeremiah closed the door behind him and walked over to the table, placing his guns next to the lantern. He moved to an open chest at the foot of the bed and retrieved a towel. As he dried himself, he studied her, noticing blood spatter on her face and clothing.

"Come, let me help you undress," he said.

Callie shook her head, and immediately his anger was engaged. Wrapping the towel about his waist, he moved to the back door, lifted the bar and leaned it against the wall. He returned to the table and turned down the lantern wick before he crossed the room and took her by the arm. He thought she would fight him, but she didn't. He unbuttoned her dress and pushed the fabric from her shoulders. The shift she wore was blood stained, and her pantaloons were torn. He lifted the shift over her head, and the torn underpants fell to the floor. She stood before him naked, and Jeremiah thought her perfect. She had gained some weight; her rib cage was no longer showing. Callie had small, but firm breasts, and her caramel hips, thighs and legs were shapely.

He led her out the back door to the pump, and when the breeze touched her skin, Callie involuntarily let out a sob. He worked the pump for her as she vigorously scrubbed herself. Jeremiah watched as she attempted to rid herself of the overseer's smell and touch. She gagged as she rinsed her mouth trying to further purge herself from the taste of Sizemore's whiskey drenched kisses.

When she was done scrubbing herself, the combination of her wet skin and the steady breeze made her shake violently. Jeremiah removed the towel from about his waist, handing it to her. As she dried herself, she began to cry, and he was at a loss. More to the point, he was not a kind man. He did not rescue her out of compassion; he stepped in because he was jealous and territorial. The overseers tasting the slave women was a common occurrence, yet never until this night did it bother him.

She shocked him when she stepped forward and collapsed against him. While they were enemies, tonight it wasn't so. He, it appeared, was all she had. He hesitated before putting his arms around her, and she broke down weeping uncontrollably. The slice of light from the open door offered a visual to her pain. Finally, when she quieted, he offered instruction. "Come inside."

They were about to go into the cabin when the sound of earth crunching under someone's feet caught their attention. Jeremiah turned, pushing her behind him. Out of the darkness came a deep southern drawl. "I heard a gunshot. Everything all right, Jeremiah?"

Into the slice of light stepped E.J., and his presence coupled with her nakedness agitated Jeremiah. Behind him, Callie pressed herself against him, trembling. Jeremiah folded his arms over his chest. "Everything is all right... now."

E.J. nodded. "The gunshot?"

While they shared much privately, they had never allowed any-one to see them like this—as brothers, rather than slave and mas-ter. After the death of their papa, they took nothing for granted. Though they were close, Jeremiah considered it a weakness to be seen like this with a woman. It was as if his jealousy was visible. Callie had been crying, and he had been comforting her. He knew his brother was seeing a side of him that he, himself had never even seen–a side, he did not care to share.

"She ain't to be tasted by no one but me. I buried the problem in the slave graveyard."

Jeremiah's tone was sharp and belligerent. He stood before his brother, naked and burning with anger. The men were silent for a time, until E.J. finally said, "Good night then."

E.J. turned fading into the night, and with his brother gone, Jeremiah turned to her and said, "Come inside."

She stood anchored to the ground, shivering. He took her hand once more and helped her inside the cabin, then he shut and barred the door. Callie was still as a statue, refusing eye con-tact. He moved to the chest retrieving one of his coarse tan shirts and helped her into it. At the bottom of the stack of clothing, he found for himself, a pair of work trousers that laced up in the front. He put them on with no underwear, and as they stood half-dressed facing each other, he was unsure how proceed.

"Get on in the bed."

She must have been tired, because she did as he asked. Callie lay staring at him, as he reached for a shirt to finish dressing. He was holstering his gun, about to leave, when she whispered, "Please don't leave me."

Jeremiah was overstimulated, and his nastiness took control, scorching her in the process. He glared at her for a moment, before dropping some truth between clenched teeth. "Let's you and me be clear. I ain't a nice damn man. Ya need to be seein' me in the proper light. You are my slave, and you will do what the hell I say."

He was so angry, his chest heaved. The first violent exchange he had with Callie came to mind. She had told him she knew *precisely* who he was. Just thinking of her words to him that day had him irritated, still, an unwanted curiosity made him ask, "What does the word *precisely* mean?"

Her eyebrows drew together in confusion as she sat up in the bed and leaned against the wall. "*Precisely* means… *exactly,*" she whispered.

Jeremiah felt inadequate in a verbal exchange with her; he knew she was more educated. This one factor made it harder for him to control the situation between them. Worse yet, he wasn't sure if he liked her when she was submissive.

She drew her legs up in front of her and placed her forehead against her knees. Callie turned her head and looked away. He too felt defeated as he tossed his gun harness on the table and his shirt back into the chest. Jeremiah stepped to the lantern and turned the wick all the way down. Darkness enveloped them as he padded on his tiptoes across the room. Seating himself on the edge of the bed, he exhaled before laying back. He found that he was drained. When he was comfortable, she laid next to him and after a time, she moved in closer laying her head on his chest.

Finally, when he could admit to himself that he wanted her nearness, he placed his arm around her, pulling her closer. She began to cry again, and he offered no words. After a time, she calmed, and all was quiet. He could feel that she was still awake, and though he was worn-out, he couldn't sleep. Into the newfound tranquility, his deep voice asked, "Callie, will you tend me in all things?"

"No," she responded without hesitation.

Jeremiah smiled into the darkness. It wasn't lost on him that he was now tending her in all things. After a stretch of silence, Callie asked a question of her own, "Jeremiah?"

"What?" he answered, snidely.

"Who is going to save me from you?" she whispered, sounding on the verge of tears.

"No damn body," he snapped.

❊ ❊ ❊

Over the next two days, E.J. spent time showing Suzanne his home. The afternoons were turning out to be real scorchers, so in the mornings, just after an early breakfast, they walked in the gardens. They talked about all manner of things, and E.J. found her beauty second only to her intelligence.

"Will you volunteer, Edward?"

E.J. smiled at his bride-to-be. "I have the responsibility to carry on the Hunter line and look after my land. I have not volunteered, but I suspect I will have to join the party sooner or later. It is the reason I am going to Virginia. I want to see how things are unfolding. Most importantly, I am going to be of service where I can."

Suzanne was wide-eyed with alarm. "Will you delay marrying me, Edward, to join a war that could get you killed?"

"I have not delayed marrying you, Suzanne. My parents died, and it has been difficult. It is your father who is delaying the nuptials, not me."

Suzanne sighed. "I know. I am sorry for all you have been through, and I am sorry for how my papa is acting."

She wore a yellow, short-sleeve day dress, and her beautiful hair was curled flawlessly. The woman standing before him was a sight to behold with her tiny waist and firm cleavage. She turned and began walking up the path, forcing him to follow her. She looked over her shoulder at him, her beautiful lips pouty. "Why haven't you tried to kiss me like you always do, Edward?"

E.J. looked back at the main house before he looked at her. "I want you naked in my bed, Suzanne. I ain't interested in playing."

She blushed, and he stifled a laugh. He had not meant to shock her. Her response almost made him pop. "Can you show me pleasure and leave me innocent until we marry?"

His voice was not much above a croak. "I can."

She stepped closer to him. "Can you show me how to make you feel good?"

"Yes."

They continued their outing, touring the garden and the stables. Suzanne was enthralled with the horses. He kept her away from the ugliness of the fields and the slave quarters. While they enjoyed the day, E.J. could think of nothing but Suzanne's creamy white skin pressed against his own. When he finally returned her to the main house, her mother and sister were on hand to whisk her away until dinner. He then lunched with Adrian Wells, discussing the running of a plantation. It was an unavoidable deed, having to listen to the hot air coming from his future father-in-law. In truth, E.J. resented Wells because he felt belittled while in his company. It irritated him that he was a man of thirty, still sneaking about like an errant schoolboy with his intended.

After lunch, E.J. excused himself from his house guests to meet with his brother. It had been two days since he'd seen Jeremiah. He was giving his brother time to calm down from the Sizemore incident. He would be leaving for Virginia soon, and he wanted to get matters handled before he left. E.J. would spend the next few days instructing his brother and the others as to what should be done in his absence. He had secured the situation with Suzanne and her family; it was now time to bring the matter of his father's death back into focus.

❊ ❊ ❊

Since the first exchange between her and Jeremiah, he had not come back to his cabin until the problem with the overseer. This made Callie even more disappointed that he had not killed her upon their first meeting. She was too much of a coward to end her own existence. She managed her bondage by keeping busy and turning off all thought. Work was the only way to make it through the day. Callie had been assigned to labor in the kitchen with Ella, who did all the cooking. Ella wasn't nice, but neither was she mean—indifferent best described her, except when it came to her brother.

Sonny was, at first, a very nasty and mean man, but he had mellowed over the past few weeks. He directed her around the mansion, showing her what needed to be done. She followed instructions, giving him no trouble. While he wasn't friendly, he had begun advising her of things to make her life easier. Callie also noticed that every day at the same time, he kept company with Eva. It became clear that he loved her, though he did his best to hide it. Eva, on the other hand, was very kind and would often come to the main house to help with the cleaning. Sonny would step in to help because Eva at times had difficulty walking.

Eva was funny and often the one bright spot of Callie's day. Ever since the incident with the overseer, Callie couldn't focus. She was nervous, as she now realized the perils with which female slaves lived. Callie was unsure which she feared more, rape or being alone at night. Jeremiah had stayed the night the overseer tried to force himself on her, but he had not returned since. She had thought he would have been dead come morning, for he had killed a white man. But she saw him the next day, standing near the edge of the fields. His back was ramrod straight with a shotgun leaned over his right shoulder.

"You's sho' in a thankin' mood today," Eva said staring at her.

Callie looked up from where she sat polishing the silverware and smiled. "I'm tired. I haven't been sleeping much."

Eva looked askance. "So ya ain't finna tell me what got ya so nervous."

"I'm fine, really." Attempting to avoid any real discussion, Callie stood and walked to the back door.

The kitchen was a huge room with a black and white color scheme. On the left of the room was a white counter where all the vegetables were handled. At the right side of the counter sat a small round black table with four chairs. The sinks were two large white porcelain bowls and just outside the back door was the pump. Behind the sink, a large bay window overlooked the vegetable garden. In order to keep the main house, cool in the summer, a large stove was housed in a separate building adjacent to the back entrance. Still, off in the corner was a smaller black stove used in the winter. There was a large walk-in pantry next to the doorway of a long hall that traveled to the front of the house. Unless cleaning, Callie spent all her time in the kitchen. Today, she was hiding.

As the day pressed on, Eva, who loved to chit–chat, was quiet but watchful. When word came that the master and his guests would take dinner in the smaller dining room off the main parlor, Callie panicked. Just before dinner, Eva stood to leave for the day. She looked at Callie as she brushed off the front of her brown dress. Her features were soft and warm, contrasting with her wild and unruly hair.

"If'n you's scared at night, you can come and keep me company. Sonny comes to see 'bout me at night, but he don't always stay," Eva offered kindly.

Callie didn't look at her for fear she would cry; instead, she just nodded. Eva squeezed her shoulder, offering what support she could, and then she was gone. Callie wondered what Eva knew, but she wouldn't dare inquire.

"All right now, gal. Time to get the masta and his guests dinna," Ella demanded as she entered the kitchen from the back door.

Callie stood and loaded the moving tray with the meal for the evening. Her stomach was in knots; the smell of the food nauseated her. As she followed Ella down the long hall, she concentrated on the white bow tied neatly at Ella's back. When Callie stepped into the smaller dining room, the master and his guests were having polite dinner conversation. They were seated at a table shorter than the one in the formal dining room. The last rays of sunlight flooded through the open French doors. A balmy breeze carried in the scent of blooming flowers, and Callie was thankful for the fresh air because she felt faint.

Ella handed Callie the plates, and she placed them before each person, trying not to engage in eye contact with the master. Her hand shook as she placed his plate before him. Hurriedly, she turned away, but not before her eyes collided with his penetrating gaze. She quickly looked away and rushed from the room. Later, after a leisurely meal, the dinner party wandered out into the gardens for a stroll.

Callie was left alone to start the cleaning in the dining room. She was down on her knees straightening the floral rug beneath the table when the master stepped through the French doors. He had removed his bowtie, leaving his white shirt open at the throat. She stood, unsure of what to expect, as he offered nothing verbal, nor did he smile. She was about to fade away from the stress, when Jeremiah's voice floated into the room from the direction of the hall just behind her. "We ready in the study."

"After you, Callie," the master said calmly, making a sweeping gesture with his hand. He spoke as if they had been conversing the whole time.

She turned, moving toward Jeremiah, who stood dressed in tan trousers, a white shirt and black boots. He had removed his mustache. His dark eyes, coupled with his jet-black skin made him foreboding. His hair had not been cut and blue-black curls stood riotous upon his crown. At his hips, hung two guns, and like his brother, he did not smile. Dread climbed through her being making her legs heavy. Still, she crossed the room to him and waited patiently.

"Come," Jeremiah commanded.

At her back, she could hear the master's booted footfalls as they struck the hardwood floors. When she stepped into the hall, the front door was open, but the natural light had long since faded. As they moved along the corridor, she could no longer make out the canvases that hung on the wall. The further they walked toward the study, the dimmer her life felt. At the end of the hall stood Sonny, who was making his rounds to light the candles and oil lamps placed strategically about the house.

The three of them entered the study—Jeremiah, followed by Callie and finally the master. Sonny closed the door behind them. Shaded oil lamps burned about the room. A portrait of a distinguished-looking gentleman hung on the wall behind the desk. He had piercing eyes that made Callie feel as if he were watching her every move. The older white man seated in front of the desk was a dinner guest from the previous evening. Callie remembered him. He rose to greet them.

"Norman," the master said, as he continued to the front of the study. Leaning his hip on the corner of the desk, he folded his arms over his chest and waited.

"Edward, Jeremiah," Norman responded.

Jeremiah moved to stand to the left of the master, and Callie was left standing in the center of the room behind Norman. She was unsure why she was there, but it couldn't be for anything good. The men began speaking as though she didn't exist.

"I will be leaving for Virginia day after tomorrow. Currently, we have thirty overseers. They are to be broken down into two groups of fifteen between you and Percy. Norman, I want you and Percy to report to Jeremiah. Do you foresee this being an issue?" The master asked.

"No. Ain't no issue. Jeremiah and I work fine together," Norman replied.

E.J. nodded. "The plantation needs to be covered at night, the same as in the day. We can't have a repeat of the last insurrection. I want all angles of my land watched day and night."

Callie listened to the exchange, but kept her head down attempting to go unnoticed. She feared hearing too much and then being punished for it. The master had a smooth voice which carried attitude, and she was petrified in his presence. Until the other night, he had not noticed her. Yet, here she stood, waiting for the next shoe to drop. She had hoped he would kill her and be done, rather than let her linger in pain.

"I will take the nights," Jeremiah said.

Jeremiah's voice was rough and deep. His anger simmered just below the surface. Callie could feel his tension, but as was her way, she offered no eye contact. The man called Norman asked, "So you will have night duty and I will handle the day hours?"

"Precisely," Jeremiah responded, drawing out his pronunciation of the word so that it dripped with authority.

Callie's head popped up, and her eyes slammed into his. He did not acknowledge the nonverbal exchange. Instead, he blinked slowly, refocusing on Norman. Dropping her head again, she went back into her shell, tuning the men out. She stood motionless in the background until the meeting appeared to be coming to an end. The air in the study was thick; she couldn't breathe.

"What's yo' name, girl?" the man called Norman asked.

Callie looked up into his cold blue eyes. She opened her mouth to respond, but Jeremiah cut her off. "Mine."

Jeremiah moved to stand between her and Norman. She was trembling and to her shame, she pressed herself against his back. As he spoke, his words were calm and measured. "She is mine, and I do not share."

Norman nodded, the message was clear. Silence hung in the

air for moments before Jeremiah added, "Sizemore came to my cabin to taste what is mine. He won't be back."

The master walked over and opened the door to the study. "That will be all, Norman."

The older man stood and looked at both men before he walked out the door without a word. Callie wanted to leave as well, but no one had dismissed her so she remained behind Jeremiah–standing entirely too close. The men continued to speak as though she wasn't there.

"While in Virginia, I will go back to the Turner plantation. It's time we begin investigating papa's death. I shall be gone a fortnight. I will send word of any developments," the master said.

"I will be here when you get back. I won't fail again," Jeremiah replied.

"I fear this war will be nastier than most think. I can only delay so long before it falls on my doorstep," E.J. went on.

"One thing at a time," Jeremiah replied.

E.J. nodded, ending the conversation, and suddenly Jeremiah stepped away from her–leaving her exposed. She held the master's stare, and he startled her when he spoke.

"Good night, Callie."

"Good night, sir," she whispered.

Jeremiah walked toward the door, and Callie followed. Once in the hall, he stopped abruptly, staring at her. An oil lamp sat on a small table midway down the hall, making the lighting soft. Callie stood with her back to the wall, looking up at him. He was agitated, and somehow, she knew why. She would not push him; she was too exhausted from holding herself together. Callie could not manage the discord between them tonight. He stepped into her personal space and leaning down against her ear, he whispered, "It's good that you understand he ain't not your master. I am."

Hostility rolled off his person, hitting her in waves. They were cheek-to-cheek, and Callie was so engulfed by his emotions, her eyes watered, but she stifled the urge to cry. Finally, when she had composed herself, she answered softly, "I don't wish to call no man master."

He stepped back and smiled at her, showing beautiful white teeth. Jeremiah's scent had collected in her nostrils. He smelled of soap, saddle polish and the outdoors. His masculinity was over-powering, and he shocked her when he leaned forward pressing his lips gently to hers. He kissed her not once, but twice, and against her lips he said, "You will answer to me, Callie, one way or another."

Placing his lips against her forehead, he kissed her a third time before he stepped back. "You are done here for the night. Go home."

Callie did not hesitate; she almost ran down the hall toward the kitchen and out the back door.

❈ ❈ ❈

Jeremiah watched her go before he returned to the study. E.J. was standing at the window. His brother turned to face him with a troubled expression. Jeremiah joined him at the window. The two of them stared out into the darkness, their reflections in the panes looking back at them in the soft light. Jeremiah finally spoke first.

"What is bothering you that you ain't shared?"

"Suzanne's father continues to delay our marriage. I will not allow her to be given to another man. If Adrian Wells continues to be a hindrance, I will kill him and take his daughter."

Jeremiah nodded slowly at his brother's reflection. He didn't understand why E.J. didn't just kill Adrian Wells and be done.

❈ ❈ ❈

Later that evening, when the house had quieted, Suzanne stood naked, facing E.J. in the soft candlelight. He wore no shoes or shirt and his blue trousers were halfway unbuttoned. Black hair trickled from his muscled stomach into his pants. His gazed was intense, and he did not speak.

Suzanne finally found her nerve. "Take your pants off, Edward, and be naked with me."

E.J. smiled, as he took in her naked splendor. She had creamy white skin with nipples that reminded him of strawberries in June. Suzanne had a tiny waist, and hips that flared ever so slightly with long, stunning legs. He closed his eyes against the thought of being buried deep within her while her taught, firm legs encircled him. Her hair was loose and fell about her shoulders—she was striking. He breathed in through his nose to calm himself. His voice was velvety. "I need my trousers, Suzanne, ain't no other way to keep you innocent."

When she pouted, E.J. stepped forward caressing her face and kissing her deeply. He groaned from the contact, before he picked her up and carried her to his bed. As she lay in the center of the mattress, her legs fell open. It was then he decided to give her father one month. If Wells did not relent in his stance about the marriage, E.J. would kill him. Leaning down, he applied his tongue to her womanhood and pleasure echoed through the chamber. Later, Suzanne proved to be a faster learner as his deep groans of ecstasy flooded the room.

Suzanne had dozed off exhausted from their sexual play; still he managed to leave her intact. E.J. doused the candles and carried her back to the guest room. As he laid her gently upon the bed, she whispered, "I love you, Edward."

E.J. smiled. Suzanne fell immediately asleep, and when he stepped back into the hall, he headed to Nettie's small room on the third floor. He found that he needed her to ease his pent-up energy, and she welcomed him.

❀ ❀ ❀

Richmond, Virginia

May 1861

E.J. journeyed with the Wells family, first by carriage and then by railroad to Richmond, Virginia. The party arrived after four days of rigorous travel—tired, but excited to have made it to their destination. They settled in at the luxurious Spotswood hotel on the second floor. The hotel spanned an entire city block and was five stories high. On the ground level, to the left of the lobby, was a grand eatery. Large round tables with pristine white table cloths filled the dining area. Each was topped with a candelabrum. The red plush carpet ran all the way to the front of the room, stopping at a stage. On a marble platform sat a gleaming, black grand piano with clawed feet.

The atmosphere was hustle and bustle, as the staff rushed about to do the bidding of the rich. In the rear of the dining room, the black doors to the kitchen swung back and forth constantly, with waiters rushing in and out carrying trays loaded with food and drink. Tall, mullion windows lined the far wall; their draperies pulled back to allow the sunlight to flood the room. Chatter filled the room with discussions of war spoken by both men and women.

Back in the lobby, a huge front desk stood adjacent to a grand spiral staircase. Behind the desk stood five men dressed in crisp white shirts, blue vests and matching blue trousers, their sole purpose–pleasing the guests. Next to the steps were several young men dressed as bell-hops; their uniforms were burgundy. On every floor a bell-hop stood at the ready. The most elite from the newly formed government were in residence, and the Spotswood was sparing no expense.

On the right of the staircase was a gentlemen's lounge with

overstuffed, velvet-covered chairs where the men relaxed with their cigars and drink. The room's color scheme was a masculine brown and beige. The lounge was never empty as the men had plenty to debate. Heated arguments over slavery, government and agriculture echoed out into the lobby. The grand hotel was the temporary home of the Confederate administration while they awaited proper housing.

On the second day in Virginia, E.J. was seated with Suzanne and her family in the dining room having lunch, when Jefferson Davis himself stepped into the lobby. On the streets, the people cheered, so happy were they that their hero had arrived. Both E.J. and Adrian Wells excused themselves to stand along the edge of the lobby to witness this proud day. President Davis was an unassuming man of average height, with dark brown hair, intelligent blue eyes, a hook nose and high cheekbones. His gray and brown beard was trimmed to perfection and framed a genuine smile. He wore a long dark blue coat, a white shirt and blue bow tie; he was fashion. The new president was immediately whisked away for his safety, and the members of his cabinet followed.

❊ ❊ ❊

Time passed slowly in Virginia with E.J. spending his mornings in the company of his intended. Adrian Wells was so taken with the daily fervor in the gentlemen's lounge, he barely paid his wife and daughters any attention. E.J. and Suzanne strolled every morning after breakfast. He loved the time they spent getting to know one another. Today, she was beautiful in her royal blue dress with a matching bonnet. Her face, however, wore a worried look.

"What troubles you, darling?"

"Now that we're here in Richmond, the war is not just some romantic notion. I fear greatly for your safety, Edward," she whispered, as her steps faltered.

"You don't have anything to be worried about. Don't be

concerned, love; I will speak with you before I do anything." E.J. reassured her.

"I know you own slaves, Edward, but don't you think at times it's wrong?" she asked, holding his gaze.

"No, I don't think it's wrong. It's all I know. My daddy died trying to protect our livelihood. How would I care for you without slaves?"

"You could be a lawyer." She smiled.

His eyes narrowed. "Do you not want to be a farmer's wife?"

Suzanne moved in on her tiptoes and kissed his cheek. "I want to be your wife no matter what you do, Edward. It's just that...."

"It's just what, Suzanne?"

"I don't think we are going to win this war. I just want you to know, if you didn't have the Hunter plantation, I would still want to be your wife," she whispered, as she stepped back.

E.J. stared at his fiancé. He was impressed by her intelligence for he too thought all the same things. Changing the subject, he said, "Come, woman! You think far too much."

They had resumed walking when Suzanne took him by surprise yet again. "I'm shocked at your stance on slavery."

"Why so?"

Suzanne looked directly into his eyes. "Because you love your brother, and he is a slave."

E.J. wondered when she had observed him and his brother together, but he didn't ask. Instead, he offered her a lesson. "To every rule there is an exception—Jeremiah is the exception to most rules."

"I see that he loves you because he is protective of you. He's frightening, the way he lurks in the dark corners of your home." She shivered.

E.J. chuckled. "You are safer because he does."

❊ ❊ ❊

The days following the arrival of Jefferson Davis were hectic in Richmond. It was also difficult to get into the gentlemen's lounge now that he was in residence. The very price of the rooms had gone up from two dollars per week to three. E.J. sat in on one debate about slavery that wasn't really a debate since everyone felt the same. The hotel started allowing people into the lounge on alternate days based on your last name. E.J. had given his pass to his father in-law to be, an act that seemed to elevate him in Adrian Wells' esteem.

E.J. let Suzanne know he would be gone for a day, explaining that he had an errand to run. He hired a hansom cab, and his first stop was the local dry-goods store. There, he sent a brief, yet simple telegram to his brother. Next, he started his journey to the Turner plantation, and he did not send word that he wished an audience. The visit would be impolite and forward. E.J. was not trying to make a good impression. He was trying to get answers about his papa, and he would not be turned away.

It was just after midday when his carriage came to a stop in front of the main house. E.J. observed his surroundings. He could still see remnants of the uprising that took place two years ago. Large piles of charred wood lay to the left of the fields where the slaves were picking cotton. Out of the carriage window, the main house came into view. It was a lot like his home with large white pillars and rolling green lawns, but he wasn't fooled. On this rebuilt estate, his papa had been put down like a dog.

The carriage suddenly became stuffy, and he tugged at his starched, white shirt collar, just inside his bow tie. E.J. felt clammy, the air too thick for him to breathe. He became concerned that he would not be able to control his rage. At this very moment, he felt as though he could kill everyone who dwelled within that wretched house.

E.J. could hear the driver come around to the side of the carriage and set the steps. The door was pulled open, and he placed his hand above his eyes for shade, giving them a moment to adjust. The day was bright and would have been considered beautiful, if he hadn't been trying to solve his papa's murder. He stepped down from the carriage and addressed the driver, his words slow and deliberate.

"You will wait just to the left of the drive, until further instructed."

The driver was a middle aged, white fellow, with wild gray and black hair tied back into a ponytail. He had dark brown eyes, a big red snout and small lips. E.J. measured the driver, who came highly recommended. He appeared to be a ruffian, yet the man answered simply, "Yes, Sir."

As E.J. approached the stairs of the main house, he could hear the carriage roll off to the side of the long drive. Before he could knock, a young male slave dressed in butler attire pulled open the front door. He was dark-skinned with low cut hair and a lazy eye. The slave spoke first.

"Who may I says is callin'?"

"My name is Edward Hunter Jr. I have come to see a Mr. Will Turner," E.J. barely contained his anger.

At the mention of the previous owner, the slave's face registered shock. He hesitated before he replied. "Please sah, wait right chere."

E.J. blinked as the slave slammed the door in his face. Moments ticked by before a tall, thin white man with brown hair, aquiline features and thick glasses opened the door. He did not match the description E.J. had been given of Will Turner. He wore a wrinkled gray suit and his appearance put E.J. in mind of a solicitor. The man stepped forward and extended his hand. "I am Anderson Wilkerson."

"Edward Hunter Jr.," E.J. replied.

"Please come in, Mr. Hunter."

E.J. did not make polite conversation nor did he apologize for showing up unannounced. Instead, he placed the burden of conversation on the man standing before him.

"You must be tired from your travels. Follow me, please," Anderson said, before directing his next words to the butler who was hovering in the background. "Fetch my wife, Daniel."

"Yes, sah," the butler said before racing off.

E.J. followed Anderson into a small sitting room located off the long hall. The color scheme was blue and gold. In the corner of the room sat a large comfortable blue couch, trimmed in gold. Two matching chairs sat opposite the couch for the purpose of conversation. The men were just about to seat themselves, when a vision of loveliness appeared in the doorway.

"Ah, my beautiful wife Rose." Anderson reached out his hand to her. "Darling, this is Mr. Edward Hunter."

"Mr. Hunter, how nice to meet you, though I wish it was under better circumstances." Rose went right to the heart of the matter.

"Nice to meet you as well, Miss Rose." E.J. felt lighter, now that he realized they weren't going to behave as though they didn't know why he had come. The urge to kill everyone in the house had subsided–for now.

"Won't you please sit and rest yourself," Rose continued, and to the servant she said, "Daniel, please bring refreshments."

Rose Wilkerson was dressed in pink and white. Under her lovely cleavage was a dark pink bow, separating the skirts from the bodice. Her black hair spilled about her shoulders, and her dark blue eyes did not falter from his stare. After seating themselves, E.J. waited until after the refreshments were served to begin any real discussion. Small finger sandwiches and lemonade was placed before him on the table, but he didn't indulge. Lunch seemed a polite formality to ease them into dialogue about the last two years.

When the door to the sitting room was pulled shut, E.J. looked from Anderson to his wife. "I want to know what happened to my father."

"I hear your plantation suffered an uprising," Anderson replied. "It could only be the same band of slaves that burned down our plantation. Did you not catch them?"

Rose's expression became one of urgent distress. She was trying to communicate to her husband, without words, the need for discretion.

"One of my men shot one of the runaways in the face. We believe he is dead, but we would like to get all of them. I did notice the similarities in the uprisings, and it brought me back to my father's death. Here's what I think, Anderson. I believe this band of runaways came here to your plantation when my father came to visit all those months back. He was killed as a result." E.J. leaned forward in his chair. "Where is Will Turner, by the way?"

When E.J. adjusted in his chair, he noticed Rose slid back in her chair, as if trying to distance herself from his words. She understood the threat, and it pleased him. He could see her alarm, though she covered it well. Mrs. Wilkerson knew the slaves in question, E.J. could feel it. The expression on her face made clear her thoughts. She adjusted her skirts to buy time before she answered, "Will is my brother. He went missing some months ago. No one has seen him since."

"So, he is dead, then?" E.J. replied, callously.

Anderson took over the exchange, oblivious of his wife's unease. "About three months ago, these runaways came and accosted my wife, demanding information as to who killed their brother. I was incensed. According to the documents my wife and I found, William believed they were holed up in Canada somewhere."

E.J.'s gaze fell to Rose. He watched her reaction, and it was clear, she was not thrilled with how much her husband was talk-ing. Nevertheless, her husband was spilling the beans. Patiently, he waited until Anderson took a breath, before he spoke.

"May I see these documents?" E.J. asked.

"You most certainly can." Anderson stood to fetch the papers.

As the door clicked shut behind Anderson, E.J. turned his glare on Rose. When finally, he spoke, his southern drawl dripped hazard. "Miss Rose, my father was murdered in your home. The idea that you would try to cover for those responsible makes me reassess you. I seek to deal with those who have wronged my fam-ily. But I could widen my list of victims to include you and your husband. The choice is yours."

Rose's hand shook as she brought it to her chest in dismay. She leaned back for a moment. "Obviously in your grief, you have forgotten your manners. It isn't polite to come to someone's home uninvited and then threaten to kill them. Lucky for you, I don't take offense easily. Understand that my brother has gone missing, and I have my own sorrows to nurse. As for covering up your father's murder, I will not apologize for being cautious as to whom I speak. I only have your word that you are who you say you are. Don't threaten me, Mr. Hunter. You and your grief can go to hell."

E.J. thought Rose Wilkerson was magnificent in her anger. When she stood abruptly to leave the room, her long black hair spilled over her right eye. Her chest was heaving with indignation, as E.J. offered calmly, "I apologize for my behavior, Miss Rose. You are correct in your assumption that my sorrow has run away with me. Can you forgive me?"

E.J. let his jacket fall open to reveal the gun holstered to his upper left side. He was still attempting to intimidate her without words. She stared at him unmoved, it seemed, by his new threat. In the distance, he could hear Anderson speaking with a servant as he drew closer. E.J. spoke calmly to Rose. "I will try to be on my best behavior, Miss Rose. But I really must know what happened to my papa."

Rose nodded slowly, as her husband stepped through the door with Will's box of documents.

❈ ❈ ❈

The Wilkersons did not offer Edward Hunter Jr. lodging for the night, though the hour had grown late by the time their visitor had reviewed Will Turner's documents to his satisfaction. The couple watched from a foyer window as E.J.'s hansom cab disappeared down the long drive. As soon as the carriage was out of sight, Rose rounded on Anderson.

"How could you speak about these things with no regard for my feelings? How could you speak with a complete stranger about my family and home this way? Are you trying to get us killed, or are you trying to see that my childhood home is burned to the ground, yet again?"

Anderson who never had a cross word with his wife was stunned. After a time, his eyes narrowed, and he couldn't help himself. A vision of his wife standing in her night wrap while three slaves ogled her came to mind. He could see in his mind's eye, Rose reaching out to touch one of them on the sleeve. She had whispered something that he could not hear, and when he asked about it, she had lied; he was sure of it. His jealousy got the better of him. "If I didn't know better, I would think you are like your father and brother. Maybe you too, like your meat well done."

"Vulgarity and jealousy doesn't become you, Anderson," Rose replied, before she turned and walked away.

❈ ❈ ❈

Two days passed, and silence continued between Rose and Anderson. When she dressed to leave for town, Anderson did not question her or invite himself. She took Bertha, a female slave with her as a companion, and they left at first light. Rose made only one stop before heading back home. She went to the dry-goods store to send a telegram, her message desperate.

5

Canada, June 1861

THE MEN RODE out to the inn to give the ambassador a message from Black. Bainesworth was disappointed that Black had not come himself. He was even less enchanted that the message sent, offered nothing. Instead of four days, the endeavor had taken four weeks. This was the second meeting between himself and the eighteen, but no progress had been made—no concrete answer had been reached.

"Black will see ya by the creek, same as before," said the man with the angry scar.

"I shall gather my men," Bainesworth responded.

"You will come alone," the man said, "Either ya trust us or ya don't."

Bainesworth stared at the three men before him. The twins looked as though they ate babies for breakfast, but the one doing the talking seemed void of all emotion. The man with the scar sat on his horse, leaning over a shotgun that lay across his lap. No, he didn't trust them, but he was in a bind. Bainesworth looked just past the men in the saddle to the people milling about. No one appeared to care that these killers were on the loose. He focused on the superficial: the warm temperature, the overcast skies, the mixture of people going from establishment to establishment, and the smell of strong coffee coming from just beyond the inn's front door. The ambassador finally mustered a nod, lest his voice give away his fear. They didn't even give him time to retrieve his horse, providing one for him.

They rode in silence for an hour, and when the creek came into view, so too did twelve more men. The three men flanking the ambassador rode up the bank, leaving him behind. Black stood off to the side having what looked like an intense conversation with a dark-skinned man, who was just a bit shorter than him. Bainesworth's steps faltered when the men all turned at once to stare at him.

"Greetings, Black, to both you and your men," Bainesworth called out as he approached.

"Ambassador," Black replied.

When Black and Bainesworth stood just a few feet from each other, the ambassador looked about. Again, he regretted coming alone. The upside, he was getting another audience with Black, but it did not look like it would go well. The men had formed a circle with him and Black at the center. The ambassador looked at the men before him dressed in all black and knew from their expressions a decision had been reached.

Bainesworth turned to Black. "Have you come to a conclusion, my good man?"

"May I ask how you came by the information that there is a scheme to kill Lincoln?" Black queried.

"Montreal has become flooded with southern factions. This is not to say that there are not those who oppose the southern position. But the men in question appear to be from the North, supporting the South's stance. They come from all walks of life. One such man is fresh out of nappies and is an actor, of all things."

Black stood with his arms folded over his chest, listening

intently. "Ambassador," came his stinging reply, "when I ask a question, I want the answer, not some sidestepping history lesson."

Bainesworth turned red and stepped closer as if to whisper, but Black cut him off. "Surely you understand that my men need to know all if they are expected to risk their lives. Come now, Ambassador, don't be coy—spit it out."

The ambassador coughed. "The queen has spies in the larger cities. These spies report their findings to the queen and her council. Based on the issue, her majesty may send orders on how to address a matter. I learned of the misfortune concerning the Union president through the spy system. I was directed to warn Mr. Lincoln."

"So you's a spy," Simon erupted.

The ambassador was uncomfortable, but he answered truthfully, "Yes."

"You have a group of men. Why don't you warn the Union?" Elbert asked.

Bainesworth could not hold eye contact with the two men speaking. The taller man had one brown eye and one gray eye; the other had lifeless, cold eyes. Still, he managed, "You men seem more likely to get the job done efficiently. You have better knowledge of the States as you have worked the Underground Railroad."

"We work the Underground Railroad because we are not free people. Why should we give a damn about their war?" Black asked, clearly irked that Bainesworth was admitting to spying on him as well.

The ambassador was growing distraught. "I need your assistance. The men with me will not ride into the States now. Perhaps I can offer you men something for your services."

"What kind of power do you have?" Black asked.

Bainesworth knew he had put his foot in his mouth. He gathered his thoughts before he spoke. "I have the queen's ear, but my power is limited. Is it money you seek?"

Black snorted, insulted by the question. He turned to walk away. Bainesworth stammered at his back. "I am just trying to fathom what will be a fair exchange."

Black turned around and glared. "You must think me unintelligent?"

Bainesworth smiled. "I am thinking many things at this moment, but you being unintelligent isn't among them. You have the upper hand, Black, and we both know it. What is it you want, my friend, so that we might move to the next level?"

"For starters, you will ride out with us. Your men are not needed. When we leave, we will take only you. We have no deal if you refuse," Black answered.

"I look rough, but it is all for show. Taking me along can't help the cause. What can I give you in exchange for your service?" Bainesworth asked.

"We have no deal if you refuse. As for what you can give us, you can't expect us to know at this moment. You only just proposed payment. We would be negligent if we answered in haste." Black said, returning the ambassador's smile.

"I see," Bainesworth said on a sigh, "When shall we leave?"

"I have some matters to handle that will take five days. We will ride out on day six. This will give you time to change your mind. But be warned, Ambassador, once we step into the plan, there is no going back. You are not in charge—I am. If you fail to follow my orders, James here," Black motioned to the man who had delivered his original message back at the inn, "will slit your throat."

"I shall be here on day six, at…" Bainesworth's questioned.

"At dawn," Black finished for him.

"I shall be ready."

Black turned, whispering something to the one of the men that escorted him to this meeting place. The man nodded and the three came together again to deliver him back to town.

❈ ❈ ❈

When they were done playing nanny to the ambassador, James, Frank, and Lou rode a little farther to a general store called "Everything." James greeted the tall, white proprietor, Virgil, with a heartfelt handshake.

"Is something the matter?" Virgil asked. "Is Black needing me?"

"No. Things is good," James answered.

James watched as Virgil's blue eyes lost their look of concern, and his thin frame relaxed. He looked about the store. James had never purchased anything but the necessities required by life. But today, with his impending departure only days away, he wanted to buy something nice for Abby.

"Can I help with something, James?" Virgil inquired.

"I would like to buy a few things for a lady." James looked nervously back toward Frank and Lou, who had posted up near the door.

Virgil smiled. "What do you have in mind?"

"Shit," James said on a chuckle, "I ain't got nothin' in mind."

Virgil laughed aloud. "So, you're courting?"

James frowned at the word "courting". It implied that Abby wasn't officially his. He was instantly jealous, and his response carried bite, "She is mine. We ain't damn courtin'."

Virgil held up his hands. "I understand," he said apologetically. "I have several items for you to consider."

After an hour of moving through the store, James settled on several items. He bought Abby two dresses—one was a bright yellow, with short sleeves, the other a powder blue with a matching bonnet. The colors would go well with her exquisite dark skin. He didn't stop there; James also purchased two bars of rose-scented soap. He had been about to leave when he spied a large, white porcelain tub. He desired it for her and lastly, he bought a small bottle of perfume. The fragrance was fresh, not overpowering like he had smelled in the pussy parlor. He made plans to have everything delivered in the morning.

"In the morning it is," Virgil agreed. "Tell Black I asked after him."

James nodded, before stepping onto the boardwalk where Frank and Lou waited. They rode hard for the fort and made it just as night fell. After dropping his horse to the stables, James broke from his comrades and headed for Black's house. When he entered the foyer, he could hear Little Otis singing with Big Mama and Sunday. He walked into the kitchen to find Sunday feeding Natalie.

"Papa up!" Otis cried when he saw him.

James reached out his arms and lifted Otis, causing Big Mama and Sunday to smile. Natalie reached out her arms and James lifted her too. Both children were dressed in nightgowns, Natalie in pink and Otis in blue. Sunday shook her head. "She ain't wantin to eat her mashed potatoes."

At Sunday's words, Natalie turned her head away, placing her head on James' shoulder. He laughed. "She knows her Uncle James will save her from mashed potatoes."

Big Mama just shook her head. He was about to seat himself when Black appeared at the hall entrance. The look on his face told James to follow him. James started to follow him when Big Mama said, "We'll keep the chilren."

"I got them, Mama. They be 'sleep after a while." James replied.

"I ain't wantin to thleep, Papa," Little Otis said as James carried him and Natalie down the hall toward the study.

James put the children down on the floor. Paul had carved several farm animals out of wood, and the babies began playing with them. Black's office had become their favorite place in the house before bedtime. The children were distracted with the toys, leaving the men to talk.

"Anthony and Luke went to the dry goods store. They go once every seven days to pick up supplies. While there, they may send telegrams for me or check to see if I have any. Today, a telegram came, and it was for you."

James' eyebrows knitted together; he could not think of a soul who would send him a message. Judging by Black's facial expression, it wasn't good news either.

What happened?" James asked, taking the telegram from Black.

"See for yourself," Black replied.

As James reached for the message, his hand shook revealing how emotionally fragile he felt. Though he and the men would handle the matter with Lincoln first, James also understood that Black had taken this mission to help *him*. It was why Black was negotiating so vigorously with Bainesworth. Since the ambassador was using them, Black was trying to see what benefit could be had from having Bainesworth around.

Black played with the children while James read the message. He read it several times, so shocked was he to discover who had sent it.

FRIENDS CAME FROM THE HUNTER PLANTATION AND INFORMED ME YOU WERE UNDER THE WEATHER I HOPE THIS MESSAGE FINDS YOU WELL THEY INSIST THEY WILL COME TO LOOK IN ON YOU AND YOUR BROTHERS I WILL BE LEAVING FOR BOSTON SOON–ROSE

James looked up from the paper and stared at Black.

"It would seem," Black said, not taking his eyes off the children, "that our issues have become tied. It was rumored that old man Hunter had two sons—one white and one colored. It appears they are both on our trail. Tim killing Hunter saved me, but we should have burned Will's office."

"Yeah, if Rose is sending this message, the new Hunter musta come to see her. He must know enough to cause her concern. Prolly the overseers, or even the slaves, been talkin'. What now?"

"I need to think on it. Let the men know we will meet in my dining room at dawn," Black replied.

James nodded, and both men turned their attention back to the children.

※ ※ ※

When the children had fallen asleep, James put Otis in Big Mama's bed and headed for Elbert's house. The night carried a warm breeze, as he walked alone in the darkness. James was forced to ponder matters he never thought of before. Now that he was a father and experiencing closeness with Abby, he feared an attack on the fort. He had always feared as much, but nowadays, he sympathized even more with Black and Elbert.

The hour had grown late, but it wasn't yet midnight. James reached Elbert's house and stood alone, thinking, until Elbert stepped onto the porch next to him. "What has you out so late? Is our son all right? Elbert asked.

"Yeah, he in bed wit' Big Mama," James answered.

The light from the window spilled onto the porch, and Elbert waited patiently for James to get his thoughts together. "We ridin' out again, but we ain't built Anna and the kids no house."

"She understands. Anna is more worried about our safety."

"Shit, I'm worried too. You and Simon just had little ones. I don't think neither of ya should come."

"I will be by your side," Elbert responded.

James nodded. "I got a message from Rose today."

Elbert turned facing him. "Really?"

"She says they has come from the Hunter plantation looking

for us. I exposed us," James went on. There was no mistaking the weariness and guilt in his tone.

"You tried to save a woman and her child. They probably would have both been killed. Now the child is with us, and Mamie got her baby back as well. I would do it again, with no damn issue," Elbert said with a low chuckle.

"They know where we are."

Elbert waved him off. "And we know where they are. I say we ride out to keep the bullshit from the fort. War got the south tied up—that gives us the advantage."

James knew his brother was right. "Black wants to meet at dawn in the dining room."

"Yeah," Elbert said.

James wished Elbert a goodnight and headed for the barracks. He planned to go and see Abby, so the first thing he did was bathe. Then, he enlisted the help of Anthony and Luke to get the word out about the meeting.

He and Abigail had fallen into a routine, and it felt good. Normally, on the days he had his son, he slept at Black's house. When Elbert had their son, he slept with Abby. Tonight, was an exception; he needed her.

She left a light burning in the front room for him. The door was pulled shut, but unlocked. In the front room, he lowered the wick and got undressed. In total darkness, he maneuvered his way to the bedroom. He climbed into bed, and Abby instantly moved close to him, placing her head on his chest.

Her whisper broke through the darkness. "I thought ya had the baby today."

"I do. He sleepin' wit' Big Mama. I missed you."

"Mmmm. I missed you too," Abby whispered back.

James smiled to himself. She snuggled closer and kissed his chest as she dozed off once again. In that moment, something happened that had not occurred in weeks—his dick got hard. Content, James fell asleep.

※ ※ ※

It was five-thirty in the morning when James made his way to the front of the fort. The men were changing shifts, and Luke would be on duty for the next few hours. He left directions for Luke to take possession of the items he procured from Virgil.

"When he get here, I'll come find ya," Luke said.

"I'll be at Black's house. We has a meetin' this morning," James called out over his shoulder as he walked away.

The morning air was warm and there was no breeze. The first rays of light were breaking through the horizon as Black's house came into view. Black and several of the men were gathered on the front porch. James shook hands with his comrades and joined Black. They waited for the others to arrive. Dr. Shultz and Elbert appeared a few minutes later. Soon, the others could be seen approaching the house. Black went inside, cueing the men to follow.

As the men filed into the dining room, Black seated himself at the head of the table. James sat opposite. When everyone was settled, Black spoke.

"We are here to help James resolve the matter of the colored overseer. I am sorry to say that we have also been saddled with the task of messenger. Since Bainesworth wants a favor, I thought to use him as he intends to use us. But I fear we have an even greater problem." Black's expression prompted James to chime in.

"I got a telegram from Rose, the sister of Will Turner. She was wantin' me to know that someone come from the Hunter plantation is looking for us. Based on the message, I think she sayin' Hunter's sons wanna know who killed they father."

Tim spoke up. "I killed him when he shot Black. It's me they look for."

"They looking for us, Tim. We are one here," Elbert said.

"Elbert is right. We ain't separate. But I understand where ya coming from, Tim. We wouldn't be exposed if I hadn't acted witout thinking," James said.

"We do what we has to," added Gilbert. "We ain't clean up well is all. But when we strike this time, we leave no stone unturned."

James, aware that Black expected him to lead, directed his next words to Simon. "Now that we know they's looking for us, I worries for the women and children. I would feel better if you stayed behind and ran the fort, Simon. You and Morgan runnin' things here would make it easier to think through this mission."

"Done," Simon responded.

Black smiled, giving James further encouragement and he continued, "In yo' place we will take Anthony and leave Luke with you. I think we needs to meet with the women as well to make them aware of what's going on. When we leave, the fort needs to be on lockdown 'cept for the men patrolling the property."

"I agree," Black said. "Because of the war, I had planned on increasing our supplies in case of an emergency."

"I say we move out by railway. While we move, we can rest. I'm hopin' to cut our time being gone, wit' us movin' by train," James said.

Black appeared pleased with the suggestion. "Since we have to go get supplies, I say we get our list of demands together for Bainesworth."

"I think we should go to Montreal and see for ourselves what Bainesworth speaks of. Our next move should be to travel from Montreal to Beacon Hill by railway—then move into Washington on horseback," James replied.

"I gotta man what can help with the horses," Simon offered.

"We can rest our bones at the old house in Williamsport before we moves out," Gilbert added.

The conversation lulled as the women served a hardy breakfast of scrambled eggs, bacon, biscuits and coffee. James looked on as Sunday kissed the top of Black's head before moving about to serve the men. Her husband briefly acknowledged her, but James could see by his expression that Black was preoccupied. James hoped his brother wasn't feeling guilty about what he considered to be his own fault.

Fannie was still a constant ache in James' soul, but she was dead, and there was nothing more he could do for her. He now had to worry about the women and children, with his son and Abby being his primary concern. He could not live with himself if anything happened to them, especially Abby. If what occurred at the Hunter plantation resulted in her being harmed, he would not be able to see life through. James decided at that moment to include her in the women's meeting. She needed to understand she could not leave the fort in his absence.

The meeting ended with several agenda items. First Black, James, and Elbert would ride out to the inn to discuss travel plans with Bainesworth. Second, they would meet with the women to discuss the safety of leaving Simon and Morgan in charge. Third, while in town, they would order supplies and have everything delivered. Fourth, Elbert would speak to Anthony and bring him up to speed. Fifth, Shultz would check on Morgan and the baby, so she could be part of the meeting. He would do the same with Anna and her baby. The doctor also ordered everyone who would be part of the meeting to bathe. His last rule–everyone could look at the babies, but only Big Mama and Miss Cora would have physical contact.

After the meeting, James, Elbert and Black headed over to Abby's cabin. Luke had just pulled up with a flatbed wagon and on the back, was the new tub.

"I see you ain't wantin' to bathe with the men no more," Elbert quipped.

"Mind yo' damn business," James chuckled.

Abby was out helping Shultz with the babies. The men lugged the tub inside the cabin and installed it next to the fireplace, hooking it up to a drain under the cabin. James left three packages containing the dresses, soap and perfume on the table for her. When they finished, they headed to the stables. James, Black, and Elbert rode out an hour later. Frank and Lou tagged along as back up.

❀ ❀ ❀

It was just after midday when the men stepped onto the boardwalk. The sun shone brightly, though occasionally, the clouds overtook the radiance of the day. Still, there had been no rain. Frank and Lou posted up at the front door of O'Reilly's inn. Black, James, and Elbert continued on inside. At the front desk sat an older white gentleman in a blue vest and bowtie. He had bushy gray hair and wore black-framed glasses that he had to keep pushing up on his flat nose. He smiled, showing bright white teeth, when he saw Black.

"Black, I haven't seen you in a good while!" Nigel, the innkeeper said.

"Nigel. Good to see you, you're looking well," Black responded.

The innkeeper nodded at James and Elbert. "Gentlemen."

"Nigel, these are my brothers, Elbert and James," Black said in introduction.

James and Elbert stepped forward and offered handshakes.

"We are here to see the ambassador," Black said. "What room is he in?"

Nigel rolled his eyes heavenward at the mention of Bainesworth. "Black, the ambassador is in room 214. Did you know he thinks I'm his personal manservant? The maids and I are ready to kill him."

Elbert let out a chuckle.

"Don't kill him, Nigel." Black's eyes were bright with amusement. "We will be taking him off your hands soon enough."

"If you say so, Black. He is causing me more gray hair," Nigel smirked. "You're in luck—his highness is in the lounge, worrying the maids."

Black nodded and moved toward the dining area. There were several small tables and chairs in the lounge. At the back of the room, a large curtain separated the tables from where the food was being prepared. Black could hear Bainesworth complaining about his tea being cold. When the men caught the ambassador's eye, he smiled and stood from his chair in greeting.

The ambassador was dressed in a dark green suit, with large black buttons. His hair had grown and was pulled back into a ponytail with a green ribbon. He wore a white lace front shirt and black boots. On the pinky finger of his left hand was a large emerald ring. He was a fop, and it was everything the men could do to keep from laughing at him.

Bainesworth narrowed his eyes. "I thought you said six days. It's only been a day. Please say you haven't come to cry off."

Black stared at the ambassador for a moment. He had to think about what Bainesworth was saying. With the mission fast approaching, Black knew he had to do better.

James stepped in. "We ain't come to say we ain't goin' to work wit' ya. We come to discuss travel."

Bainesworth stared at James, unable to understand his southern accent. When he finally figured out what James was saying he asked, "Travel?"

Black looked about before his eyebrow popped. The ambassador took the cue. "Shall we go to my room?"

"Yes, we need privacy," Black replied.

A young white maid walked toward Bainesworth with a cup in her hand. "Later, Trella, the men and I need to be about business."

The maid rolled her blue eyes and pushed her black hair behind her ear. She was plump with keen features and very large breasts. Bainesworth called to her. "You can bring the tea to my room later."

The maid pursed her lips and walked away, her brown skirt swaying with her generous hips.

The men followed Bainesworth to the top of the stairs. Floral carpet ran the full length of the corridor. The ambassador led them down the hall to the third door on the left. He placed his skeleton key in the keyhole and opened the door. The brothers followed.

The room was large and colorful. At the center of the chamber, the bed was draped in a purple spread with gold fringe. Next to the bed, there was a water closet. Through its open door, a stand with a white basin was visible. In the corner was a purple privacy screen to make the chamber pot decorative. Across the room to the right was a large oak desk that had seen better days. The floors were polished hardwood. Under the desk was an area rug that matched the carpet in the hall. Elbert, the last man into the room, closed the door behind him. He walked over to the window, posting up to watch the street.

"We have other business to be about in the States," Black began. "I have decided that travel shouldn't be exhausting. If we traveled by rail, we could rest while we moved. Can you secure travel by train?"

Bainesworth gave Black a curious look. "I can. How many will I need to make plans for, and dare I ask the route?"

"We got eighteen and yoself make nineteen," James answered.

"We will go on horseback to the outskirts of Ottawa. There we will catch the train to Montreal. When we have gathered the information needed, we will move by railway into the States. We will ride from Montreal to Boston and change to horses on Beacon Hill," Black added.

"I shall take care of it," the ambassador said. "I'm sure it will take me more than six days. Can I notify you when I know more?

As the queen's man, it shouldn't be an issue getting passage. I need to deal with my contact and discuss scheduling."

Black nodded as his brain turned over every possibility. The extra days wouldn't hurt the situation because he needed to add another phase to the plan. He would send messages to Charlotte, North Carolina and New York. This move was vital, as he could now see the plan coming together. He was about to turn and leave when Elbert spoke up.

"Did you dismiss the men you came with, Ambassador?" Elbert's gaze was fixated on the street below.

The ambassador shot a look in Black's direction. "I haven't yet. They will watch over me until we leave," he explained.

James walked over to the window to see what Elbert was looking at. Bainesworth's men were all over the place on the street below, trying to look nonchalant.

Black looked at the ambassador and smiled. "You know I will kill you if necessary, right?"

"I can assure you, my good man, it won't be necessary. Please understand this is a rough place. Until I ride out with you, my men are needed," Bainesworth's voice shook.

Black eyed the man thoughtfully for a moment before he headed for the door. James followed, but Elbert remained in place.

"You wouldn't need men for protection if you didn't dress like that," Elbert said.

Black, with his hand on the doorknob, turned to look at Bainesworth, whose face was flushed in indignation. "My good man, my apparel is the height of fashion in England. I'll have you know my tailor comes highly recommended."

It took all their effort for Black and James not to fall to the floor laughing like schoolboys. Elbert however wasn't done. "Yo' tailor don't care if you get yo' ass beat—is what it looks like. Burn those clothes and put back on the clothes ya had when ya came to the fort. You ain't going with us dressed like that."

Bainesworth opened his mouth to speak, but Elbert stopped him. "From now on, when you got something to say, speak slow 'cause I can't understand shit ya saying. Understanding each other could be the difference between life and death on this mission. If you don't know what I mean, now's the time to say."

The ambassador looked annoyed, but he nodded his understanding. Elbert, Black and James quit the room, and once in the lobby, James and Black could not stop laughing. Elbert smiled shaking his head. The three met Frank and Lou on the boardwalk, and together the men headed for the dry-goods store.

They walked the length of the boardwalk, watching as the people moved about. Periodically, white people and colored people ventured forward to speak with Black. He was gracious as always, asking after their well-being and that of their families. The twins, Elbert and James hung back allowing Black the room to be the legend he was.

They crossed the roadway to the store, and Black greeted the clerk. "Good afternoon, Melvin."

Melvin's dark eyes lit up. "Afternoon, Black. It's good to see you."

"Same here."

Melvin was a tall, middle-aged white man with pasty skin and bad posture. His voice was soft and patient. "What can I do for you, Black?"

"I would like to place an order." Black handed Melvin his list.

While Melvin read through the list, Black turned and whispered to James. "We got the Lincoln issue to deal with first. I think the Hunter plantation needs to be watched. We need to know what's going on before we go there."

"I sees it the same," James replied.

"I'm going to send Jeb to the Hunter plantation to get work as an overseer. I will advise him to respond by sending his message to the Hill. His answer should be waiting for us once we get there. I will also notify Moses," Black said.

James helped Black compose the coded messages before they headed back to the fort. The supplies would be delivered in the morning. The men made it back to the fort as the sun started to set. They rode straight for the barracks to speak with Simon, who was at the front desk with Philip, handing out supplies.

Simon saw Black and the men and stepped toward them.

"I have ordered the supplies. They will be delivered tomorrow. I am trying to get eyes on the Hunter plantation; we don't need to approach blindly," Black said.

"Who ya gon use for that?" Simon asked.

"I have sent word to Jeb, Miss Esther's son," Black answered.

James chimed in. "I wants the men on Beacon Hill to keep being changed out every two weeks. When we gets to the Hill, we will send word to ya. I thinks when the next men go to the Hill, they will need to take supplies and extra horses. It would be slow going, but wit' the war, horses may be hard to come by. And we ain't needin' to spend no monies if we ain't got to."

Simon nodded.

"I will keep you posted as we progress," Black said.

Elbert turned and started walking toward the bathhouse. Looking back over his shoulder, he said, "I'm going to start working with Anthony."

"The women folk and the eighteen gon meet in Black's house tomorrow at noon," Simon called after him.

"Yeah," Elbert said before disappearing through the back door of the barracks.

Black spoke with Simon and James a few more minutes before he dismissed them to head their separate ways.

❈ ❈ ❈

It was dark when James made his way to the house to see about his son. Big Mama and Sunday were seated at the table, and they both smiled when he stepped into the kitchen.

"Where is the babies?" he asked.

"They's 'sleep now. Me and Big Mama had them out in the garden," Sunday answered.

"Where yo' brothers?" Mama asked.

"Black went to speak wit' Tim and Elbert went to find Anthony."

The women nodded.

"Imma go and see 'bout Miss Abby if that's all right?"

Big Mama eyed him thoughtfully for a second. "Go on. We got the boy," she said. "He sleep in my bed."

James looked at the women sheepishly. He knew they were worried, but he didn't know what to say. "It's gon be all right. I promise."

Sunday and Mama just nodded their heads. James turned on his heels and left the house.

James felt the weight of their worry as he walked to Abigail's cabin. He was tired. It had been a long day, and he still had to discuss his leaving with her. Abby had gotten better about his comings and goings from her place, but she was still uncomfortable about their age difference. Getting her to this meeting could prove difficult, for she would be openly admitting she was his. But her safety was far too important to him. He would insist on her being by his side. It was time to bring her into the fold.

James took a shortcut to get to Abby's quicker. Though it was June, the night held a chill. When he reached her cabin, he noticed it was dark. She always left a light on for him. He stepped up onto the porch, thinking she might still be with Shultz. The door was unlocked. He entered the front room and noticed the dim light just beyond the curtain. Closing the door behind him, he moved quietly toward the light. He heard what sounded like crying. When he pushed back the curtain and looked into the room, he found Abby seated at the foot of the bed. She looked up at him. The two dresses he bought, lay next to her. The plain brown wrapper was on the floor at her feet and in her hands, she held the soap and the small perfume bottle.

James did not speak; instead, he stood just inside the curtain with his arms folded over his chest. He was at a loss, so he waited. Abby's hair was braided in two plaits and pinned neatly at the crown of her head. She wore a brown dress and her feet were bare. When she looked up at him, her eyes were red and swollen from crying. His chest constricted at the sight of her pain. Silence hung between them until she finally found her words.

"I am from the Patterson plantation in North Carolina. We ain't do much in the way of cotton, but we growed vegetables and tended the animals. I worked sometime in the fields and other times in the main house. I ain't begin to question being a slave 'til the masta took a wife."

James just nodded, afraid to speak. She was opening up to him, and he didn't want her to stop. He wanted to know about Abigail from Abigail. What Black told him had helped, but tonight he would hear it from her. He only wanted happiness for her, but she didn't seem pleased with his choices. He waited for her to go on.

"I smelled foul all the time. There was never no soap and we ain't get but one set of clothes. The masta's new wife had perfume and soap. He treated her nice enough—he seemed taken with her. Harold, my husband, was picked for me. We ain't know each other, but he was kind. I come to care for him. But if'n I had been allowed to choose, I cain't say it would have been him." Abby began crying again.

She wiped her face with her handkerchief before she went on. "I ain't never felt beautiful before, 'til you. I thought smellin' fine was for white women. I thought being wit' a man that you wants and what wants you back was for white women only. I thought my dark skin made it so I would never truly be wanted or loved."

James spoke, his voice deep and raw, "You are so beautiful to me, Abby. All I think about when we ain't togetha is you. Yo' dark skin is lovely."

His words made her cry more, but he gave her time.

"I washed my hands wit' soap that belonged to the masta's wife, and she caught me. She told her husband that I stole the soap. I just wanted to smell good one time. I was wit' child and Harold ain't want the masta to beat me, so we ran. They run us down, and Harold led them away from me. He faced the catchers alone. I watched him hanged, 'cause I stole soap."

James hadn't expected her next words, he was almost sorry he bought the damn soap. He searched for the right words. "Baby, they hung him 'cause the world is cruel—not 'cause ya stole soap. There ain't no justice in slavery, and there ain't no sense you can make of what happened."

Abby stared at him like she hoped what he was telling her was true. James opened his arms to her. She dropped the soap and perfume on the bed and stepped into his embrace. James held her as she continued to cry. He whispered words of encouragement and love. At that moment he knew he could never live without her, and he would always protect her.

When Abby calmed down, he moved the items from the bed, and they lay together fully clothed, holding each other until she slept.

❀ ❀ ❀

It was almost midnight when James got up from the bed and started a fire. The chill was still present in the air. He went outside to the pump and filled the tub halfway with cool water. Then he filled both large pots by the fireplace with water and set one on to boil. Next, he removed his boots, gun, and shirt, before making himself comfortable in a chair by the fire. He thought of the sadness Abby carried, and he was beside himself with grief.

He uncorked the bottle of whiskey and took it straight to the head as he watched the flames dance under the pot. James was deep in thought when he heard movement to his left. Abby stood in the doorway, and he reached his hand out to her. She had removed her dress and was wearing a night wrap. The glow of the firelight and the lantern turned down low cast the cabin in gold and blue hues. She was hesitant to move toward him, and he knew why. He turned his attention back to the fire, giving her a moment. He feared she would turn him away; he could feel Fannie and Harold in the room.

He was tense until he felt her soft hand on his shoulder. When he looked up, her eyes held pain. He felt it too—the guilt of Fannie's death rode him. Still, he reached for her hand and the new memories they would create. He didn't think she would speak, but she did.

"I carried a baby. I ain't beautiful naked."

He smiled as he stood and placed the bottle on the table. Turning the wick up a bit, he then took Abby in his arms. He loosened the belt of her night wrap. Underneath, she wore a white cotton shift and matching pantaloons. He laid the wrap across the back of the chair before he touched her.

Sexual contact for him had always been with prostitutes, save for the intimacy he shared with Rose. Pleasuring the plantation owner's daughter had been nerve-wracking, but he had left her whole. James had never been inside her. He feared Rose having a colored baby drop from her belly. He had walked away from the Turner planation the year Black had taken Youngblood's eye, and he had not looked back. Now, with Abby standing before him, it was a point of reference.

He desperately needed to kiss her, because he didn't kiss the girls at the whorehouse. Leaning down, he asked, "May I kiss ya, Abigail?"

"Yes," she answered breathlessly.

He roughly shoved his tongue into her mouth and groaned. He thought she would pull away, but she shocked him by gently cupping his face. She was soothing him, while deepening the kiss. He had never wanted a woman like this. Abruptly, he backed away and stared down at her. His breathing was labored, his voice hoarse. "I wanna see all of ya."

Stepping back, he lifted her shift over her head and tossed it to the floor. He stared down at her. Taking in her lovely, dark skin, he was moved. Abby had delightfully firm breasts, and her nipples were like blackberries. He reached out and touched her nipple. She breathed in sharply from the contact. Letting his hand fall away, James reached for her underwear and pushed them down over her hips. Instinctively, she tried to cover herself, and he pulled her hands away.

Her eyes watered. "I tell you I ain't beautiful naked. Can ya turn the wick down?"

"Shhh." He placed a finger over her lips.

He moved to the chair and pulled her along with him. When she stood between his legs, James drank in the sight of her naked beauty. Abby had a flat belly and well-rounded hips. Her legs were a deep chocolate and very shapely. On her hips, thighs, and at the bottom of her belly, she had stretch marks. Abby was exquisite, and he couldn't help feeling jealous that the stretch marks weren't from carrying his seed. Pushing her back from him, he got down on his knees and kissed her juicy black skin. She reached down and ran her fingers through his hair. Tears fell from her eyes, and he had never experienced the like.

"Bathe wit' me," he asked.

When she nodded, he grabbed a towel and moved to the fireplace. James mixed the steaming pot of water with the cool water in the tub. He tested the temperature with his hand; it felt right. He hung the other pot over the fire, before placing the empty pot in the corner. Abby had gone to the bedroom to retrieve more towels and soap. She was nervous when he finally gave her, his attention.

James smiled, then turned down the wick before stoking the fire. He removed his pants, and when they stood naked together, he reached out a hand to her. With no hesitation, Abby moved into his arms. She turned her face up to his and he kissed her deeply before saying, "Come."

James led her over to the water. Abby dropped the towels as he lifted her in his arms and stepped into the tub. He eased her down into the water, and she leaned back against his chest. He had filled the tub so high some of the water sloshed over the side.

James was aroused, but there was much to cover, so he paced himself. He laid his head back and relaxed; he could feel her do the same. The warm water felt good after the day he had. They let the bath soothe them in the quiet of the wee hours.

James broke the tranquility with a dose of reality. "I has to leave to handle some business. I will be gone for a good while."

Abby turned to face him. "Is somethin' wrong? Why ya has to leave?"

He was trying to decide what to tell her and decided on the truth. He told her how he had been shot in the face, adding the facts about Jeremiah. Abby kneeled between his legs, keeping her hands on his chest as he spoke. He could see the anxiety on her face, and he hated that he was upsetting her. After he had told her everything, she leaned forward and kissed him.

"I know y'all go out and help folks. It's how I come to be safe here, but I'm still worried for ya."

"We has no choice but to go. This matter will spill to the front gate if it ain't dealt wit'. I wants you and the boy safe. There ain't no other way."

Abby nodded at his words.

"Simon and Morgan will stay on at the fort," he told her. "They job is to keep everyone safe. We meets midday tomorrow. I wants you to be there. I wants the family to understand what you mean to me."

Her facial expression softened, and he knew at that moment she understood what he was asking. He was ready to make it known that she was his. Though most people already knew or suspected, he wanted there to be no doubt. He could see the uncertainty in her eyes, and he guessed the cause.

"I ain't carin' 'bout yo' age, Abby. I want you to stop carin' 'bout mine. Woman, you belong to me."

"James, I just..."

James cut her off; his patience had worn thin. Black's words popped into his head, about there being men at the fort who wanted more from her. He became irritated with jealousy. "Is there someone at the fort closer to yo' age you would rather be wit'?"

Abby smiled and moved in, straddling him. She reached out and cupped his face, water dripping through her fingers. "Ain't no one else," she whispered. "I never been in love before ya, James. I cared deeply for Harold; we was friends, but not like what I feels wit' you. I'm just scared."

The kiss that followed dissolved his jealousy. He pulled her to him tightly, and she whimpered. He palmed her ass in his large hands and was undone. Abby leaned over the side of the tub and reached for the soap and cloth. She lathered herself and him with the rose-scented soap. James had to work to compose himself. It was so sensual watching her bathe herself as she continued to straddle him.

The cabin smelled of roses, and the chill had gone from the room. When she rinsed the soap from her body and his, he said huskily, "I wanna be inside you."

"I wanna be one with you too," she whispered tenderly.

He breathed in sharply. Abby stood, and the water cascaded down her lovely dark skin. James laid back and enjoyed the view as she stepped from the tub. He closed his eyes as he listened to her move toward the back room to ready herself for him. Fannie popped into his head, but he didn't back away from the thought; instead he embraced his sorrow. Tonight, he would connect with Abby, both physically and emotionally–tonight he would *live*. James stepped from the tub and wrapped a towel about his waist. He stood in front of the fire, reflecting. He had never made love to a woman he actually loved. Though he tried not to be, he was anxious. When he entered the back room, he found Abby standing next to the bed, clutching her towel.

He smiled at her. "You changin' yo' mind on me?"

"No," she said.

She was standing between the dresser and the bed. He stepped to her, but he did not touch her. Instead, he pulled the covers back. "After you, Abigail."

She dropped her towel and climbed into the bed. James followed her, but not before turning the lamp all the way up. He climbed between her welcoming thighs. She reached up, cupping his face, and he leaned down to kiss her beautiful lips. He kissed her nose and her forehead before moving to her neck and shoulders. He listened as her breathing became labored; all he wanted was to please her. She arched her back as he placed soft kisses between her breasts. He licked at her nipple–biting it lightly—before taking it into his mouth. Abby moaned her pleasure, and when he offered the same treatment to her other nipple, she cried out.

Hearing how much she enjoyed his touch sent waves of ecstasy pulsing through him. James couldn't get enough of her; his body was ready, but he wouldn't dare rush. He kissed her all the way down her belly and when he came to her sweetness, he plied his tongue to her. Abby tried to close her legs, but he placed his hand flat against her belly, and she calmed. Grabbing her by the hips, he yanked her closer so he could apply more pressure. He allowed his tongue to hit her clit to a rhythm. And when he thought she would shatter, he backed away only to restart the process.

"*Oooo,* James," she panted.

James felt her body tense, and he knew she was on the brink of euphoria. He pressed her legs farther apart and continued tasting her. Abby arched her back one final time just as her sweet nectar burst forth. He was hypnotized as he watched her climax, and she was stunning. She began weeping.

"James...James...James..."

He kissed her, sharing the flavor of orgasm with her. Tears spilled from her eyes, rolling backward into her hair. James had never experienced such oneness with anyone. Taking himself in hand, he placed his manhood at her opening and pressed forward. Abby was tight and wet. His voice was rusty. "Bend yo' legs for me."

She complied, offering him a better angle. His ragged breathing filled the room, and when he could go no further, he closed his eyes for a moment trying to control the sensations splintering through his being. Abby was moaning, whimpering and crying; she was driving him mad. The pace he set was slow, but intense. Every stroke he dealt her caused him to die a little. He kissed her again, wanting to stay engaged with her, but Abby began meeting him stroke for stroke. She wrapped her arms about his neck and her legs about his hips. He groaned from the physical and emotional friction.

"*Ahhhhh,* woman, I love you so damn much," he ground out.

He tried to be gentle, but Abby grabbed him by the ass and pulled him deeper within her. James could hold on no longer and began pounding into her. She stayed with him, accepting him, welcoming him, loving him until he became frenzied in his strokes. His body needed release, though he fought losing his connection with her. His seed erupted violently as he drank in her cries of pleasure. Abby wept and promised to always love him. James collapsed in her arms, allowing her to embrace him. When he regained his strength, he pulled her on top of him. He wasn't willing to relinquish the tenderness he had found with her. As he held her in his arms, his eyes watered. Abby leaned up and kissed his face, lingering on his scar.

The lovers slept for a time, until James woke her just before dawn. He wanted more of the intimacy he had achieved with her. When the first rays of light climbed through the cabin windows, James had spilled his seed again and again. The sounds of ecstasy and rose soap permeated the air. As the lovers lay holding each other, James had only one thought: *mine*.

❊ ❊ ❊

Abby sat on the bed with the sheet wrapped about her nakedness. They had spent all morning lying in each other's arms. She had never thought such things happened for slaves. James was strapping on his gun and smiled at her over his shoulder. Abby thought him handsome, but it was the confidence with which he carried himself that made him striking. As he turned to face her in his black shirt, trousers, and boots, he was different this morning and so was she.

James stood between the bed and the dresser, arms folded over his chest, beaming at her. "Wear the yellow dress. I wanna see ya in it. Be back in one hour to get ya for the meetin'."

Abby smiled and nodded. James kissed her, and then he was gone. When she was alone, she gathered her toiletries and headed to the front room. James had again filled the tub with warm water and Abby stepped in. Seating herself, she leaned back to soak. She closed her eyes, and Harold popped into her head. Leaning forward, she placed her head against her knees and wept for Harold.

When she had cried herself out, she stepped from the tub and dressed. She donned the yellow dress as James had requested. The top of the dress was form fitting, while still offering modesty. At her tiny waist the dress belled out, dropping to her ankles. She looked in the mirror and smiled; she didn't recognize herself.

Abby had never felt so dainty. She styled her hair in two cornrows, pinning the ends of the braids at the back of her head. When she finished dressing, she seated herself on the foot of the bed to wait for James. As her thoughts centered on him, she became anxious.

She thought of his pain over Fannie, and she felt sorrow for him. In the light of day, she had been shy with him, but after last night and this morning… Abby's face warmed when she thought of the pleasure he gave her. If she closed her eyes, she could see him over her, his muscles glistening with his efforts. She loved running her fingers through his curly black hair. In the throes of passion, he had told her he loved her—she could still hear it echoing in her head. He made her feel young, beautiful and worthy. She felt delicate; she cried some more, but managed to calm herself before he came back.

An hour later, Abby heard footsteps on her porch. The door opened, and little Otis came running in ahead of his father. James took his son by the hand, but he never took his eyes from her. She looked at the floor because she couldn't handle those green, penetrating eyes.

"Hi, Mith Abby," Otis said.

"Hello, Otis. Don't you look handsome!" Abby said.

Otis grinned broadly as he held his papa's hand. He was dressed in black boots, black trousers and a tan short-sleeved shirt. His face glowed from the olive oil rubbed into his dark skin. Abby kept her attention on the child. Otis held up his toy, a carved horse. "Mama gimme dis horsie."

"How nice!" Abby said.

Otis got down on his hands and knees to play. When she looked up into James' eyes, his gaze was direct. "You look lovely, Abby. Yellow becomes ya."

Shyly, she answered, "Thank you. I never had nothin' so fine."

James smiled. "Ready?"

He leaned in and softly kissed her before ushering them to the door. The day was bright. One of the men, who was outside waiting with the carriage, jumped down to set the steps for her.

"Hello, Miss Abby! Nice to see ya," Luke said.

"Hello…" Abby said, uncertain of the man's name.

"Luke, ma'am," he filled in for her.

"Hello, Luke."

She climbed into the carriage, followed by Otis and James. They rattled down the path, going the long way to Black's house. Still, the ride was short. Luke set the steps once more, and James climbed down first, helping the boy and then her. The carriage moved off, leaving the three of them standing at the foot of the porch steps. Abby did not look at James; she didn't want to lose her nerve and back out of the meeting.

James reached out his hands to lift Otis and carry him up the steps.

"I do it, Papa."

Abby giggled. Otis was such a sweet baby. How could anyone want to harm him? "Will ya help me on up the steps since ya such a big boy?" Abby asked him.

"Mhmmm," Otis answered, taking Abby by the hand.

She could feel James at her back. When they entered the house, he moved in front of them, leading them to the dining room. When he saw Big Mama, Otis broke and ran to her. Around the room the men stood about talking, their facial expressions serious. She of course recognized Black, Elbert and Simon. Sunday, Big Mama, Iris, Cora, and Morgan were seated at the table, along with Elbert's wife, but she did not know her. Mary and Sarah were also there. Sunday and Dr. Shultz came over to greet them.

"Miss Abby," Dr. Shultz said.

"Hello, Doctor," she replied.

"Hello, Miss Abby. I loves yo' dress," Sunday said.

"Hello, Miss Sunday. How you been?" Abby asked.

"I been good," Sunday returned.

"Excuse me," James said, as he walked over to Black and Simon.

Shultz followed the men, leaving Abby with Sunday. As she stared at the younger woman, Abby felt her insecurities and doubt mount. Sunday was a beautiful young woman with cocoa brown skin and huge, expressive eyes. She was also a very kind person.

"Won't ya come sit wit' us women, Abby?" Sunday asked her.

Abby followed Sunday to the table, where she introduced her. "Everyone, this here is Abby."

"Hello, Abby," the women replied in unison.

"This here is Sarah," Sunday said, motioning toward the woman. "She Tim's wife, and ya knows Mama. Anna is Elbert's wife and ya knows Morgan. I's sho' ya knows Mary. And 'course, ya knows Miss Cora and Iris."

Abby acknowledged each woman with a nod. They were all very young, except for Mama, Cora and Iris. The women were dressed in an assortment of blue, brown, pink and green dresses. They were lovely, and she became more intimidated. She seated herself between Morgan and Sunday. Morgan held her sleeping infant in her arms. She was wrapped in a pink blanket, with only her black curls showing.

"How is ya, Abby?" Morgan asked.

"I'm fine, Morgan."

When Abby was about to ask after her, more men dressed in black stepped into the dining room. Abby lived on the fort, so she knew about the eighteen. But this was an intimate view of who they were and what they did. These men were a scary bunch, yet she had never felt safer in her life. A light skinned man, along with the twins, came in last and with them were two more women.

Sunday made the introductions. "This here is Hazel. She Gilbert's woman, and this here is Carrie, she is Frank's woman. This here is Abby."

Both women wore brown dresses, and their hair was braided in two cornrows. Abby smiled at them in greeting. The women seated themselves and the men moved around the table. Some stood behind their women and others sat on the floor. Little Otis climbed off Big Mama's lap to go sit with the men. The women continued to chat until Black moved in, standing behind his wife. When he raised his hand, the room quieted. The meeting was now underway.

Black's voice was full of authority when he spoke. "An issue of safety has come to our attention. The men and I take your well-being and that of our children seriously. The security of Fort Independence is important. As I'm sure you all know, when we men ride out, we do so to set other colored folk free. This has caused us to make a few enemies, but we stand strong in the face of such adversity. Our bold deeds are a direct result of the brave women who stand by our sides. We men will stop at nothing to keep you from harm's way."

Black looked to James, indicating he should take over. James surveyed the women. Abby could see he was uncomfortable, yet when he spoke, his words came forth with strength. "The last babies we moved was from the Hunter plantation. They has tracked us here. As men, we plans on meeting the matter head on and away from the fort."

James paused for a moment, but Abby couldn't take her eyes from him. Gone was the gentle soul she had lain with just hours ago. Unlike Black, James wasn't polished. Still, his power radiated through the room. There was anger in his voice when he said, "Black and I has decided that Simon and Morgan, who is more than capable, will stay behind to help you women folk defend yoselves in our absence."

James looked to Morgan, who had passed the baby to her husband. Simon stood behind his wife's chair and cradled his daughter as Morgan spoke. "If'n ya feelin fear, you's wastin' yo time. We's women, but we ain't victims. This thought keeps our chilren from being victims. Me and Simon will organize ya, and see to it that ya stays safe. Us women will go out to the fort and help the other women and chilren while the men patrol. If ya cain't shoot, we will fix that, too. As for the older chilren, they will help us keep our guns loaded. And when yo mens return, you will be right chere where they left ya."

"Cora, Iris and me will keep the babies wit' us while yawl moves about," Big Mama said.

"When the men leave, I will move into James' room to help in our efforts. I need to learn how to shoot," Anna said.

"Me, Sarah and Mary will be workin' wit' the women folk here at the fort," Sunday said.

"I cain't shoot," Hazel, Gilbert's woman said.

"Me neither," Carrie, Frank's woman added.

"I cain't shoot neither," Horace's woman, Beulah said.

Morgan nodded. "As I say, me and Simon will fix that."

James took over the conversation once more. "Black has ordered mo' supplies. I know ya don't do this, but I feels like it needs speakin' on. No one in this room is allowed outside of the gate til we comes back. We has men what will be outside the gate for yo' safety, but ain't no one else allowed to come or go. Do you all understand?"

The women all nodded. James stood at the head of the table, arms folded, and feet spread apart. The scar on the right side of his face only enhanced his strong, handsome demeanor.

"We men will die 'fore we let anything happen to ya," he said.

As Abby watched him, two things ran through her mind: first, she was sad to hear him speak of his own death; second, she realized she couldn't live without him.

❈ ❈ ❈

When the meeting ended, Anna and Morgan retired to Big Mama's room to feed the babies. Sunday took Natalie and Otis to the kitchen to feed them. Abby volunteered to help. Cora and

Big Mama went to help Anna and Morgan. Sarah, Mary, and Iris helped serve the men an early dinner. The meal consisted of collard greens, stewed goat and sweet potatoes.

As the day pressed on, Abby felt a real sense of family. Even with danger looming in the background, she was enjoying herself. There had been an elderly woman who cared for her as a child; but, Granny died before Abby reached womanhood. Harold had been her only family until his untimely death. Still, her life with Harold had been nothing like what she was witnessing here today. Everyone was so warm and kind. Abby hadn't known she needed this type of interaction until this very day. Her life was becoming a series of revelations.

They partied until the hour grew late. James came and stood next to her. Abby smiled up at him. Elbert approached them, holding a sleeping Otis in his arms. "Simon and Morgan are going to stay in yo' room, so they don't have to take the little one out so late. Me and Anna are going to stay in Cora's room for the same reason. It's my week with Otis. I got him from here."

"Yeah," James said.

Elbert smiled. "Night, Miss Abby."

"Good night, Mista Elbert," Abby replied.

When Elbert walked away, James turned and looked at her. His gaze was so intense, his eyes so penetrating, Abby had to look away. James pressed his lips against her ear.

"Is ya feelin' shy wit' me, Abby?" He whispered.

She breathed in sharply before she whispered back, "Yes."

"I wanna see ya take yo' dress off. I wants ya to sleep naked wit' me, Abigail. Will ya do that for me?"

Abby closed her eyes for a second. "Whateva ya want, James."

It was his turn to breathe in suddenly. Standing to his full height, he stared down at her. "I'm hungry for ya, Abby. Are ya too sore?"

Though she felt shy, she wanted him just as badly as he wanted her. She had never felt such things. She looked into his eyes. "No, I ain't too sore. I wants to feel yo' touch."

James smiled at her before taking her by the hand. He began the process of telling everyone good night. When they finally stepped onto the porch of Black's house into the balmy night air, Abby felt something she had never felt before–sexual excitement and anticipation.

6

Horry, South Carolina
June 1861

IT WAS JUST past daybreak as Jeremiah walked the cotton fields of the Hunter plantation. His presence made the slaves uneasy, but he wanted to see first-hand the progress being made. He walked from row to row making certain every hand was busy. The earth was soft under his booted feet from the previous night's rain. As he stood in close proximity to several male slaves, he could smell the unwashed bodies on the breeze. They never met his gaze, but he could feel the animosity that dripped from them. Small bugs fluttered through the air as the sun made its ascent into the sky. It was promising to be an uncomfortable day.

As for the female slaves, they made plenty of eye contact with the black cracker. Their hope was to please him sexually, thereby making life easier on themselves. It was why he didn't deal in the weakness called love. In this life, a colored man could not afford such luxuries. Callie came to mind as he moved about. She had his attention, but she had not tried to capitalize on it. In fact, she tried to stay clear of him, and he appreciated it. Jeremiah felt his interest in her was dangerous and, in order to control it, he would begin tasting the new female slaves. It was the simplest way to rinse her from his thoughts.

As he looked toward the edge of the fields, he could see the overseers on horseback keeping watch. Moving toward the end of a row, he noticed the key man speaking with Norman. When he stepped from the cotton, Sonny addressed him.

"We has a message for ya."

Jeremiah frowned at the older slave. Sonny handed the telegram to him and waited. The message read:

VIRGINIA IS MAJESTIC I WILL EXTEND MY STAY ACCORDINGLY AS I GO VISITING I WILL SHARE YOUR HEARTFELT CONDOLENCES

When he finished reading the message, Jeremiah looked up into the sky, and then abruptly walked away. He passed the stables, a small shed, and a large pile of burnt wood before he found a hidden path that circled the working part of the property. He was paranoid about being overtaken by the same band of runaways. Though they left not a trace, he knew they camped in the deep woods. It was the only way they could have gotten the drop on him. His brother was headed to the Turner plantation, and Jeremiah was anxious to hear what he had discovered.

The trees were in full bloom with fat, green leaves. As he rounded the front of the property, the rolling, verdant lawns were a welcomed distraction. He saw Callie and Eva working the gardens in front of the house. As he approached, he heard them giggling. When they noticed him, they grew quiet. Callie never looked up, and though Eva looked him in his eyes, she did not speak. He was about to walk away when he noticed a male slave pushing a wheelbarrow full of topsoil. He was brown-skinned, standing about six feet, and he looked to be closer to Callie's age. Jeremiah gauged him to be about twenty-five summers.

When the slave brought the dirt, he smiled at Callie before

asking her where she would like it dumped. Callie directed him to the side of the flower bed. Still, she did not acknowledge him, causing his jealousy to become engaged. He stood for a time staring out ahead of him, while listening to the exchange between her and the male slave, named Festus. After a time, Festus walked away to get more dirt, and she attempted to follow him.

"Callie!" Jeremiah called out.

She stopped in her tracks, and Eva kept her head lowered. Inside his person, Jeremiah's emotions were out of control, warring with his calm exterior. Callie did not speak; she just stared at him. It was a subtle form of disrespect.

Managing his temper, Jeremiah said, "You are done here. Go to the kitchen and help Ella."

Callie had been about to reject his direction. He saw it in her eyes. It was why he didn't deal with her out in the open. He realized he would have to hurt her to get her to follow his orders. She made him soft, and he hated it. But today—today—he would do her harm if she refused. Jeremiah watched as Eva looked up and whispered something to her. Callie at once walked away and disappeared into the house. Eva offered him a weak smile before she returned her attention to the flowers.

Jeremiah turned and calmly walked off, but he was not done with Callie. He had let her go too long thinking she could decline his direction. *It was time to break her.*

❊ ❊ ❊

As night fell, Jeremiah walked the property. He was pleased to see the overseers doing the same. Now that his brother was gone, he got very little sleep. He made his rounds before heading back to the main house. Entering through the kitchen, he discovered all was quiet. Except for the three slaves on the top floor, the house was empty. He ate an apple while he stood in the kitchen, thinking. All manner of things ran through his head. He thought about his papa, his brother and, for the first time, about who he was as a man. There was no question he had achieved much, but she, Callie, did not appreciate all that he had accomplished.

Exiting the house, the same way he entered, he headed to his cabin. He could avoid her no more. Jeremiah took the long way, and now that the sun had gone down, it was pitch dark. The only relief was the light cast onto the paths from the candles and lanterns that burned brightly from the cabin windows. When finally, he made it to his own cabin, it was dark. Callie was not home. Still, he stepped onto the porch and walked inside. He lit the lantern on the table. Jeremiah experienced a moment of panic that she might have run off. Thinking of the number of men he had roaming the property, he realized she wouldn't have gotten far. His mind traveled to the possibility that she was with the male slave, Festus. The thought was more than he could stomach.

Turning on his heels, he headed to the one place he hoped Callie would be. He walked with purpose as he headed down through the slave quarters. Because the hour wasn't late, a few slaves sat on their makeshift porches. They laughed and spoke with each other, but when he passed, all went silent. The male slaves thought he was after one of them for punishment. The female slaves knew if Jeremiah was among them, it was to pick a mate for the night.

He ignored them all as he continued on to the big oak at the end of the path. At the left of the tree was Eva's cabin. Jeremiah stepped up to the door, but did not knock. Instead he pushed the door open to find Callie seated at the table with Eva and the key man. The three were smiling about something being said. He first focused on the key man. Jeremiah had never seen him smile. Second, he noticed that Callie was smiling, though she never smiled at him. They all three stood when he stepped into the cabin. He let the silence linger, trying to convey his displeasure, while at the same time promoting unease.

Upon seeing him, Callie's smile faded. She was not pleased to see him, but Jeremiah was pleased to see her. When he finally spoke, his words sounded desperate even to his own ears, and he knew they heard it.

"You don't have permission to be here. Let's go." he informed and ordered.

Callie placed her hand on her hips and scowled at him. She also did not move. He assessed her for a moment—taking in her tan dress, with dirt on the hips from her work in the garden. Her hair was combed neatly in two plaits pinned on top of her head. She was attractive, and he tried not to notice. He was clear about where they stood, so he did not ask her again. He was prepared to drag her back to his cabin. Tonight, he would begin the process of breaking her.

Callie stood in the center of the room in front of the small brown table. At the back of the cabin was a bed that looked large enough for only one person. On the left of the room was the fireplace with a black pot hanging just above the neatly stacked wood. A lantern hung from the ceiling on a hook suspended just over the table. Jeremiah calmed himself before he stepped toward her. She did not move because she did not fear him. But the key man knew his temper and moved to stand in front of her.

Jeremiah smiled, because he would rather beat the key man than her. In this instance, however, he knew he would beat them both, and he would start with the immediate threat—Sonny.

"You sure 'bout this?" He asked the older slave, his voice smooth and even.

Sonny looked hesitant. Callie gave in and stepped around Sonny, moving to stand before Jeremiah. He snatched her by the neck, but never took his eyes from the key man. He reached for his gun, and Callie gasped, "Please don't."

Jeremiah appeared composed, yet his eyes were ablaze when he looked at her. He released her neck and grabbed her by the upper arm, shaking her violently. Eva let out a nervous cry, but neither she nor Sonny moved. Still holding her by the arm, he stepped to Sonny, standing nose to nose. Callie reached out and touched his cheek as she spoke.

"I'm sorry, Jeremiah–please."

Eva burst into tears, as Jeremiah looked down at Callie and then at Sonny. "I will deal with you in the morning."

He dragged Callie from the cabin and down the path while the other slaves looked on. As he walked along swiftly, his anger would spike, and he would shake her periodically for good measure. When he reached his cabin, Jeremiah kicked open the door and flung her inside. Callie fell to the floor, crawling backward on her hands, feet and elbows. Jeremiah slammed the door so hard, the whole cabin shook.

"You will do what I say, when I say it. Ain't no more talking back, Callie. Ain't no more ignoring me. You will not cause others to question my authority."

His chest was heaving as he recalled Sonny's audacity. She stood, facing him. Defeated, a sob escaped her. "I can't take anymore. Why won't you just kill me? My very existence depends on you. I don't want to need you. Yet, if I don't bend to you, I stand to be abused by the overseers. I'm a coward because I can't take my own life, kill me–kill me, please!"

Jeremiah didn't dare approach her, for fear he would fulfill her request. He had been living under a great deal of stress, and it was all coming to a head. Callie had added new feelings to his emotional collage: jealousy and possessiveness. They were overpowering him; it was why he steered clear of her, though he constantly watched her from a distance.

"I *will* kill the key man, but not you," he promised.

Her eyes flashed with rage, but before he could think, Callie ran forward, hands fisted and punched him square in the nose. He saw stars from the impact. He attempted to grab her hands but missed, and she punched him again, nailing him right in the nose a second time. Blood spurted from his person. Jeremiah tussled with her before slamming her against the back door. He had her wrists pinned above her head with one hand and with the other, he squeezed her face.

His lips touched hers as he spoke through clenched teeth. "So, you worry for the key man? You will watch me kill him since you caused this."

She began weeping and attempted to turn her face away. He squeezed her cheeks harder and forced her to continue facing him. Callie whispered between sobs, "I can't take anymore."

Jeremiah suddenly released her and stepped back. "Tonight, will be a long night, Callie. Everything about you belongs to me, and I will beat you until you understand it."

He wiped his nose and blood stained the sleeve of his shirt. Callie had blood on her dress and her right cheek. The sight of blood on her repulsed him—even someone else's. The thought of beating her made him weak, and to himself, he admitted that he desperately wanted her to comply.

She was still crying softly, looking at him—waiting. He began pacing, trying to work through his frustrations to no avail. Jeremiah tried to get away from her, but her voice followed him.

"What can I give you to make you leave Sonny and Eva alone?"

Jeremiah stopped mid-stride, before turning back to look at her. He was incredulous at her damn nerve. He calmed himself, and when he spoke his voice was like velvet. "What could you give me? You little bitch. You can't give me nothing. I own you. You have nothing to barter with."

"I won't be difficult no more," she said calmly.

"I could beat you and break you!" Jeremiah yelled.

"You can beat me, but you won't break me."

He knew she was telling the truth, and it galled him. He began pacing again. Except for his boots hitting the wood floor, there was no other sound in the cabin. Callie had him tied in knots and all reasonable thought fled his mind. He ignored her as his thoughts wandered to the uprising that had taken place on Hunter soil. All at once, it occurred to him. *You can't stop a woman. How can you stop another uprising?* Jeremiah had to concede to the truth–he, the black cracker, got his ass whooped by a woman. He realized that she won, but just as he decided to kill her and the damn key man, Callie offered him what he wanted.

"I will tend you, Jeremiah, in all things," she whispered.

He was frozen where he stood, and to his shame, he comprehended something that he had not understood until that moment. He loved her, and it had weakened him. She had run him out of his home. He had killed an overseer out of jealousy, and he had not taken up with a willing slave woman because he wanted *her*. *Shit.* It was he who was tending her in all things.

As he stared at her, they both knew she was offering him an illusion. The burning question now–could he accept the illusion as the new reality? Could he act as though he were in charge, when in fact she was? The concept aroused him.

He knew she was waiting for his next move. And though his right mind told him to choke the life out of her, he stepped forward crowding her. Jeremiah leaned in and kissed her softly, while searching her eyes for rejection. But there was none. He kissed her a second time and suckled her bottom lip. Callie breathed in sharply, and when she opened her mouth, he offered his tongue. The kiss was deep and all-consuming. She burst out crying while hungrily kissing him back.

Jeremiah stepped back staring at her, and he was dazed by her willingness. He regarded her for a time before trying out his new-found power over her. He, the black cracker was buying into the illusion, and it was time to see if Callie could obey her new master.

"Undress for me," Jeremiah commanded.

Callie didn't hesitate. Sliding her dress from her shoulders, she pushed it down over her hips until the material pooled at her feet. Removing her shift and shoes, she stood before him naked. He could see that she was emotional as she stared just past his head, refusing a visual exchange. There would be no more disengaging from him—he would no longer allow it.

"I want even your eyes. Don't look away or we have nothing."

She brought her glassy eyes up to meet his, doing as he requested. Curtly, he grabbed her by the upper arm and moved her to stand in the center of the cabin. Opening the back door, he pulled the tub in from the porch. Then stepping into the night, he began pumping water and using two buckets at a time, he filled the tub to overflowing. Callie did not move. Lastly, he walked over to the lantern on the table and turned it down, before moving it to the floor.

Jeremiah felt overstimulated as he turned, headed for the back door. The air within the cabin was stifling, thick and hot. He had one last order to give before he stepped out into sweltering summer night.

"Bathe yourself," he said, and then he was gone.

❈ ❈ ❈

Callie watched him go, before moving to do his bidding. At the chest, she fumbled for a cloth and towel. Then reaching under the bed, she retrieved a small box that housed the coarse soap she hated. Though he had stepped into the night, she knew he was nearby. Callie could feel his presence as she immersed herself in tub. The water was a welcoming relief from the hot, stickiness of the cabin. She sat quietly for a time, until the emotional strain became so great, she wept.

She was terrified that Jeremiah would kill the key man. Callie had been angry when he ordered her to the hot kitchen to work with Ella. It also infuriated her that she needed his protection from the other overseers. She did not want to need such a man.

At night, the cabin was frightening and visiting with Eva was a godsend. She had been on the Hunter plantation since April, and Eva was the only friend she made. Sonny was kind to her because he loved Eva. The other slaves wouldn't even speak to her unless it was necessary because she lived in *his* cabin.

As she washed herself, she recalled the events of the evening. She had known the exact moment he decided to kill her, and she was pleased. The problem—he had also decided to kill Sonny. She saw it in his dark eyes, and she couldn't live or die with someone else's demise on her head. She had tried to bargain with him, but he wanted all or nothing. Jeremiah was a man who had trained himself to go without, the minimum would not do. Again she wept, but this time it was for the key man.

Callie looked up when she saw movement just beyond the back door. She watched as he seated himself on the steps of the porch, giving her his back. He was waiting to test her obedience. Callie understood that if she pushed him, the key man could meet his end tonight. There was nothing else to do but stand and step from the tub.

She dried herself, before rubbing the cream Eva had given her on her body. It smelled of peaches and helped to soothe her dry skin. She did not dress. Instead, she wrapped the towel about herself and waited. She was at his disposal. He did not rush either, but remained on the back porch staring into the darkness. An hour passed before he finally stood.

He entered the cabin and began undressing. Callie did not look away. Jeremiah removed his guns, placing them still holstered on a hook to the left of the table. Seating himself in a chair, he removed his boots and then his shirt, dropping it to the floor. He unlaced his trousers, revealing that he didn't wear underpants. Jeremiah was an extraordinary specimen of a man. He had broad shoulders, his belly lay in eight bricks and his legs were muscled. Dangling at the juncture of his powerful thighs was his rather large maleness. The shock of black curls that was his hair had grown riotous upon his crown. He was clean—shaven, with the beginnings of a mustache. The black cracker was statuesque and grand in his masculinity; a fact that could not be denied.

She had seen him naked before, but tonight was different. Jeremiah, Callie noticed, had a busted top lip and two swollen eyes. Under normal circumstances, she would have felt sorrow for harming another human being. But in his case, she felt nothing as she watched him sink down into the tub. Leaning back, he closed his eyes as if to disengage from her.

Callie sighed as she stood and picked his clothing up from the floor. She neatly folded everything he took off and placed his boots under the bed. Coming to stand on the side of the tub, she asked softly, "Would you like me to wash your back?"

Abruptly, he opened his blood-red eyes and glared at her. Callie could feel the venom dripping from him. She almost faltered and looked away, but continued to hold his gaze. When he didn't respond, she adjusted the towel wrapped about her and knelt beside the tub. She fished out the cloth and soap and began washing his chest. He sat up, allowing her to scrub his back. Jeremiah turned facing her. They were nose-to-nose. Boldly, she leaned in and kissed him. He groaned. Callie suddenly backed away, worried she hurt him. She reached out and fingered his lip, and he allowed it. They stared at each other until she gently leaned in and kissed him again.

Without warning, he stood. The water cascading down his body, and Callie rushed to get him a towel. Stepping from the tub, he accepted the towel and promptly ignored her. Indifference had settled in the cabin as he moved to stand at the back door. They continued on in quietness until she got up the nerve to stand behind him. Still, he did not acknowledge her presence, and she worried that compromise wouldn't happen. She leaned in and kissed his back softly, causing his muscles to tighten. Finally, Jeremiah turned and looked down at her.

"Please forgive my actions tonight," she whispered on a sob.

"You are sorry because of the key man. You ain't offerin' me nothin' real. Your gift is broken."

"I am broken. It's all I have to give you," Callie replied

He closed the cabin door, but he didn't lock it. She was startled when he reached out his hand and loosened the towel wrapped about her. As she stood before him naked, she wanted mercy. Letting his own towel fall to the floor, he leaned down. "Put your arms around my neck."

Callie did as she was told, and he stood lifting her into his strong embrace. She wrapped her legs around his waist, before whispering, "I don't know what you are wanting."

"Yeah, ya do."

Callie looked deep into his eyes. "Can you forgive me and Sonny?"

"I ain't wanting to talk about Sonny," he responded.

She felt his body tense and knew his temper was rising. Nodding, she conceded to his wishes and hugged him tightly to her. After a time, she realized, he was holding her just as tightly as he slowly moved about the cabin. He paced for some time until finally he stopped in front of the table. Bending, he set her naked upon the surface.

"Lay back," he demanded.

The surface of the table was cool against her back. Callie stared up at the ceiling as the urge to cry suffocated her. Jeremiah bent over her and kissed her until she was breathless.

"Can I taste you?" He whispered in her ear.

"Yes," she panted.

He captured one caramel, nipple in his mouth, before moving to her other nipple and doing the same. Jeremiah kissed her collarbone and neck, before kissing her lips once more. She stopped breathing when he moved to the side of the table. He kissed her belly and then bit her nipples lightly. He was relentless. A spell had been cast about the cabin, and she was trapped in his sensuality, his masculinity and her own desperate need. Jeremiah was in charge, and to her shame, she liked it.

He circled the table twice, before sitting in a chair and pulling himself right up between her thighs. He grabbed her legs and yanked her down the table to meet him. She lay open to him, feeling exposed and enslaved. Callie stared at the ceiling until she felt him lean in placing his mouth against her hot flesh. He plied the very tip of his tongue to her clit, and she cried out his name.

"Ohhh, Jeremiah…ohhh."

He stopped unexpectedly, rubbing his face against her inner thigh. Focusing once again on her womanhood, he restarted the process. He licked at her, wringing soft cries of pleasure from her until she didn't recognize the sound of her own voice. Sensations mounted within her, and suddenly he backed away again leaving her unfulfilled.

"Please, don't leave me. I need you," she begged, arching her back.

Jeremiah leaned in, and Callie grabbed his curls, wrapping her fingers in his hair. He stayed with her until her body was awash in an orgasm so sweet, she felt weightless. She had never experienced the like. When he moved to stand over, his gaze was piercing. He licked his lips, as if he enjoyed the taste of her. Reaching out, he touched her belly, before palming her breasts in his hands. Callie arched her back involuntarily as her body responded to him. He pressed her thighs apart, and his hands trailed down her legs. He was breathing harshly, as he licked one of his fingers and slipped it inside her. She moaned.

Callie closed her eyes against his intense stare and welcomed his touch. He moved his finger slowly, back and forth. The feeling was so exquisite, her breath caught. She heard him speak as if off in the distance. His voice was hoarse–ragged, "You tight."

He pushed a second finger into her sweetness, and she squirmed from the discomfort. Brusquely, he backed away from her and narrowed his eyes. "Have you never taken a man inside you?"

"No," she said between heartbeats.

He closed his eyes for a moment and then stepped away from the table. When he came back, he had Eva's cream. Callie looked away when he rubbed some on his hard member. She felt the coolness of the cream against her skin and closed her eyes. He pulled her closer, resting her legs against his chest. Taking himself in hand, he placed himself at her opening. As he pushed into her, she turned her face away. She felt him stop when she whimpered.

"Don't hide from me, Callie. I want all of you," Jeremiah said on a groan.

She reached out her hand, offering acceptance of his touch. Callie entwined her fingers with his. His eyes blazed with desire, and she was mesmerized. He pressed forward leaning on his free hand, breaching her. She called out her pain, but never let go of his hand.

"Ahhh…it aches–Jeremiah, it aches," she sobbed.

He held his body completely still but turned his face to kiss her legs as they rested against his chest. She moaned and tried to adjust, causing him to call out in pure delight. His words soothed her, "Callie… Callie… I promise the hurt will stop."

Jeremiah untangled his fingers from hers and began smoothing the palms of his hands over her belly. When he got to her breasts, he rubbed his work roughened hands over her nipples. Callie concentrated on his touch, and her pain began to ebb. She watched as he moved one of his hands down between her legs. He manipulated her clit with his fingers, and she breathed in sharply, moaning and crying out. She wiggled her bottom, adjusting herself—trying to get closer to him. He clutched her hips trying to still her.

"Shit, woman—you so damn tight," he ground out in a strangled voice, "Hold still."

But Callie couldn't hold still, his fingers were like magic. She wiggled again, and his grip tightened on her hips. He began to move slowly within her, and she was lost. She watched as his stomach muscles contracted and released with his efforts. His jet-black skin glistened with a light sheen of perspiration. When he threw his head back and closed his eyes, his Adam's apple bobbed.

Callie moaned because he was making her feel so good. She moaned because he was beautiful in the throes of passion. She moaned because she did not want the joining end. She moaned because he closed his eyes, and she did not want to be shut off from him in this moment. Brazenly, she spoke to him between gasps and pants.

"Jeremiah... don't close your eyes—please," She breathed, "Ooohhh, Jeremiah... Jeremiah, I want all of you too."

He opened his eyes and grabbed her hips, bringing her to him thrust for thrust. And Callie received him as he pounded into her. The table scraped the floor from his rough, frantic movements. Finally, when release was upon them, they called out each other's names. Callie began to cry and the black cracker—well, his eyes watered as he found release. He slumped over onto the table, and Callie just held him.

When he finally caught his breath, he backed out of her. Callie laid her arm over her eyes, not because she felt shy, but because she did not want him to leave her body. She listened as he moved about; she heard him wringing a cloth out in the tub. He came to her and cleaned her tenderly. The cool cloth stung, but she made no sound. When he was finished, the cabin grew quiet. After a time, she uncovered her eyes to find him staring at her. She could not read him, and she was afraid to speak. All at once, he picked her up and, cradling her like a baby, placed her gently on the bed. After lowering the wick completely, he opened the back door. She felt the night breeze fill the cabin.

After a moment of silence, she felt the bed dip under his weight. Jeremiah pulled her onto her side and nuzzled his face between her breasts. They continued in quietness, until his deep voice broke the darkness.

"You will not take another man inside you. I will kill him," his voice was aggressive–hostile.

Callie could feel his emotions running away with him. She could also feel her own emotions doing the same. She ignored him, and the action caused his anger.

"Do you understand me, Callie?"

She knew her words would shock him. Still, she spoke honestly, "I have rules too, Jeremiah. You will not place your gun inside another holster or I will kill her and you too."

He backed away from her in the bed and flipped her onto her back. It was pitch dark, but she could feel his smile. Sadly, she could not smile, because she was serious. The thought of him coupling with another, after what they had shared made her belly hurt. She turned her head away, not wanting to face her feelings. He climbed between her thighs and eased into her. Callie breathed in sharply, as he moved within her. His pace was steady and slow as he pulled himself all the way out, before slamming forward to the hilt. He repeated the action until she moaned with pleasure. Her lips found his, and his kisses were delicious. Jeremiah had her nose open–it was her last thought before ecstasy claimed her.

Callie's breath came in short spurts. "Ohhh, Jeremiah, my heart pains me–we feel so good together."

"Callie–I can't hold it, you feel too damn good. Fuck me back–stay wit' me," Jeremiah groaned, as he slammed into her.

And Callie did as she was told–she fucked him back.

❊ ❊ ❊

Two hours past, and Jeremiah did not sleep. He lay awake holding Callie in his arms while she slept. The temperature in the cabin was hot, even with the back door open. But, he could not let her go. He had never lingered with a woman after lovemaking. Everything he was feeling was new, and he was again, overstimulated.

He smiled, because she still didn't understand that he was the man—the master of their situation. She had threatened to kill him if he took another, and he knew she did not jest. He did not want another, but he wouldn't admit it. Callie had him open; he both loved and hated it.

The key man popped into his head, and his anger instantly flared. He pushed Sonny from his head, thinking instead of all he had to do. Jeremiah sighed as he released her before slipping from the bed. He dressed in the dark, as he had done so many times in his life. Stepping out the back door, he closed it quietly and faded into the night.

❊ ❊ ❊

Daylight was dripping into the cabin when Callie opened her eyes. Looking around the room, Jeremiah was nowhere to be found. She jumped from the bed frantically and began dressing. Callie's stomach pained her for she knew Jeremiah had killed Sonny while she slept. When she finished dressing, she raced out the back door and ran to Eva's cabin. She rushed inside, finding it empty. Backtracking, she headed for the main house.

The sun was coming up, and the plantation was coming alive. She ran up the path and around to the back of the house. Callie was crying as she stepped through the door. She was so anxious that she didn't see Jeremiah standing under a tree in the distance, watching her.

❊ ❊ ❊

Sonny had made peace with what was to come. He knew Jeremiah would come for him. He would have run if not for Ella and Eva. Though he wanted freedom, he did not want it without Eva. She could not manage a long-distance journey on her bad hip. He had only two regrets: that he had shown fear when he faced Jeremiah, and that Eva would suffer in his absence.

He was standing in the kitchen with Ella and Eva when Callie came rushing in. She was breathless and crying. Her face lit up when she saw him.

"Sonny! Eva! I am so sorry for the trouble I caused you both," Callie said on a sob.

The three of them stood there looking at her. Sonny knew it wasn't her fault. He had been tired for a long time and when Callie stood up to Jeremiah, it brought his own manhood into question. He had not liked Callie in the beginning. But she had been kind to Eva, and his feelings had softened.

"I knowed you was nothin' but trouble when ya came," Ella sneered.

Before Sonny could respond, Jeremiah stepped through the back door. Eva and Ella moved closer to him; Callie stood between him and the black cracker. Sonny felt like urinating on himself, but he held eye contact. He noticed that both Jeremiah's eyes were swollen, and his top lip was busted. The girl, from what he could see, had no marks on her. Jeremiah was dressed in tan trousers and a tan shirt, with a gun holstered at his right hip. Holstered at his upper left side was a second weapon. The black cracker stood with his arms crossed and his feet spread apart, glaring at him.

Callie turned to Jeremiah and whispered something that Sonny could not hear, but the overseer's penetrating stare never wavered. While on the Hunter plantation, Sonny had seen the real Jeremiah in action. He had witnessed the black cracker put down several male slaves for less. The girl did not seem to understand who she was dealing with. Sonny worried for all three of the women, but he did not dare speak. The damage was done and there was no turning back.

"Key man!" Jeremiah addressed him. "We got us a problem that Callie here ain't going to understand. She is new here and did not know that we never liked each other. You all know me, and ya all know how I handle issues that smell like revolt."

Sonny nodded. Next to him, Eva and Ella cried softly. Callie's back was to him, but he could hear her sniffling too. Jeremiah looked down at Callie. When she spoke, her words were humble.

"Please, Jeremiah," Callie begged, "I am so sorry for my actions."

Eva squeezed his hand twice; Sonny realized that she saw it too. Jeremiah loved the girl. It was why he wasn't dead already. He now saw Jeremiah's appearance at Eva's cabin last night differently. The overseer had been relieved to see Callie. He probably thought she had run. As Sonny watched the exchange between the two, he was sure of one thing. Jeremiah was making clear his love for the girl. Silently, he was threatening them on her behalf. Shit, poor Callie really didn't understand the power she held.

When Jeremiah looked at him again, Sonny knew he wouldn't be killed, but he would be punished. Jeremiah's voice was dead calm. "I don't see how we can move forward. The feeling to kill you ain't left me."

Sonny continued to hold Jeremiah's stare, but did not respond verbally. He knew the overseer was not looking for an answer. Callie, who was already distraught, dropped to her knees at Jeremiah's words. She leaned her forehead against his thigh and wept softly. Jeremiah let his eyes fall to where she knelt before him. Reaching down, he placed two fingers under her chin, bringing her eyes up to meet his.

"I am angry about being a slave," she told him. "I am angry

about needing your protection. I am angry about being left alone in that cabin after what happened with the overseer. Last night, I gave into you because I didn't want Sonny hurt. Today, I am giving in because of my feelings for you. I am yours and there will not be another. Please, Jeremiah, see that you have won. Please see my pain."

Sonny looked on, awed by the girl. Though Callie was crying, he saw her strength. He saw the courage it took to bare one's self to a man like Jeremiah to save someone else's skin. When Jeremiah locked eyes with him, Sonny was embarrassed to have witnessed such intimacy.

"Go away, Sonny, and take those two with you." Jeremiah's voice was tight with hostility and resentment. Callie broke him with her words, and it was obvious to everyone in the kitchen.

Taking Eva by the hand and Ella by the elbow, Sonny ushered the women out of the kitchen and down the hall.

Jeremiah watched as the three rushed from the kitchen, leaving him and Callie alone. He helped her up from the floor and sat her on the counter in front of him. Standing between her legs, he regarded her intently. When he spoke, his voice wracked with emotion.

"You are plenty angry, I see."

"I am."

"These feelings you have—do they include you seeing me in the proper light?"

She looked him in the eyes. "What I see is not good."

"But you gave into me anyway?"

"You want to own me. I don't want a master. My thoughts and feelings are all jumbled up," she whispered.

"You want me to see your pain, Callie, but do you see mine?"

"No, I don't see your pain. You are the one in charge."

He took a step back. She had a way of making him think too much about matters he had previously been sure about. Everything about her showed her to be smarter than he. Callie was hard to converse with, because for every thought he had, she had two working against him. He changed the subject.

"Old lady Parson learned you to read?"

Callie's eyebrows drew together in confusion. "She did."

"My pain, Callie, comes from wanting a woman who is difficult. My discomfort, Callie, comes from giving that woman orders that she does not follow. My hurt, Callie, comes from having to think through not killing the woman I want, even though she pushes me to do so. My ache, Callie, comes from feeling the hate that woman has for me, but still I want her."

"Just because I don't want to be owned, doesn't mean I don't want to feel you in my life. Because I want to feel you in my life doesn't mean I agree with how you live your life. Because I don't want to be a slave, Jeremiah, doesn't make me difficult. Oh, I see you in the proper light, but you have coupled with me and turned my body against my head. My body wants things from you—I never knew a woman could want from a man. I ache, because I am not who I was yesterday."

"You match words with me even when you know it will make me angry."

"Why would you want me, if we can speak about nothing?" she asked.

"I want peace from your words, Callie."

"I want forgiveness from you, Jeremiah; I wish for Sonny to be safe from punishment for my actions."

He stood there, thinking on her boldness. Fatigue was setting in, and he no longer wanted to engage in dialogue about Sonny. Callie had a way of making him feel defeated. He had figured out that it wasn't her goal to best him. She was just clever. He supposed she couldn't just turn it off and therein lay the problem. He could see the uncertainty in her eyes. He turned his back on her to give himself a moment, but she would not give him a reprieve.

"Jeremiah?"

He turned back to her, and she reached out her hand. "Last night, when I hit you, I felt no remorse. In the light of day, I feel nothing but shame."

He stepped back between her legs. Callie reached up and touched his injured lip with her index finger before kissing him. His lip ached, and he groaned when she cupped his face in her hands and kissed him harder. It occurred to him that outside of a sexual moment, he had not experienced human contact unless it was violent. Certainly, he loved his brother and father, but this was different.

"If Sonny should breathe wrong, I will kill him. He is to stay the hell out of my way," he warned.

"Yes," Callie responded, as she kissed him all over his face.

Finally, he backed away from her and left through the back door.

Richmond Virginia

June 1861

It was five in the morning as E.J. stood in front of the Spotswood Hotel, thinking. He had employed the same driver he had used for the trip to the Turner plantation to handle other delicate matters. Simpson had proven to be discrete. As E.J. pondered his next move, Simpson appeared out of the darkness. His eyes glistened from the small amount of light that streamed through the glass doors behind them. He greeted E.J. in his refined manner that contrasted so readily with his rough and dangerous exterior.

"Good morning, sir," the driver said.

"Good morning, Simpson. What have you got for me?"

"You were correct, sir. Mrs. Wilkerson sent a telegram the day after your departure."

"Really?" E.J. replied with piqued interest. "And to whom did she send this message?"

"The clerk at the dry-goods store was unorganized and disinterested. He couldn't be sure."

E.J. gave the driver a thoughtful look. "I see."

"There is more, sir," the driver offered.

"Please continue."

"Mr. and Mrs. Wilkerson left the Turner plantation headed for Boston yesterday. It seems they left Mr. Wilkerson's brother, Walter Wilkerson, in charge. Miss Rose wasn't pleased, but the overseers tell me her husband put his foot down."

E.J. nodded. "Do you know where in Boston?"

"Anderson Wilkerson is a litigator. He will not be hard to find as he has a shingle out front his door. The overseers did seem afraid of the runaways who burned the place down. They wanted to make certain their names weren't used."

"What about the slaves, were they forthcoming?" E.J. inquired.

"Most of the slaves they have are from a replenished workforce. The elderly slaves seemed too old to care about consequences from me or anyone else for that matter. So, I got nothing more from the slaves. What's next for you, sir? Will you stay on in Virginia?"

"I will be leaving tomorrow for South Carolina. The battle of Aquia has hit too close for my taste. I will be traveling with my intended, along with her mother and sister, by train. I need to get them to safety. Please be here at first light tomorrow to carriage us to the train." E.J. said.

"Certainly, sir," said Simpson, and turning on his heels, he walked off into the pale light of early dawn.

✵ ✵ ✵

Charlotte, North Carolina

June 1861

Jeb Woodard was standing on his porch one sunny afternoon when his younger brother Gerald rode up on horseback. The men resembled one another with blond hair and green eyes. Gerald was younger by two summers, and the two were close. They had followed in their mother's footsteps and become abolitionists. Their father had died in the fight for freedom when they were still very young. Jeb was quiet as he watched his brother swing down from his horse.

"Been at the dry-goods store tryin' to stay abreast of the goings-on," Gerald said.

"We at war is what's going on. I'm glad Mama went north," Jeb replied.

"Yeah. Me too."

"Shit about to get hard 'round here." Jeb stared off into the trees.

"A telegram came for ya. The storekeep sent it wit' me." Gerald mounted the porch and reached into his pocket, handing Jeb the message.

Jeb unfolded the paper, his eyes scanning the page.

I AM SORRY TO HEAR YOU HAVE FALLEN ON HARD TIMES I HAVE A FRIEND IN SOUTH CAROLINA WHO IS LOOKING TO REBUILD HIS PLANTATION. PERHAPS YOU CAN FIND HONEST WORK AS AN OVERSEER WITH HIM. I INTEND TO VISIT A FRIEND IN BOSTON BEFORE COMING SOUTH IF THERE IS ROOM I TOO HOPE TO PUT IN WORK ON THIS PLANTATION

Jeb grinned as he looked up from the message.

"What is it?"

"We going to find us some work." Jeb chuckled.

"The Hunter plantation?" Gerald asked, wide-eyed.

"Yes."

Gerald could hardly contain his glee. "I missed out on all the damn fun last time, running errands for Mama. I ain't missin' shit this time."

"Ya moved two families to freedom. From where I sit, that ain't nothing to sneeze at." Jeb responded.

"But this sounds like more fun."

"Yeah, it does."

"When do we leave?" Gerald probed.

"Soon–real soon. I have some loose ends to tie up, and then we can go."

The men grew silent for a time, each in their own thoughts. The Hunter plantation had been a sore spot for abolitionists for many years. Black and his men had brought the Hunter clan low, but they were attempting to rise again. They could not let that happen.

Jeb was deep in thought, as he mumbled again, "Soon–real soon."

7

Canada, July 1861

IT WAS JUST after noon on a hot July day. Black, along with James, Elbert, Tim, and Simon, stood at the front of the barracks speaking privately. When Luke appeared they, all looked up at once.

"The ambassador is at the gate. He askin' for ya, Black," Luke said.

Black did not ask any questions. Instead, he headed for the gate, and the men followed. Outside the main entrance of the fort, the men surrounded Black, as he spoke with the ambassador.

It seemed the ambassador had taken Elbert's advice. He was dressed in plain brown trousers, a white shirt and brown boots. He wore a brown leather hat that shielded his eyes from the sun. Two of his men waited off to the side.

"Ambassador," Black said, by way of greeting.

"Black–Gentlemen," Bainesworth offered.

The men behind Black nodded. Black also noticed that Bainesworth had not made the same mistake he had on his initial visit. He had come with two men who waited at a non-aggressive distance. He spoke to move the conversation along.

"Ambassador, have you come to discuss travel?"

"I did. My friend was hard to track down, but there is a 2:10 train leaving Ottawa for Montreal in seven days. We would be in Montreal for three days before the next train leaves for Boston. By my calculations, we will have to account for travel. Ottawa is about a day and a half from here."

"We will need to leave in five days," James said.

"Yeah," Elbert agreed.

"We will meet you at the inn on day five at dawn," Black said to the ambassador.

"I shall be ready." Bainesworth said, before he and his men departed.

Black was deep in thought, as the men spoke about last minute details that needed tending. Sunday, his child, Mama and his new extended family were his concern. The idea of them being hurt was more than he could take. Elbert stepped away from the bunch and clapped him on the back to get his attention. Black turned and looked at him.

"You worry for the women and children as you always do," Elbert said.

"You and Simon just had new babies. Then, there is my Natalie and little Otis to consider. We won't even speak about all of the children we just brought home."

Elbert offered a sympathetic smile. "I have the same thoughts. I am uncomfortable with this situation as well, but leaving is the best thing we can do for our women and children. We need to contain this thing away from the fort. Even if one of us dies, it would be worth it."

"I agree," Black said, looking away.

"You will look after Anna and my boys if something should happen to me–the thought keeps me standing. The people here need you more than me," Elbert said.

James had moved to stand next to Elbert. Tim and Simon had walked away giving the brothers a moment.

"Ain't no sense in beatin' 'round the bush. The fort can't run without you, Black," James said.

The conversation irritated Black. His eyebrows pressed together as he regarded both Elbert and James. "We will ride out together, and we will touch this subject no further."

They stood quietly, each man up in his own head. Their thoughts the same–to spend time with their families. They would take these few days to find peace in the arms of the women who loved them. And when the time came to leave–they would make certain the bullshit did not touch home.

※ ※ ※

Later that day, James stopped by Elbert's cabin to bring water in for Anna. Elbert was at the barracks, working with Anthony. Anna was seated on the porch, holding his nephew when he arrived. He almost couldn't face her, so great was his guilt about ripping Elbert away when they just had a new baby.

"James, are you bringing Otis home today? Junior misses his big brother," Anna said with a smile.

He stared at her for a moment before looking away. Finally, he answered, "Elbert is picking him up from Big Mama when he leaves the barracks."

Anna's expression changed to one of concern. "Is something wrong?"

James exhaled. "Anna, I am sorry about this mess. I know Elbert wanted to build you and the baby a bigger house. Now we leaving again, and I done brought another baby for you to have to fuss over."

Anna looked at him with compassion. "Come sit."

Placing the buckets by the door, James seated himself in the chair next to her. Anna turned and handed him the baby. Little Elbert was a plump, brown-skinned child with curly black hair. Anna had him dressed in light blue short pants with a blue short sleeved shirt. There was a light blanket over his legs. James could not help smiling down at the adorable boy.

"You are not just Elbert's brother; you are my brother, too. I love Otis as if I had birthed him from my own body."

"I know that ya loves Otis—"

Anna cut him off. "I love you too, James. I know you men work hard to keep us safe. I understand what's happening, and I understand some things can't be helped."

James looked at her. She wore a short-sleeved, pastel green dress and her hair was pulled back into a French braid. The sincerity in her eyes made him feel better about the situation. But his feelings of regret did not go away. Anna must have read his thoughts.

"I am so glad you are well; I was beside myself with worry when you were shot."

He touched his face. "Looks worse than it is."

"I never said it before, but thank you for helping me when I needed it most. Above all, please stay safe. When you come home, you will help Elbert build a home for the children we share."

Little Elbert began to fuss, and James handed him back to Anna. Overwhelmed by her gratitude, he could no longer speak. He kissed her on the cheek and then went about filling the tub for her. Once the task was complete, he left for the barracks.

Elbert's cabin was off the beaten path. James walked for some time before any other cabins came into view. The late afternoon sun filtered through the trees. Suddenly, he changed directions and the cemetery came into view. He wound through the graves until he came to her resting place.

Fannie represented his fear of failure, and his inability to protect those important to him. He lingered until the sun disappeared behind the tree tops. When he exited the black wrought iron gate, his chest tightened, but thoughts of Abby alleviated the pressure.

Thoughts of the black cracker did the very opposite, causing his blood to race. James was angry about being shot in the face, but it was the death of little Otis' mama he could not get beyond. Why would Jeremiah kill her in cold blood simply because she did not want to be separated from her child? James had learned much in his time as a slave, and he was sure of one thing, Jeremiah was a rogue dog that needed to be put down. There could be no other way to deal with such a man.

As he walked the path that would carry him back to the center of the fort, James paused to stare up at the sky. Summer was in full swing, the weather hot and sticky. The pathway was lined with large trees on both sides. At the base of the trees, green grass grew to the edge of the worn path. He was surrounded by beauty at Fort Independence, but he remembered a time when he found this life a burden.

They had just become free, and unlike Black, he did not want the responsibility of sustaining freedom for others. He smiled at the wild existence he and Elbert had lived. Still, when Black needed them, they did as he asked. Otis' death was a turning point for both him and Elbert. Now, as he strolled along, he could think of no other place he would rather be. Whenever he played the last few months in his head, all he could think about was exposing the fort and its people. It was a painful thought—he needed to fix it before it careened out of control.

Once at the center of the fort, he walked down a hill past the school and then up another. Black's house came into view. The sun had stopped working for the day when he entered the long hall. The house was peaceful as he made his way to the kitchen. Seated to the table alone was Miss Cora. She looked up sensing his presence.

"James. How's Anna?"

James gave her an incredulous look. "How you know I come from Anna?"

"You go every other day to see if she needs something. Anna told me so, is how I know."

"Anna is good. Where is everyone?"

Miss Cora gave him a welcoming smile, "Well, Black is in his study. Your mama is in her room with the children, and Sunday is in her room folding clothes."

James nodded, and then backtracked to the front of the house. Once on the porch, he sat on the top step. Thirty minutes passed before Elbert joined him. James remained quiet, leaving the weight of conversation to his brother.

"I come to take Otis home with me tonight." Elbert said.

"He inside wit' Big Mama."

The men sat in comfortable silence. After a time, Black joined them, and still there were no words. Otis came running down the hall yelling, "Mama–Papa."

James and Elbert moved just a tad to allow their son to sit between them. Sunday, Big Mama, and Miss Cora appeared, seating themselves in the chairs on the porch. Black stood holding his daughter. An hour of quietness passed before he reached out his hand to Sunday. They exited the porch headed for the privacy of their room. Big Mama and Miss Cora soon followed. Elbert stood, shaking James' hand. He took Otis into his arms and headed home. James remained seated, watching Elbert and his son until they faded into the night. Finally, he stood and closed the front door to Black's house before heading to Abigail for the night.

As James walked alone to Abby's cabin, he felt time running out on him. Now that a departure date had been agreed upon, he was overcome by the prospect of goodbye.

❈ ❈ ❈

Abby spent the day cleaning her little cabin and washing clothes. The place now showed signs of his presence, she thought, as she straightened his boots neatly in the corner. She cooked a hearty meal of cornbread, country fried steak and cabbage. After completing her chores at home, she went to help Dr. Shultz with patients. While with the doctor, Anthony had come to inform him of their leave time. The news turned the day hectic, as the doctor attempted to see his more serious patients, along with his expectant mothers.

It was after dark when she made it home, tired from her work with the doctor. The hour had grown late, when she heard his heavy footsteps on the porch. He never came inside. Abby understood why he delayed facing her. James didn't want to discuss leaving. She didn't want him to go, but she wouldn't verbalize such feelings. It would make matters worse on him and her. Seated at the table, she reached into the basket at her foot, folding the last articles of clothing. She then moved about, putting everything away before she headed to the front door and him.

Abby found him standing with his back to the door, his right shoulder leaned against the post, feet crossed at the ankle. She stepped onto the porch, barefoot and stood beside him in silence. He had his flask in hand and took a sip before handing it to her. Under normal circumstances, she would have refused, but his impending departure changed her mind.

She turned the flask up to her mouth, taking a small swallow. It was like fire. Abby breathed in slowly to soothe the burn before handing the flask back to him. The whiskey had given her the nerve to share her thoughts.

"Is you avoiding me?"

He turned, leaning his back against the post, offering his undivided attention. The lantern light highlighted the pain between them as she considered him. He had unbuttoned his shirt revealing his beauty and maleness. She almost looked away from the intensity in his green eyes. James had shaved. He had also hacked off his curly hair, and she felt remorse. The shorter he cut his hair, the more intimidating he appeared. Still, there was no denying he was a fine-looking man. When he finally spoke, she realized she missed him already.

James smiled at her. "I am avoiding *me*."

His low, deep voice always seemed to rub up against her skin. She turned away to give herself a moment. Time slipped by in quietness. "We leaves five days from now," he said.

"I know," Abby replied, turning back to him. "I was wit' the doctor when Anthony come to tell him."

James nodded his head and continued to study her. She mustered the strength to hold his gaze, his words echoing uncomfortably in the pit of her stomach.

"I miss you already." he said.

She knew what he needed to hear. "I will be right here waiting for ya to come back to me."

James opened his arms to her, and she stepped into his embrace. "Damn, woman," he whispered against her neck.

Abby cried as he held her. Moments passed, before he said, "Come inside."

She served him as he sat at the table. They ate their meal leisurely and engaged in small talk. Abby loved looking at him across the table, but it wasn't just his striking appearance that captivated her. What kept her enthralled was the fact that he did not know how remarkable he was.

James waited as she cleared the table. He stood and stretched. "Imma fill the tub."

Later, as they soaked in the warm water, she remained quiet, preferring that he be the one to speak and ease his mind. She leaned back against his chest, feeling the tension in his muscles. His whole body was rigid.

"I been selfish, Abby."

She turned and straddled him, looking at him in surprise. "Why would you say such a thang?"

"I needed you so bad for me. I ain't push you and my son together. Now I has to leave, and he don't know you like he should."

Abby reached out, tracing his scar with her fingers. She smiled. "Don't be worrying 'bout Otis and me. I intend to help Anna and Sunday wit' him. I wants to spend time wit' him. He's a sweet boy. Me and him will be fine—we gonna wait for ya togetha."

She thought he would say something; instead, he looked away. She cupped his face in her hands and kissed him. When their lips parted, James whispered, "I can't see life witout you, Abby."

Abby hugged him to her, and water slipped slowly over the rim of the tub. He deepened the kiss, pushing his tongue roughly into her mouth. She felt his large hands trail along her back, until he palmed her bottom. His hard member pressed against her rear, and she found she wanted him just as desperately. Leaning up on her knees, she positioned herself and eased down onto his shaft. The joining made them both moan.

"Woman, you is perfect," he groaned.

It was his touch and his words that pushed them toward fulfillment. As she rode him, Abby threw her head back, allowing the powerful feelings of ecstasy to claim her. James took control of their lovemaking, lifting and dropping her onto him. They were mindless in their oneness. She felt his body stiffen, and James called out in sheer delight. Abby kissed him, tasting his promises of love and commitment.

"I can't never let you go," he breathed.

James rubbed her back as she cried. When she quieted, he whispered against her ear, once more, "Perfect."

❀ ❀ ❀

James opened his eyes and looked about. Abby lay quietly next to him, but he knew she was awake. Climbing from the bed, he headed for the front door. At the tree on the side of the cabin, he took a piss and then splashed his naked body with cold water from the pump. He was offering Abby a moment of privacy.

Back in the cabin, he shut the door softly behind him. He

dried himself with the towel hanging from the back of the chair, before heading to the room. Abby was laying out their clothing for the day. He was not ready for their private time to end.

"I don't wanna do nothin' but lay in bed wit' you all day."

"Ya has important thangs to handle. We can't lay 'round all day," she admonished gently.

James walked over and took the clothes from her hand, laying them at the foot of the bed. He frowned down at her. "Woman, I ain't wantin' to see nobody but you today."

Abby smiled up at him, offering nothing verbal as she untied her wrap and stood before him, naked. He pulled back the covers, allowing her in bed first. Once they were settled, he reached over turned the lantern down completely and pulled her close.

"Did I ever tell ya 'bout the time I stole cookies from the big house and Big Mama caught me?"

"No," she giggled.

"Big Mama was helping out in the kitchen. I's 'bout six summas and when Cook laid out dem cookies, I took five when wasn't nobody looking."

"*Five?*" Abby laughed. "No wonder ya got caught."

"Yeah, I took five—took one for Otis, Black and Elbert. I took two for me, since I was the one doin' the stealin' and all. Big Mama warmed my buns—I couldn't sit for two days."

Abby laughed so hard, he began to laugh with her. When she could finally speak, she asked, "Did you get in trouble all the time?"

"Me and Elbert did. Black and Otis was a couple a goodie damn two shoes."

"It's hard to thank of you big men as children afraid of Big Mama," Abby said, still giggling.

"Shit, we all still 'fraid of her."

The couple laughed and spoke softly with one another. Dawn

had come again before James stepped from the cabin ready to face life.

❧ ❧ ❧

Simon had already taken over running the fort, and when James stepped into the barracks, the shift in power was evident. He could see Black, Elbert, Tim, Gilbert and Shultz standing at the front desk, talking. Tim handed him a slip of paper, and he read the message.

OUR GOOD FRIEND GOT YOUR NOTE WHEN HE IS SETTLED HE WILL DROP YOU A LINE HE IS HOPEFUL HE WILL FIND WORK IN THE NEAR FUTURE

James looked up, confused. "From Moses and Miss Esther," Black said.

"What if Jeb can't get work at the Hunter plantation?" Shultz asked.

"They will need overseers and slaves. The plantation is almost starting from scratch. If they don't hire him, Jeb will keep watch anyway," Black replied.

"Do we have a plan in place for the Lincoln issue?" Elbert asked, looking from Black to James.

"I has the beginnings of a plan," James said.

"I still ain't seein' why the ambassada think Lincoln gon listen to us," Gilbert said.

"I think Bainesworth wants our company because we know the States," Black explained. He then asked James. "How do you think we should proceed?"

"Is you expectin' somethin' in Montreal to show you how to plan this mission?" James inquired.

"I am expecting no great revelation from our time in Montreal. But we will be thorough, leaving no stone unturned," Black responded.

James smirked. "I got two possibilities on how to go about

this. One, we dress Tim and Shultz as Union soldiers, so we can move freely in Lincoln's circle. We waits for a chance to catch him alone to warn him or—"

"Or *what?*" Black asked. He too had a smirk on his face.

"Or we take the Union president against his will. My mind says it ain't no tellin' him. We gonna has to show him," James said.

Before Black could respond, Shultz said, "Shit, I hate to say it, but James' plan will work. I know firsthand."

The men burst out laughing, and Elbert clapped the good doctor on the back. Black added to James' plan. "I think we can use some of both possibilities to get the job done."

"Yes," Shultz agreed.

Each man fell into his own thoughts for a bit, thinking on the severity of the days ahead. The men then began the task of getting the replacement group ready to carry extra supplies to Beacon Hill. They added more men for the trip and loaded the wagons themselves. The back-breaking work was welcomed; it gave the men a chance to disengage from all thought and use only their brawn. As the day pressed on, all of the eighteen stayed busy with the tasks at hand. The togetherness of the men was a rehearsal of the days and months to come.

The eighteen had been stepping through the plan hatched by James. Elbert, Black, and Simon attempted to poke holes in everything James proposed. It was the strategy used before a plan could be executed. When the men felt they had a foolproof scheme, they took it to Morgan for her approval. Twice she sent them back to the drawing board. They met with Morgan for a third time in Black's dining room, and when they ran through the scenario, she smiled, offering one piece of advice.

"This ambassada seem like he gon need some nannying. I

thank ya need an extra man 'cause he a hindrance. Add one mo' to the group and thangs will flow well."

Simon stood behind his wife's chair, holding the baby. His look was serious as he surveyed the other men. In his arms, little Lettie stared up at him, cooing and gurgling with her deep brown skin and curly black hair. The men chuckled at her in intervals. She began to suck her fist and in a short while dozed off.

"Since ya think we should add another man, ya must has someone in mind," James said.

"I do. I thanks y'all should take Luke," Morgan replied.

Black turned to Anthony, nodding curtly. The younger man immediately exited the dining room to fetch Luke. Elbert chimed in. "I'll go and start bringing Luke up to speed."

The men filed out of Black's house, leaving James, Simon, Shultz and Tim to further discussion.

"You got yoself a beautiful little one," James said to Simon, looking on Lettie with adoration.

"Yes, she is," Black added.

"She looks just like Morgan," Tim chuckled.

Simon laughed. "Hell wit' you, Tim."

Shultz moved in to stand next to Simon. Black noticed right away that the doctor seemed different–agitated. Black asked, "Doctor, may I see you in my study?"

Shultz stared at Black for a moment, before nodding. Black said to the remaining men, "Same time tomorrow?"

"Yeah," the men answered in unison.

Black, followed by Shultz, headed for his study. He closed the door and sat down at his desk. Going straight to the point, he asked, "Is something wrong, Doctor?"

Shultz opened his mouth, but no words came out. His face turned red.

"Have you changed your mind about riding out with us?"

Black pressed him. "It's understandable if you choose not to accompany us."

"Riding out is not my issue."

"Then what is it?" Black asked, concerned. He did not need anyone riding out, who was in doubt.

Shultz coughed and turned red again. "I stay upstairs in your house, and I have my cabin where I see patients, but..." His voice trailed off.

"Out with it, Doctor," Black said impatiently.

"When a man has no woman, riding out is simple. But when a man *has* a woman, he worries for her," Shultz looked more and more uncomfortable.

Black did not speak. He could feel the presence of Otis in the room. Shultz rushed on, "In light of Otis–I didn't want to say, but I worry for Mary. I love her."

Black recovered from his thoughts. "Otis is gone. I wish nothing but happiness for both you and Mary."

Shultz walked to the window and stood, looking out.

"You are sure," Black went on, "you wouldn't rather stay here and help Simon? I understand the worry. I feel the same about Sunday."

Shultz turned to face him. "And let you bastards have all the fun? No, I will ride out. When you have a problem, I have a problem. Your enemy is my enemy."

Black nodded as he assessed the doctor. Shultz wore brown trousers, a white shirt and black boots. The doctor had even begun wearing a gun holstered to his upper left side. He adjusted his glasses twice, while he stared out the window.

Shultz spoke, offering painful honesty. "I have no place to be alone with Mary. Herschel is always home or not far from home. As a doctor, the reality of death stares me in the face, and I want more time with her. I was taking it slowly, because I thought life would calm down for us. I have had no time to move her into a cabin with me. I was also attempting to allow her time to reconcile her life with Otis. I don't mind sharing her with his memory. But now, it is almost time to leave again and…"

Black scribbled something on a slip of paper and handed it to Shultz. "Will you please ask Herschel to come see me? I have some last-minute matters to go over with him. Please let him know that I will need him most of the morning."

Shultz took the message and stared at him. Black understood his plight.

Once alone, Black bowed his head, thinking of his brother. In his sadness, he managed to smile. Shultz was a good man and Mary deserved some happiness. Turning his mind to his paperwork, he began his day.

❀ ❀ ❀

Shultz felt less than a man for having to get Black's help to spend time with Mary. As he walked to Mary's cabin, he knew he needed to clear the air. He knocked on the door a little too forcefully, and Herschel answered. Over Herschel's shoulder, he saw Mary come out of the back room.

"Doctor, good morning to you," Herschel greeted.

"Good morning, Herschel. I have a message from Black for you," Shultz said.

"Nicholas, good morning. Have you eaten?" Mary asked.

Shultz smiled at her. Mary was lovely in her yellow, short-sleeved dress. Her blonde hair was pinned back, revealing the full effect of her haunting eyes that changed from blue to gray depending on what color she was wearing. In that moment, he realized the intensity with which he desired her.

When he informed her that he had already eaten, Mary's expression fell to one of disappointment and he quickly added. "I would, however, like some coffee."

Herschel turned to Mary. "Black needs me. I will see you much later this afternoon."

The doctor watched as Herschel reached for his black hat on the peg by the door. He left the cabin without a backward glance closing the door quietly behind him. Moments and heartbeats passed as Shultz gazed at her. When he could form the right words, he nervously offered his thoughts.

"I didn't think we would be leaving again so soon. I want you to be my wife, Mary. I have tried to go slow to give you enough time to feel comfortable. But things have changed so quickly and I..."

"You what, Nicholas?"

Shultz swallowed hard. "I love you, Mary."

Mary's cheeks turned red. Still, she shocked him when she said, "I love you too, Nicholas. I am worried about you leaving, especially since James was shot."

"When I *come home*," he emphasized the words to reassure her, "will you marry me? Will you leave this cabin and live with me?" He held his breath, waiting for her answer.

"What about my uncle?" she asked, as if thinking aloud.

The doctor now understood Elbert's wanting to live only with Anna. He smirked. "He can stay in this cabin. I just want you."

"Yes, Nicholas, I will marry you."

Shultz took her in his arms and kissed her. As he backed away, he felt like a schoolboy. "Black asked your uncle to come to his house so I could be alone with you."

Mary's expression went blank. "I want to lay naked with you, Mary. I don't want to leave without feeling your skin against mine."

The awkwardness was unbearable. He looked away as she whispered, "I have not been with a man other than my late husband."

Shultz was embarrassed by his forwardness. His eyes snapped back to hers when she said, "My room is in the back of the cabin."

The doctor looked past the oak table and three chairs by the fireplace. His eyes bounced off the green sofa and landed on the wooden door at the back of the cabin. He felt faint when she reached out her hand and led him to her room.

The doctor was plagued by his insecurities. He was not like the other men—confident with the women. He had only one sexual encounter in his life, and it was for pay. It had been a great three minutes for him, but for his companion, not so much. There had been no other carnal encounters for pay or otherwise, mostly because while he accepted hams in exchange for medical services, prostitutes did not accept hams for sexual favors. He was, however, clear about one thing; he wanted Mary more than he wanted anything in his life.

He had never been in her room and just stepping over the threshold was an intimate act. A large bed sat in the middle of the room with a colorful quilt that lay across the foot. On the left of the bed was a window with blue curtains pulled back. Sunlight flooded the room, brightening the best moment of his life. The door swung closed behind him, squeaking on its hinges. Next to the bed sat a wooden nightstand, with a white pitcher and basin. Mary turned to face him; her cheeks were still flushed.

Shultz wanted to take the lead, but he couldn't move for fear he would stain his trousers without her help. He was paralyzed by the fear of failure. Mary, who seemed to comprehend his plight, smiled. Shyly, she unbuttoned her dress, pushing it down over her shoulders and hips. She stood before him in a white cotton shift with the sun kissing her skin. She hesitated for seconds, before lifting the shift over her head and dropping it to the floor. When she was completely nude, his eyes watered.

Mary was wonderfully slender with soft white skin. She had full, firm breasts, with rosy nipples, that hardened in the stillness of the room. She had shapely hips and legs, causing the doctor to breathe in bursts. Reaching up, she loosened her hair allowing it to fall about her shoulders. Shultz was hypnotized and did not move. He realized something he had not before–Mary was slightly taller than him. She stepped forward cupped his face and kissed him. When she attempted to remove his glasses, he grabbed her hand.

"Not yet," he exhaled, "I can't see a damn thing without them. You are lovely, Mary."

She helped him remove his gun and place it on the nightstand. He stood motionless, as she unbuttoned his shirt and smoothed her hands over his chest. Finally, his mind and body began to work, and he finished undressing, without looking at her. When they stood naked facing each other, she kissed him again, and his hard member pressed against her belly. Unable to help himself, the good doctor groaned. Mary deepened the kiss, pushing her tongue into his mouth. She felt so good, Shultz once again feared he would express himself prematurely.

He felt the need to explain himself and whispered hoarsely, "Mary, I want you so bad. I don't know–I don't want to disappoint you."

Against his lips, she answered, "Oh, Nicholas, you can't disappoint me. You have all morning to prove your point."

She took his glasses, placing them on the nightstand next to his gun. She kissed him and this time the doctor responded hungrily. He clumsily walked her backwards until they fell onto the bed. Desperate to be one with her, he took himself in hand and found her core. The lovers had not made it to the center of the bed when he eased forward to the hilt.

"Oh, Mary, I'm so sorry. I need you," he groaned, breathlessly.

"Nicholas," she panted.

His movements were frenzied and choppy, because he couldn't get himself under control. And there was one other problem the doctor hadn't thought of–Mary was tight. He tried to concentrate on the curtains, the nightstand, and the colors of the quilt. The exercise was futile. She lifted her legs giving him a better angle, causing him to sink deeper. He was unable to withdraw from her because the friction was torture, and he exploded, filling her with his seed. The doctor collapsed on top of her, and Mary just held him as he cried out.

"Sweet, sweet, Mary."

The room was filled with the sounds of their labored breathing. When he could catch his breath, the doctor moved them to the center of the bed. He kissed her, and his body began to react. Mary was welcoming when he climbed back between her legs. As he slipped inside her, she whimpered.

"I think I'm ready to prove my point," he whispered.

"I love you, Nicholas," Mary moaned.

The couple made love twice more and the doctor—well, he really did prove his point.

❀ ❀ ❀

Elbert had just made it home from the barracks. He sat in a chair on the porch instead of going inside. It was after midnight, and even though it had been a long day, he wasn't sleepy. After lighting a cigar, he took out his flask, leaned his head back and drank deeply. He could hear Anna moving about inside the cabin, and he sighed. They had not been intimate since the birth of their son. He was now feeling the pressure of his departure, but he was fearful of rushing her. The thought of leaving without making love to his wife made him ache. He took another puff from his cigar and stared blankly into the night.

The door creaked open, slowly. Anna walked over and put her hand on his shoulder.

"Elbert," she said softly, "I've been waiting for you."

He craned his neck, attempting to see into the cabin. When he turned back, he found Anna gloriously naked. His eyes narrowed. "Where are the little ones?"

"Your mama and my mama have them for the evening," Anna

replied, giving his shoulder a gentle squeeze. "Come make love to me, Papa. I miss you already."

Snuffing the cigar out on the porch floor, he followed his wife inside. After closing the door, he removed his gun and laid it, along with the flask, on the table. He lifted her and carried her to their bed. Anna helped him undress as she kissed him hungrily. When he was naked, she lay back on the bed and he climbed between her thighs. She wrapped her legs about his waist and Elbert eased into her, trying to pace himself.

"I love you, Papa," Anna moaned.

It had been so long since they had been physical, her words pushed him to an early completion, but he did not leave her. He remained inside her, kissing her and basking in her love. Elbert made love to his wife until he was weak from pleasure. When sleep finally claimed him, it was dreamless.

❀ ❀ ❀

Black had moved his easel into their bedroom. It was nearly two in the morning, as he stood naked, paint brush in hand concentrating on his subject. Sunday lay in the bed on her belly, propped up on her elbows with her chin resting in her hands. She too was naked with one leg kicked up behind her. She was a vision of loveliness. Black had to suppress feelings of sadness for having to leave her.

"When ya gonna let me see, Nat?" Sunday asked impatiently.

"Hmmm. I'm almost finished," he answered, as he applied a dab of paint to the canvas.

"I been posing for days," Sunday said in mock frustration.

"I'm not quite done, but you may come see it," Black said, as he stepped to the side of the canvas.

Sunday hopped up from the bed. The light from the oil lamp danced off her beautiful, mahogany skin. Black watched as her eyebrows popped at the sight of his latest creation. He began to laugh.

"You ain't paint me! Ya painted the whole damn room, but ya ain't paint me! Ya even painted the dent in the bed where I lay— but not me!"

He stared down at her, his arms folded over his chest. Sunday was spitting mad, and he could not love her more. "I was too jealous to paint you naked. I don't want anyone to see you like this."

"If'n ya weren't gonna paint me, why ya make me pose for ya?" she asked, glaring at him.

"I love seeing you naked is why I had you pose."

"Oh, *you*!"

"Where would I hang such a portrait of you in this house? We are never alone." He chuckled.

She looked in his eyes and smirked. "In yo' study, sos'n people can see my beauty."

Black imagined the eighteen meeting in his study with a painting of his naked wife on the wall. The thought did not amuse him, and he was about to tell her so.

With her hands on her hips, she cut him off. "I has decided you ain't gonna see me naked neither, Nat."

She was about to walk away when Black sprang into action and swept her up in his arms. Sunday squealed, pretending to be angry. "Put me down, Nat!"

Black tossed her onto the bed, and Sunday giggled. Pressing her legs apart, he entered her. And when he could go no further, he did not move. Instead, he allowed himself to soak in all her goodness. Black closed his eyes and groaned.

"*Ohhh,* Nat," Sunday sighed.

He wanted to be gentle and savor the moment, but Sunday was moving to meet his every thrust. The room was filled with the sound of their lovemaking. When they climaxed together, Black was mindless.

Later, as Sunday lay asleep on his chest, he had one final thought before he drifted off. He somehow knew that when he returned from his mission, his wife would be with child.

❃ ❃ ❃

In the early dawn, Gilbert made his way to the cabin he shared with Hazel. He had taken her from the Bridges plantation when Elbert had taken the overseer Billy hostage. At first, he had taken her under his wing because it was the right thing to do. When they left the plantation that fateful evening, it was the way she had ridden in front of him on his horse. It was the very way she had leaned into him seeking his warmth and protection that had moved him.

Gilbert had been living with Hazel for six months, but they had not been sexual. Several issues plagued his thoughts. He had not cared about much since his wife and child died—taking his ease with a woman had been part of life. Now, with Hazel, everything was changed. He could not wipe from his mind the image of her fixing her clothes as she stood behind that damn overseer. He had contemplated letting her go, but he had been too weak to follow through. His reasoning for not coupling with her was elementary; he wanted to know without a doubt that the seed she carried was his. And so, he waited, allowing her woman's blood to flow three times before he could be sure. But when that time had passed, and he was sure she did not carry the overseer's child, he still could not make the connection.

Though no words had passed between them on the matter, she somehow understood his feelings. Still, she had been nothing but loving toward him as she worked through her captivity issues. He had even gone to the pussy parlor once, but it had not helped. It had only complicated matters, making it difficult for him to face her. He hid at the barracks for three days until his guilt subsided. And when he had finally come home, she was there waiting—happy to see him.

This morning, as he stood in the darkness facing his cabin, Gilbert had finally come to some conclusions on the problem of Hazel. Though he loved her, he would let her go. He hurt over his wife and child, but he was wounded over Hazel. He wanted to go back to feeling numb–Gilbert wanted to go back to where he was before she had climbed up in front of him on his horse–the dead place. Today, he would let her know that she could keep the cabin. Once the mission was over, he would move back into the barracks. Gilbert was ready to leave; he was ready to put some distance between them.

When he pushed the cabin door open, he was met by soft candle light and Hazel, who was seated at the table. She must have just finished braiding her hair. She looked up and smiled. As he fixated on her, he noticed she wore only a sheet wrapped about her slender body. Hazel had deep brown skin, small brown eyes, a fat nose and plump lips. She wasn't pretty, but she had unforgettable appeal.

The cabin was simple; a small black stove sat to the right of the door and to the left was a large bed. They had a brown table with two chairs. Next to the fireplace was a tin tub large enough for only one person. A black cast iron pot sat next to the tub, evidence that she had bathed.

"Ya hungry?" She asked.

"No."

"Come rest yaself," she said, gesturing to the other chair at the table.

He allowed the door to close behind him, but he did not move toward her. When she spoke, the air between them became stifling. "Has ya come to tell me ya don't want me, Gilly?"

Gilbert had not expected her to say such a thing. Stunned, he had to look away to get his emotions under control. Still, his anger was apparent when he said, "I cain't move the thought from ma head of you fixin' yo' clothes behind him."

He felt shame when he saw tears form in her eyes. "I cain't move it from my head neither," she said.

"I know it ain't makin' sense, but I's so damn angry and bitter 'bout him touchin' you. I cain't damn think right." Gilbert said, and to his embarrassment he was almost yelling.

Hazel began to cry in earnest. "I hates seeing ya hurtin. I loves ya, Gilly."

"Damn you, Hazel–don't!" He shouted. Unable to escape her words, he turned his back to her and leaned his forehead against the door.

He heard the chair scrape the floor, her soft footsteps approaching. She inserted herself between him and the door. Hazel was a little over five feet to his towering frame, yet he felt smaller than she. Gilbert placed his hand with its missing fingers on the door to steady himself.

"I ain't choose this life, Gilly. It chose me. I's tryna live it the best I know how."

"I know," he whispered; his voice raw.

Gilbert wanted to taste her, but when he leaned in to offer his tongue, she turned her face away. He stepped back, bracing for rejection, and Hazel offered a dose of reality. "I cain't change what happened."

He leaned down, kissing her deeply and impatiently. Gilbert burst out crying, and Hazel did not turn him away. He wept for his wife, his child and his need for her. She pushed his wild hair back from his eyes and cupped his face. Against her lips, he whispered, "I *do* love you."

Gilbert stepped back, wiping his eyes, and she came forward to help him undress. Hazel placed his gun on the table and helped him remove his shirt. He was a light skinned man with brown eyes, a sharp nose and small lips. His face was clean shaven, but his hair was long and wild upon his head. He had broad shoulders, a well-defined chest and carved belly.

"Come," she said, softly, "Let me plait yo' hair."

He smiled weakly; Hazel was giving him a moment to think. He sat at the table and allowed her to brush, then comb, and plait his hair in two fat cornrows to the back of his head. When she finished, he reached behind him, grabbed her by the hand and pulled her between his legs. Unwrapping the sheet from her body, he let it fall to the floor. He pressed his lips to her belly, and she hugged him. His emotions got the better of him and again, he began to cry. It seemed the more he tried to quiet his pain, the more sorrow he felt. Gilbert hadn't wept in years, and it was a shoulder shaking moment.

"Damn," he offered brokenly, "I stayed away 'cause I wanted you to carry my seed—not his. I needed to be sho'."

She caressed his face. "I needed to be sho' too, Gilly."

Gilbert gently pushed her back from him and removed his boots and trousers. When they stood naked, he pulled her to him, hugging her. He picked her up, carrying her to their bed. He kissed her lips, neck and collarbone. Gilbert kissed between her breasts, before taking each erect brown nipple into his mouth. He continued down her stomach until he came to her core. He licked her clit, but not for the purpose of orgasm. Plying his tongue to her, he waited until her back arched, and then he pulled away.

"I ain't wantin' you to come witout me." His voice was strangled as he leaned back over her. He took her mouth in a stormy, emotion filled kiss.

Placing himself at her opening, he pushed until he could go no farther. He didn't break the kiss, and when he felt her tightness about him, it caused his eyes to water once more.

"Aaahhhh… shit, you mine," he ground out.

"Ohhh, Gilly… yes, I's yours," she breathed.

At first, he couldn't move for fear it would be over before it started. It was the way her body accepted his, and the way she called him Gilly—it was the way she had acknowledged being his woman that pushed him to frenzy. He pounded into her, unable to hold himself. It had been months of waiting to make certain she was his and months of depriving himself of her body. As darkness began to recede and the beauty of dawn leaked into the little cabin, the sounds of pleasure filled the room. He groaned, and she whimpered. Added to their labored breathing was the sound of the headboard banging against the wall on his every stroke—finally when completion flooded his being, he called out, speaking the truth.

"I love ya, Hazel… forever," he promised between pants.

"Ooooo, Gilbert…Gilbert. I loves ya more. Only you," she reassured him.

He was sorry that he couldn't give her more—he was sorry that he was losing the link. Gilbert was sorry that he couldn't be gentle. He slammed into her, and Hazel wrapped her arms about his neck and her legs about his hips holding on through the ride. And when his seed burst forth, Gilbert begged her to never leave him. Before collapsing on top of her, he promised to always take care of her.

As the last vibrations of orgasm splintered through them, Hazel called out, "I cain't never leave ya, Gilly."

Gilbert and Hazel did not leave the cabin for the whole day. They spoke about all manner of things while helping one another heal from the tragedy of slavery. They made love again and again until fatigue set in. Gilbert was still hurt, but when thoughts of the overseer popped into his head, he could now replace those images with memories of his woman in the throes of passion from his touch. It was the beginning of a new thing.

❧ ❧ ❧

Tim stood naked staring out the window seeing only his reflection against the dark night. He had worked around his cabin all day with the help of his son and Mamie's boys. The night hours were reserved for his wife. Sarah had not said, but he knew she was concerned about him leaving. James coming home injured, and Simon being left in charge of the fort added to her stress. Still, Tim had to admit that Simon and Morgan would keep his wife and child safe in his absence.

James had taken responsibility for exposing them, but it was he who had killed Edward Hunter Sr. Tim had his own guilt, and it wasn't about killing Hunter. He had left too many loose ends, and now the fort was visible to their enemies. There was no choice; a cleanup was necessary, and he knew it would be violent. Black had known of his guilt, but he didn't mention it. Instead, Black had told him he appreciated his friendship. Tim knew Black was saying so much more, but it did not stop his worry.

Sarah, his wife, had walked the children over to Mamie's cabin. Their son Daniel would spend the night with Mamie's family to give them time alone. He could see his wife as she stepped onto the porch and pushed the door. Tim turned facing the door when it opened. The lighting in the cabin was dim, but he could see her anxiety.

"Come, be naked with me."

She nodded and unbuttoned the top part of her blue dress and pushed it down til it pooled on the floor. As she removed her shoes and stockings, Tim came to her, helping to pull her shift over her head. When she was naked, he gazed down at her.

"There, that's better," he said.

She giggled. "Why do you like to be naked as the day you were born?"

Tim laughed softly. "I like it when you are as naked as the day you were born. I take my clothes off to make you do the same."

Sarah walked into his embrace, and he felt her trembling. Tim, who was just over six feet with pale white skin, black hair and coal black eyes could feel his wife's fear. He felt shame for leaving her. Against her ear, he whispered words of comfort.

"You will be safe here in my absence."

"I know," she answered.

"What is troubling you?"

"I worry for your safety. I try not to think too much, but I can't help being concerned," Sarah said.

He led her into the bedroom, and they lay down together. When she settled in his arms, Tim thought it was time to be honest.

"If ever there was a time I needed to go with Black– it's now. Some of what is happening is my doing."

Sarah's forehead wrinkled in confusion. "How so, Timmy?"

He had not meant to sound so worried. Pushing her onto her back, he moved between her thighs. "I don't want to talk anymore."

Sarah kissed him as he slid inside her. He grunted at the feel of his wife's creamy white skin against his own. He began to move and realized he was emotional. He would miss his wife more than words could say. He tried for a slow pace, but couldn't manage it. Their pace became quick and unsteady, but every stroke offered sensation after sensation. Backing out of her, Tim pulled her on her hands and knees. He needed the change to keep the connection, but it did no good. When he entered her from behind, all thought emptied from his mind. It didn't help that his wife was cheering him on.

"Ooooh, Timmy. I never want it to end," she panted.

He was already struggling, but her words brought the matter to a close. She pushed back against him on every thrust, and he cried out, "Sarah… Sarah."

As they climaxed, he grabbed her hips and pulled her to him. His body was seized by the orgasm. And when ecstasy released its tight grip on them, they fell to the bed in a tangle of arms and legs.

The couple made love until dawn.

❁ ❁ ❁

It was dawn on the day before the men would leave for Ottawa. They met in the barracks after a shift change, and with the inclusion of Luke and Anthony, they were now the nineteen.

"Everyone will answer to me and Black. Is it any questions?" James asked, and when no one spoke, he began assigning teams.

"Black, you gon work wit' Shultz, Josiah, John, and Gilbert," James said. After pausing to look at his list, he added, "Herman, Horace, Ephraim, Tim and Jake is yours, too."

Black gave a nod as James finished assigning the men. He left nothing to chance. "Elbert, Anthony, Luke, Frank, Lou, Emmett, Jesse and Ralph—you all wit' me. Our extra man is Bainesworth; I will watch him or kill him, whichever is needed."

Black also went over last-minute items. When he was finished, the men dispersed. James noticed Tim seemed agitated when he approached Simon.

"Can I speak with you out back?" Tim asked.

"Yeah," Simon responded. He looked over and smiled at Black.

When Tim and Simon stepped out the back door of the barracks into the cloudy morning, Black and James followed. They watched the exchange from the doorway. Once out back, Tim moved in aggressively to stand toe-to-toe with Simon. James was about to step in to break it up, but Black shook his head. Following Black's lead, James refrained.

"Sarah is still afraid of you," Tim barked.

Simon's eyebrow popped over his gray eye. "I have taken yo' wife's feelins for me into thought. Morgan will be dealin' wit' her directly. But, if'n the condition becomes unsafe, yo' wife gonna have to deal wit' me. My job is to keep her and yo' boy safe, and I will."

Tim glared at Simon for a moment before he nodded and backed down. When Tim relaxed, Simon offered one more piece of realism, "Sides, it was you I was wantin' to kill—not Sarah."

Simon smirked and then stuck his hand out to shake Tim's hand. Tim exhaled before accepting. Simon clapped him on the back. "I ain't like leaving Morgan behind neither."

Again, Tim nodded. As for Black—well, he didn't think he could feel any better about leaving Simon in charge, but he did.

❄ ❄ ❄

The men spent the last few hours with their women and children. They bathed, ate well and rested. The day had progressed with the men tying up all loose ends. It was three in the morning when they left their homes headed for the front of the fort. At the gate, two covered wagons drawn by a full team of six horses waited. The men loaded their supplies and saddlebags. Black and James separated, each climbing onto the back of a wagon. The men followed suit, breaking down accordingly. When the wagons pulled through the gate, the men were silent as they made for the inn.

Three hours later, daylight broke. And though it was July, a small breeze offered some relief as the inn came into view. On the boardwalk, in front of O'Reilly's, stood the ambassador. The wagon came to a halt, and Bainesworth threw his saddlebag and supplies up first before climbing in.

The group made it to the outskirts of Ottawa at eleven the next morning. They set up camp along the train tracks where they planned to meet the train. Several hours went by until they heard the distant rumble of the locomotive.

Bainesworth, Black, James and Elbert met with the engineer. He was a short white man with thick glasses dressed in striped overalls, his lips sunken where his front teeth were missing. As he conversed with the ambassador, he spit tobacco in long streams to the left of where they stood.

The man acknowledged only Bainesworth, his anxiety obvious. He walked them down alongside the train. When they reached the third and fourth cars, they stopped. Black noted two more railcars.

"I left the two middle cars empty for you and your men," the engineer said.

Bainesworth knew Black did not want an introduction for reasons of discretion. He nodded before saying to the engineer, "Thank you, Mr. Franklin. Your help will not be forgotten."

"We will be leaving in twenty minutes. The train will not stop inside the city of Montreal. I will bring the train to a halt thirty minutes outside the city. I will return in three and a half days to the same spot bound for the States. We pull out at 4:10, and my schedule will be tight. I can't wait more than fifteen minutes; if you and your men are not there, I will be forced to leave you," the engineer explained.

"We will be there, my good man, I can assure you," the ambassador answered.

The men loaded the railcars with their supplies and climbed in. The cars smelled of pine, and the floors were covered in wood chips and sawdust, indicating the previous cargo had been lumber. The men relaxed against their saddlebags for the three-hour ride.

The sliding doors on either side of the cars were left open to create a cross-breeze. Black stood guard at the doorway of the third car, holding onto a metal handle mounted to the frame. He watched the countryside roll by. They were now stepping through the plan and there would be no turning back.

8

The Hunter Plantation
July 1861

E.J AND JEREMIAH stood at the French doors off the dining room. The day was shaping up to be overcast, and the possibility of a downpour was great. Jeremiah stood quietly listening as his brother gave an account of his time in Virginia.

"This band of runaways has struck fear in the hearts of many. Will Turner's sister seemed worried when speaking of them. While she was sympathetic about Papa, she was not forthcoming. Her husband, however, was very informative. Though his motivation was jealousy."

"This war is gon' make shit hard for us. We need men if we are to deal with things suitably. No temporary fix will do for this group of runaways," Jeremiah stated.

"I have several men coming to be interviewed," E.J. reassured him. "I would like you to sit in on the meetings. We need overseers and a separate crew to protect the plantation. I will also try and assemble a team to go to Canada, if necessary."

"I don't think we should spread ourselves too thin. We need to assess what's in Canada before we travel all that way."

"I have a man watching Rose Wilkerson," E.J. said. "He has followed her to Boston. I believe she has contacted this band of runaways to warn them. If she has done as I suspect, then we will hold our position here. She is a very beautiful woman, but I will instruct Simpson to kill both her and her husband just the same."

"We need a plan if we are to be prepared when they strike. There will be no recovering if handled wrong."

"I agree. I will send my man in the north to Canada to assess the situation if needed. Somehow, I see this group coming to seek out the Wilkerson woman. There is something not correct about her."

Jeremiah turned to face his brother. "I don't understand—and if you are right, what will it mean?"

"If they come to her, then they will come to us. We will be ready. I must resolve this matter, because come the New Year, I will have to enlist."

Jeremiah stared at his brother. He was not pleased with the thought of bullets flying about E.J.'s head. His brother would have enlisted already had their father still been alive. E.J. had expressed that he would not need a damn valet during the war. But Jeremiah would go anyway to watch his brother's back–still today was not yesterday. Now he had Callie, and he worried about her safety. He struggled not to make his love for her obvious to others. Jeremiah didn't want to share anything about her. Callie was his weakness.

E. J. seemed to read his thoughts. "I hear you have begun sleeping in your own cabin."

"Why would you care about something so small?"

E.J. smirked, "So you will not answer?"

"No."

It started raining, just as Jeremiah turned quietly and walked away.

❀ ❀ ❀

In his study, E.J. sat reflecting on his time in Virginia and, most importantly, his time with Adrian Wells. Suzanne's father had become obsessed with being in the thick of things. He had become less and less concerned about his wife and daughters. The man had stopped spending any time with his family, preferring to sit in the gentlemen's club day and night. When E.J. suggested bringing Suzanne, her mother and sister back to his home, Wells had looked relieved. Julia, Suzanne's mother, had been hurt and concerned about her husband's decision to stay in Virginia. Edward had tried to get him to reconsider, but it had not worked. Wells said he would be along later to fetch his family.

E.J. wanted his soon-to-be bride safe. They had been home a little under two weeks, and Suzanne had already begun her duties as a wife around the mansion. She directed the slaves who staffed the main house. He ate three meals a day with the women. It was beginning to feel a lot like a home. The loneliness he felt since his father's death was starting to ebb. He was deep in thought when he heard satin rustling, and Julia appeared in the doorway. Her face told him she had much on her mind.

Edward, I have come to ask if I may use the stables."

He smiled. "Certainly, but the weather is not up to par today."

"When will you marry Suzanne?"

Shocked by her question, he leaned back in his chair and regarded her carefully. "I was hoping to work through this matter with your husband."

"Are you one of those, Edward?" She asked with a smile.

"Those?"

"Yes. A man who thinks a woman is too flighty of mind to make decisions."

E.J. looked at her, amused. But he did not answer. He did not think Julia unintelligent; still, he had not expected this. When he didn't respond, she went on. "My husband is a very smart man, but he allows shiny things to distract him. Because he is that kind of man, even if I wanted to deal in fashion and furniture, I cannot. I am forced to think of every matter concerning my girls. Don't get me wrong—I love Adrian. But I love him for who he is—not who I want him to be. So, with that said, I think you and Suzanne should marry by week's end, *unless...*"

"I have not changed my mind if that is what you are inferring. Old man Jackson is the minister on the neighboring plantation. I will send word to him to get a time and date. In the meantime, I will speak with Suzanne."

Julia clasped her hands in pleasure, her brown curls bobbing with excitement. She was yet an attractive, youthful woman, with a fine figure. E.J. could see what he had to look forward to. He stood from his chair and gave her a bow.

"I'll let you get back to work. And thank you for the use of your stables," Julia said appreciatively.

"Please enjoy."

As she floated to the door in her powder blue dress, she turned suddenly. "Oh, Edward, I almost forgot. The slave woman, Nettie—don't you think it would be best if you moved her to a cabin and found her other duties? I can tell by the look in your eyes that you won't sell her. In this market, well, it might prove difficult even if she *is* a nice piece."

E.J. just smiled, unshaken by her words. As a man, he would not discuss his desires with a woman who was not tending his needs. Still, he did offer his thoughts on her insight, "No, I won't sell her."

❋ ❋ ❋

The barn had been converted into a makeshift office for interviewing potential candidates. Jeremiah stood behind his brother, quiet, watchful and somewhat agitated. Both men were seeing the effects of war as some of the applicants appeared to be deserters. E.J. did not question them about their histories, and those men were not hired. Out of twenty applicants, ten were hired; two were brothers.

"What's yo names and where you all from?" E.J. addressed them.

"I'm Jeb, and this here is Gerald. We was born in North Carolina, but we was raised up in Tennessee."

Gerald stepped forward and shook E.J.'s hand. "Folks call me Gerry."

"I'm Edward Hunter. Folks call me E.J., and this here is Jeremiah." E.J. nodded in Jeremiah's direction.

Jeb stared just over E.J.'s shoulder at Jeremiah. He held eye contact with the black cracker, but neither man spoke. Jeb had been aware of these two, but he had never seen them close up. Colored overseers weren't uncommon, but this man looked more like a man that would run with Black, himself. Instead, he was helping to oppress. Jeb slowly turned his eyes from the black cracker, offering the right amount of contempt, making real his stance as a white—more superior man.

"Jeremiah knows the ins and outs of this plantation. If there is going to be a problem taking direction from him, I can't use you," E.J. cautioned.

Jeb nodded in Jeremiah's direction, offering the humility that comes with hunger and needing work. "I got no issues. I just need work."

Norman, the older overseer, stepped forward. "You men can follow me. Hope ya don't mind sharing a cabin; it'll make more room for others."

Gerry smiled at his brother. "Looks like I ain't gonna never get away from sleepin' wit' you."

Jeb chuckled as he stepped forward and offered E.J. his hand.

The new hires followed Norman from the barn. When the brothers were alone, E.J. asked, "What do you think?"

"I think if this group of runaways struck tonight, we would be in trouble," Jeremiah replied.

EJ nodded and stood behind the desk, stretching. As he moved down the center aisle, the horses snorted. At the front of the barn, the hay on the floor was wet. The doors were pulled back, and the rain was heavy. Both men stood for a moment, and it was Jeremiah who broke the silence.

"Make certain the new men understand that Callie is mine or we will need more men."

E.J. chuckled as both men stepped into the rain headed in opposite directions.

9

Canada, Montreal
August 1861

ON THE SOUTH side of town, just before the area became questionable was a little eatery called Ruby's. The restaurant specialized in down home cooking. The proprietor Ruby was an ex-slave from Alabama, who made it to Montreal with Black's help.

Black had not seen her in about three years, but she had not changed. Ruby's skin was like the darkest of berries, making the name "Black" just as suitable for her. She had light brown eyes, with a perfect nose and beautiful plump, heart shaped lips. She was older than he by nine years and absolutely gorgeous. Her hair was plaited into fat braids all over her head and pulled up into a ponytail, making her eyes even more expressive. She stood five feet, five inches and was curvy of frame. Ruby was *almost* irresistible.

It was dark when Black, Elbert, James, and Tim entered the establishment through the kitchen at the rear of the building. Ruby looked up from chopping garlic, and her eyes slammed into Black's gaze. She did not speak.

"Good evening, Ruby." Black smiled.

"Hope. I thought you forgot about me. They tell me you married," she answered in a deep southern accent.

"I didn't forget about you. And, yes, I have married."

She nodded, her pain evident. "Please give us a moment." Black asked, never taking his eyes from her.

The three men promptly exited the kitchen. Black and Ruby continued to stare at each other. Time seemed to stand still, and he was reminded of his life with Ruby. He had not long begun his work as an abolitionist when he helped her to freedom. He remembered being young, lonely and hurt because his mama was still on the Turner plantation. It was the shit he couldn't share with anyone. Ruby had seen his hurt and offered him intimacy with no strings attached. She was everything he needed, and most importantly, she could not have children.

Ruby had been his first sexual experience. Their couplings had been intense, yet filled with patience. He had changed from a boy to a man in her bed, but life was still happening, and he had a calling. He had Herschel purchase the building in which she lived/worked, and over time his visits had waned. Sex and intimacy had stopped between them long before Sunday. If he were truthful, he backed away because she made him feel too good, and he refused to be ruled by his dick. As a man of color, he had to put everything in perspective in order to survive and maintain freedom. Pussy *was* high on his list of priorities, but he would not be governed by it. Along his travels, there had been many women and many great moments, but he remained a thinker. He smiled, because when he thought he had it figured out, he had succumbed to love.

"It's good to see you, Ruby."

She laid aside her knife. "I have missed you, Hope. You look well. What brings you away from home?"

"I have important business. Can my men and I stay for a few days while we figure things out?"

"Of course, Hope. All this really belongs to you. I have three ladies who work different days, but they are discreet. If it will be better, I can close for a few days."

"If you could close, that would be better. The men and I will sleep between the dining room and the barn. I will pay you for housing and feeding us for the next three days."

"Whatever you want, Hope." When she got up the nerve, she asked, "Will you come to me at night while you are here?"

They had always been open with each other about everything. Conversation had flowed between them with ease. She always made him feel wanted, and he had reciprocated. He regarded her for a time before he finally spoke. His deep voice rolled around the kitchen, offering a hard dose of truth.

"If I came to your bed, I would not be alone. My love for her and my guilt about her would be with me. It would not make for a pleasurable evening. Also, when I am on a mission, I need a clear mind. I will sleep with the men."

Ruby averted her eyes and wiped her hands on her stained apron. "I will lock up and put the sign in the window."

Black followed her to the dining room. There were little black wooden tables, with three matching chairs polished to perfection, arranged about the small eating area. A candle sat in a small dish in the center of each table. On the far-right wall was a painting of a lake with swans floating on its surface. He had painted it more than seven years ago.

He watched as she pulled the curtains closed and opened the front door to bring in the lantern that lit the doorway for patrons. She turned the sign to read "Closed" and pulled the small curtain on the door, turning the lock.

"Would you rather we find someplace else to use as a base of operations?" he asked, understanding the rejection in his words.

"No, Hope. You are always welcome here," Ruby answered without hesitation.

He stared at her for a moment, as if testing the sincerity of her words and then nodded. He walked back through the little kitchen, past the large black stove in the corner and continued out the back door. Black found his men standing quietly in the dark. He began giving orders.

"James will break down the groups of those who will rest, those who will keep watch and those who will seek out information. Some of you will stay in the barn and some will sleep on the floor in the dining room. Tim, Shultz, and Bainesworth will meet with me in the kitchen to go over the plan."

The men began to move about. Black stepped back into the kitchen, followed by Tim, Shultz and Bainesworth. Ruby had cleared and wiped the table in preparation. When the men were seated, she began placing bowls of food in front of them. She served the men shrimp and grits with a side of warm biscuits. The aroma of coffee filled the room and she poured each man a cup before leaving them to talk.

When they were alone, Black addressed Bainesworth. "What is the name of this group? Who is the leader?"

"The name of this group is 'The Preservers of Southern Life,'" Bainesworth replied. "I wish I could point out the leader, my good man, but I have not been privy to such information. I have also not been invited to any private affairs."

"Then how do you know they wish to harm the Union President?" Tim asked.

"I know they are plotting to abduct Lincoln because they have been quite vocal about it. They believe the war will end if he is removed—leaving America to be two countries or leaving Jeff Davis in charge of everything. This one act alone could rejuvenate the expansion of slavery. If Lincoln is abducted, I do not believe they will ransom him. I think they will kill him to further their agenda." The ambassador looked from man to man. He reached into his pocket and produced a small crumpled pamphlet. "Here is an example of their work."

Black took the pamphlet and examined it. The leaflet had a purple border and in the center, was a caricature of Lincoln tied up and blindfolded. When he opened the booklet, there were itemized steps on how to abduct the president in order to cripple the northern army. Black whistled as he passed the leaflet to Tim.

Bainesworth went on. "The queen has ordered this type of activity stopped, but to no avail. Some have been arrested and deported back to the States, but more rise up. She has declared that we are neutral in the War Between the States, but it has done no good. A large number of Canadians have joined the war on the Union side. Equally, there are meetings for those opposed to this group, and in favor of Lincoln, but they do not appear as strong."

"Maybe the South plans to abduct the president because they think they will not win otherwise," Shultz offered.

"There is a meeting held almost every day at the Buckingham Theatre. You must come witness for yourself what I speak of," Bainesworth suggested.

"Tim, I will leave you in charge of this matter," Black said. "Report back to me when you have more. Remember, the train leaves in three days."

Tim looked at Bainesworth and Shultz. "The three of us will attend the next meeting."

The men finished their meal in silence. Black was worried that this war could affect his wife, daughter, and mother. Yet, he admitted to himself, he saw it coming. Based on what he had read about Lincoln, ending slavery did not seem to be his priority. Gauging the words of the Union president, along with his actions, it seemed keeping the country whole took precedence over every other thing. If it were about freeing an oppressed people, why would Lincoln not allow ex-slaves to be soldiers and pay them a just wage for their service? As Black weighed the questions before him, he wondered if the Union president was worth his trouble since people of color did not appear to be worth Mr. Lincoln's time.

Black pushed back from the table and stood. "Elbert, Gilbert and I will move around to determine what is happening in the colored sector."

The other men nodded as Black walked toward the back door.

"The three of us will be at the theatre by noon," Tim instructed.

Montreal was a small metropolis, the equivalent of three city miles. There was theatre, fine dining, grand hotels and more. On the south side of town, just before the farmlands, was a seedier element that offered its own excitement. It consisted of a saloon, a whorehouse and a few cheap rooming houses. It was the theatre that doubled as a town hall in the daylight hours that made life and politics fascinating in the city. And though Montreal had suffered flooding in April, it was still thriving.

It was noon, and the weather was mild for an August day. Tim, Shultz, and Bainesworth were dressed like gentlemen as they stepped into the theatre for a town hall meeting. The room was packed and though the temperature was mild outside, it was suffocating inside. The lighting was dim, yet the stage was bright. A fat, white man of medium height and build stepped into view. Based on the brilliance of the candles surrounding the podium, his attire was a white suit. He had dark hair and wore glasses. Tim leaned back in his chair, crossing his right ankle over his left knee and waited. The room quieted as the man took center stage. When he spoke, they were transported back to the oppressive, Deep South.

"My name is Maynard Smith. I am from Missippy. I am here to discuss the efforts of those brave Confederates who refuse to back down from that tyrant in the North," he said, with an educated southern twang.

The crowd applauded, and the speaker raised his hands once more. He adjusted his glasses and shuffled his papers.

"My friends, I am here to ask your help. I am here to ask you to take up arms with the men of the South who fight to preserve our very existence. It may appear that we fight to maintain slavery, but nothing could be farther from the truth. We fight for family; we fight for our livelihoods; and we fight for our homes. We in the South fight for an economy that has benefited both the South *and* the North. Our system is formed on the back of hypocrisy. Did you know that the banks in the North will lend landowners in the South money using slaves as collateral? Yes, they do. Because they recognize that slaves are a commodity. Did you know that when cotton is picked by our slave labor and shipped to other ports, northern-based shipping companies help to move our product for gain? Are you aware that when that tyrant Lincoln offers his thoughts against slavery, his very suit is made of cotton? No, my friends, we did not break from the Union to maintain slavery, because we are not asking permission to live how we see fit. We broke from the duplicity of an administration who speaks out against slavery while living in the very luxury it offers. We in the South have formed our own government based on truth. And most particularly, we in the South don't need no damn Yankees telling us how to live."

The crowd once again erupted in applause, and the three men exchanged looks. The speaker raised his hands, and the crowd quieted. He offered his last few thoughts. "In the lobby, we are serving lemonade, and there will be literature for your review. Thank you for your time. We must stop tyranny before it spreads and that starts with *you!*"

The people filed out of the theatre row by row and spilled into the burgundy and brown lobby. Tim took up his post by the front doors and watched as Bainesworth and Shultz worked the gathering. The crowd was mostly men and, strangely, the mix of southerners ranged in low numbers. An indication that the South was soliciting help from the Canadians. It also appeared that the Canadians were taking the request and this war seriously. The doctor signaled him, and Tim moved forward.

The doctor and Bainesworth stood making conversation with three men of various ages. The first man Tim recognized as the speaker. The man standing next to him was dressed in brown trousers, a white shirt and black tie. He looked to be in his late fifties with unfriendly blue eyes, gray hair, a broad nose, and thin, almost frowning, lips. The man standing to the left of Shultz looked to be about thirty summers with brown hair and brown eyes. When he smiled, his front tooth was missing. He too wore brown trousers, a white shirt and gold rim glasses.

It was Bainesworth who made the introductions. "Maynard, Howard, and Kirk, I would like you to meet my good friend, Dr. Morgan and his cousin William."

Tim stepped forward in his new identity and shook hands. Shultz did the same, now answering to Dr. Morgan. The speaker smiled and addressed Tim.

"Well…William, did you say?" asked Maynard Smith.

"Folks just call me Willie," Tim responded.

"Your southern accent tells me you are from Georgia or the Carolinas. Why are you in Canada? You wouldn't be hiding from your duty, would you?" Maynard asked.

Tim did not address Maynard. Instead, he directed his words to Bainesworth as he placed his hand on his hip, pushing back the jacket of his brown suit to reveal his holstered weapon. "I thought you told me this movement was about solving real problems."

"Will, I can assure you it is," Bainesworth responded nervously.

Shultz chuckled as Maynard inquired, "I'm sorry, ah, Willie. Am I missing something here?"

The men stood next to the doorway leading back into the just emptied theatre. The room was now dark, save for the light emanating from the lobby. Tim stepped forward pulling his gun swiftly, shoving the barrel into Maynard Smith's face. He nodded curtly, directing the other man toward the dark theatre. The other two men with the speaker raised their hands slightly. Forcing the now frightened Maynard into the dark auditorium, Tim pressed him against the wall while still holding the gun to his head.

"Yes, Mr. Smith, you are missing something. I don't take kindly to polite insults. Do you understand me?" Tim asked.

Maynard nodded, and Tim uncocked his gun before hitting his victim hard upside the head with it. When his legs buckled, Tim held him in place. "I am in Canada to solve the problem of war, not to chat like bitches in a salon."

Maynard held his bleeding skull as Tim frisked him. "Do you have a gun, Mr. Smith?"

"Y-yes," Maynard replied.

Tim found his piece and took it, showing Maynard Smith the utmost disrespect. Placing the weapon at his back between his pants and belt, Tim took a step back and scowled at Smith. "You only have one time to make a first impression. I don't like you, Mr. Smith."

Tim went back into the crowded lobby with Shultz, Bainesworth and the other men. Without hesitation he asked, "Either of you have a concern that needs my attention?"

The younger man, Kirk, spoke up. "We can use a man like you, Will. If you can get past Maynard's rudeness, maybe you can join us."

Maynard re-entered the lobby. His shirt was wrinkled, and he held a white handkerchief to his forehead where he had been knocked with the gun. Tim turned, directing his attention to Maynard, and Shultz stepped in with perfect timing.

"Cousin, you can't kill everyone just because you're angry about your lands in the South."

Tim glowered at Shultz, before he relented and looked away.

"Kirk," Shultz said, "my cousin and I will be in touch if we are interested in working with you. Sorry for this inconvenience. Although, in my cousin's defense, I thought we were here to shut down the tyrant—not hurl insults."

Maynard kept his eyes on his shoes.

"Here is my card," Kirk said, handing it to Tim. "We are staying at the Grand hotel, diagonally across the street on the second floor. We plan to meet in five days."

Shultz and Bainesworth were distressed. The train for Boston would leave in two and a half days. Five days would put them out of their schedule. Tim helped closed the gap, "Gentlemen, it was nice meeting you all. But I need to be heading back to Virginia. I leave here in a little over a day."

As Tim turned to leave, the older fellow, Howard spoke up. "We could have suppa demorro night in the lobby of the hotel we stayin' in."

Tim cocked his head. "What makes me so special? I ain't interested in yo' cause—it ain't my cause."

"We here askin' the Canadians for help. But a southerner has somethin' to lose—and somethin' to gain—in this matta. Ya can't beat true southern loyalty. Maynard is sorry. Ain't ya, Maynard?" Howard said, cajoling his friend.

Maynard cleared his throat before mumbling a sheepish apology. "I certainly meant no harm."

Tim stared at them for a few seconds. "I will think on it," he finally replied.

When Tim turned to leave, Maynard said, "Ahhh, my gun..."

Tim stared daggers at Maynard and then strolled away. Behind him, he heard Bainesworth say, "We shall attempt to persuade him to change his mind, but we can make no promises."

As Tim stepped into the late afternoon sun, he could see people milling about. It occurred to him that the nastiness of this war was spilling into Canada. Shultz and Bainesworth joined him as he moved down the staggered stone stairs onto the street.

"I must say, that went well," Bainesworth said.

"Those three need to be put down," Tim replied, thinking aloud.

❊ ❊ ❊

The men moved in groups of five throughout the city's night life. Black found that the "Preservers of Southern Life" were well known in the colored sector. The presence of such a faction elicited concerns of recapture for ex-slaves. Many of the colored locals knew of or had had some type of dealings with Black. There was relief at the sight of him and his men.

Black, Elbert, and James, along with Frank and Lou systematically went through colored areas collecting information. At a church on the edge of town, they listened to the concerns of the people who still had loved ones in the south. Their next stop was the saloon where piano music, accompanied by loud talking, floated to the street. When Black stepped through the swinging doors followed by Elbert and James, the atmosphere came to a sudden hush.

Frank and Lou remained at the swinging doors, watching the street. As the music and life resumed, Black looked about, locking eyes with the barkeep. Sidney was a brown skinned fellow, who was balding on the top. He was just about six-feet and the eyes that bulged in his head had a yellow tint. He had a wide nose and a full black beard. The barkeeper was dressed in a brown homespun shirt with short sleeves.

As Black glanced around, there was a collage of brown faces, and all eyes were on him. At the left of the room sat a dusty old piano, and the old man playing was just as dusty. He wore a tan homespun shirt like the barkeep and brown matching trousers; on his head, sat a worn black hat. Jimbo was a bright skinned fellow of about sixty summers with dark hair and brown eyes. He had a scar about his neck that started at one ear and ended at the other. He grinned at Black.

When standing on the street, the saloon and pussy parlor were side-by-side. On the inside of the saloon, near the piano, was a wide entrance that connected both establishments. Black could see the women as they catered to men. The décor was plain with brown tables and matching chairs throughout the saloon and whorehouse, though the ratio of chairs to tables was not proportionate. In fact, there were some tables with no chairs at all. Black looked to Sidney, the barkeeper once again. He did not smile as he wiped the bar with a towel that appeared less than clean.

Sidney nodded curtly in the direction of a small hall that led to a brown door. Black looked back at James and then Elbert. They had separated. James stood next to the piano and Elbert stood by the bar. As Black moved toward the door, the piano player started humming. Jimbo's voice was deep and rhythmic as he let fly a couple bars of a song Black hated.

Hope has come and he aint fraid. Hope has come, we 'bout to be diggin' a few graves.

Black glowered as the old man played with gusto. Jimbo's shoulders were to his ears, his arms outstretched, and his fingers spread wide as he banged the keys. But what annoyed Black most was Elbert–tapping his foot to the beat. Shaking his head at a smiling James, Black headed toward the back of the bar. When he came to the door, Black noticed two bullet holes in the wood. The door creaked on its hinges when it swung open. Behind a roughly made desk sat Ike, who looked up when Black strode into his office.

Ike was of medium build with brown skin, dark eyes, and wild unkempt hair. His nose was wide and kind of flat. His mouth was big, with a slightly pink bottom lip, bringing attention to the perfection of his very white teeth. He was about thirty-five summers and nearly six feet. Ike was from the Bedford plantation in Georgia and over the years, his name had changed from Ike to Spike. The name change was due to the incorrect pronunciation of the elderly slaves where he was raised. The name had stuck.

"Spike," Black said in greeting.

"Hope, been a long time," Spike replied.

"It has been."

Spike stood and walked over to Black, limping ever-so-slightly. He wore a gun holstered to his upper right side. The two men shook hands.

"What got ya so far from home?" Spike asked.

"A little of this and a little of that," Black responded.

Spike leaned his hip against the desk, giving Black a wary look. "You goin' ta have ta do betta than that."

"The group the 'Preservers of Southern Life'—what do you know about them?"

"Hmmm, so you's on a mission." Spike chuckled.

Black, not liking to be questioned, offered nothing. Spike threw up his hands and sighed. "I thanks its a way for the South to box in the North in this thang they calls a damn war."

"Who is their leader?"

Spike shrugged his shoulders. "They's seen, but they ain't seen. They gathers a lot, but the leader of the gatherins be different each time. I cain't pin down who would be the leader. But what I can say is, it's mo' than one man. They's clever, so ya cain't track 'em or stop 'em."

Black stood, arms crossed, feet apart. He listened carefully to the other man's detailed accounting. Spike was known for his intelligence and his deep attention to the world about him. When he finished speaking, Black nodded curtly toward the door. "Someone mad at you?"

"Shit, dems exit holes. The fellow on the other side of the door ain't do so well."

Black laughed as Spike continued, "I has a friend what works at the Grand Hotel. He works odd jobs ya know, as a server, cleaning chamber pots and what not. He say he heard talk of stealing that new president...what he name?"

"Lincoln," Black filled in.

"Lincoln, that's it. Fred say he was cleanin' one room and heard a heated dispute 'bout it through the wall from the next room. He say they was arguing on the best time to take him. Fred say it scared the shit out of him. He ain't want them to know he was listenin'."

"Where can I find this Fred?"

"Fred just be three places–wit' the whores, wit' the men dranking, or workin'. Tonight, I thanks he workin'. You and me can go to him or I can brang 'im to you. What's today?"

"Tuesday."

"Fred lowda be to the hotel all night. We can go to him, if'n you wantin'."

"Yeah," Black said as they exited the office.

When Black stepped back into the bar, Jimbo was still banging the keys, but the song had changed. He continued to the street, followed by the men. Once in the cover of darkness, he heard James whisper, "Spike, how the hell is ya?"

"I cain't complain," Spike whispered back.

"Spike, been a while," Elbert said, shaking the man's hand.

"Sho' has," Spike replied.

Frank and Lou exchanged greetings as well.

As the men moved through the night towards the Grand Hotel, the hour had grown late. The weather was hot and muggy. They stuck to the shadows, away from the lampposts that lined the sidewalks. The area along the theatre was deserted. Once at the hotel, they blended into their surroundings and disappeared down the alley. The side passage smelled of rotted garbage and when the path let out behind the establishment, a warm breeze highlighted the unpleasant odor of emptied chamber pots.

The Grand Hotel took up most of the city block, with a few small businesses crammed in beside it. Still, the smaller commerce was there to cater to the occupants and employees of the hotel. The men stood on the edge of the light originating from the gigantic back doors. The goal: to see without being seen.

The kitchen was still bustling, even at such a late hour, as the workers prepared to offer another day of luxury. People of color moved about with purpose, dressed in maid, butler and chef uniforms. They were busy cutting, peeling, or decorating food. The smell had changed for the better, yet just two feet in the opposite direction would curdle one's belly.

The other man hung back as Spike whistled. A few people closest to the door looked up; others didn't hear or acknowledge him because the noise level was so high. "Ya seen Fred? I needs 'im," Spike said to a young woman in a maid's uniform.

She pointed, as she moved back into the busy, well-lit kitchen. Fred was seated on a stool peeling potatoes and speaking with a young woman seated next to him. Upon seeing Spike, he stood excusing himself.

"What you doin' here?" Fred asked.

"We was needin' to speak wit' ya, Freddy," Spike replied.

Fred looked over his shoulder and then back at Spike. "Who is *we?*"

As if on cue, the men appeared one by one on the edge of the light. Fred's eyes widened when Black said. "I need to speak with you, Fred."

"This here is Black," Spike said.

Fred was about twenty-five summers. He was dark of skin with a thin frame standing about five-feet, seven-inches. The younger man's features were shadowed, as the light from the kitchen was behind him. Yet, Black could feel his apprehension.

Fred mumbled, "I heard a ya, Mista Black. But I cain't thank of a damn thang I know that would interest ya."

Black grinned, "Let me be the judge of what's interesting, Fred. I'd like you to come with us, away from here, so we can speak freely."

"Yes, sah. Give me one moment."

Stepping back toward the kitchen entrance, Fred removed the apron he was wearing. Black watched as he stopped and spoke to a maid. She nodded, and he turned back toward the men.

"Follow us," Elbert instructed.

Darkness swallowed them as they trekked back down the alley toward the street. Frank and Lou took the lead, while Black and Elbert brought up the rear. The men crossed the roadway to the opposite side and traveled soundlessly down the walkway for about a mile. Lou lifted Frank, so they could snuff out several of the lampposts along the way, securing privacy from prying eyes. They were almost to Ruby's when the men stopped and formed a circle around Fred.

Black's voice floated on the night air. "Working at the hotel like you do, I'm sure you have seen much."

"Yes, sah, I has," Fred responded.

"I am interested in one group, the 'Preservers of Southern Life.' What can you tell me about them?" Black asked.

"They's a mean bunch, Mista Black—they hates colored folks. They speaks free 'bout what they thanks. I don't look 'em in the eye when I be havin' ta deal wit' 'em. You hears all sorts of stuff when ya servin' 'em or cleaning they rooms." Fred replied.

"What sort of things have you overheard?" Black probed.

"They talks about the meetins' they holds. They talks about the war. And, they ain't all southerners neither, Mista Black. Couple of the people I seen is from the North. Mostly I hear yo' regular shit, 'bout niggers ain't meant to be free. I did hear 'em talkin 'bout stealing that new president to make the North surrender. When I heard that, I got real scared. Thought they was gonna get ta shootin', they was so angry." Fred answered and then grew quiet for a moment.

"When did this happen?" Black pressed him. "Did you hear any names?"

"I ain't hear no names. It was a few months back—tried to push it from my head. I don't need no shit. But I did hear one man say, you's from England, you ain't got shit to lose. It was 'bout three men, one was tryna keep the peace. The other was sayin' they should have taken the president 'fore war broke out. The man what was from England said it wasn't too late. I had my ear pressed 'gainst the wall. When I back away, I knock the vase off the nightstand. Shit, they stopped talkin' and I heard the door to their room open when I made it to the stairs. I kept goin', and I ain't look back."

"Anything else?" Elbert asked.

"Yeah," Freddy went on. "I heard one man say, if they take the damn yankee president now, we won't lose ground."

"These men," Black said, "if you heard them speak again, you think you would recognize their voices?"

"I thank so—but I cain't say fo' sho', Mista Black," Fred answered nervously.

❅ ❅ ❅

Bainesworth, Tim, and Shultz stood at the front desk in the main lobby of the Grand Hotel. Shultz and the ambassador were attired in suits; Tim was dressed in black boots, black trousers, and a white shirt with the sleeves rolled up. At his upper right side, his gun was holstered in plain view. Tim was not dressed for polite company. The bellhop had gone to fetch Kirk Flanders and

Howard Shepard. While the men waited, Tim observed the hotel. It was truly "grand".

The plush burgundy carpet in the lobby ran from wall to wall. Against the far wall of the room was a row of throne-like chairs. The chairs were burgundy, with big claw feet and arms carved intricately in rich, dark wood. The front desk was made from the same wood, and beside the front desk was a large, winding staircase. On the left of the lobby was a spacious dining room. Tim gazed around the room and caught his reflection in a huge, gilt-framed mirror on the far wall. The hotel was well lit from the candles on the tables and the sunlight that danced through the windows.

"Will! Good to see you," Kirk said by way of greeting, "Dr. Morgan...Bainesworth."

"Kirk," Tim replied with far less enthusiasm. He then looked past Kirk, searching for his partners.

"They're at the theatre," Kirk said, reading his mind.

Tim nodded. The men exited the hotel and crossed the street. People strolled about in the afternoon sunshine, going from store to store. On the roadway, expensive carriages with fine horses moved to and fro. A small group of gentlemen, accompanied by their ladies, stood in front of the theatre. There was an array of different colored suits, dresses and hats. The weather was hot, and no breeze blew, yet the people standing about managed to look cool.

Several signs hung in front of the theatre announcing a performance of Shakespeare's *Romeo and Juliet*. Show time wasn't until seven that evening—it was not yet four-thirty.

Kirk, Tim, Shultz, and Bainesworth walked up the steps and into the theatre. Once inside the lobby, Tim could see the place was as busy as a beehive. Music drifted from the stage out to the common areas. Actors and actresses paced the lobby, saying their lines, readying themselves for the evening ahead.

Tim hung back with Shultz and Bainesworth. He watched

as Kirk headed toward the stage; Maynard and Howard were on hand to speak with him. Two other men jumped from the stage and stood next to Kirk. They chatted for a few seconds, and then suddenly Kirk was strolling purposefully back up the aisle. He waved Tim and the other men over.

"Follow me," he said.

They trailed Kirk down the center aisle with Tim bringing up the rear. When they reached the stage, the lighting was brilliant. The actors stood in clusters talking, and no one seemed to be paying them any mind. On either side of the stage were two gray doors. Kirk took the swinging door to the right and as they stepped into the corridor, Tim felt uneasy. Still, he continued with the knowledge that Shultz was strapped. The lighting was dimmer in the hall, but he could see more gray doors when his eyes finally adjusted.

Halfway down the corridor, a door to the left opened. Maynard Smith stepped into view and waved them forward. Tim entered the small dressing room last, where four other men were present. He only recognized Howard and Maynard. On the left side of the room was a large oval mirror with a tall chair in front of it. The room was lit with a couple of dingy oil lamps, making the room hot and stuffy.

Howard made the introductions. "Dr. Morgan, Bainesworth, Will—I would like ya all to meet John and Samuel."

The men all shook hands, but once the formalities were out of the way, Tim became watchful and quiet. Samuel was of medium build and looked to be in his late thirties. He had dark hair and mean eyes. He sported a mustache and beard and was dressed in a wrinkled, blue suit. John was a fair-skinned, raven-haired man with alert dark eyes. Other than a big bushy mustache, his face was clean shaven, and he was dressed in a white robe.

"I think we have the beginnings of a great operation," Kirk began. "We will continue to form our plan here in Montreal and then move it to Washington, where it will be executed. Part of our hold-up is having the right men in place."

Tim, deliberately sounding bored, spoke up. "I'm all for planning, but a time frame is needed. The war is underway. Bainesworth here directed me to you all because he thought your group was serious. I am leaving for Virginia in a few hours—from what I can see, you all don't even have a plan. I ain't heard shit that sounds like a plan."

The man called John chimed in. "Kirk, as much as I hate to agree, he's correct. We don't have a plan in place, and it's making me tired."

"Will, Booth, you both need to be patient. We do have a plan, Booth, and you know it. Stealing a president and ransoming him is not light work," Maynard added.

"Why are we ransoming Lincoln? We need to kill him and be done. The "Preservers of Southern Life" have done nothing toward getting rid of that tyrant," Booth spat.

Tim's eyes fixed on the man. "John...aahh, Booth—"

"People call me, Booth," John said.

"Booth, if you don't mind my asking–how long have you been dealing with this group?" Tim asked.

"I have been dealing with this foolishness since May, but I have grown weary," Booth complained.

Tim turned to Kirk. "If your group has a trust issue, then I don't want any part in this thing that's going nowhere." He looked to Bainesworth and Shultz. "Gentlemen, I am ready to go. I have wasted enough time."

Howard interceded. "We has a plan that we's gonna work through in Washington—late Septemba, early Octoba."

"We plan on taking the Union president and ransoming him in October," Kirk confirmed.

"I say we kill him."

Booth's words hung in the air, and the room grew quiet.

Maynard's cold eyes searched the group. "We *are* considering killing him."

Tim smirked. "How many men do we have?"

Maynard's eyes lit up. "We? Does this mean you will join us?"

"It means, if you all have a plan, I'm in. If the group is like you, all talk and no action, I ain't," Tim responded, stepping up on Maynard threateningly.

The rest of the men laughed nervously, but to further intimidate Maynard, Tim did not. Kirk steered the group away from the tension between Maynard and Tim. "The Preservers of Southern Life have a huge following, but for this mission there are about ten of us. We have three men in Washington that watch Lincoln's every move. They follow his daily pattern; we are almost ready."

Tim saw that even Booth was surprised at Kirk's revelation. He looked back at Kirk. "Where will we meet in Washington?"

"We will meet in Fredericksburg first and backtrack to Washington when ready," Kirk replied.

"When are we looking at?" Samuel inquired.

"We will be leaving Montreal after the meeting a week from now. The men and I should be in Fredericksburg no later than the first week of September. I am hopeful we will be there sooner. There is an old farmhouse owned by Howard's family that is not in use. We will shoot for September tenth at Lily Farm," Kirk said.

Shultz opened his mouth to say something, but there was a knock at the door.

"Makeup, Mr. Booth," came a man's voice from the corridor.

"Just a moment, Peter," Booth replied.

"How will we get in touch?" Shultz finally asked.

"We would like for Willie to go to the Union capital and make contact with our men. There is a dry goods store on Tenth Street. If you should decide to take the job," Maynard addressed Tim, "when you are settled in Washington, go to the store. The proprietor's name is Herbert. He will also handle any messages between us."

"I have something to handle at home, and then I will be in Washington, straight away," Tim said.

"I will be in Washington before month's end. I look forward to working with you, Will," Booth said.

"Same here," Tim replied.

There was another knock. The invisible Peter's voice called out with more urgency. "Mr. Booth, we need to start your makeup."

"I hope you all will stay for the performance," Booth said as he opened the door to a skinny man wearing thick glasses and a black tam.

The men shook hands as they filed out of the dressing room.

"I ain't staying for the show," Tim whispered to Booth. "I will see you in Washington."

"I understand–until Washington, then." Booth answered.

❊ ❊ ❊

As night fell, the men posted up around Ruby's eatery. Anthony and Luke took the front door, Emmett and Ephraim took the back. Gilbert and Elbert stood on the corner under an extinguished lamppost. At the opposite corner, Herman and John did the same. The men rotated to offer relief to the men outside. Inside the restaurant, Black conducted an experiment that could end in blood shed.

Ruby had cooked and was serving cabbage, fried chicken, rice and gravy. She had also baked several cakes and pies. The tables were pushed together, and Black sat facing Bainesworth. Next to the ambassador, and on the right, sat Fred–on his left, James. The conversation in the room was hushed as Black engaged Bainesworth in small talk.

"How long have you been in Canada, Ambassador?" Black inquired.

"Let's see, I made it from London town to Montreal in March. The weather was terrible, I might add," Bainesworth replied.

"Did you travel alone?"

Bainesworth shifted in his chair. "The queen's business can be lonely business. Yes, I voyaged alone."

Black raised his eyes; his expression conveying hazard. "When you arrived, where did you take rooms?"

"My rooms were at the Grand—marvelous food," Bainesworth said.

As Black stared at the ambassador, he could see Fred shaking his head from his side view. He was confirming that the ambassador's voice did not sound familiar. Black nodded and began eating, cutting the conversation rudely short. Bainesworth pushed back from the table and stood. He walked to the back door where Shultz chatted with Emmett and Ephraim. The doctor smiled, before handing the ambassador the handkerchief from his shirt pocket. Bainesworth immediately mopped the sweat from his brow.

❋ ❋ ❋

On the morning of the third day, well before dawn, the men packed up their belongings. The dining room had been put back to rights and the men were now standing about outside keeping watch. Black leaned against the kitchen counter, watching Ruby go about her business. She would not look at him.

"I left the deed to this place on one of the tables in the dining room. I have turned the restaurant and the land it sits on over to you."

Ruby stopped in her tracks. "Why would you do such a thing?"

"You do all the work—it's better this way."

Black was severing all ties, and he knew that Ruby understood. She looked away, nodding her acceptance. "I can't say when I will see you again, and the way life has been going for me–I would just prefer you be treated fairly. I apologize, I hadn't thought of it sooner."

Ruby's voice was shaky. "Hope, you are too generous. You have nothing to seek forgiveness for."

Black stood to his full height; he was just about to end the conversation when Spike entered through the back door. Though Spike tried to hide it, he was jealous and because of Sunday, Black understood the feeling. The kitchen suddenly became too small. Black was about to excuse himself, when Spike addressed him.

"Brought two wagons—me and Fred is doin' the drivin'."

Black smiled. Spike was interrupting his conversation with Ruby to tell him what he already knew. "I'm guessing you would prefer I not be alone with Miss Ruby."

"You would be guessin' right," Spike replied, he would not bitch up.

"Spike!" Ruby's tone was one of both embarrassment and shock.

Spike turned to her. "I ain't start it Ruby; Hope did. I ain't 'shamed neither. I be here for ya every day, but ya ignores me for him."

Black coughed, but it was Ruby who surprised him with her next words. "Why would I chase wit' you, Spike? Yes, you come every day to see me and leave every night to be at that damn whorehouse. I ain't sharing wit' no whores."

Black had never heard Ruby swear. She was standing with her hands on her hips, glaring at Spike, who appeared momentarily flabbergasted.

"That ain't fair, woman! I would do anythin' ya ask of me, but ya keeps pining over him. Ya keeps this place like he gon' walk through the door any minute. Hope ain't so damn special," Spike said, pointing an angry finger at Black.

Black's eyebrow arched, and he was about to say something when Ruby declared loudly, "Hope owns the place!"

Spike scowled at him, and Black held up his hands. "I don't own the place anymore. But you are incorrect about one thing…"

"Yeah, and what that is?" Spike asked sarcastically.

Black's eyes gleamed with mischief. "I *am* special."

Spike narrowed his eyes, and Ruby burst out laughing. Black opened his arms, and she came to him, giggling as she hugged him. Over her head, he smiled at a disgruntled Spike.

"Be safe, Hope, and thank you for everything," Ruby whispered.

Black looked at her affectionately. "You be safe too, Ruby."

As he passed Spike in the doorway, Black said, "I'll be outside."

Black stepped through the back door into the pre-dawn and heard Spike say, "I loves ya, Ruby. Shit, I loves Hope too; he helped me get free. But he can't have ya!"

❄ ❄ ❄

The sun was just coming up when Black and the men made it to the checkpoint. They camped out in the trees until the 4:10 train arrived headed for Boston. Black and Spike did not speak about Ruby again, instead they turned their mind to the matter at hand.

Black began thinking. They needed to find Rose and hear firsthand what information she held. Lincoln was next on the list. Their goal was to not get killed while trying to do a good deed. And then, there was the matter of the Hunter plantation—they needed to contain the problem in the South. Lastly, they needed to retrace Fannie's steps.

Black and James stood in the doorway of the railcar, watching the countryside roll by. Black's thoughts were on the people of Fort Independence. As for James, a muscle in his jaw spasmed constantly as he looked out at the green mountains of New England. Black could only assume he was ready—for anything.

10

Hunter Plantation
August 1861

OLD MAN JACKSON, the local pastor, had come to the Hunter plantation to join Suzanne and E.J. in holy matrimony. The ceremony took place in the study and was simple, yet beautiful. Suzanne wore a white day dress with black slippers. Her mother and sister both wore powder blue dresses as they stood in support of the bride. E.J. wore a blue suit, and next to him, stood Jeremiah dressed in slave attire. As the brothers stood side by side, no one dared question E.J.'s choice in support.

The slaves who cleaned and lived in the house also attended the nuptials. They looked on with elation as the master took a wife. Nettie, however, did not smile. The sight of E.J. and Miss Suzanne squeezed the very life from her.

The gray-haired pastor appeared rickety in his bearing. But his voice was strong when he commanded, "Repeat after me."

In just a few short moments, the couple was pronounced man and wife. The small, yet intimate crowd clapped as E.J. planted a chaste kiss on Suzanne's lips. The gathering then moved to the informal dining room off the gardens, and the French doors were propped open, allowing in the late morning sun. The slaves had gone back to work, serving the wedding party. A few of the over-seers offered well wishes as they joined in the celebration. Jeremiah did not mingle with such company; still, he was pleased for his brother. He was about to take his leave when E.J. excused himself from his young wife and approached.

"Where you going?"

"I'm going to my cabin to sleep. I been up all night walking the plantation. I ain't slept in days." Jeremiah replied.

"I wanted you to stay a little longer. The women need to get used to your presence," E.J. said, looking over his shoulder.

Jeremiah assessed his brother. "What troubles you?"

E.J. hesitated. "Nettie."

Suzanne suddenly appeared and took hold of her husband's hand. "Good morning, Jeremiah," she said softly.

She had never spoken to him before and, quite frankly, he liked it that way. He did not wish to be mistaken for a damn but-ler. Jeremiah also did not need his brother's new wife to be a point of contention between them.

"Good morning, Miss Suzanne," he replied woodenly.

Suzanne looked up into his eyes, and the black cracker could smell her fear. Her voice shook when she said, "Your brother tells me you're mean and that you only like him."

Jeremiah hadn't expected her to say such a thing, nor had he expected E.J. to tell her that they were brothers. He chuckled. "I don't like Edward all the time, and he is meaner than me."

"I see that you have already switched loyalties, brother," E.J. said.

Suzanne smiled. She was about to comment when her mother called her away. She excused herself.

"What about Nettie?" Jeremiah asked when they were alone.

"Never mind, I will handle it," E.J. said, watching his wife from across the room.

Jeremiah nodded. He knew exactly what troubled his brother. E.J. cared for the slave girl, and those feelings were causing him angst. Jeremiah did not envy him. He couldn't handle Callie; the last thing he needed was another woman complicating his life.

"I will see you tonight; sleep is calling me," Jeremiah said.

Jeremiah strode in the direction of his cabin and saw two slave boys helping an emotional Nettie move her scant belongings to a cabin on the far end of the plantation. It was the natural order of things between a master and slave woman. Jeremiah's mind did not linger; he had his own problems to manage. When his cabin finally came into view, he welcomed the thought of rest.

He walked around to the back of his cabin and finding the door open, he smiled. When he entered the small space he shared with her, he was greeted by a foul odor and the vision of Callie with her head in a bucket. The sound of her heaving echoed throughout the cabin. He was instantly worried for her. She had not looked well for days. But when he asked after her well-being, she had responded that it must have been something she ate.

Callie pulled her head out of the bucket and looked up at him. "I am not getting any better. I feel like I'm dying," she croaked.

Jeremiah quickly removed his guns and shirt before lifting her into his arms. She tried to push him away, but she was too weak. As he carried her out to the pump, he noticed her clothes were stained with the contents of her stomach. He steadied her on her feet and began working the pump.

"Drink some and clean ya face," he instructed.

Callie splashed the cool water on her face, but she didn't drink. "My belly can't take anything," she moaned.

Jeremiah carried her back inside and helped her removed her soiled clothing before wrapping her in a towel. He sat down in one of the chairs and pulled her onto his lap, cradling her. Later, he filled the tub and helped her into the water. She looked thinner, and he could not recall when he saw her eat last. He lay on the floor next to the tub staring up at the ceiling while she bathed. Callie was ill, and he was afraid.

When she stepped from the tub and vomited onto the floor, he decided to go for help. Jeremiah went to find Eva.

❈ ❈ ❈

Eva and Sonny had just made it to her cabin. The fading sun offered no relief from the unbearable heat.

Sonny had been different with her of late. He was now more affectionate. Eva suspected it was the incident with Jeremiah that had caused his change. She was sure the thought of dying and leaving her alone worried him. Normally, she walked home before dark by herself, now he accompanied her nightly. She wasn't complaining—she loved his attention. He was also more carnal, and she loved that too.

"Ya hungry, key man?" Eva asked with a giggle.

"You knows I hates it when folks call me 'key man,'" Sonny complained.

"I's sorry; I couldn't hep myself. Imma behave, I promises."

Sonny kissed her. "I's very hungry, but it ain't for no food."

Eva thought him handsome as he smiled down at her. She had been about to tell him so when there came a loud banging at the front door. The reality of being controlled by outside forces came flooding back. Sonny squeezed her hand gently before moving to pull the door open. Eva was anxious as she stood at the back of the cabin, trembling.

Jeremiah stood in the doorway, shirtless; his guns holstered at his right hip and upper left side. A light sheen of perspiration caused the rippling muscles in his shoulders, chest and arms to glisten. There was tension in his bloodshot gaze, and his wild unruly hair only added to the threatening vision that was the black overseer. Eva could taste her fear when his eyes locked on her. He spoke, directing his velvet voice to her.

"Eva, I need your help. Please come with me."

"Yes, sah, Mista Jeremiah," she whispered.

Sonny gave her a worried look as she limped out of the cabin with Jeremiah in her wake. On the makeshift porch, Eva held onto the rail and slowly descended the two steps onto the path. As they walked along, Jeremiah modified his gait to match hers.

Eva chose her words carefully. "Sah, if ya don't mind my askin', what happened?"

"Callie ain't well."

"Oh."

Jeremiah stopped short. "I'm going to carry you. Will that cause ya any pain?"

Eva was still shaking her head when he scooped her up in his arms. She had never seen Jeremiah as a man, viewing him only as vicious. And though she had never directly experienced his wrath, it had been scary to witness. She wished he would put her down, but she wouldn't dare say so. While she was attempting to think through this uncomfortable circumstance, he spoke.

"Put your arms around my neck, Eva."

Awkwardly, she did as he instructed, and Jeremiah began to run. When they arrived at his cabin, he stood her on the porch.

"Callie is in the bed," he said.

Eva nodded.

Once in the cabin, she was assailed by a sour smell that clung to the room. She looked about, gauging the situation, and when she turned back to him, Jeremiah was visibly afraid. "Come empt the pail and tub. Rench 'em both and fill 'em both."

While Jeremiah did as she ordered, Eva limped over and pulled a chair close to the bed. Callie's eyes fluttered open when she began to speak softly, "What's goin' on wit' ya, dear?"

"I can't eat anything; my belly can't take anything, not even water. I'm weak."

She felt Callie's forehead—there was no fever. "When the last time ya come 'round?"

Eva could see her question shocked the younger woman as she tried to recall. "I don't recollect. I think May."

"Ya been coupling wit' him?"

"Yes," Callie replied, looking away.

"Since when?"

Callie swallowed hard. "Early June."

"Ok, we'll get ya fixed up," Eva stood and walked to the back door.

Jeremiah was at the pump, cleaning a pail when she stepped onto the porch. When he noticed her, he came to her instantly. Eva spoke slowly so he would get it right.

"I needs ya to go to the main house and ask Ella for these thangs. We needs some ginger water and mint water. Tell Ella to send some crackers and a small plate of food. And tell her I say to send two apples."

He didn't move, causing Eva to say, "She ain't dying that's fo' sho'. We'll talk when ya gets back. Brang the small pail of water 'fore ya go."

Jeremiah did as she requested before rushing off to the main house. While he was gone, Eva helped her from the bed, dressing her. Seating Callie to the table, she combed her hair and spoke frankly with her.

"Is he the first ya couple wit'?"

Callie's voice was weak and faltered as she spoke. "Where I come from, there was no time for such things. The mistress was elderly; she needed tending day and night. The only men I saw were my brother and father. The mistress' husband died years before I was born. Aside from the other servants, it was just me taking care of her. Though helping her was hell, it was still an easier life than most had."

"How old is ya?" Eva inquired.

"Twenty-five summers."

Eva took Callie's chin in her hand and made her look up at her. "Ya knows you is wit' child, right?"

"I figured it out when you asked about when I come around," Callie said, pulling away and leaning her forehead on the table.

Eva patted her back. "This will pass. Ya gonna be fine."

Eva began cleaning up. She opened the front door to get some cross ventilation, and the bad smell began to dissipate. Jeremiah returned with a small wooden box and placed it on the table. He stared down at Callie before going to sit on the back steps.

Eva coaxed Callie into drinking a small amount of the ginger water, while forcing her to eat a cracker or two. Callie relieved herself twice and Jeremiah was on hand to remove and clean the bucket. Finally, Callie climbed into bed to sleep, but not before Eva got her to eat a few spoons of the chicken soup Ella had sent.

Eva gathered Callie's and Jeremiah's soiled clothes in a sack. She would take them home to wash. Dropping the bag at the front door, she looked out into the dying sunlight to see Sonny standing next to a pine tree a few yards away. She signaled for him to come take the bag, and when he came forward, she smiled to reassure him.

"Wait for me. I has to talk wit' Jeremiah," she said, keeping her voice low.

Sonny picked up the bag of clothes and returned to his position in the shade of the pine. Eva walked back through the cabin, past a sleeping Callie to face Jeremiah. He stood when she came outside, and his eyes were filled with emotion. Jeremiah offered his intense, undivided attention causing Eva to look to the ground.

"Her belly gon bother her for a few mo' weeks. But it will stop soon enuff."

Jeremiah's expression changed to one of alarm. "A few more weeks? What's wrong with her?"

Eva was both incredulous and embarrassed to have to speak with him about such matters. As she stared at him, she realized how beautiful Jeremiah was. The ugliness of his being a colored overseer was all she had seen until now. Here he stood, nervous, hurt, and in love. Life was settling a few scores with the black cracker. She almost hated to see how it would play out.

"Callie is wit' child. She carries yo' seed. From what she say, the baby should be here in February," Eva carefully explained.

His eyes welled up, and his voice was raw. "Carrying my seed is killing her."

"It ain't. She just don't eat like she should. She be all right, but she gotta eat."

"I know that some of the women do things to take the child out of them. Can you do that for her, Eva? Can ya stop this?" Jeremiah's desperation was palpable.

"Ya loves her. Why would ya want such a thing?"

"Life is getting even with me. I don't want her hurt."

Eva smiled and reached out to touch his cheek. "She loves ya *and* this child. She ain't gonna do it. But you's right—some women do thangs to remove the child and many of 'em don't live neither."

Jeremiah sighed and leaned back against the side of the cabin.

"When she wake," Eva instructed him softly, "see to it that she drank and eat, even if it's a little. Imma take her thangs and wash 'em. I'll be back in the mawning. If ya needs me, come get me."

Jeremiah pursed his lips and nodded. "I'll carry you and the sack home."

Eva smiled. "Sonny out front; he will carry the sack and help me. The key man cain't take no mo' tonight."

Jeremiah gave her a weak smile. "Thank you, Eva."

Eva put her hand on his arm before heading out the front of the cabin to meet Sonny.

❊ ❊ ❊

Jeremiah stood outside for a while after Eva left. It was nighttime again, and he still hadn't slept. He exhaled, as he walked through the back of the cabin, heading for the front door. He closed it and when he turned back to the room at large, Callie lay awake staring at him. Crossing to the table, he poured her some ginger water in a wooden cup and brought it along with a few crackers to the bed. She waved him off.

"Eva said you have to eat and drink."

Callie looked at him for a moment, before she nodded and took a cracker from his hand. She nibbled and sipped the ginger water. Immediately, she wrinkled her nose.

"It don't taste good."

"You have to eat." He snapped.

Callie's expression grew serious. "I want our baby. I won't take anything to remove your seed from me."

Jeremiah felt so overcome with emotion, he looked away. He needed a moment, but she wouldn't relent. Callie cupped his face and whispered, "I won't, Jeremiah."

The tenderness between them was clouding his judgment. As he glared at her, he knew he should weigh his words, but his feelings were out of his reach. He offered the truth in large doses, his voice severe.

"You can't be thinking me, you and this damn baby gonna live happy. Shit, you smarter than me—why would you let yourself be tricked by feelings? I only want you. I don't want this baby. I don't want to share you with no damn body."

"Your words contradict your actions. You should have killed me like I requested, rather than couple with me," Callie replied evenly.

She stared at him, as if counting his shortcomings, until

finally, she disengaged from him totally. Callie lay back in the bed and turned herself to face the wall. He glared at the small of her back. Jeremiah was so damn angry, but what annoyed him most was her use of the word, *contradict*. It galled him to wonder at the meaning. He turned the lantern down and began to pace the back porch. E.J. appeared, and Jeremiah found he didn't want to talk.

"You are here on your wedding night?" Jeremiah asked, sarcastically.

"Ella thought Callie must not be well," E.J. replied, standing at the bottom of the back steps.

"I will sleep tonight. We can meet in your study in the morning. Will you hire more men?"

"You, all right? Is Callie all right?" E.J. pressed him, not allowing the subject to be changed.

Jeremiah's response was brief and final. "She is resting."

"I will hire more men, and yes, we can meet in the study around ten."

Jeremiah nodded, but said nothing further.

"You don't talk about the girl," E.J. said. "If there is something you need, you have but to say."

Jeremiah studied his brother's face. "Ella tell you she is wit' child?"

"Based on what Eva requested, Ella thought Callie might be in a family way."

Jeremiah couldn't respond; his emotions were still too high. "I will see you in the morning,"

The two men stood for a time staring at one another in the slice of light provided by the back door. Finally, E.J. nodded, and as he turned to leave, Jeremiah whispered, "I can't keep them— they deserve better than me."

E.J. frowned. "I don't understand."

"I will have to take them somewhere safe."

"Where could be safer than here with us?" E.J. asked.

"I'm done E.J.–I'm done for tonight."

E.J. nodded and walked away. As Jeremiah watched him go, he noticed his brother was headed in the direction of Nettie's cabin rather than home.

❀ ❀ ❀

Callie lay facing the wall; she cried when he left the room. Hearing him say he didn't want the child hurt, but what pained her most was understanding that he was right. When she backed away from her emotions, she could see his anxiety for her and the child. They were both now at fault for breeding in such conditions and offering the legacy of slavery to their unborn child. She had allowed herself to believe that she could have what white women had–a man with choices. Jeremiah's words had jolted her back to the harsh reality of their situation. His words had reminded her of who he was as a man.

She recalled their conversations over the last few months, and though he spoke very little, she knew it was the most he had conversed with anyone—other than his brother. When they disagreed, they did what they were doing at this moment. They disengaged. The anger he carried was still simmering within him, and she believed he backed away at times to keep from hurting her. She was always able to see when she had ignited enough anger within him to cause fire. What she never did was set out to hurt and upset him; she always offered him the truth. She also realized, he didn't engage in physically punishing her because he could respect the sincerity of her words.

Jeremiah kept a strange schedule, working all night and then sleeping during the day. He seemed obsessed with being ready at all times. It was clear, he anticipated some type of danger, but he did not discuss it with her. They had learned to coexist in the cabin, and he no longer slept in his room at the big house. During the night hours, he checked on her and it made her feel safe. In the daytime, she checked on him to see that he didn't want for anything. Some days, she lingered in bed and he would make love to her. She had become accustomed to tending him in all things.

They also had moments when he would burst out laughing at something she said. The first time she heard his laughter, she thought it strange—and she realized he thought it strange as well. They had argued because she wanted to work in the gardens again, rather than in the hot kitchen with Ella. She knew he was jealous of the male slaves who helped in the gardens. He had forbidden her while throwing the word master around. He put his foot down, reminding her that she had agreed not to be difficult. She conceded to keep the peace.

Her mind flashed back to the conversation they had the day after that argument. It had been just before dawn. She was seated at the table, folding clothes, when he appeared at the back door. He filled the tub and she helped him undress. They did not speak because she was still angry. He soaked in the water, ignoring her. When she finished with the clothes, she knelt beside the tub and waited for him to acknowledge her.

"I am tired, woman. I don't want to fight," he finally said.

"Why would you think I want to fight, Jeremiah?"

"Because you ain't like my use of the word 'master'."

She looked him straight in the eyes. "Your use of the word 'master' doesn't bother me."

"Really?" he scoffed. "I thought you didn't want a master—and certainly not me."

"It doesn't bother me, because…"

He looked at her with suspicion. "Because *why*?"

"It doesn't bother me, because I have figured out how I can become *your* master," she replied boldly.

He sat straight up in the tub and burst out laughing. Jeremiah was extra handsome when he laughed, and she couldn't help it, she giggled too. His hilarity rolled around the cabin, lightening the mood.

"Let's hear it," he said.

"When we couple, and you put your mouth on me, it feels so good; it enslaves me to you. I think if I take you in my mouth–if I licked and sucked on you, it would make me your master," she explained slowly, while holding his eyes.

"You figured that out all by yourself?" he asked, his voice raw.

"I did." Jeremiah's facial expression became blank as she went on. "Do you think it will work? Will it help you to see that there is only you? Will it help you understand that I want no one but you? Would taking you in my mouth make me master for the day?"

"It–ah takes some getting used to," he explained.

"I understand; but, I promise to stay with you and not back away, the same as you do for me."

"So, you want to control me?" he asked, actually smiling at the thought.

Callie chose her words with care. "I seek to *share* control with you. I don't want the burden of mastering you totally."

"I see," he said, appearing deep in thought.

"May I ask a question?"

"Yeah," he replied.

"Is it possible for me to master you *some* of the time?" You have not made clear if I could," she said softly.

"Yes, Callie, if you took me in your mouth, you would indeed be the master," he replied, his gaze penetrating.

Callie was snatched from her reverie when Jeremiah pulled the tub back into the cabin and began filling it. She pretended to be asleep because she could not face him. She would not get rid of their child. They had not spoken much about feelings, but she loved him. In truth, she had loved him since he saved her from Sizemore. She had not said as much, but she suspected he knew.

She listened and could tell he was removing his clothes. Soon, she heard the water sloshing and the sounds of him washing himself.

When she could take no more, she turned over to face him. He had washed his hair and was using a dipping cup to rinse the soap from his curly locks. His eyes were squeezed shut against the water and soap, allowing her a moment to observe him. Using his cloth, he wiped his hair of the excess water and then his face before opening his eyes. Their gazes collided. It seemed like an eternity before he spoke.

"I'm afraid for you and the child," he said, as if to answer her question.

"I know," she whispered.

"We need to talk. I just need time to rest and think."

Callie nodded. Still, she felt the need to make clear her feelings. "I won't remove your seed from me."

"I know."

"You angry with me?" she asked.

He stood abruptly allowing the water to cascade down his beautiful black body. Jeremiah stepped from the tub, but he did not reach for a towel. Instead, he allowed the hot summer night to dry his skin. He walked to the back door and stood for a moment. Callie had given up on the conversation because he took so long to answer.

He turned to her. "I love you, Callie, and I am *so* afraid for you."

His unexpected words caused her to burst out crying. He turned the lantern all the way down, and then walked to the edge of the bed. Scooping her into his arms, he began to pace back and forth, from inside the cabin to the back porch. She wrapped her arms about his neck while her legs encircled his waist, allowing herself to be comforted.

"*Sshhh*, don't cry, Callie," he whispered.

When she finally quieted, she asked, "Don't you see why I want this child?"

He spoke slowly. "Life is punishing me, Callie, because I am not a good man. I have done things for which I feel no shame."

She looked into his eyes. "Maybe life offers you another chance."

"No. Through *you*, life is showing me what I can't never have."

She opened her mouth to argue his point, but he cut her short. "No more—I have not slept in days. I'm done for now, Callie. Come eat and drink something for me."

He put her down in a chair at the table, and she ate half an apple, some crackers and then sipped a little mint water. She still felt weak and queasy. Jeremiah had gone outside to give her some privacy. She climbed into the bed, and soon he came back. She waited until he was settled in next to her before she spoke again.

"Jeremiah."

He sighed. "Yes, Callie."

"I love you," she said softly.

He sat up on one elbow. "*Never* say those words to me again and never tell anyone about your feelings for me. Do you understand?" he snapped.

She could hear his agony, anxiety and fear, still she said, "I will tell no one else. I won't need to because some things can't be hidden, Jeremiah. I haven't told Eva I love you, but she knows. She has not told me she loves Sonny, but still I feel it when they are near. I will, however, tell you that I love you, and you will not control my words."

"You are a damn hardheaded woman," he said in vexation.

Callie snuggled closer to him and kissed his chest. "I love you, Jeremiah," she said once more.

He flipped her onto her back, and she welcomed him between her legs. She wore only his shirt and no underclothing. Callie knew it was weak to step away from reality to engage in the fantasy of freedom and happiness. But, she wanted him—she wanted this child, and she did not want to choose between the two.

He broke into her thoughts. "Can I have you, Callie? I know you ain't feeling well, but I need you. I won't be rough, I promise."

"Yes."

Their coupling was not about sex, it was about intimacy. Their coming together was about emotional tension and their need to release it. As his lips found hers, he entered her slowly, and when he was planted deep within her, he groaned. She could sense he was holding back. His touch was tender—his rhythm, magic. Jeremiah's breathing was labored as he moved inside her. She wrapped her legs about his waist, and the action caused him to cry out.

"Callie... Callie, you so damn sweet," he whispered between kisses.

His words pushed her toward orgasm. She unlocked her legs from his waist so that she might assist him to completion. Though she was still weak, she met him thrust-for-thrust. When the sweetest of sensations splintered through her, Callie was euphoric.

"Ohhh, Jeremiah—I love you."

Jeremiah kept the pace and most importantly, he kept it tender. His stride quickened and when his seed burst forth, he buried himself deep within her. His kisses were violent, and she did not miss the taste of his tears. The black cracker tried to hide his pain under the cover of darkness, weeping *almost* silently. But Callie heard his hurt and shared his ache.

She was aware of the very moment when sleep claimed him. Jeremiah was exhausted, and Callie knew when morning came the beast inside him would be evident for all to see. The only thing she could do was weather the storm, while reassuring him that she loved him.

❈ ❈ ❈

Jeremiah lay in bed listening for sound in the cabin, and there was none. He was alone. Opening his eyes, he thought it early morning. The sun was bright, and the heat of the day was already consuming. He pissed in the bucket that sat in the corner, and then emptied the tub and the bucket, bringing in fresh water. When he finally dressed, he stood for a moment in thought. He was not pleased that Callie wasn't resting.

She left him alone, giving him a moment to face himself. He had not cried when his mama was taken from him, and he had not cried when E.J. told him of their papa's death. And though he had been hurt in those instances, he offered no reaction. He could not allow his weaknesses to be used against him. But last night, when he connected with her and his child–he had never experienced the like. He still felt emotionally joined to her, and the feeling would never subside. Shutting the back door behind him, Jeremiah headed to the study to meet his brother.

As he walked through the slave quarters, he could see the elderly slave women seated on their porches. Some were tending the children; others sat peeling vegetables to send back to the kitchens for Ella. Everyone played a part in the mechanics of plantation life. When he reached the big oak by Eva's cabin, he made a right, moving past the last line of slave cabins into the openness of the plantation. He could see the slaves picking cotton off in the distance. On the left of the fields, a group of female slaves huddled together washing the bed linen and the children all at once.

Jeremiah entered the kitchen and saw Callie seated to the table stirring the contents of a large bowl. She looked much improved from the evening before. Callie smiled at him weakly, but he did not reciprocate as his focus fell to Eva who was seated next to her. Jeremiah felt gratitude toward her. Ella stood at the counter wearing a black dress with a clean white apron tied about her waist. She was chopping vegetables and did not acknowledge his presence. The old woman made sure he ate and saw to his clean clothes before Callie took over those duties, but she didn't talk to him unless he spoke to her. Sonny appeared suddenly at the pantry door holding a bag of flour in his arms.

They had all stopped breathing except Eva, who smiled at him when she said, "Good mawnin', Jeremiah."

"Eva," he replied with a smirk, before asking Callie, "Have you ate anything?"

"I did," Callie whispered in return.

He nodded and stared around the kitchen for a moment. Everyone went about their duties as if he were not there. He walked out of the kitchen and headed for E.J.'s study. When he arrived, he encountered Suzanne, along with her mother and sister, clustered just inside the doorway. They were all dressed in riding habits. It occurred to Jeremiah that he had never seen slave women take their leisure. He was quiet and patient as he waited for E.J. to finish speaking with the women.

"Edward, please come with us," Suzanne asked.

"Darling, I have business to handle. Jeremiah is waiting for me," E.J. replied, nodding in his direction.

The three women turned to face him. Jeremiah was stone-faced, as he stared from woman to woman. E.J.'s wife wore a blue riding habit; her sister wore a similar outfit only in a lighter shade of blue. Their mother was dressed in a burgundy ensemble. In Jeremiah's opinion, she was the handsomest of the three. Unlike her daughter's, she did not fear him. Jeremiah knew the look, and if not for Callie, he would have indulged in the forbidden.

"Good morning, Jeremiah," Suzanne uttered timidly.

"Good morning, Miss Suzanne," he replied.

Suzanne's sister Maryam only offered an apprehensive nod. Their mother did not speak to him, but kept her eyes locked on his for a moment or two longer. Then she turned to her new son-in-law.

"We will get out of your way."

"Yes, Edward, we will be on our way," Suzanne echoed. She was pouting, clearly disappointed her husband was not joining them on their morning ride.

"Later," E.J. promised, kissing his wife on the forehead. The women filed out of the study headed for the stables.

When they were alone, Jeremiah looked over at his brother who had seated himself behind his desk. E.J.'s expression had changed from convivial to worry.

"What bothers you, brother? Are you not pleased with married life?" Jeremiah asked on a chuckle.

E.J. did not return his humor. "I have a list of damn difficulties."

Jeremiah closed the door and gave his brother his undivided attention. E.J. continued, "I have been going through Papa's papers since my return from Virginia. He and I did not talk much. I ain't telling you anything you don't already know. Reading through his paperwork offers some insight into the man. Some of it ain't pretty–a lot of it ain't pretty."

"What could you be reading that we couldn't see with our own eyes?"

"I've been looking closely at his paperwork," E.J. indicated the pile of documents on his desk, "to match it with what I was shown at the Turner plantation. I see dates and entries concerning a slave called Black. Papa was in the thick of it with Turner; he was even helping Turner hire bounty hunters for the capture of this runaway. What I can't figure out is if they were able to hire such men."

The expression on E.J.'s face indicated he was far more upset than he was letting on. "Give it all to me, Edward."

"What will you do about Callie? Will you leave her here?" E.J. asked, changing the subject.

"I won't discuss her right now," Jeremiah took a step closer. "Are you worried my loyalty ain't with you?"

E.J. turned away from him and walked to the window. He looked out on the day and sighed. "When we were children, I knew you were my brother even though no one had told me so. You favored him. I don't ever remember you not being around. I saw that our life was different; still, Papa kept you near. My mother hated it, but Papa constantly left me in your care. As we got older, I realized you were sad about your mama. Only one time did you let slip that you would find her, and I never forgot it."

Jeremiah *had* ached about his mama. But he was a man now, and rarely, if ever, did he think about her. Today, he was unable to help himself. "Do you know where he sold her? Is that what this is about?"

E.J. turned from the window and looked directly at him. "It does not appear that he ever sold her."

Jeremiah's eyes widened. "Are you saying she is here still?"

"I came across four private journals. They speak about a slave woman named, Flower. He states she born him a son whom he named Jeremiah. There were more notes about how and where he purchased her. It seems she died," E.J. said tersely.

Jeremiah was weary, about Callie, about his child and about facing this gang of runaways. He did not want to discuss his mother. Gathering his thoughts, he offered no emotion when he asked, "Why would you question my loyalty? What has one to do with the other?"

"It looks as though Papa killed her in a fit of jealousy," E.J. went on. "She began to take up with a male slave after my mother came. He refused to share her, killing them both. He writes that he was madly in love with both the slave girl and his wife. Callie is with child, and you seem distraught over the fact. I thought you would leave when you found this out."

Jeremiah did not react to his brother's words. His speech was slow and steady when he asked, "How long have you known about all of this?"

"About a week. Your loyalty is not what I question."

"Yeah, ya do. You think if I hate Papa, then I will hate you. We are men. Your behavior is that of a jilted lover," Jeremiah chuckled, halfheartedly.

E.J. looked deeply at him for a moment as if trying to read his thoughts. "I will help you keep them safe," he said finally.

Jeremiah was unresponsive, keeping his eyes fixed on his brother.

"There is more in the books than I care to speak on. You can take the journals to your cabin, if you want to look over them in private."

"Leave the books here in the study. It ain't shit I can do about 1831 now. I will look over them later. Did you find anything that would help us with this situation?"

"No, I didn't. Do you understand what I have said? Why are you not troubled by what I have found?" E.J. pressed him.

Jeremiah laughed. "I am a colored man and, in truth, a slave. I am used to tragedy; it is happiness that has my head tangled."

The sound of pounding hooves, accompanied by two gunshots, interrupted them.

"Suzanne," E.J. breathed.

Jeremiah pulled open the study door and stepped into the corridor. E.J. followed as he strapped on his guns. Sunlight spilled into the house at the end of the hall where the front door sat ajar. The brothers could hear yelling, an indication trouble was upon them. Jeremiah hung back just beyond the door as E.J. walked onto the front porch. Moving to the front room, he peered out the window past the curtains without pushing them aside.

In the front yard was a posse of about fifteen men on horseback. Each man was dressed in various degrees of a Confederate uniform, their faces denoting menace. At the center of the group sat Suzanne, along with her mother and sister. Their horses reined in by two men from the posse. The women did not speak.

Jeremiah backed away from the window and turned, rushing for the kitchen and Callie. Behind him, E.J. could be heard addressing the situation. "Gentlemen, welcome to Hunter Manor."

At the end of the hall, Callie, Eva, Ella and Sonny were huddled. They too heard the commotion. Taking Callie by the hand, Jeremiah said to Sonny, "The storage room—unlock it."

Sonny hurried to the end of the hall and pushed at the wall; it bounced open. Behind it was a door, and Sonny used a skeleton key from the ring he carried. Callie was about to speak, but Jeremiah cut her off, and against her ear he whispered, "You want the child safe, and I want you safe. Now ain't the time, woman."

Sonny ushered Eva and Ella inside the storage room. Once they were inside, he looked at Callie and said, "Come, girl. Thangs 'bout to get ugly 'round here."

"Go, now," Jeremiah said, and then he looked at Sonny, "Lock up and don't come out til I come for ya."

Sonny nodded. Jeremiah removed the gun from his hip. Placing it in Sonny's hand, he said, "No one enters here but me or E.J."

Shoving Callie into the dark, dank room, Jeremiah pressed the wall back into place before exiting through the back of the house. He followed the brush around to the fields, staying out of sight. When he spotted Norman, Jeremiah immediately started barking orders as he continued on into the rows of cotton.

"Every slave here will step out of the field and lay face down! If you lift your head—we will blow it off. Move now!"

The slaves started filing out of the fields to lay face down as instructed. Five overseers were on hand with shotguns. Jeremiah locked eyes with a young white man—a new hire. He stood about six feet with short brown hair, brown eyes and a sharp nose. He looked panicked. When Jeremiah addressed him, the young man glared at him, and his expression changed to one of offense. He did not wish to be directed by a slave.

"You, what's yo' name?" Jeremiah asked.

"Hank," he said.

"Go round up five men and meet me at the back of the main house," Jeremiah ordered.

The young man stared at him for a moment before nodding and running off to do as he was told. Jeremiah then turned to Norman, "Have ten men meet E.J. at the front of the house. We have unwelcomed and unfriendly guests."

"Will do," Norman answered.

Jeremiah was about to walk away when he had an afterthought. "Send the remainder of the men down through the slave quarters. Make it known, anything that smells of rebellion will be shut down."

Norman hurried off in the opposite direction. Jeremiah then headed for the back of the house. He broke into a run, and as he moved along, he made a mental note to kill Hank. When he arrived at the back of the house, Hank was there with five other men. Everything from that point was a blur. The men followed Jeremiah into the kitchen. When they entered the hall, he could see E.J.'s back as he stood on the porch. His brother's voice was calm, but his stance was aggressive. Jeremiah blinked as he stepped outside, letting his eyes adjust to the sunlight.

Jeremiah stood to the left of his brother. Behind them, the six overseers stood with their weapons drawn. Out in front, Jeremiah could see the fear in Suzanne's eyes as she looked from him to E.J. Her sister kept her head down as did her mother.

E.J. brought him up to speed; his southern drawl pronounced, as he stepped through the explanation. "Mr. Ricks has graciously informed me that he and his men will be confiscating whatever the group needs in the name of war. He has also advised me that I should be thankful he has brought the women home. Do I have the right of it, Mr. Ricks?"

The man holding the leather leads to Suzanne's horse spoke up, "Ya has it right, Mista Hunter."

The men standing with Ricks laughed. It appeared he was the leader of this band of misfits. He had a red mop and full flaming beard. Jeremiah gauged him to be about thirty summers. He turned his green eyes on Jeremiah, causing the black cracker to smile. Ricks had been about to speak, when he noticed more of Hunter's men closing in on his group; their weapons drawn.

"I respect the war effort, Mr. Ricks—I really do. But I'm afraid I can't allow you to seize anything here at Hunter Manor." E.J. moved to the edge of the top step and continued, "What I can do is allow you to be on your way. Try the next plantation, gentlemen. You'll get nothing here."

A man with blond stringy hair, gold rimmed glasses and a gash on his right cheek swung down from his saddle. He moved to stand next to Ricks' horse. The other men with them drew their weapons. The blond fellow sneered and spoke confidently, "We got ya women. You ain't gonna shoot, and we all knows it."

As the man spoke, Jeremiah pulled his gun from his left upper holster and shot him in his left eye. Maryam's light blue habit was splattered with blood as the man fell dead between the horses. The stallions sidestepped anxiously as the leader of the group drew his gun, but E.J. was quicker. He pulled his weapon and shot the leader with precision in the face.

"Drop ya damn guns!" Jeremiah yelled.

Suzanne and her sister screamed, as tears streamed down their faces. E.J. rushed down the stairs as their men yanked the unwanted guests from their saddles. Jeremiah followed his brother while barking orders.

"On the ground! If ya lift yo' head, we'll blow it off!"

E.J. helped his distraught wife from the saddle. She clung to him, as her sister threw her arms around their mother. Jeremiah locked eyes with Julia.

"I think we got us a rogue group of deserters," E.J. said.

"You ain't gotta guess. Pick one and I will find out for sure," Jeremiah replied.

E.J. nodded, and Jeremiah stepped to the nearest man lying face down on the ground. Roughly, the black cracker reached down, flipping a boy of no more than twenty summers onto his back. Jerking him by his brown locks, Jeremiah asked with no emotion. "You wanna live?"

The boy's dark eyes blinked wildly. "Yes, I wants to live. We ain't mean no harm."

"What regiment you from?" Jeremiah asked.

"We from the 9th regiment, but we mostly buried the dead. We left 'cause we got tired of living like vultures. We been going from farm to farm, taking thangs, but we ain't never hurt nobody," the boy's voice cracked.

"How many more of you is there?"

"Ain't no more of us, we's it," the boy answered quickly.

Jeremiah looked to E.J. who nodded curtly, and it was the signal he needed. He reached into his boot, pulled out his hunting knife and, without hesitation, slit the boy's throat. Blood sprayed up at him, and when the boy lay dead, Jeremiah cleaned the blade on the boy's shirt before he stood.

"Put them all down," E.J. ordered, "and take them to the slave graveyard!"

Their overseers began walking among the men lying on the ground, offering one shot to the back of the head. Two of the rogue group tried to make a run for it, but they were brought down with ease. A flatbed wagon was brought around to the front of the property. As the men loaded the dead bodies, E.J. helped the women up the stairs.

"Julia," he addressed his mother-in-law, "take them inside away from this. I'll have Ella come to you. I have to see this through."

"All right, Edward," Julia responded.

Jeremiah mounted the steps and stood next to his brother. "It ain't noon yet, and I see we got us a problem."

"What is it, you see?"

"The overseers ain't organized; this group shouldn't have made it to the front of the house," Jeremiah replied.

"Agreed."

As Jeremiah watched the cleanup, he did not consider them ready to face the runaways. The death of his papa no longer held any significance. His mama popped into his thoughts, and he felt deep remorse. Strangely, his next thoughts were of Callie, and he felt sorrow that he had allowed himself to taste love. Her presence in his life forced *truth* upon him, and he found it painful. The question now–how could he give her up? Turning away from the scene before him, he went to fetch Callie.

❀ ❀ ❀

Callie sat quietly with the others locked behind the wall. She had become inaudibly hysterical as she heard muffled screams off in the distance. The small storage room was dank, dark and smelled musty. She couldn't see the others and was relieved in turn that they could not see her. Callie cried but offered no sound. She worried for Jeremiah and faced with the thought of losing him– she could not breathe.

When she was sure that she would go mad with worry, a thumping sound came from outside the door. Callie heard one of the other women let out a sob and fear seized her. A scraping sound came next and then Jeremiah's voice, "Open, key man."

Callie heard the jingle of keys and then the lock turning. A small amount of dim light spilled into the little room along with Jeremiah's next words, "My gun, Sonny."

Sonny stepped forward and handed him the gun. "Callie, you will come with me," Jeremiah ordered.

Jeremiah grabbed her by the wrist and pulled her along in his wake. She could feel the tension in his sticky touch. In the hall, at the opening of the storage room, the lighting was poor. But when they entered the kitchen, she realized why his touch felt wet. When they stepped into the sunlight at the back of the house, Jeremiah was covered in blood.

His stride was long–swift. Callie had to run to keep up. As they crossed the plantation, she could see the disturbing activity in both directions. The slaves filed back into the fields, looking about with fear. In front of the main house, bodies were being piled onto the back of a wagon.

Abruptly, she stopped and pulled her hand away from him. Callie wiped the transferred blood on her dress before she looked up at him. Jeremiah's homespun tan shirt was blood stained, and on his face, was dried spatter. His hair was curly and wild upon his head, adding to his ominous appearance. Rage burned in his eyes, and Callie trembled with alarm.

"Are you hurt?" she asked him on a whisper.

"No," he answered. Jeremiah studied her for a moment before he perceptively said, "So, today, you fear me. You have never been afraid of me even during our most unstable moments."

"I don't like seeing you covered in blood."

"A time will come again when I will be covered in blood; unfortunately, it *will* be my own. Ain't no future in stepping away from reality. You are afraid of me at this moment; your body speaks what you don't say."

"I worry for our child," Callie admitted.

"Ain't no reason to fear, you are the master between us, and we both know it." His ire was evident.

Callie reached for him. Jeremiah looked down at her hand, but he did not move to touch her. All at once, his eyes diverted to something behind her. Callie turned to see what had gotten his attention. An overseer was walking briskly toward them; a new wave of fear overtook her.

The overseer was taller than Jeremiah, and his features were rough. He had blond hair, greenish eyes and a very crooked nose. When he addressed Jeremiah, his demeanor was calm and his southern accent prevalent.

"Mr. Hunter is wantin' us to meet in the barn when the bodies is buried."

"Tell Mr. Hunter I'll be there," Jeremiah replied.

The overseer turned his attention to her. She looked down at the ground.

"What's yo' name, girl?"

She looked up, just as Jeremiah stepped between her and the overseer. "*Mine*," he said. The threat in his one-word response unmistakable.

She could only see Jeremiah's back, but the verbal exchange ended as quickly as it started. Jeremiah grabbed her hand and immediately dragged her away.

❊ ❊ ❊

Jeb stood watching the retreating back of the black cracker. He shook his head. The man was impressive, and Jeb was sorry about how all this would play out. The abolitionist movement could use a man like Jeremiah. Jeb sighed, as he thought about Black and his men. Jeremiah would not live out the year, and his death would be a waste. But one thing did bring a smile to Jeb's face. The black cracker had a woman, and it appeared he could be controlled through her.

11

Beacon Hill
August 1861

JAMES AND THE men had been on Beacon Hill for two days. They blended with the folks and life on the Hill as if they had not been away. Anna's old house was still their base of operations, and Black received reports of the goings-on in his absence. The atmosphere had changed with the arrival of war. Many of the men attempted to enlist, but were told colored soldiers were not needed. Still, the people of Beacon Hill remained hopeful.

On the second day, the men spent the daylight hours watching the townhouse of Will Turner's widow. It was a long shot, but they banked on the fact that Turner's widow had his child. The feeling was that Rose would not be able to resist seeing her baby niece. Just after midday, a luxurious carriage rolled up in front of the house where Turner's widow resided. The driver set the steps, opened the door, and Rose appeared. He helped her down, and in a blink of an eye, she disappeared into the house.

James and Shultz kept watch while Tim, disguised as the driver of a hansom cab, parked at the end of the street. The temperature was hot, but not unbearable, as they waited in the alley between two homes opposite the widow's house. It was early evening when the same carriage came back to fetch Rose. James could see her hugging a red headed woman before she bounced down the steps and climbed into the vehicle. Tim rolled the cab along slowly, allowing him and Shultz to get in. The men followed her to a home a small distance away. Just outside the wrought iron gate surrounding Rose's home hung a shingle that read: **Anderson Wilkerson Attorney at Law**

Now that they knew where she was staying while in Boston, they returned to Beacon Hill. James decided he would not approach her right away. Instead, he would observe her habits to determine her situation. He would not be careless like he had in the past, acting on impulse. There was no room for error; he had to get this right.

The men were acting in a small window of time. James watched Rose's home for an additional two days, while Black and the men handled other concerns on the Hill. He witnessed her husband leaving both days at noon with a leather satchel in hand. On both occasions, he returned home by 5 pm. The widow of Will Turner also visited with the baby. Rose's delight at seeing them again was evident, even from a distance. Unlike the neighborhood where Turner's widow lived, Rose's community was busy and transient. Still, he had made up his mind he would seek her out while her husband was away.

※ ※ ※

It was noon the next day when James, Black, and Elbert gathered in the alley opposite Rose's townhouse. Sutter Street boasted of professional residents. At almost every home, a shingle hung from the wrought iron gate. Along with Rose's husband, there was a doctor, a banker, and a minister. As the men went about their days, their women tended the children with the help of colored women from places like Beacon Hill. Rose had a staff of servants from what James could tell, so they couldn't use that angle to gain entry.

In a pattern on either side of the street, trees and lampposts lined the curb. The trees were placed strategically in front of the alleys to cover the unsightly dirt roads beside the stately homes. This helped conceal the brothers while they waited for the right moment. On the left side of the roadway, hansom cabs lined the street, the drivers anxious for business. The male residents used these hacks to handle daily business, leaving their personal carriages for their families. Tim stood among the drivers, leaned against the side of the hansom cab they would use for a getaway. Rose's husband had been gone just under an hour.

As the men stood in the alley across the roadway, a mild breeze blew. The aroma of freshly, baked apple pie floated around them from an open window above their heads. The sun shone brightly on Sutter Street, but was eclipsed in the alleys because of the way the homes were situated. When it was time to move, the brothers didn't head toward the street. Instead, they hastened through the backyards, trekking through the small gardens allotted for each house. They were careful not to make a sound. The smell of flowers and wet dirt from the rain of the night before assailed them. The men stepped onto the main thoroughfare disguised as gardeners in brown homespun clothes, toting hoes and shovels. They traveled west on Broad Street, crossing Sutter at the top.

They moved through the backyards of the homes on Rose's side of the street. When they arrived at the back of her townhouse, James carefully pried the back door open. He peered up a long dark stairwell that led to another door. The raised corridor smelled of polish and leather. Next to the door, at the top of the stairs, hung a slicker. He nodded sharply at Black and Elbert before stepping through the door.

In the backyard, Black posted up at the door. Elbert posted

up in the alley, watching the street, where he could see Tim, who stood facing him by the hansom cab. At the top of the stairs, James forced the second door and stepped into the kitchen. The room was white-washed, except for the black potbelly stove to the left. Even the table and chairs were painted white. A porcelain vase painted with pastel blooms sat in the center of the table. It was filled with pink roses.

At his right was an open window, allowing a soft breeze to penetrate the hot room. The doorway opened into a formal dining room. There was a long mahogany table lined with several chairs, along with a matching breakfront. Beyond was a sunny parlor with furnishings upholstered in pale green. There were plants in ceramic pots near the tall windows, and the green drapes were pulled back to allow the sunlight into the room. On the left were two doors that opened onto another long hallway. James heard voices—a man and woman's words echoed into the parlor. He peered around the doorframe where he saw Rose standing at the foot of a wide staircase, on her left was the front entrance.

"I'm not in need of anything, Alfred. Please take a moment for yourself. I will be in the family room, reading," Rose said, her voice drawing nearer.

"Yes, Miss," the masculine voice replied.

"Oh, and Alfred," Rose called up to him, "my husband will be about thirty minutes late for dinner."

"Yes, Madame," the butler answered dryly.

James admired Rose from his position at the threshold of the parlor. She wore a yellow, short-sleeved dress that fit snug over her breasts. The dress belled out at the hips and fell below the ankles. Her black hair was pulled into an elegant chignon, pinned neatly around the edges. As always, Rose was beautiful.

When she turned for the hall, she looked right into his eyes. The color drained from her face, and she placed her hand defensively to her breasts. Alfred's voice reverberated from the top of the landing.

"Is something wrong, Madame?"

James held her gaze as she responded, "No, Alfred. I'm fine. I just remembered I'm in need of vellum and ink. I have correspondence that I must get out. Would you be so kind as to go the market? Bertha has gone visiting."

"Certainly, Madame, I could use the walk."

"Thank you, Alfred."

James disappeared behind the door, giving Rose time to let the butler out. When he heard the door creak on its hinges and the lock click, he stepped back into view. Rose remained with her back to him. It was quiet except for the sound of horse's hooves drifting through the open window in the front parlor. He gave her a moment to collect herself.

"I came as fast as I could."

She turned around to face him. "I know that Black travels without you. I have never seen Elbert without you..."

She was emotional as she regarded him. Shit, he felt it too. But he remained focused on the business at hand.

"Ain't you gonna come closer?" he asked.

Rose smiled weakly, and walked hesitantly toward him. James moved back from the doorway to give her room. The hall was darker in contrast to the parlor, and when she stepped over the threshold, he was speechless. Folding his arms over his chest, he gazed down at her. James suddenly remembered why he had stayed away. He still had a soft spot for Rose, but it would never have worked.

Rose's face went pale, and her breath caught as she reached out to touch the scar on his right cheek. The color came rushing back just as quickly as tears spilled from her eyes. She whispered, "I knew you were hurt."

James closed his eyes and turned his face, kissing the palm of her hand. He pulled her close to him, kissing her forehead. He could feel his heart pounding as she wrapped her arms around him.

"*Shhh*," he said, trying to calm her. "It ain't as bad as it looks."

Rose stepped away and pulled a handkerchief from the pocket of her dress. She dabbed her eyes. "I thought I would never see you again."

"Me neither," he answered honestly.

She moved past him to stand at the window, giving them both a moment to gather themselves. Realizing that he had lingered long enough, James got down to business.

"Ya said someone come to visit you from the Hunter plantation. Who come to ya?"

She turned to face him once more. "Edward Hunter Jr. came to visit. He wanted to know who killed his father. Mr. Hunter wanted to know who burned down his plantation and freed his slaves."

James looked at her calmly. "And what did you tell him?"

"I told him nothing. My husband, on the other hand, told him what he *thought* he knew."

"What could yo' husband know to tell 'em?" James queried. He could see she was uneasy.

"Anderson showed him William's papers."

"Is ya finna keep making me ask ya every damn question or you gonna just tell me?" James said, growing mildly impatient.

James almost smiled, when her temper flared. "Don't be rude to me about events I didn't cause," she snapped.

Getting his impatience under control, he responded, "I'm sorry."

"Mr. Hunter came to the plantation demanding to see Will. Anderson shared Will's papers, but there wasn't much in them. He wrote of Black and his home in Canada, but it appeared my brother had never been to Black's home, so he was unclear about the location. He spoke of wanting Sunday and being unable to have her." Rose hesitated for a moment and glanced out the window. "He also spoke of being deceived by Tim."

James stared at Rose, to his way of thinking, Will's papers held a lot. She must have read his thoughts.

"My husband is harmless, and I have been careful not to tell him too much. His actions are born of jealousy because I asked for you discreetly. I promise Anderson hasn't a mean bone in his body."

"I ain't finna ever be a slave again, so if yo husband's words get between me and freedom, I will kill him."

"I am tired of being threatened," Rose's face grew flush. "I have warned you, even against my husband's wishes. You have always been a man to me. Anderson has not spoken again of the matter between Black and Will. I will give you Will's papers, but don't you dare threaten me!"

"I ain't threatened you. I wouldn't never harm you and ya know it."

"Harming my husband would harm me," Rose replied.

James sighed. "Who threatened you?"

"Mr. Hunter promised to kill me *and* my husband if he didn't get what he wanted. I did not allow him to see that I was frightened, but I was. He waited until my husband went to fetch the papers, because he suspected I knew more than I was saying."

"It's wartime now. I think you's safe."

Rose looked as though she would like to say more and thought better of it, causing James to ask, "What ain't you saying?"

"I am afraid that Mr. Hunter may have been about more than words."

"Tell me," James pushed.

Rose motioned for him to come to the window. James went to her, standing scandalously close as he peered over her head onto the street below.

"There is a man who watches me and my home. I am sure he was Mr. Hunter's driver. I know that is where I have seen him before. He tries to play the role of a hansom cab worker, but has never taken a fare that I have seen. He watches me, and he watches my husband. I have said nothing to Anderson."

"Which man?"

"Tim is parked in front of the house. Look at the hansom cab driver parked three spaces up from Tim's carriage. His horses have white around their hooves. He is always out there early and most times before the other drivers," Rose answered.

Indeed, James saw a middle-aged, white fellow with graying hair pulled back into a ponytail. His face was only visible from a side view, but he looked rough. James moved away from the window. "Where are your brother's papers?"

"Please follow me."

As James followed her down the hall, he noted the perfectly polished floors and the fancy blue-gray wallpaper. Rose was living well, but her husband was oblivious to safety. He would change all that and bring her husband to a new reality. At the end of the hall was an elegant family room with a large black piano, thick brown carpet and a fancy burgundy sofa. She continued past a black chair to a wooden desk that was almost an eyesore in the room. Using a key, she unlocked the drawer before handing him a ledger and what looked like a journal.

James walked over to the piano and placed the books on the stool. Opening the piano's top, he pulled a large knife from his waist strap and cut a lengthy piece of wire. Coiling the cord, he shoved it into his trouser pocket.

Alarmed, she hissed, "What are you doing? You will ruin the piano!"

James walked toward her and took her face in his hands. He kissed her deeply. He knew he shouldn't engage in any kind of familiarity with her, but when he left Massachusetts, he would never see her again. She must have felt the same for she did not fight him. Rose returned his kiss with equal passion.

Abruptly, he stepped back. "Don't leave the house or have guests until I says so. You ain't got to worry about this man again."

James did not wait for a response. Instead, he turned and left the house the same way he entered. When he opened the back door, Black was standing quietly, looking about. Upon seeing James, Black stepped to the end of the alley, notifying Tim and Elbert they were done. Tim nodded. James, Black and Elbert retraced their movements through the backyards headed for Broad Street. The four men met up farther down the boulevard.

Inside the carriage, Black asked, "What did you learn?"

"Hunter is watchin', and he got Rose afraid," James replied.

Elbert leaned forward. "Who is watching?"

"One of the drivers parked on Sutter Street. Rose believes he workin' for Hunter."

The other men looked at James who pressed on. "We deal wit' him and then be on our way."

"Yeah," Elbert agreed.

❋ ❋ ❋

The men waited until nightfall to execute the simplest of plans. They would overtake the man with the ponytail, question and then kill him. The plan, though uncomplicated, held a degree of danger. The rub–they did not know if he worked alone or if he had an accomplice. James suspected he was alone, for Rose's husband was so oblivious, he posed no threat. Anderson could be killed on his way to the office, and Rose murdered in their home. Since the man with the ponytail had not yet acted, he must have been told to watch their habits. This man could have been told to watch for Black and his men.

Later in the evening, Frank and Lou posted up outside Rose's home. Emmett and Gilbert posted up on the opposite side of the street. After the lantern lighters illuminated Sutter Street, they pressed on to the next roadway. James and Elbert extinguished the lampposts opposite Rose's house. Along with Emmett and Gilbert, James, Elbert, Tim, Black and Shultz stood just beyond the light, watching for any sign of the man who worked for Hunter.

The hours ticked by slowly, and just before dawn, two hansom cabs rolled onto Sutter Street. The quietness was broken by the springs of the carriages, the wheels traveling the cobblestone and the clopping of horse hooves. One driver positioned his carriage and horses at the top of the roadway, several houses up from the Wilkerson residence. The second carriage and horses came to a stop just a few feet away from Rose's front door. One of the horses blew his breath and shook his head as he got comfortable. The drivers each gave the horses a feed bag. When they were finished tending the animals, they approached one another, stopping under one of the lampposts.

In the dim light, the men's features were indistinct. James readily noticed, nonetheless, that one of the men had a ponytail.

"Looks like we was wrong. He got him a friend," Elbert said.

"We need to take them both," Black added.

"Ain't no other way," James responded, while pulling a pair of work gloves from his back pocket. As he put on each glove, he flexed his fingers, adjusting his digits for comfort. There was no turning back.

The men took their places as darkness began to recede. At the opposite end of Sutter, Shultz could be seen in the company of Frank and Lou, who carried a ladder. At the first lamppost, Frank climbed the ladder while Lou held it steady. Shultz could be heard yelling at them.

"Hurry up! We don't have all day! Your kind is so damn lazy!"

The two hansom cab drivers were leery, turning their attention to the white man and the two-colored men with him. The men were untrusting of the trio and moved to stand together at the carriage closest to Rose's house. As Shultz and the twins drew nearer, the man with the ponytail spoke, and his aggression could not be missed.

"You three are not the regulars. You are here too early. We still have an hour before daybreak—do you plan to leave us standing in the dark?" He barked.

Shultz turned to the man. "Who might you be?"

"Who I am isn't important; your incompetence is the issue."

"Unless you are the mayor of our fair city, your identity and your thoughts are of no consequence to me. Please remove yourself from our path, so we can continue in our efforts," Shultz responded.

"I'm afraid I'm going to have to ask you and your niggers to be on your way. And don't come back—we'll take care of lighting and extinguishing the lampposts on this street," the man with the ponytail threatened, as he drew his double-edged blade. Behind him, the other driver drew and cocked his gun.

Shultz stood for a moment and glared at both men. "So, you are nothing but a ruffian with fine speech."

Shultz held the two men's attention, while James moved in swiftly behind the man with the gun. There was a whistling sound, followed by a gasp and then a struggle. The man with the ponytail turned toward his partner, who was trying to free himself of James' hold. He sprang into action, trying to help his friend but to no avail.

Shultz pulled his gun and cocked it. "Down on the damn ground!"

Frank came forward and forced the man with the ponytail to the ground. Lou stepped in tying his hands behind his back. Elbert removed the gun from the other man's hands, as James continued to strangle the life from his quarry with the piano wire he took from Rose's home. The man wheezed and kicked violently. And even when his victim began to expire–James did not relent.

Dawn was fast approaching when Tim stepped in becoming the driver of the hansom cab closest to Rose's home. Elbert grabbed the feet of the man James put down. Frank and Lou got the man with the ponytail to his feet, and they all moved toward the carriage on the end of Sutter Street. Shultz dumped two buckets of rain water meant for the horses on the ground, washing the blood into the roadway beneath the carriage. The doctor took over driving the cab which carried James, Elbert, Frank and Lou, along with their captives.

Later, when the early morning sun rose on Sutter Street, nothing appeared out of the ordinary. As it had been every morning, the hansom cab drivers began showing up for work, hopeful for a fare. Among them stood Tim, who waited patiently for noon and Rose's husband to emerge from the town home. Inside the carriage sat Black, who also waited quietly. The cab was hot and uncomfortable, the only relief–an inconsistent stream of air that crawled between the curtains.

❄ ❄ ❄

Black actually relaxed enough in the carriage to work mentally through many of the obstacles he and the men would face. He had a few concerns that needed tending before they could press on to Washington. As his mind made mental notes, he finally heard Tim speaking.

"Right this way, sir. I can take ya where ya needs to go."

"Thank you. I'm headed for Main Street. Is it possible for you to wait for me?" Anderson Wilkerson asked, as he walked up to the carriage. He was reading some papers as Tim pulled the door open.

"Absolutely sir, whatever you needs," Tim responded.

When the carriage door opened, Black could see a tall thin, white man dressed in a charcoal gray suit. It was just as James had said; Anderson Wilkerson was oblivious to his surroundings.

Black smiled and shook his head, for with privilege came the lessening of basic instincts. He recalled Wilkerson as the man who stood at the top of the steps with Rose the night they found out about Otis. He closed the folder of papers in order to step up into the carriage. He wore very thick spectacles, and when he finally focused on the task at hand, he came face to face with the barrel of Black's gun.

"Join me," Black commanded and when Anderson looked as if he would cause a scene, Black warned. "Don't bother, there are two men at your back door. They are in place to murder your wife if you should cause a commotion. I'm Black, in case you hadn't already guessed."

Anderson climbed into the carriage, and Tim shut the door. Black could see that the other man was visibly shaken. The carriage started rolling and slowed when it turned onto Broad Street. Both doors opened abruptly, allowing Gilbert and Emmett into the cab. They sat opposite Black on either side of Anderson Wilkerson; the ride to Beacon Hill was silent.

When the carriage finally pulled in front of Anna's old house, Emmett and Gilbert opened the carriage doors. Out of one door stepped Emmett, Anderson and Gilbert; from the other door stepped Black. The people of Beacon Hill went about their day as though it were an ordinary day. As the men led Anderson up the walk, James appeared in the doorway. He held a white towel that he used to slowly wipe his hands free of excess blood.

Anderson turned to Black and whispered, "Please don't kill my wife. This is my fault; she had nothing to do with it."

His steps faltered, causing Black to offer some sound advice, "Your wife's safety is up to you."

Anderson appeared confused, and Black didn't attempt to enlighten him.

❋❋❋

Anderson wanted to shit himself, he was so nervous. He had been taken hostage by slaves, and he was now certain of what happened to Will Turner. A thought bloomed in his mind. How had this group known he had spoken of them? He wondered if the wife he had been trying to save not five minutes before had summoned these savages. The very thought made him ill. When he examined the truth, he and his beautiful wife had not been getting along. They had not even shared a bed since these runaways stormed the Turner plantation. Anderson had only one wish before he died here today. He wanted to know if his wife had betrayed him.

He entered the house flanked by two slaves. At the far wall was a brown couch that needed brushing. Behind the couch, a mattress stood leaned against the wall, bare of any bed dressings. The fireplace was to the left of the couch, and the way the sparse furniture was situated did not promote coziness. On the right of the fireplace was an opened door, but he could not see into the room. There was a brown wooden table in the center of the room with two chairs. At the table facing the front door sat a man who appeared to be dead.

A bright skinned slave with a nasty scar on the right side of his face stood glaring at him. He wore a blood stained, tan shirt. Over his left shoulder was the white towel he used to wipe his hands free from the gore. He was shorter than Anderson and though his demeanor was laid back, there was no mistaking the vicious nature of the man. Anderson recognized Black and the slave standing next to him with the dead eyes. But this savage, he was sure wasn't with them on that fateful night when they came to the Turner plantation demanding answers.

"Anderson," Black said, "please have a seat on the couch. Allow me to make the introductions. On my left is Elbert and on my right is James. We are brothers."

Anderson sat down before he passed out. Black continued speaking, though he was no longer addressing him. "Did you kill him?"

"I ain't kill him yet," James answered.

"Shit, he looks dead to me," Elbert said.

James stepped over to the prisoner and slapped him twice on either side of his face. The man moaned. His right eye was swollen shut. Anderson thought he recognized the poor soul, but he couldn't put a finger on where he knew him from. James doused the man with a bucket of water, and he sputtered as he sat up straight in the chair.

James looked at Anderson. "I sees it in yo face. Ya knows him, don't you?"

"I have seen him before, though I can't say from where," Anderson responded, and to his shame, his voice shook.

"Would ya like to know if'n he knows you?" James countered.

"Y-yes, I would like to know," Anderson replied.

Turning to the man in the chair, James demanded, "Me and Anderson is wantin' to know how ya knows him."

The man peered around the room with his one working eye, but he did not speak. The white shirt he wore was stained in blood at the neck. Even in his battered state, he offered insolence and nothing else.

James shook his head. "I guess we finna see whose will is the strongest. You should know I ain't plannin' on shootin' you. I plans on takin you apart limb by limb."

The prisoner's eye bounced in James' direction. His face suddenly looked apprehensive, but he said nothing. James' next words were directed at Anderson.

"I thinks I has an idea where ya knows him from."

"Help me, please. I'm unclear and can't place him," Anderson said cautiously, unsure of where this was going.

"He a hansom cab driver what parks on yo' street but never

takes a fare. We removed him from in front yo' house this mornin' and took his cab. If we ain't show, ya might have been riding wit' him," James said.

Anderson leaned forward, removing his spectacles. He wiped his eyes, before placing the glasses back on his face. His eyes locked on the man, and in his mind's eye, he could see this man standing in front of his house daily. He drove an expensive, black carriage with two fine horses. Yes, he had seen him before, but his connection to this stranger he didn't understand.

"Did ya speak to Hunter when he come to ya lookin' for answers?" James asked.

Anderson wasn't bold enough to not answer, but he was afraid to admit he had. He had to collect himself before he responded. "Y-yes...I showed him Will's papers."

"Did you now?" Elbert asked.

Anderson couldn't even look Elbert in the eyes, so he looked to Black, who stood well over six feet. He had a bald head, perceptive eyes and an aggressive stance. Black wore a tan shirt with the sleeves hacked off; his arms folded over his chest. And one could not miss the gun holstered at his upper left side. Anderson decided to look to the floor.

James continued, "Do you remembers him as Hunter's driver?"

Anderson's eyes bounced back to the driver. He did remember him as the man that drove the Hunter carriage. But he didn't know exactly what that meant for this circumstance, and he was afraid to inquire. It seemed James had dismissed him focusing on the man at the table.

He watched as James stepped into the back room for a moment and came back with another blood-stained towel. When he unrolled the towel, a bloody razor and double-edged knife appeared. Most alarmingly, Anderson saw what looked like a piano wire wrapped around and nailed to two sticks on either end. He shut his imagination down at that point.

James addressed the man at the table. "Me and Anderson wants to know what you is about. I ain't finna ask again."

When the man didn't respond, James nodded to his brothers. Black stepped forward untying him, and Elbert forced his left hand onto the table. James then grabbed the knife and plunged it into the back of the man's hand, pinning it to the table. He grunted and began to sweat profusely, but he didn't cry out—not at first. When James twisted the knife ever so slightly, it caused his prisoner to scream. The sound was gut-wrenching.

"Shit," the man groaned until the pain began to stabilize.

But James' goal was not to let the pain ease, so he calmly informed his captive, "I'm 'bout to start cutting yo' fingers off one by one. Ya looks like a man what knows this process. First you gotta cut, then burn so's yo' victim don't bleed out. It's already hot in here, ya sure ya won't change yo' mind?"

"I was sent by Hunter," the man groaned.

"Imma need a little more than that," James chuckled. "Let's start wit' yo' name."

"Simpson," the prisoner said, his voice tight with pain.

"Well, Simpson, me and Anderson is all ears. Right, Anderson?"

"Yes," Anderson said, his nervousness forgotten.

"I was sent to watch the Wilkerson residence and kill them if necessary. I was sent mainly to kill Mrs. Wilkerson. Mr. Hunter was concerned that she wasn't forthcoming about the death of his father," Simpson grunted.

Upon hearing what the man had to say about Rose, Anderson became enraged. He jumped to his feet and knocked James out of the way, giving the knife a good turn. Simpson started screaming again, and Anderson yelled, "You bastard, why would you think to harm my damn wife!"

James laughed and stepped in front of Anderson. "Easy. You gon kill him 'fore we get the whole story."

Anderson stared blindly at James for a moment before giving in. He did not sit down again, but remained standing as James resumed the interrogation.

"How many of ya is there?"

Simpson was panting. "It was just me and Eddie. I mostly work alone; Eddie was there for back-up and to earn a few coins. He was actually taking fares."

"How long have you been watching us?" Anderson asked.

"June," Simpson replied.

"June," Anderson repeated and looked at James incredulously.

Three white men suddenly entered the house. He recognized the driver but not the other two. The driver moved to stand next to Black; the other two posted up at the door to watch.

"Has ya been in touch wit' Hunter since ya been here?" James asked.

"I sent a telegram to say I located Mrs. Wilkerson," Simpson admitted.

Anderson stepped forward punching him in the face. Blood splattered onto his clean white shirt. Simpson was weak and could barely moan.

Black interjected. "What is the code used to make certain the message is from you?"

Simpson spat blood. "The code is 'Rose sends her love.'"

"You son of a bitch!" Anderson growled and hit the man again.

When he looked to James, he hadn't expected it, but James handed him a gun. Anderson's hands shook, as he pushed the table aside to stand directly in front of Simpson. Placing the muzzle right between his eyes, he pulled the trigger. Simpson's body went limp, and the blow back further stained his shirt. Anderson had to remove and wipe his glasses.

Elbert handed him a bottle of whiskey, and he drank deeply. The men started the clean-up and James led him around back where he handed him a shovel. They didn't speak for a time, until Anderson asked, "How did you know about all that was happening?"

"Yo' wife was worried Hunter would murder you. She was also 'fraid we would kill ya for shooting off yo' big mouth. Miss Rose sent for us 'cause she wanted us to know you was innocent. She let us know if we harmed you, we would be harming her. She say you was jealous. Why?"

"I love my wife and…I just love my wife." It was all Anderson could say.

James stared at him for a moment, taking in his disheveled appearance. Anderson had loosened his black tie and unbuttoned the collar of his white, blood-stained shirt. His glasses were smeared, and his hair was drenched from sweat. As they stood in the hot afternoon sun with shovels in their hands, James had one more point to make before bringing this matter to a close between him and Rose's husband.

"I loves Rose too. I got the feelin' you ain't been all that nice lately. You wanna adjust yoself or we could adjust thangs for you," James leaned on his shovel, staring at him.

Anderson understood the threat. When he could gather his thoughts, he said, "I won't share my wife. Rose is mine."

James glared at him before smirking. He reached out his hand and offered a truce. Anderson accepted. In the bloody hand shake, the two men found a mutual respect.

It was well after nightfall. Rose paced the house, her fear mounting. She noticed that the man with the ponytail was no longer outside their home. When five o'clock came and went, she was sure her husband had been abducted. She feared ending up like her brother's wife–they still didn't know what happened to Will. Amber, his widow, had not wanted to live after his disappearance, but she pressed on for the sake of their daughter.

Rose's heart ached. She was sure her husband no longer loved her. As for her part in this debacle, she loved two men; but she wanted to grow old with her husband. She also understood that though James loved her, he could not bear to look her in the face at times. His pride would not allow him to trade his demeaning past as a slave for the possibility of forever with her.

The lanterns had not been brought in so that she could see what was going on outside. She was about to contact the police when a carriage pulled up in front of her house. Tim jumped down from the driver's seat as Black, Elbert, James and Anderson emerged from the coach. Rose had to lean her back against the wall to keep her legs under her. She stood at the edge of the parlor watching for the door to open.

Anderson stepped through the door first, and he seemed different from the gentle husband she had come to know. He held his jacket in his hand and his glasses were crooked on his face. His shirt was blood-stained, and his hair was plastered to his head from perspiration. James stepped into the doorway behind Anderson, and he too was covered in blood. Black and Tim began extinguishing the lanterns as they stood guard at the front door. Elbert pulled the door shut, leaving her alone with James and Anderson in the foyer.

"Are you hurt?" she whispered to her husband.

"Just my pride," Anderson responded, his voice thick with emotion, "Why didn't you tell me you were afraid?"

"Things have been different between us. I wasn't sure–" Rose's voice trailed off. She was uneasy, standing before both men discussing feelings. Still, she was clear on one thing, her husband knew she cared for James. They wouldn't be standing together in this awkwardness, if he didn't. She looked to the floor; it was all too much.

"I'm sorry, Rose. I truly am," Anderson whispered.

Rose looked up abruptly at her husband, and then at

James, whose facial expression was closed. "I'm sorry too," she answered softly.

Finally, when she could get up the nerve, she asked James, "Are you all right?"

"I'm well," he answered, and to Anderson he said, "Come let me show ya, what I means 'bout them two back doors."

Anderson nodded, and they walked off toward the kitchen. Rose heard the back door open, and then she heard James telling her husband that they needed better locks for both doors. She wandered to the family room, trying to hide. But when she looked up, James was standing in the doorway alone. She looked for her husband, but he was gone.

"He's gone to change his clothes." James said reading her mind, "Cain't say when Imma see you again. The war only gon get worse from here. Be well, Rose."

Rose wept. She knew they wouldn't see each other again. There was nothing left to say. She went to him, hugging him, even as he stood covered in blood. James held her and kissed her forehead, before curtly releasing her. He turned, headed for the front door and did not look back.

Beacon Hill

Black and the men spent another day and a half on Beacon Hill. The men stayed just long enough for him to handle some last-minute business. Shultz and Bainesworth sent messages for him from the dry-goods store. They also retrieved any communications that awaited Black's attention. Word had come from the Hunter plantation—the plan was coming together. The message from Jeb was simple and to the point.

WE ARE IN AND WE LOOK FORWARD TO SEEING YOU

Black smiled and handed the message to James who then handed it to Elbert. It was midnight when twenty men rode out for Washington and the next leg of their journey.

Fort Independence

August 1861

Simon stood at the front of the barracks, watching the shift change. Security at the fort was tight and, aside from the men patrolling the perimeter on schedule, no one left the compound. Now in Black's shoes, Simon felt the weight of the task handed to him. He did not sleep well, but he did have some bright spots in his life. His wife and child were thriving, which took a large burden from his shoulders. But what really moved him was how resilient the women were in the absence of their men.

It was mid-morning, as he slowly made his way to Black's house. The temperature was mild, and as he strolled along, he could see the children playing in the distance. When Black's house came into view, he saw the women standing on the porch waiting for him. They were his new posse, and in truth, they showed signs of being a little more vicious than the men, if pushed.

When the women were sure he saw them, they walked back into the house. Simon and his ladies met every other morning to discuss the goings-on at Fort Independence. It was the way he made certain he wasn't missing anything. Once at the house, he climbed the steps two at a time and headed to Black's study. Sunday sat behind the desk, while Morgan, Big Mama, Iris and Miss Cora were seated on the couch. Extra chairs were brought in for Sarah, Abby and Anna, who were seated to the left of the room. On the right of the room and next to Black's desk sat Beulah, Mary, Hazel and Carrie. As for the children, Big Mama held Otis, Miss Cora held little Elbert and Sunday held Natalie, all three were sleep. Morgan was burping their daughter, who was wide eyed and staring around the room. Standing next to the couch and just left of the portrait of Big Mama was Paul, who wore his gun on his right hip.

All the women had taken turns working with him in the barracks except the older women and Tim's wife, Sarah. Simon sighed before saying, "Good mornin', ladies."

"Good morning, Simon," the women answered in unison.

"Good mornin', honey," Morgan said, her eyes twinkling.

Morgan had been teasing him over his difficulties with Tim's wife.

Simon began the meeting. "Imma let y'all tell me which one of ya gon work the barrack wit' me."

Sarah cleared her throat. "I believe it's my turn, Simon."

Simon paused for a moment and then nodded.

"I will go with you to the barracks after the meeting," Sarah added.

"Good," Simon said, feeling relieved. "What we got next?"

Sunday piped up with her report. "Ain't been no major changes. The peoples is well and the chilren we placed is thriving. Everyone is careful not to waste since we on lock down. Ain't been no complaints neither, so we's good. When Sarah finishes her time at the barracks, I will start my time."

"The older children know how to load the rifles, and we have them broken down into groups. They will keep the guns loaded for us, while we do the shooting should it come down to it," Mary said.

"In every home is a shotgun on the rack. We ready, if'n we needs be," Abby added.

"I'm making three out of five shots, so I'm making progress," Anna said.

"I ain't as good as Anna, but I's getting there," Hazel said.

Simon looked around the room at the women; their dresses

were beautiful shades of yellow, blue, pink and green. But right up over the pretty dresses, were their holsters. The women were all strapped and Simon couldn't help but smile. He was so proud of them. Still in the back of his mind, he would consider it a fail on his part if they had to engage in combat. His job was to protect them, and he would do so, with his life.

"All right, ladies. Ain't no changes at the barracks, neither. The mens is patrolling the inside and outside, so'n we ain't surprised. Long as we keeps our heads, we should be fine," Simon informed them.

Sunday spoke up. "Guess we can go on 'bout our day. We meets back here day after tomorrow in the mornin'. If'n ya got a problem, you can come find me, Simon, or Morgan."

As the women adjourned, little Otis began to cry. He had been inconsolable in Elbert's absence. Anna took him from Big Mama and tried to calm him.

"*Ssshhh*, what's the matter, honey?" Anna asked the boy.

Otis' answer was the same as it had been every day since Elbert left, "I want my mama...I want my mama."

"Awww, sweety, your mama will be home soon," Anna assured him, as he hiccupped and looked around the room for Elbert. "Come let Mama Anna wash your face."

Otis hugged her and continued to cry softly. Anna looked at Sunday and Simon before she left the study to deal with him. Abby followed to help Anna with the children. When it was just Simon, Morgan and Sunday, they spoke of the news from the front gate.

"Black sent word. Giddy brung me the messages," Sunday said, handing a piece of paper to Simon. He read the message.

MONTREAL WAS UNEVENTFUL I WORRIED FOR OUR FRIEND'S HEALTH HE IS STILL ABOVE GROUND

Simon looked up. "I'm figurin Black ain't had to kill the ambassador."

"The plan is movin' like we thanks it should," Morgan added.

Sunday was quiet as she handed Simon the next message.

BOSTON HANDLED MOVING ON

Simon could see that Sunday was shaken. "The mens has handled two matters, and they has two mo'. They be home directly," he said, reassuringly.

Sunday tried at a smile. "I hope so."

Morgan handed Simon the baby and gave Sunday a hug. As Simon held his daughter, he thought of Black and the others. The next two steps in the plan were the most dangerous. He said a silent prayer.

Boston

Sutter Street

Rose and Anderson had separate rooms from the very first day of their marriage. Now, he insisted she share his bed nightly, using her room as a dressing area only. They had not made love in weeks, and when they had been intimate in the past, she had been shy, but receptive. Anderson had been gentle and patient, placing no demands that made her feel uncomfortable. On the night he came home with James and the other men, he did not sleep. Still, he insisted she sleep in his bed while he paced the house.

He had not spoken of what happened when he was with James. She thought it best if she didn't push him. The day after the incident, Anderson sat at the kitchen table working on a will for a client. He made notations as he moved from law book to law book. At lunch, he had a glass of whiskey and went back to work.

When night fell, and she could no longer take the silence, she asked, "Are you hungry?"

He looked up from his work and stared at her for a moment. "No."

She was about to walk away, when he asked, "Are you sorry you married me?"

"No," she whispered.

Anderson put aside his fountain pen. His eyes were piercing, and his voice thick. "I share your heart with a slave, and he has shown himself to be better at seeing to your needs than I."

Her eyes welled up, and softly she said, "Anderson, I love you."

"Do you wish you could be with him?"

"I wish to grow old with you."

He removed his glasses and rubbed his eyes. Anderson looked away, his voice hoarse when he asked, "Will you come naked to our bed tonight? Please?"

"Yes."

He stood suddenly, crossing the room to her, but he did not touch her. She turned on her own, heading for their bedroom. They climbed the stairs in silence; his room was the first door on the right. Two oil lamps sat on the nightstand and chest. The wicks were turned down, offering a soft light. In the center of the room was a large four poster bed with burgundy bedding and many pillows. On the left of the bed and next to the window was a brown dresser with three long drawers. In front of the bed, sat a large porcelain tub and just beyond the tub was the door to her room.

When she reached out to snuff one of the lamps completely, Anderson's words stopped her, "I don't want to fumble around in the dark. I need to see you."

She did not respond with words, instead she began to undress, and he did the same. Anderson was thin, yet muscular. In his suits, he appeared tall and lanky, but standing before her nude, his body was chiseled and well-defined. She realized that in the two years they had been married, they had not been open about their nakedness. Rose had never actually seen her husband's erection, but tonight was different. His white skin was pale, his brown hair wild and his blue eyes intense. Anderson was a lawyer who spent no time in the sun. Still, he was handsome. When she looked away out of shyness, he spoke again.

"I'm not trying to shock your sensibilities, but I want you to see me—not him."

She brought her eyes back to his, as she stood before him naked. Rose reached up and unpinned her black hair, allowing it to fall about her shoulders. Anderson breathed in sharply and whispered, "You are so beautiful."

He stepped to her, lifting her into his arms and carried her to their bed. When he laid her gently upon the mattress, he climbed between her legs. As he stared down at her, his hair hung forward and she reached up pushing his hair from his eyes. Anderson leaned down and kissed her deeply, causing her to whimper. Pressing her legs apart, she felt him at her core. When he entered her, Rose realized just how much she missed her husband and told him so.

"*Ohhh,* Anderson. I have missed you," she sighed, breathlessly.

From the onset of their coupling, Anderson's movements were feverish. He took her mouth in a scorching kiss, and he stroked her as if his very life depended on it. His rhythm was that he had no rhythm; still, his every stroke was exhilarating. When Rose felt the first spikes of ecstasy stab through her, she opened her legs wider, wanting all of him. But he withdrew from her and leaned back on his knees. His breathing was tortured, and his erection glistened from her juices. Rose had never seen her husband like this, and it was titillating.

"I don't want it to end," he whispered, his voice rusty.

Before she could respond, he leaned down kissing her chin. He took an erect nipple into his mouth, sucking, licking and biting her. Unable to help herself, she sobbed at the pleasure he gave. Anderson continued kissing her down her body, lingering where she hoped his seed would one day grow. When he came to her womanhood, he took her into his mouth, and she cried out in pure delight.

"Anderson… Anderson, ooohhh."

He stayed with her, pleasuring her. When she fell into an orgasmic state, he leaned back over her and kissed her deeply. Anderson shared the flavor of their coupling, and while she was still weak from ecstasy, he slipped inside her again.

His attempt to calm himself by offering his mouth did not work. He ground out, "Shit, Rosie, I'm still on the edge."

Rose had never heard her husband curse. She vaguely heard his declaration this time, so euphoric was she. Anderson hammered into her trying to get all he could from their joining. As completion seized him, he stroked her until his seed burst forth. In an effort to cling to satisfaction, he withdrew from her one last time. He then pressed himself forward as far as he could, before collapsing on top of her. Rose just held him.

✹ ✹ ✹

At breakfast the next morning, Rose sat across the table from her husband. Anderson's head was down as he thumbed through a law book. Even in her shyness, she noted the changes in his outward appearance that could not be missed. He wore a white shirt and brown bow tie, but markedly, he now wore a gun holstered to his upper left side. He had not shaved this morning, and it added to his appeal. Anderson looked up from his work, and his blue eyes locked on her. Rose felt as if she had been caught stealing. He smiled, but his gaze was different, and she felt pinned to the chair.

She thought he would speak, but a knock at the front door changed the direction of the morning. Alfred came to announce they had a visitor.

"Sir, the constable is here. He is in the foyer. He wishes to speak with the man of the house."

Anderson wiped his mouth with his napkin before he stood

headed to the front of the house. Rose followed. At the threshold of the front parlor stood an older gentleman wearing a blue uniform with a matching hat. Gray hair could be seen around the edges of his hat. He had dark eyes and sunburn on his nose. The officer also had a thin, gray mustache and when he spoke it danced. Rose was nervous.

"Good morning, officer," Anderson said smiling. "Are you here to collect for a charity?"

"I wish I were about other business, sir," the constable replied.

"Oh? What seems to be the trouble?" Anderson inquired.

The officer looked at Rose with apprehension.

"You may speak freely, Officer." Anderson instructed.

"I'm Officer Michaels, and why I'm here is not good. We found a hansom cab driver known to work this street, dead. His body was found about a mile up Broad Street. We are canvassing the area to see if anyone has seen or heard anything."

"Poor fellow. How did he die?"

"He appears to have been strangled with a wire of some sort. No one we have spoken with has seen anything out of the ordinary."

"I'm sorry to disappoint. I have seen nothing of import either," Anderson responded.

The constable nodded. "Well," he said, "if you see anything, please notify law enforcement. In the meantime, please take all precautions. We are unclear who did this, so we are warning residents to be aware."

"I will and thank you." Anderson shook the officer's hand.

When he closed the front door behind the officer, Anderson walked into the parlor and gazed out the window. He watched until the older man disappeared down the street. Rose stood quietly regarding the new man that was her husband.

"I did not kill this man," he said.

"I know," she responded.

"I replaced the piano wire while you slept."

Rose looked away. Anderson was saying much with few words. She needed to escape for a moment to gather her emotions, but there would be no respite.

Anderson swallowed hard as he looked at her. "James and I dumped him where he could be found. We thought to send a message that I am no easy mark."

He vibrated with anger as he continued, "We buried the man with the ponytail. He will never bother you again."

Rose tried to reassure herself and her husband, "I feel safe with you, Anderson."

Anderson stepped closer, his expression pained. "I have but one regret."

Rose was afraid to know his remorse. She thought he was bemoaning loving a woman who loved another. Insult was added to the injury because James was a slave by social standards. Still, she felt obliged to ask, "What is it your regret, my love?"

"I killed the man with the ponytail, but James killed his partner. I regret that I did not kill them both."

Rose heard what her husband did not say—Anderson regretted he was not the only man willing to kill for her.

12

Hunter Plantation
September 1861

THE RAIN HAD stopped when E.J. walked out of the kitchen and into the night air. The smell of wet earth assailed him as he made his way to her cabin. He had been avoiding Nettie. Twice had he gone to her cabin since his marriage—but he hadn't the nerve to see her. In truth, he was shaken over who he was as a man. Reading his father's personal papers, as well as the manifest of slaves who had come and gone from the Hunter plantation had enlightened him against his will. His love for his brother was also a factor.

He realized that his perception of his father was based on his own needs, rather than the man himself. E.J. saw himself as weak for several reasons. First, reading about the death of his brother's mother troubled him. While he knew he should have viewed her death as business, he could not. Her demise represented a hypocrisy perpetrated by his father. He had been trying to live his life at the standard he thought his father had lived. What he now understood–his father wasn't who he thought him to be. Secondly, he was his father's son, for he loved the slave girl Nettie. His love for Suzanne had not diminished, but it had changed.

E.J. suspected that his change in feelings, stemmed from being controlled with regard to Nettie. It didn't help that since the incident with the deserters, Suzanne had taken to sleeping with her mother and sister. He knew he should exert his power as her husband, but he did not want her in his bed, if she did not wish to be there. E.J. did not want forced sex from his wife. Still, every night that she spent away from his bed furthered his feelings of resentment. Though he understood her trauma of the situation, he was annoyed that she sought safety elsewhere. He loved his young wife deeply, but he was becoming impatient.

The insects played their symphony as he walked under trees, while raindrops dripped from the fat leaves. A quarter moon hung in the sky, offering no relief from the darkness. He came to Nettie's cabin and stepped onto the porch before knocking the mud from his boots. He pushed at the door and found Nettie sorting the laundry for the main house.

She looked up from her task and glared at him. The pain he witnessed in her eyes forced him to see her as a woman rather than a slave. When she spoke, her jealousy was tangible, and he couldn't look away.

"Yo' wife must ain't well cause ya here."

She stood, removed her tan dress and waited in the center of the one room. E.J. ignored her anger and stared about the cabin, collecting his emotions. When he got himself under control, he looked up at her, and their eyes collided.

"Ella and Sonny spectin' the laundry in the mornin'. Ya need to do yo' business so'n I can get back to work," she hissed.

E.J.'s anger flared at her disrespect. "You forget yourself, Nettie. Don't make me beat you."

"I's wishin' ya would beat me. Maybe I could learn to hate ya. I ain't got no business lovin' you," her voice cracked.

His irritation dissolved at her words, and he sighed, "It was that way in the past, it ain't the case now. I'm here because I miss you."

"They tells me ya wife is sleepin' wit' her mama not you. I's sho' ya do miss me." Nettie folded her arms over her bare breasts.

"I could force my wife to my bed, Nettie, the same as I can force you. I love her, I won't lie. I ain't want you moved from the main house, but I thought it would be best for all concerned. I had you moved because I love and want you too. I am the master here at Hunter Manor. I could seek my ease elsewhere–that is not the only reason I am here. Understand I don't owe you an explanation. You are my slave."

"Masta, where is ya wantin' me to lay? I has other chores what need tendin'," Nettie said, unmoved by his words.

He took in the sight of her deep chocolate skin. Nettie was flawless, and her nudity moved him, but he would not make love to her. He wanted to be welcomed, and she was unimpressed.

"Get in the damn bed," E.J. demanded.

He placed his gun on the table and removed his clothes. When he was naked, he climbed into the bed next to her. He didn't touch her. They lay silent for a while until he finally turned on his side, pulling her to him. Her body went stiff.

He spooned her and against her ear, he whispered, "I want to be welcomed into your heart and body. I am asking you to be mine. I promise to care for you and protect you, along with any children that will come from us. I will not mistreat you. I will try and make you happy if you let me."

She kept her back to him. "What choice I got?"

"I won't force you, Nettie. I will stay away if that's what you want."

"I's so jealous it's squeezin' the life from me," Nettie said, choking back tears.

E.J. stroked her hip. "I will make time for you. You are important to me. I promise, Nettie."

"Whateva ya wants, Masta."

"You have to say you want me, Nettie—aint no moving forward unless you say it," E.J.'s tone became more insistent. He forced her to face him.

She looked past him as she answered in a soft monotone. "I wants you, Masta."

"Edward—my name is Edward." His voice was gravelly.

"I wants you, Edward," she said, shy about using his given name.

They did not make love. Instead, E.J. was thankful that she was receptive. He loved her so much, yet the weight of his responsibilities was drowning him. When he enlisted, he knew he would have to set her free. It was the only way to ensure her safety in his absence. It was what he had really come to tell her, but he couldn't let go. He would settle her somewhere safe and come back for her after the war—if he survived.

E.J. had not slept in days. He found peace in her arms and finally drifted to sleep. At dawn, Nettie woke him with her mouth, and he returned the kindness. He entered her slowly, and the world fell away. His sweet Nettie showed him just how much she missed him. When he felt her body tighten around him, he tried to back away from completion. She felt so good he never wanted it to end, but her words and touch broke him down.

"Ohhh, Edward, don't stop it, let it be. Please, Masta let it be," she moaned.

It was her body's acceptance of his, her tightness and her words that caused him to spill his seed. He groaned and cried out, "Shit, Nettie, I can't leave you now if I wanted."

The little cabin echoed with the sounds of ecstasy as E.J. collapsed on top of her. He pulled them onto their side shifting his weight. Nettie's leg rested on his hip, and they lay facing one another. As the sun rose, he took in the sight of her dark skin against his white skin. The image signified a truth that could not be denied. The system under which they lived could not continue as it had—the lines between black and white would have to be redefined.

He made love to her once more, and later when he sat eating, there was a knock at the door. E.J. stood wearing tan trousers, black boots, his guns at his hips and no shirt. He and Nettie had washed each other at the pump behind her cabin. His hair was still wet. Pulling the door open, he came face-to-face with Sonny.

"The laundry is not ready, Sonny. You can come back later."

"Yes, sah," Sonny replied and quickly disappeared.

It was nearly noon when E.J. kissed Nettie deeply and headed for the main house. He strolled leisurely as a breeze wildly tossed his curls. The white shirt he wore was unbuttoned, revealing his muscled chest. E.J. reeked of sexuality and release. He entered the house through the French doors off the gardens. Ella was serving Suzanne, along with her mother and sister when he appeared in the doorway of the dining room. They all looked up at once, except for Ella.

Suzanne and her sister blushed and looked away; Julia, however, did not. E.J. gazed at his wife, and his irritation was back.

He addressed the room. "Good day, ladies."

"Good afternoon, Edward," Suzanne said softly.

"Edward," Julia said, hiding her face in her cup.

Maryam smiled demurely. "Hello, Edward."

Suzanne lifted her eyes to him. She was nervous; still, she asked, "Won't you join us, Edward?"

"No, thank you. I am not hungry," he replied, failing to achieve the casual tone he wanted.

E.J. stepped passed Ella and headed for his study. He walked into the office and was surprised to find Callie seated by the window, reading one of his father's old journals. When she saw him, her hands shook as she clutched the journal in her lap.

She looked to the floor. "Jeremiah sat me here and told me to read, sir."

E.J. looked at her for a moment before he smiled. "Good afternoon, Callie."

His brother was attempting to share his life, by leaving her in his study. But Callie, he was sure, wanted nothing to do with him.

"Would you prefer to take the books to your cabin?" he asked her calmly.

"Yes, sir," Callie replied, offering no eye contact.

His curiosity got the better of him, as he thought aloud. "Why is he having you read the journals? He can read."

Callie wore a plain tan skirt with a matching shirt. She had large brown eyes, full lips and her hair was braided in two neat plaits pinned at the top of her head. The beauty of her deep cara-mel skin was magnified by the natural light from the window. Her anxiety and fear of him were evident from the way she wrung her hands together over the book. E.J. wasn't expecting her to answer, and he was shocked when she spoke.

"I think he wants me to read because I carry his child," she whispered.

E.J. could think of nothing to say–he knew she was correct. He had offered her a way of escape, and she took it, "You can leave and take however many books you want with you."

Callie stood, and E.J. could see she was truly with child.

"I will take this one for now, if that's all right," she said timidly.

He smiled at her once more. "That's fine with me, Callie."

Callie was unresponsive to his kindness. She squeezed past him in the doorway and made a run for it. E.J. chuckled as he seated himself behind his desk. He had been working for an hour when Jeremiah appeared.

"I see ya ran her off. I ain't expect her to stay when you came around," Jeremiah said.

"She is leery of me, and I ain't the least bit offended by it."

Jeremiah changed the subject. "The men have done better, but we still got us three issues."

"What do you see?"

"Deserters, the war and that damn gang of runaways."

"I see a fourth matter," E.J. clarified.

"And that is?"

"I am not as interested in avenging Papa's death as I felt before reading the journals. I am still bothered by his tragic exit, but I also miss my mama dearly. The matter of your mama angers me," E.J. held his hands up as he acknowledged, "I know this is weakness on my part, but still I feel some kind a way."

"It don't matter how you feel, there is no backing away from this situation." Jeremiah replied.

E.J. handed Jeremiah two telegrams and the first read:

I AM IN BOSTON I HAVE LOCATED THE PROPER COUNSEL

The second message read:

BOSTON IS UNEVENTFUL ROSE SENDS HER LOVE

When Jeremiah looked up, E.J. said, "The first message is from my man in Boston. The second is not from him. I think he's dead. He would never have used her actual name in the message. He was far too discreet to make such a blunder. So, I understand there is no turning back. The second message is a warning, and I am clear about it."

"Are you clear they ain't in Canada?" Jeremiah asked.

"Rose Wilkerson did as I suspected and summoned them. I should have killed her and her husband."

Jeremiah's tone was sympathetic. "If it will make ya feel any better, they would have come back, anyhow. This is not about the

Wilkerson woman. This about me shooting one of their men and killing the slave woman they thought to save."

E.J. leaned back in his chair and stared at his brother. Jeremiah had no immediate reactions to the news about his mother, yet, he had Callie reading the journals. "You don't expect to survive the encounter with this group of runaways, do you? You are having Callie read Papa's papers for more reasons than I originally thought."

Jeremiah smiled. "I am having her read because she don't talk to me unless she has a reason. The journals make her have to talk to me. Papa's old papers don't interest me, but it gives her something to do when she ain't working."

Jeremiah turned around and promptly left the room. E.J. chuckled to himself. His brother had given all he was willing to share for one day.

❊ ❊ ❊

Jeremiah went through the dining room to the gardens. When he emerged into the sunlight, he found Suzanne, along with her mother and sister, taking a stroll. The women had paused in the shade of a magnolia tree and were in close conversation. Suzanne and Maryam looked up, acknowledging him with curt nods. Julia turned, after speaking with her daughters, and began walking in his direction. She wore a yellow muslin dress that was off the shoulders. He thought her striking.

He stopped on the stone pathway between two flower beds. Julia stood in his way, and Jeremiah glared down at her. The black cracker was attempting to intimidate, but she was unfazed.

Julia flashed him a smile. "Jeremiah, I wanted to say thank you for keeping my daughters and myself safe."

"You're welcome, misses."

"In the future when I go riding, you will accompany me

for protection," she responded, tossing her long brown hair to one side.

The image of her skirts tossed up, while bent over in front of him holding on to a tree came to mind. Jeremiah actually smiled. "I take my orders from Mr. Hunter. Please speak with him, and he will have someone else ride with his wife and her guests."

She placed her hands on her hips and glowered at him. Her anger made her even more attractive, but he was absolutely not interested. He had bigger problems to deal with and an extra piece of ass, he did not need. Although he was looking her right in the eyes, his silence was dismissing.

"I will speak with Edward. I'm sure he won't mind lending you to me for a few hours," she said with authority.

"Good noon, misses," Jeremiah said as he stepped around her.

Jeremiah checked on the men that reported to him before taking the long way to his cabin. They had a total of sixty men, but that number was now diminished by one. E.J. had not inquired about Hank, and he had not volunteered. It seemed Callie being with child made him even more brutal. His brother had been correct; he did not think he would survive an interaction with the runaways. But he would try for her sake. He had also decided that if he had to die, he would kill as many of them as he could. Lastly, he did not feel the same about his papa, in light of what happened to his mama. Yet, he continued to offer no reaction; it was better that way.

He had hoped to search this group of runaways out before they came looking for him; but that had not been possible. Jeremiah now understood that what looked like unorganized chaos was actually a well thought out plan. He and his brother had been on the defensive since the uprising. They had been retraining new slaves, rebuilding the plantation and spending time hiring new overseers. The war was adding to their inability to get ahead, and if that wasn't enough, women had been added to the mix.

He felt shame because he had become fixated with Callie. She was constantly in his thoughts, and this took away from his sharpness. When she shared her body with him, it became clear that he was no match for the group of men seeking his death.

Jeremiah was experiencing great resentment toward E.J.'s mother in-law for treating him like a stallion. He watched as his brother anguished over his feelings for his wife and Nettie. When considering his own situation, he had done a poor job of managing his own feelings of love. Like any man, he enjoyed variety, and he *could* handle more than one piece of pussy. But he could not handle the complications of life brought on by love. His seed growing within her made clear that he was not privileged like his brother. E.J. could monetarily afford two women. He could not afford one woman and a child.

The door to his cabin was open, and he could see Callie seated to the table reading. She didn't look up, but she did acknowledge him.

"Your food is still warm, and I have some lemonade for you."

Jeremiah didn't move or speak. He wanted her undivided attention, and he conveyed his wants through silence until the quiet made her look at him. She smiled weakly, as he stood just inside the doorway. He assessed her; Callie looked troubled. He spoke his thoughts to open the lines of communication.

"If reading the journals is going to saddened you, I'll take them from you."

"Can we speak about what I read?" She set the book aside.

"We can. Do you have something to discuss with me now?"

"I thought you would eat and sleep now," she said.

"Did you eat?"

"I ate with Eva."

He nodded as he removed his shirt and threw it in the basket near the door. Crossing the room, he seated himself in the chair opposite her. On his plate was a helping of collard greens and mashed sweet potato. He did not care for meat, and she served him accordingly. The process was slow, but Callie was tending him in all things.

Leaning back in his chair, he studied her as he chewed his food. Callie was different with him–she had become skittish. Seeing him covered in blood had shaken her. He knew that she suspected he had killed someone. This was the matter he wanted to discuss. Instead, he would let her speak about the journals, while he gauged her love for him. She had not told him that she loved him again. He had forbidden her to say such things to him, but today, he needed to hear it.

He placed his fork down on the wooden plate. "Ain't no sense in waiting to talk about what you're reading. Please tell me what concerns you."

"Do you plan on reading his writings?"

"No."

"I see, but you're sure you don't mind talking about his writings?" she asked again.

"'Contradict…what does this word mean?"

She was looking down at the table, and her head popped up suddenly at his words. Callie cleared her throat and whispered, "You said you don't want children."

"I don't."

"But coupling makes babies–you say you don't want babies, but you couple with me as if you want them. The way you act doesn't go with your words."

"I think this word don't fit me," Jeremiah said after some thought.

She gave him a curious look. "Please explain."

"I couple with you because it feels so damn good. All I think about is being between your legs. Your body tricks me and makes me a fiend for you. Feeling the results of a child never came to me."

Callie looked to the back door, "So you should not be held accountable?"

"I am forced to the outcome of my actions. I think it's this way for everybody."

"If you stopped coupling with me, this worry would be gone from us," she said, appearing hurt.

"I ain't *never* willingly going to stop wanting or touching you."

Callie's voice wavered. "Will our baby be sold from us?"

He had hoped their talk would be light–funny. It soon became clear what troubled her, and it also explained her skittish demeanor. Callie's belly wasn't large, but one could see she was with child. She had started avoiding being seen naked. He worried she had stopped loving him, but it was far worse than he could have imaged.

Callie thought he would be instrumental in the sale of their baby. The part that hurt–he understood why she would think such a thing. They were slaves and had no business breeding in these conditions. Their child wouldn't be sold because of his relationship with his brother. Yet, there was no comfort in the thought. It meant his brother held the power over his family, and she could see it.

She wasn't breathing. "I would not allow you to be separated from our child."

Callie's eyes became glassy. "Will I be separated from you?"

"I don't think ya have room to worry about me. I want you to think of keeping yourself and the child safe at all times."

Her eyes searched his. "Are we going to be together?"

Jeremiah looked away, his inadequacies as a man and slave weighing him down. Callie whispered, "Please talk to me."

"My aim is to keep you and the child with me. But if it comes down to safety, we will separate for your well-being. I have done things that may cause my death; I won't let it spill on you," he paused for a moment. "You are different with me, why?"

"I am different with you because we can be mean and unstable with one another. This could harm our child." Callie answered, before adding, "I don't want to think of your death."

Jeremiah sought to change the subject. "You don't let me see you naked. I want to see your changes."

"I try not to make you uncomfortable with this situation."

"Tell me you love me," he asked, feeling weak as he waited for her to answer.

"I thought I wasn't allowed to say such things to you."

"I thought you said you would say it anyway, whether I like it or not. You don't say it. Is it now that you are with child you don't love me? You ain't been listening to me," he replied, his voice deep and his dark eyes intense.

Callie smiled showing pretty white teeth, still she remained silent.

"Have I said something amusing?"

"And you don't think the word '*contradict*' fits you?"

Jeremiah just stared at her, feeling terrified. Callie had not confirmed her love for him. He turned away from her.

"I love you more than I did yesterday," she whispered.

Abruptly, he turned back to her. "You are sure about this?"

She giggled, "I have loved you since the day you saved me from the overseer."

Jeremiah did not say, but he loved her since the day his brother purchased her for him. He was drawn to her and the unbalanced, violent nature between them kept him excited. He had learned to back away from his anger to keep her safe. Callie also backed away from volatile exchanges, and it helped him to better control his temper. His jealousy was still not easily harnessed, and she worked with him doing as he demanded.

"Did you want to talk about the journals?"

"Not now–later." Callie stood and took his face in her hands. "You haven't said you love me."

"I love you, Callie."

She kissed him before backing away. Callie headed for the door and over her shoulder, she said, "Going to help Ella with dinner. I'll bring you back some fruit."

Jeremiah watched as she disappeared out the back door. When he was alone, he removed his boots and climbed in bed. He rested, but he did not sleep. His thoughts were busy with the safety of his woman and child. A plan for her exit from the plantation had not been explored because he was weak–unable to let her go. He dozed off amid thoughts of love and unworthiness. As he lingered between sleep and awareness, he hoped to find a way to keep the life he was making with Callie. Betsy and the boy came to mind– he had too many failures.

13

Baltimore, Maryland
September 1861

WHEN JAMES AND the men arrived in Baltimore, the unrest could be felt by all. Even though most of the colored folks in the city and state were free, the city was divided in its stance on slavery. Maryland had not seceded from the Union, but the local government had Confederate sympathies. Black used his connections in the colored sector to arrange lodging for the group. They would rest for two days before they headed to nearby Washington and the next step in the plan.

They settled about a mile inland from the Patapsco River, where the men were welcomed by Andy Murphy and his family. Black had not seen Andy in a great while. Andy was kin to Mary and Herschel. He and his wife had been invaluable in the struggle for freedom. Andy was a mulatto, the product of Herschel's uncle and a slave woman. He was just over six feet and rail thin. His skin was so light he could pass for a white man, which he did to help the struggle. He had close-cropped salt and pepper hair, dark brown eyes and a very wide nose. When he smiled, there was a gap where a front tooth had been.

Mable, his wife was a small white woman. Her thick brown plait was streaked with gray. She looked younger than her fifty summers and had produced two colored sons. Both young men had followed in their parents' steps in the fight for freedom. They all lived on a stretch of land, farming and working the docks of the Patapsco.

Andy and his sons had met Black and the men about a half a mile in from the river. Daylight was just breaking when the two groups intercepted one another.

"Andy, it's good to see you," Black greeted warmly.

"Black, how ya been?"

"I can't complain."

Andy's sons stepped forward as Black swung down from his horse. The oldest, also named Andy, spoke up. "Been a while, ain't it?"

"Yes, it has, Junior," Black replied.

"How is ya and how is Mary?" Andy's other son, who was named after Herschel, asked.

"Mary and Herschel are well."

"We's sorry 'bout Otis," Herschel offered.

"Yes, so are we," Black said.

Junior turned to Elbert. "Elbert, ya mean son of a bitch. How you?"

Elbert chuckled. "I'm good."

"Jim, glad to see ya still standin'," Junior said to James.

"Shit, I'm glad I'm standing too," James answered as he swung down from his horse to shake hands.

Both of Andy's sons looked like him. Herschel was about twenty-seven summers and Junior about twenty-nine. They were tall, strong young men. They and their father were dressed in blue overalls and black work boots. They toted shotguns and pistols—there was no fear in them.

The men got reacquainted, and Black introduced Bainesworth, Shultz, Luke, and Anthony. The other men had all worked together before.

"This here is Dr. Shultz," Black said, pointing to the doctor.

Andy smiled—his missing front tooth was like a darkened window. "You's the one sweet on our Mary. Herschel sends word when he can."

Shultz smiled in greeting. "Good to meet you all."

"I don't guess we needs to worry about Mary," Herschel said bluntly. "They would kill ya if'n ya mistreats her."

"I love Mary. I would never mistreat her," Shultz responded good-naturedly.

"This here is Bainesworth—he is a friend," Black said.

"Good day to you all," Bainesworth said in his thick British accent.

Andy and his sons stared at the newcomer, looking perplexed. Elbert translated. "He says 'good day'."

"Oohh, he's a fancy ass," Junior quipped. "He ain't from these parts."

Black cleared his throat, trying not to laugh. "Yes, he is a fancy ass."

Bainesworth looked at Black and getting their humor, laughed with the others. The ice had been broken. After introductions were made, the entourage headed in the direction of Andy's farm. When they arrived, they set up in the barn. After they determined shifts and schedules, Black and James went in search of Mable. When they opened the front door of a small cabin, she was waiting.

"Miss Mable, good to see you," Black said as he leaned down and kissed her cheek.

Mable had a proud bearing. The plain brown dress she wore

did not hide her inner opulence. She beamed at both men, and James gave her a kiss as well.

"Glad seein' ya, Miss Mable," James said.

"Come sit. We will talk," the woman ordered.

The cabin was plain and spotless. At the rear was a wooden door, pulled shut. Two rocking chairs sat facing the hearth where a small fire burned. The table was large with two benches on either side. There were three windows, two at the front and one at the back. The wooden shutters were open, letting in the sunlight and cross ventilation of a glorious morning. A breeze came from the river and the smell of fall was in the air.

Mable fixed both men a hefty bowl of stewed meat with garden vegetables and potatoes. Black did not think too hard on the type of meat; instead, he spooned in a mouthful and chewed. Mable giggled. "We butchered a calf—you are safe."

Black chuckled and continued to eat.

"This sho' is good, Miss Mable," James said.

She brought the cornbread to the table, along with honey and coffee. After serving them, her expression grew serious. "I have two names for you," she said.

She was about to say more when her husband stepped though the cabin door. Mable turned to him. "Are you hungry, dear?"

"I could eat something, Mother," Andy responded.

She nodded, and as she moved to fix his food, Andy seated himself opposite Black and James. "The men got them a fire going; ma sons been stewin' beef and cookin' over an open pit for two days. Yo' men finna eat well."

"We appreciate you all," Black and James said in unison.

Mable placed a plate of food in front of her husband, and then picked up the conversation where she left off. "You asked for names of colored folk doing well in Washington. The preference was that they be women. Is that right?"

"That is correct," Black said.

"There is a colored woman named Elizabeth who has become Miss Lincoln's modiste and companion. Lizzie lives in the executive mansion and has Wednesday afternoons off. I have met her in passing. She is sharp; I'm sure she is what you will need," Mable informed them.

"Who is the other person?" James asked.

"The other person is a young colored girl named Music. She is about twenty summers and works in the kitchens. The girl is quiet and private; you will definitely be able to use her. She also appears to be unattached," Mable added.

Andy grinned and looked at Black. "Can I knows what you's about?"

"Believe me, you are better off not knowing," Black replied, leaving Andy's words hanging in midair.

Mable stood suddenly, waving her hands and sounding giddy. "Oh, I almost forgot."

She moved swiftly to the back room and returned with a pile of what looked like blue clothing. Handing Black the clothes, he saw it was the Union uniforms he had requested.

"Have your men sort these out, so I can do any mending needed," Mabel said.

Two hours went by with Black discussing at length with his friends what to expect in Washington, D.C. He learned the city was more like a military base where Union soldiers were camped out in the streets around the executive mansion. Mable confirmed what he already knew—the soldier's encampment went on as far as the eye could see. Still, Black did not worry. For he also knew that because of their numbers, the soldiers would take for granted the safety of the Union president.

"Every unionist ain't for niggers. Ya needs to know that," Andy said with concern.

"We is clear on that," James answered.

"Colored men lined up to enlist, and they was turned away

like children. Hell, white folks ain't clear 'bout likin' one another, so's they cain't like us," Andy declared.

"Colored men *will* fight in this war when white folks realize they have no choice. White man's worst nightmare is a nigger with a gun, but he will have to bow to the reasoning to save his own women and children. This whole damn war will be humbling for all," Black said to the room at large.

"I agrees," Andy said.

"Lincoln has suspended *habeas corpus*. He has started arresting government officials here in Maryland to keep the rails open to the troops. It's all here in the paper," Mable said, handing the newspaper to Black.

Black studied the news, trying to glean relevant information to their plan. He was about to put it aside when he came across the society page. The top of page three spoke of Mrs. Lincoln's lovely dresses and the tea parties she would have at the executive home. But it was the middle of the page that caught his eye, for it spoke of the president's habits when trying to alleviate stress.

Black's head popped up suddenly, and he looked over at James. Mable readily took notice.

"Page three grabbed you the same as it did me. Imagine, the president walking alone in the evenings to clear his head. Andy takes me to Washington to give me a break and show me a good time. I *actually* saw him...very tall fellow. He's taller than you, Black. That paper is about two weeks old, by the way."

Black grinned. Mable was too witty for her own good.

❋ ❋ ❋

Later when James and Black completed their meeting with Mable, they went to check on the men. The smell of seared meat floated through the air as half a calf turned over an open pit. Next to the pit sat a black, cast iron pot hanging over a fire. Junior was tending the food, as the men stood about talking and drinking. James stood alone, leaned against an oak, observing his surroundings. Since leaving the fort, he avoided moments where he thought too much. But today, he was unable to help himself, and so his mind wandered.

His thoughts drifted to his woman and his son, whom he missed greatly. Still, in the midst of those draining emotions there was Rose, and he was left tired from the myriad of feelings happening to him. Sleep had eluded him, and his need to feel Abby's body next his overwhelmed his senses. As he stared around the camp, he could see that some of the men were set to different tasks. He, however, could not get focused as he tried to track the lay of the land.

Black and Elbert approached with Shultz, Tim and Bainesworth in tow. The men formed a circle and began serious talks about the Union president. James was thankful for the distraction.

"Gentlemen, how shall we proceed?" Bainesworth asked.

"We let you all make the connection when we gets to Washington. Where is yo' check-in?" James said.

"Maynard advised me to go to a dry-goods store on Tenth Street when I arrive. I'll know more after the meet." Tim replied.

"We need to observe the activity at the dry-goods store. I say we locate the fellow with the British accent. His involvement in such matters could make for a terrible end," Bainesworth added.

"I agree," Elbert said.

"First, we got to admit that we has two issues. There is a lot of ground to cover," James warned.

"Absolutely," the ambassador said. "We need two schemes—there is no other way."

"Lincoln needs to be captured, warned, and released. The group from the dry-goods store needs to be handled. We need to make certain the two problems never meet," Black instructed.

"I agree," said Bainesworth. The men looked at him in unison.

"I concede I was uncomfortable in Boston—nervous even. But I suspect Mr. and Mrs. Wilkerson will not expire at the hands of some hooligan. I can't help but feel good about that."

"We need to step through the motions with this group until they show their hand. Our timing needs to be right," Tim said.

"If we put them down discreetly, the message will be clear," Elbert said.

"Shit, it's settled then," James said.

"Do we need to establish a place for cleanup?" Tim asked.

Black was about to speak, but Bainesworth cut him off. "I think we need to make certain the message is seen. If we are too inconspicuous, they will appear to have gotten away. These men need to be left to public speculation and the crows."

"The ambassador speaks the truth," Black concluded.

Two colored women appeared to help serve and clean up. One was plump and the other thin. James thought they must be the brothers' wives. The river was at their backs, cooling the air while the sun beat down. Five small children ran about, playing. In the clearing, three identical cabins stood, with interconnected well-worn paths, between them. There was a barn with a corral connected to it. Sheep and goats roamed and grazed. Each cabin had a garden as well.

Mable approached and to Tim, Bainesworth and Shultz she said, "Please follow me so we can work on your uniforms."

The ambassador bowed. "Good day to you, madam. My name is Bainesworth."

"Oh, you *are* fancy, just as my husband said. You handsome too," Mable responded with a smile.

"Hello, Miss Mable. I'm Dr. Shultz."

Mable embraced him. "Welcome to the family, Nicholas. Our Mary is a sweet girl."

"Yes, she truly is." Shultz replied.

Tim stepped forward and kissed her on the cheek. "Good to see you, Miss Mable."

"Nicholas…" Elbert snickered.

"Yes, *Nicholas*," Shultz said, annoyed. They all began to laugh.

Before they turned to follow Mable, Bainesworth said, "I feel I should just get this out of the way, so it doesn't come up later. My first name is Laverne."

The men all exchanged looks. It was too much. They broke out in hearty guffaws. As Bainesworth and Shultz stormed off behind Mable, the ambassador looked over his left shoulder and groused, "Silly bostards!"

When darkness fell, the men did a shift change. It was decided they would leave for Washington at the stroke of midnight the following day. Before they left for the capital, Black would handle one last matter. He would send correspondence to Sunday to keep her from worrying. He tried to push away all negative thought, but in his quieter moments, he considered it unrealistic to think they would all make it home. Still, they would press forward, knowing that if they got caught, they would all hang.

14

Hunter Plantation
The Passage of Time

CALLIE HAD JUST stepped from the tub and dried herself when lightning flashed, followed by a loud clap of thunder. It was early morning, yet dawn wouldn't come for a few more hours. She lit a small fire to fight off the chill as the September mornings grew cooler with each passing day. Jeremiah had filled the tub the night before and she had added some hot water for her bath.

Their routine had not changed; Jeremiah moved about the plantation at night and Callie worked during the day. She had taken to bathing at night after he left or in the morning before he came in to rest. The changes in her physical appearance made her self-conscious, and she shied away from being seen naked. She knew this troubled him, but he didn't push. When she finished rubbing the homemade cream on her skin, she wrapped herself in a sheet and sat before the fire.

She had been slowly reading the second journal when she heard his booted feet on the back porch. Jeremiah was home early, but Callie wasn't surprised considering the weather. When he stepped inside the cabin and removed his hat, water fell from the brim. His clothes were soaked. She smiled.

"Good morning, Jeremiah."

"Callie."

"I have fruit for you this morning. When day breaks, I will fetch you something from the main house."

"I ain't hungry for food," he informed her.

She looked away as he moved to the table and began undressing. He did it the same every time. First, he removed his guns, then his shirt, boots and trousers–he never wore underpants. Callie listened as he moved around behind her. When he spoke, his deep voice brought the cabin to life.

"Will you shave me and cut my hair?"

Callie observed him; his beautiful hair had grown even wilder than usual. Jeremiah had tired dark eyes, a thick mustache and the beginnings of a beard. His appearance was rough–rugged and in his nudity, he radiated power.

"You have gray hair in your beard. How old *are* you?"

He had moved to the chest at the foot of the bed and was wrapping a towel around his waist. Jeremiah stopped at her words and gave her a stony glare.

"Is you saying I'm an old man?"

She looked away as if afraid. "I'm saying young people ain't gray like you."

Jeremiah burst out laughing and she smirked. The black cracker was the very definition of beauty and maleness. The muscles in his stomach and arms contracted and released with his every movement. Callie was shaken by how much she loved him.

She knew his age; it was recorded in the journals. Still, he surprised her when he said, "I think I was about five or six summers when E.J. was born. He is thirty; I believe I am about thirty-five or thirty-six."

"You aren't sure?"

"No, I ain't sure." He glanced down at the journal. "But you know *precisely* how old I am, don't you?"

"I do. He recorded your birth to a young slave girl named Flower."

Jeremiah crossed his arms and sighed. "So, tell me, how old am I?"

"You are thirty-five summers. Your guess was correct."

"I don't think there is much in those journals that I don't know. How old are *you*, Callie?"

"I'm twenty-five summers."

"You have not talked to me about his writings. Do you fear upsetting me?"

"You have much on your shoulders; I don't care to add to the burden. You don't talk to me, so I don't know what I'm afraid of. I know that you want me to worry for myself, but I..."

She stared at the fire, and Jeremiah's voice caressed her from behind, "About two years ago our papa left here to handle some business. E.J. and I were later notified that he was shot to death on the Turner plantation. The next year there was a raid on the Bridges and Mickerson plantations. It was a band of runaways that caused all of it. When they got to Hunter Manor, they caused an uprising like I ain't never seen. E.J. was gone and I was left in charge. I gave the order to round up the women and children."

He stopped talking, causing her to turn and look at him. Jeremiah appeared deep in thought and regretful. She didn't want to push him for fear he would stop talking. Instead, she asked on a whisper, "Do you think you can lose my love?"

"Yes."

He nervously ran his fingers through his hair. She smiled up at him. "It is not possible for me to stop loving you."

Jeremiah held her gaze for several heartbeats before he picked up where he left off. "I shot one of their men in the face, but that is not what bothers me. I shot a female slave and killed her, while she held onto her child. When we sorted out the dead, their man was not among them and the child that Betsy was fighting to keep hold of was also missing."

Callie looked away to gather her thoughts. She figured he had engaged in the punishment of the slaves–she also believed him to be ruthless. What she had not expected to see was remorse for his actions. He looked at her fearfully, waiting for the results of his confession.

"You have not told me anything that I didn't already guess about you," she said. "It is why I tried not to love you, but that did not work. You saved me from being forced into unwanted acts; I cannot deny the safety you give me. As your seed grows within my belly, my heart grows with affection for you. I have been clear about the real you since I first saw you in the crowd at the slave mart. Upon our first meeting, I told you what I thought of you. I wasn't confused then, and I am not confused now. The one request you had of me ensured my love and loyalty to you. You asked that I see you in the proper light–I have done so, but still I love you."

Callie was gentle, but she pressed. "I don't understand what you see that I don't. What results is coming?"

"This gang of runaways will be back for me. They want revenge for my killing the slave woman and shooting their man. They seek my death," he replied, backing away from all emotion.

The thought of him being killed–of losing him– took Callie's breath away. "We could leave here and start a free life."

"I can't just leave E.J. in a condition that I caused. This is his land, and he will not leave. It ain't that simple."

"So, this white man is more important than me and your child?" Callie hissed.

"You see a white man, but he is my brother, no matter his color. He has asked that I not send you away. He has promised to help me keep you safe. I will send you away anyhow. His whiteness

makes him naïve, and that is dangerous. No one is more important than you and this child. I fear for your safety."

"I want to be with you and our child. I won't leave you."

"Oh, Miss Callie, you are my one true love. I never want to part
with you. But, I need to settle you elsewhere and come back for you
later–*if* I live. I thought to help Sonny and Eva to freedom so that
you will not be alone. I don't like Sonny, but you love Eva."

Jeremiah's hair fell into his eyes. Running his fingers through
his hair, he pushed the strands back from his face and crossed his
arms. She could see the tension in his body.

"Sonny and Ella are in the journals," she whispered abruptly.

"They should be–they been on the Hunter plantation for a
long time. They are brother and sister. Before you came, Ella saw
to feeding me and washing my clothes. She also cleaned my room
in the big house. I think she tries to keep me and Sonny apart
because she loves her brother. Ella is afraid of me and does not
give me trouble. She don't really speak to me neither."

Callie thought she should back away from talking about the
journals. She was thinking of something else to say when Jeremiah
said, "Speak freely, Callie."

"Ella came to the Hunter plantation with two children."

Jeremiah frowned. "I don't recall no slave children belonging
to Ella."

"Sonny is not her brother–he is her son."

Jeremiah paused for a moment, digesting the revelation. He
shrugged and then said, "It makes sense for why she tries to keep
Sonny out of my way."

"Yes, it does."

"Her other child must have been sold," Jeremiah speculated.

"No."

He smiled, "You feel sorry for the old lady, even though she
don't like you."

"I do."

"Let's hear it," he said, intrigued.

"Her daughter, Flower, fell in love with the plantation owner and bore him a son. He named that son Jeremiah. The older Hunter then took a wife when Flower believed he wouldn't because of his love for her. In her hurt, she took up with a field hand named Wilbur, and in a fit of jealousy, Hunter Sr. killed them both. Ella begged to be his cook so she could look after her daughter's child. Hunter gave her the job to keep you out of his wife's hair. Though you worked in the house, E.J.'s mama did not want you in her home. But she could not override her husband's wishes, so she tolerated you."

"His writing is far more interesting than I thought," Jeremiah smirked, but Callie didn't miss his hurt.

"Can I ask you a question?"

"Yes," he answered.

"I know you understand E.J. to be your brother, but did it never occur to you that the people you oppress are your kin as well?"

He walked slowly over to the window at the front of the cabin and looked out on the other slave cabins. "It never occurred to me. I thought Mama was by herself and when she was sold, old man Hunter took me into the main house. E.J. and I became close, and it has remained so. He taught me to read, write and figure—me and him are devoted to each other. Over the years, I have even had to give him a good thrashing once or twice, but he never told. We have a loyalty, me and him… No, it never occurred to me."

"Can you see the disconnect in which you live?"

Jeremiah's voice grew agitated. "You will not let me hide from the truth."

His temper did not sway her. "I wish to live free with you. We don't have the luxury of ignorance. Who are these men that you call runaways? Do you know who seeks your death?"

"I ain't believed this runaway to be a real person, but my mind has changed. I reasoned these ex-slaves run with a man–an ex-slave called Black."

Callie felt faint at his words. She had heard of Black. When she lived on the Parson plantation, she often dreamed he would come and free all the slaves. She never doubted that Black or his men were real. Her papa had spoken of Black, educating both her and her brother of a new type of nigger–one that had taken a stand against the system. Callie was terrified. She did not think he would survive against Black. She looked away, but Jeremiah was too discerning.

"So, you have heard of this ex-slave called Black?"

"Yes, I have."

"Do you understand why I must send you away?"

"I will not leave without you. I have had enough talk for now," she answered, cutting off all discussion. She stood adjusting the sheet about her. Callie placed the journal on the table and reached to the shelf on the wall above to retrieve the razor and other shaving items. Jeremiah walked over, seating himself. She groomed him carefully, lovingly, and he leaned back and closed his eyes.

Callie completed the task of grooming him and moved to the chest to begin dressing. Jeremiah's voice was deep–gritty, as it floated around the cabin. "Rest with me for a while before you leave to help Ella."

Jeremiah stood and dropped his towel, stepping into the bath water. Callie moved to the side of the tub to help him bathe. When he was done, she fetched his towel, as he stepped from the tub, moving to stand by the fire. Callie draped the sheet wrapped about her over the bed and climbed in naked.

The cabin was quiet for a time, save for the crackling of the fire. She watched as he moved to turn the lantern down, casting the one room into a dim light. At the side of the bed, he pulled back the sheet and climbed in. He did not attempt to cover them once he was settled.

Callie lay on her side facing him; she smiled when he reached out and caressed her shoulders. His hands moved down and cupped her breasts. She moaned. Callie felt awkward when his hands trailed down her body. He palmed her belly with both hands–their child moved, responding to his touch. Jeremiah's eyes bounced back to hers, visibly shaken by the intimacy. No words passed between them, as she allowed him to continue exploring the different levels of love happening between them. Leaning over, he kissed her deeply, and she heard him groan.

When he leaned down and kissed her belly, the baby moved just as his lips made contact. He chuckled, and she could see that he was fascinated. She too was captivated by the tenderness they were experiencing. He shifted his weight, pulling her close to cuddle with her. Callie held him and ran her fingers through his hair.

"You are so beautiful," he whispered.

"I don't want you to see me getting fat."

"I never thought to feel the child move." His wonderment was evident.

"Me either."

Jeremiah pulled back suddenly and settled with his back to the headboard. She allowed him to pull her onto his lap. She sat astride him, feeling exposed. She attempted to cover herself, but he wouldn't let her hide from him.

His voice was desperate, when he whispered against her lips. "Please don't. I want you to share yourself wit' me."

She moved her hands away, and he fingered her right nipple. The baby had stopped moving, and he seemed disappointed. Callie could feel his hard member pressed against her backside and she found that she wanted him just as badly. Outside, the rain continued in a steady downpour. She had never felt so loved, and she didn't want the moment to end. She leaned forward and kissed him. Jeremiah whispered two words that she felt in the pit of her belly.

"Ride me."

When she slid down onto him, it felt so good she threw her head back and moaned. Jeremiah's large hands cupped her rear, lifting and dropping her effortlessly onto him. She clutched his shoulders to steady herself as she settled into a delicious pace.

"I love you, so much."

"Easy, woman, ya feel too damn good." Jeremiah's voice was gravelly.

He pinned her to him on the downstroke to stop her movements. Callie leaned forward brazenly and bit his lip. He released her, and she began moving up and down until he pinned her to him again. She rode the edge as she felt the buildup happening between them. She didn't want him to leave her, but she knew her climax would make him follow.

She leaned in and whispered without shame, "Can we change positions?"

"Yes," he groaned.

She thought he would move on top of her, but he didn't. Instead, he pulled her up on all fours and entered her slowly from behind. When he was planted firmly against her womb, he pulled her back onto her knees. Jeremiah snaked his arm around her and began to apply pressure to her clit with his fingers. Against her ear, he told her his thoughts, and his words enflamed.

"This ain't help none, I'm 'bout to burst."

Mindlessly, she moaned as he instructed, "Hold onto the headboard for me."

She entwined her fingers with his, as he helped her reach out for the head of the bed. Roughly, he pulled her waist out just a bit, for better access. His movements brought tears to her eyes as pleasure splintered through her. There was no place Callie would rather be at this moment than connected to the father of her child. And she told him so.

"Shit," she hissed, "I love when you're inside me."

On the edge pleasure, Callie heard him half chuckle and half groan. She felt his grip tighten on her hips as his movements became frantic. She shuddered. Every stroke was amazing as he brought them to conclusion. She leaned her head forward in complete surrender as orgasm rode her being. She felt him stiffen. As they called out their love and need for one another, thunder clapped in the background, accentuating the intensity of their coupling.

They collapsed with Jeremiah spooning her from behind. He snuggled close to her, placing his large hand on her belly. Against her ear, he whispered, "I love you, woman, more than words can say."

As Callie lay drinking in the smell of him, the sound of his heartbeat and the feel of his skin against her own, she realized she would die without him.

❀ ❀ ❀

It had been two days since Jeremiah had gone to the main house. He couldn't face Ella, and though he had never been *unkind* to her, neither had he been kind. Discussing his papa's papers with Callie had opened old wounds while shining a light on memories long forgotten. He could see Ella helping him as a child when he had fallen and scraped his knee. He recalled her dressing him warmly in the winter and making certain he had eaten. Looking back, he now remembered being sick as a child and Ella nursing him back to health.

At the tender age of ten, he had been pushed into the fields and life had become hard. E.J. had become his constant, and he had not looked again to the old woman. Still, she cleaned his clothes, fed him and did her best to keep him away from Sonny. He did not like the key man, and now he remembered why.

Jeremiah recalled seeing his mother arguing with Sonny. What they argued about was unclear. In his mind's eye, he could see angry facial expressions from the past, but no words came with the memory. His mama had cried, while Sonny yelled. As a child, he feared Sonny, but as a man, anger had replaced fear.

Ella was always anxious whenever he and Sonny shared the same space. As a field hand, he had not seen much of Ella–she was a house nigger. He had his own cabin and a slave girl who hauled his dirty clothes to Ella for laundering. She would send food back to him, but they did not converse unless they had too. Eventually Hunter Sr. had given him two guns and a room on the second floor. His job was to safeguard the interests of his white family. He was the only nigger with a gun for miles–he used it to protect and keep order among the slaves.

It was a tactical move by Hunter Sr. to put him in place, and Jeremiah had taken to being ruthless without issue. When E.J. had returned home and taken his rightful place as heir, his slave brother had become the new heavy. Now, both he and his brother could care less what happened that fateful day to their papa. Still, he could not leave the plantation. He had no real skills. How would he care for his woman and child? There was only one choice available to him: accept the help of his brother to keep his little family safe. He could not straddle the fence any longer on whether he would send her away. He would indeed send her and the child to safety–against her will.

Jeremiah had come home early, bathed and went to bed. When he awakened, he dressed and headed for the main house. It was late morning as he moved slowly through the slave quarters. He found that he was emotional about all he had learned. Still, he pressed on until the main house came into view. He circled to the back of the house and stepped into the kitchen. Callie was chopping vegetables at the counter. Ella was seated at the table peeling potatoes, and Eva was sweeping the pantry.

Sonny appeared at the opposite door, pushing a tea tray. When

Callie noticed him, she stopped working and came to him. She smiled and touched his arm.

"Is there something you need?"

He gazed down at her. Callie's hair was parted down the middle and braided in two fat cornrows. She was perfect in motherhood. His woman was trying to offer him support; she knew his pain, though he never voiced it.

"I needed to speak with Sonny," he said.

Jeremiah could see Callie's displeasure. She knew what he was about, and she did not like it. He also knew she would curse him later—for now, she would hold her peace. She turned away and resumed the task of chopping vegetables. Everyone continued to move about as though he wasn't there until he spoke to Sonny from across the room.

"Key man, I need to talk with you. Come wit' me."

Sonny stopped working to stare at him, before moving to follow him. As Jeremiah turned to walk out the back door, his eyes locked on Ella. Her hands shook as she worked the potato, but she did not look up from the chore. He sighed; he could not speak with Sonny without first speaking with Ella.

"Meet me at my cabin in two hours." Jeremiah said.

Sonny nodded, about to turn back to his chores, when Jeremiah said to the room at large, "I need to speak with Ella—alone."

Ella's eyes popped up to meet his, and he stared at her for a moment. He was seeing her differently as she sat before him in her black dress and white apron. Her hair was plaited in two braids and pinned at the crown of her head. In his peripheral, he saw that Sonny was reluctant to leave the kitchen. Eva and Callie gently encouraged him into the hall. When they were alone, he stood for several more moments collecting himself. His grandmother broke the silence.

"Has I done sumfin wrong?"

He was unsure how to proceed and asked tersely, "Am I your grandson?"

Ella instantly covered her mouth before looking away to gather herself. He worried that he should go get Callie, since he didn't know what he was doing. They had not even started dialoguing and the old lady was about to cry.

She cleared her throat and whispered, "Yes, I's yo' grandma."

He crossed his arms over his chest. She seemed to be holding it together, so he continued, "I suppose you ain't tell me because you find me to be unkind."

"I ain't tell ya cause I ain't want to speak on Flower."

He nodded and swallowed hard. "I loved my mama."

"And she loved you."

"When I thought she was sold, I figured to see her again."

"I knowed ya thought she was 'live. I ain't speak on her to keep ya going—wasn't nothin' we could do."

"Somehow, thinking she lived helped me. Now, knowin' she been dead all this time..." He turned his back to her and stared out the open back door.

"As a man ya has to see separating a mama and child weigh two pounds. Killing yo' child's mama weigh two pounds. The deeds measure the same, there ain't no relief here."

Ella struck a nerve with her words. He was more like his papa than he thought. Jeremiah could see the changes he needed to make, but time was not on his side. He stepped away from the subject of his mother.

"I was wantin' help from Sonny. It ain't nothing for you to worry after."

He saw her visibly relax, and he felt shame. Ella was right, selling his mama and killing her weighed the same. Jeremiah was about to leave the kitchen, he needed space. "Yo' mama loved him. I couldn't get her to see reason. I was sad when the masta laid eyes on my chile. Hunter Sr. was a mean man. I knowed my chile wasn't gon survive him. When he taken a wife, yo' mama cried for weeks. She began courtin' wit' Wilbur, an old field hand. Hunter Sr. hanged po' Wilbur and ya mama..." Ella paused as if reliving the pain— "he stabbed her til' she bled out."

Jeremiah turned and stared at her; he could find no words to add to such a story. When he found his voice, he said, "Can't be much better for you wit' me being just like him."

"I feels worry between you and Sonny. Yo' uncle cain't handle you," she whispered.

"I saw Sonny arguing with my mama when I was little. I guess I ain't liked him since."

"Ya did. Sonny wanted for Flower to stop seein' Wilbur. He worried Hunter Sr. would kill her. But yo' mama wouldn't listen to reason. Like she ain't understand she was a slave," Ella said, wringing the corner of her apron and staring off into space.

"I understand ya love Sonny. I am sorry for my conduct wit' him. It ain't to be your worry no more. You have my word."

She nodded. "I loves you too; ya just mean as hell. I figure it's what's keepin' ya above ground. I know some slaves that been dealt worser hands. I's still standin' and Hunter Sr. ain't. I felt glee when they tell me he passed on."

She whispered the last part, and Jeremiah chuckled. It was better that his papa was dead, for he would have killed him and been hanged. Ella read his thoughts. "I know ya woulda killed him. I ain't tell ya to keep ya live. Callie rubbed me wrong–now I sees she good for ya."

Jeremiah grinned at the mention of Callie. He did not comment, but he nodded as he headed for the back door. He lingered in the doorway for a moment; he wanted to say so much more, but his words and emotions were again out of reach. Turning back to Ella, he gazed intently at her before disappearing into the noon sun. As he walked back to his cabin, he realized life was ending for him. It was why answers to unasked questions were being revealed. Still, he was at peace with his death, for he knew his brother, Eva, Sonny and Ella would help Callie. He had to trust they would keep her safe, because he could feel the rapid passage of time. Lastly, he stayed away from all thoughts of the uprising–Betsy's missing child and her death at his hands.

15

Washington D.C.
Life in the Capital City

JAMES, BLACK AND the other men arrived in the capital city at midnight. The men moved about the city's main thoroughfares under the cloak of darkness to get a feel for the atmosphere. James observed that it was just as Mable said it would be. Throughout the main drags were large and small camps of soldiers with bonfires burning. The weather was stifling and the small breeze that blew off the Potomac River offered no respite. The capital smelled of unwashed bodies and horseshit—military life was sobering.

By daybreak, the men had located a place to set up. Their campsite would be further upstream on the banks of the Potomac River, along with several other groups of colored men and women. These clusters of ex-slaves represented colored people who wanted to join the war effort. Yet, the patriotism shown by ex-slaves and free Negroes was overlooked by the powers that be. Colored camps were pushed to the outer limits of the city, but Shultz pointed out the positive.

"Our position further up the bank of the river will ensure disease free water."

James stood on the sidelines and listened as Black, Tim, Bainesworth and Shultz conversed about their next steps. He took in what would be his home for the next few weeks. The men pitched small tents for sleep and shelter against the mosquitoes and flies. The campground was some one hundred feet from the river, convenient enough to deal with the needs of the horses. As James stood in the shade, he noticed the leaves had begun changing colors. The sun was breaking through the trees, dappling the ground with radiant patches of golden light.

A small gathering of camp dwellers had formed, causing the men to become alert. After some time, it became clear that Black was recognized. Ex-slaves or kin of loved ones who had received his help in the past lined up to greet him. As always, Black was gracious as he moved into the crowd greeting people and shaking hands. There were also white abolitionists in the midst of the gathering who had heard of Black or had worked with him in other endeavors.

Elbert spoke softly to James. "Black hates this part, but he handles it well."

"He does." James agreed.

"He wants to remain a ghost, but that is not happening, and this is only day one," Elbert continued.

"Shit, he gon make this easier for us; ain't no sense in him being a ghost," James scoffed.

As James stared around, he noticed the men had begun silently breaking down into shifts and groups. It was a sign that they were ready to execute the plan. His eyes moved to Black, who was now speaking with a young dark-skinned woman. She looked to be about eighteen summers, and she was lovely. He was taken by surprise when, without warning, Fannie entered his mind. James had successfully pushed the pain of Fannie from him by keeping busy. He had Abby and his son; he had even taken care of Rose's safety. Still, at this moment, he felt sorrow, and it compromised everything.

He stepped away from the group and walked toward the bank of the river. His hands shook, as he pulled his flask from his back pocket and drank deeply. He tried to breathe, but his chest constricted. Outwardly, he appeared his normal, calm self, yet inside he had become unglued. Staring at the water and listening to the tranquil sounds of its movement helped him. He needed Abby, and he wished he could hold her. Once more he pulled in a deep breath, and his chest finally loosened. James turned back toward the camp and the mission with a renewed vigor.

Tim, Shultz and Bainesworth had taken one large room at the Willard Hotel. The room was on the second floor and the window faced 14th Street. The ambassador made use of his status as a diplomat to secure them lodgings. It was late afternoon on the first day when the trio walked four blocks to 10th Street. Capital City Dry-Goods was wedged between Roth's Haberdashery and Aunt Betty's bakery. Its storefront boasted of two large windows with the words "Capital City" painted decoratively in orange. The haberdashery, on the right, had one large window and a narrow entranceway. The advertisement on Roth's front window read "Gentlemen's Apparel" in white block letters. At the bottom of the window sat a handwritten sign that read, "We dress soldiers." To the left of the dry-goods store was the bakery and like Roth's, it had one large window. The words on the window were simple and inviting. "Welcome to Aunt Betty's Bakery."

Tim did not rush into the store. Instead, he looked about taking in his surroundings. Directly across the street was a park. At one side of the common area were camps of soldiers. On the other side were families strolling along in the late afternoon sun.

Trees with leaves of green, gold, and red lined the pathways. Opposite the trees were benches for those who enjoyed the outdoors, although the air was quite stale. On the next street was a large public stable that stretched on for two city blocks. The banging sounds alerted Tim to the presence of a blacksmith. He could also see the comings and goings of several different horse drawn vehicles.

Tim shielded his eyes as he looked in the direction of the stable. Three colored men were working outside the entrance. Black could be seen shoveling horse dung from the walkway. Gilbert was moving a buggy, and Frank was sliding the great stable door to an open position. The men were already assuming their posts. Turning back to Bainesworth and Shultz, he nodded to let them know he was ready to enter the store.

The bell over the door chimed when Shultz entered the store. Tim followed him, and the ambassador trailed behind. The store was set up like a maze of shelves, and the hardwood floors were covered with sawdust. The place smelled of leather and saddle soap. On first glance, the store was organized and clean. At the front of the store, standing behind a high counter stood the proprietor. The clerk was a tall thin, white man of about forty-five summers. He had short gray and black hair with frosty blue eyes. His lips were set in a hard, thin line. He wore a crisp white shirt with a black bowtie and strapped to his upper right side–his gun. Tim noticed dried blood on the handle, a testimony of this man's ability to do violence.

The clerk did not smile or greet them. He stood stone-faced, as he stared from person-to-person. If the man were not standing, Tim would have thought him dead for his pallor did not speak to health. Stepping forward, Tim reached out his hand and made the introductions.

"Good afternoon, I'm Will. I come to look in on Maynard."

The clerk looked down at his hand but did not extend his

own. Tim looked over his shoulder at Shultz before exaggerat-edly examining his hand. The clerk's voice was deep with an air of menace.

"Is there something I can help you gentlemen with?"

Tim was jumpy in the company of such a fellow. In the inter-est of safety, he thought the public would be best served if this man were murdered. There was something so alarming about the clerk's energy it could not be missed. Tim could also see that the man was sizing him up. In an effort to gain control, he stared at the clerk for a few moments before addressing Shultz who stood behind him.

"Doctor, it seems we come to the wrong place," Tim said.

Turning on his heels, Tim walked past his two comrades. "I ain't got no time for bullshit," he said, heading for the exit.

"I'm positive Maynard said this is the place," Bainesworth called out after him.

"I see taking direction from Maynard was our first mistake," Shultz added.

Tim was almost to the door, with Shultz and the ambassador quickly following, when the clerk spoke up. "Maynard is my kin. I'm Herbert."

Tim turned back and stared at the man; he could see no resemblance to Maynard. Tactically, he stood, leaving the burden of conversation to Herbert. As he weighed the clerk's demeanor, Tim realized that once the deed of taking Lincoln was done, this man would likely kill all involved, *except* Maynard. Herbert was in place for cleanup, and he looked the part.

"After dark tomorrow, we will meet here in the store." Herbert's southern accent dragged on each word.

"Who is we?" Tim asked.

"After dark is when we will meet. At the end of the corner, there is an alley that will lead you behind the buildings. Do not come to the front of the store. Either you will be here, or you won't," Herbert responded, his voice as dead as his appearance.

The three men left the store. Once on the street, he saw Black and Gilbert look up from their tasks. They would not make open contact with Black and the men again until this matter was brought to a close. Tim did not rush away from the dry-goods store; his goal was to look nonchalant and comfortable in his skin.

Tim looked up the block in both directions, then turned toward the bakery entrance. The sweet smells of cookies, cakes and breads stimulated his senses. He had not eaten in hours, and his stomach growled. Out in front of them was a glass counter with all types of delectable treats. Standing behind the counter was a portly white man with gold wire glasses. His hair was completely gray, and he was bald on the top. He had dark eyes, a fat nose and a genuine smile. The atmosphere was airy and filled with life—the opposite of the dry-goods store. Next to the man stood a colored woman. She had very dark skin, dark eyes, and thick lips. Her hair was plaited in two thick braids hanging on either sides of her face. She was thin and slightly taller than the man. They both looked to be about sixty summers.

Upon their entrance, the woman moved in a little closer to the man standing to her left. They were both dressed for their profession. He wore a white shirt with a white apron and she wore a brown serviceable dress with a white apron. Both aprons were smeared in what looked like strawberries.

"Good day," the man greeted them warmly. "Welcome to Aunt Betty's Bakery. I'm Benjamin, and this here is Stella."

"Are you saying there ain't no Aunt Betty?" Tim asked with a chuckle.

"My aunt died when I was still a child. I use her recipes and have created some of my own. Stella is marvelous at baking," Benjamin replied casually. Apparently, he'd been asked the question before.

Stella smiled. Bainesworth stepped to the counter. "The place smells delightful. I would like a scone."

Stella reached for a napkin before sticking her hand in the glass case and pulling out a scone. She handed it to the ambassador, and he took a large bite, rolling his eyes with pleasure as he savored the treat.

"We has tea if you would like," she offered.

"Tea? Oh yes please," Bainesworth responded with enthusiasm.

Over in the corner were two small white tables with two chairs each. Bainesworth seated himself as Shultz surveyed the confections. "Is that an apple pie?"

"Yes, sah, it sho' is," Stella replied, "Would ya like tea too?"

"Absolutely," the doctor said with a smile.

I would like a slice of pie myself," added Tim, salivating.

"Sho' thang," Stella said.

When they were all seated, she served them. The pie was mouthwatering, and they ate in complete silence as she moved about refilling tea cups. When Tim was halfway through his second slice of pie, Stella began to make small talk.

"Y'all new 'round here?" she asked.

"We just passing through," Tim responded.

"Where ya headed, if ya don't mind my asking?" Benjamin asked.

"We are here to enlist. We're headed wherever military life sends us," Tim replied.

As if on cue, the ambassador said, "We went to the dry-goods store next door. He wasn't a very welcoming fellow."

The woman breathed in sharply, but said nothing. Benjamin moved closer to the table and whispered, "Stella is afraid of the man next door. She thinks he isn't safe to be around."

Shit, Tim thought the same and casually asked, "Looks like you all been here for years. Do ya not get along with the owner of the dry-goods store?"

"Mista Archie was a wonderfa man. Cain't says I knows this man," Stella replied.

Benjamin dismissed her with a wave of his hand. "Stella thinks the man next door killed Archie and took over the store. But Archie was getting old and decided to hire help. He went to visit some family."

"In all the years we been here, Mista Archie been steady 'bout opening the sto' everday. He ain't never spoke on no kin. He love that sto'. I cain't see it—him going on a holiday for three months. He come by ever mawning for his coffee and warm buttered bread. I just thanks he woulda told us," the woman opined.

Tim exchanged looks with Shultz and Bainesworth. The conversation changed to small-talk once more as the men finished their pastries. Shultz and the ambassador strolled over to the bakery case one last time to get goodies to take with them. Tim looked out the window. It was getting late and the sun was low on the horizon. He pondered what Stella had said about Mr. Archie. Tim had no doubt he was dead. This was a variable they hadn't figured on in the execution of their plans.

Stella walked them to the door as Benjamin cleared their table. She leaned in and whispered to them, "Be careful 'round here. Ole Benny thanks I's crazy, but I'm ain't."

The men promised to be careful and also promised to return. Once on the street, they walked in the opposite direction of the dry-goods store so as not to cross in front of the large glass window. They took the long way back to the hotel. As they moved along the street, the lantern lighters were fast at work illuminating the area. They stopped just before they got to the hotel.

"I think it's safe to say the owner of the dry-goods establishment is dead," Bainesworth offered. "Whoever this man is to Maynard, I don't see him as trustworthy. I believe he is aware that you roughed Maynard up."

"I agree about Maynard. Is this man part of the plot to kill

Lincoln or is he part of a plot to kill us? It could be that they decided not to work with us and want us dead. Shit, I can't make it out," Shultz said.

"All of that crossed my head. Herbert don't look like he gives a damn about politics. I believe we need to act fast or it won't just be Lincoln's ass that gets knocked off," Tim said.

"I must agree. Shall we meet with Black?" The ambassador asked.

"Yeah," Tim said, "I say we make contact with Black and the men at midnight."

It was past midnight when Black and the men stood on the edge of the camp speaking in low tones. Tim, Bainesworth and Shultz rode in on horseback and joined the group. They kept a small fire and all of the twenty were present. This was not a scheduled meeting, and it was clear that a problem had arisen. Some of the men stood, while others sat on the ground with their arms wrapped about their knees. The fire danced offering a dim light of gold and blue hues. Visibility wasn't perfect, but Black didn't need more light to discern that the structure of their scheme had changed. Tim was the first to speak.

"We made contact at the dry-goods store. The man running the store is unstable. After speaking with the people running the bakery next door, the woman believes he killed the owner and took over the store."

"Is he the contact you all were supposed to meet?" Black asked.

"He says he is—and he gave the correct name," Shultz replied.

"Then the fact that he killed the owner is of no consequence. They needed a set-up, and he made one," Elbert reasoned.

"Bollocks. I say we put him down—it's one less cog that will need managing," Bainesworth asserted.

"The ambassador got him a point," James said.

"We are to meet with him in the coming evening. The problem—if we kill him before we can get them all together, it could ruin the plan and expose us," Tim said.

"Ain't the plan to kill 'em?" Lou asked.

"Yes, but the plan is to put all of them down. If we kill him too soon, we leave the job unfinished. The extra point here is that I shook up the fellow, Maynard. I saw it in the shopkeeper's eyes; he was sizing me up," Tim said.

"Kirk did say they had three men watching Lincoln's every move," Shultz said, as if just remembering the fact.

Black listened as the men tossed around different possibilities. When he finally spoke, his thoughts were methodical. "These men are a small part of a bigger group. Even if we kill the men in this smaller sect of the Preservers of Southern Life, more will rise up. Still, we intended to kill them to neutralize the immediate threat. We will not get them all—that is just a fact. I say we put these men down swiftly. Even if we don't get all six of them, we will cripple their operation and create doubt. This will give us time to caution Lincoln on the issue of safety. The goal here is to warn the Union president of the plot on his life and put him in charge of his own protection—he has the means, we do not."

Black glanced from man to man, waiting for a response. When none came, he asked, "Is there any among you who does not understand what I am saying?"

"May I try for clarity's sake?" Bainesworth asked.

"Of course," Black responded.

"The good doctor, Tim and I should take this meeting. If Maynard, Kirk, and Howard—along with Booth and Samuel— are present, we should kill them. Is this correct?"

"There are several issues which need to be addressed," Black said. "There are camps of soldiers set up all over the city. We can't just go in shooting the place up. As Elbert stated, discretion will be key. The statement about the three men who watch Lincoln's every move is vague. If they have men close enough to watch his every move, we will not see them. They are in the fold and cannot risk being found out. The men in close contact with the president will not be part of this meeting."

"Agreed," Tim said.

Black went on. "There will be signs that will let you know how this meeting will go. It is their actions that will determine if we kill them at this meeting or the next."

"Signs?" Shultz asked.

"If he is there with all the players you recognize, then we can listen to their plan. If he is there alone, then he has not been truthful, and it is a trap. If all the participants are there *except* Maynard, then it is still a trap and the possibility of other threats are real," Black explained.

"We will be at the back of the dry-goods store around nine-thirty pm," Tim said.

"And we will be in place at nine," Black affirmed.

Tim, Bainesworth, and Shultz headed back to the Willard Hotel to ready themselves for the night ahead. Black and the others continued to strategize about how they would move forward. Though Black remained calm, he realized that colored men in the throes of even a good deed could end up paying with their lives. This thought plagued him. Still, to offer even indirect assistance to the queen was better than a refusal. There was too much at stake to stand on pride–he and the people needed Fort Independence. He did not wish to be challenged for his land.

❊ ❊ ❊

The men rested in shifts and when dawn broke they readied themselves for the day ahead. In the few hours since they set up camp, other groups had begun blending with them. The people wanted to be near Black, which made it difficult for the men to discuss matters. But there was still an upside to it all. The people were eager to help them find jobs that set them up in ideal places for the mission. The belief among the colored folks was that Black was there waiting for the opportunity to soldier alongside them.

Women had joined the camp; they cooked and washed clothes for the men. Still, the men understood Black's rule about mixing work and pleasure. James had taken fresh clothing from the hand of the sweet, dark-skinned girl who reminded him of Fannie. She smiled at him, but he did not reciprocate. The young woman had three large plaits in her hair, with the front braid pinned away from her face. She had huge eyes, a wide nose and thick kissable lips. Unlike Fannie, she was curvy. She wasn't Fannie, but she favored her enough to make James uncomfortable. He made it a point not to ask her name. He bowed his head to her in thanks and turned away, almost running for the river.

The temperature was chilly even as the sun made its way into the sky. But James couldn't feel the coolness in the air. As he made his way up the riverbank to a secluded spot, the only feeling that registered for him was the tightness in his chest. He removed his boots and gun first, then the rest of his clothing. Stepping from the bushes, he walked nude to the river's edge. A small wave wrapped about his ankles, and the water was shockingly cold. It was just what he needed. He moved further into the water before completely submerging himself. Silence enveloped him as he drifted along with the current. Finally, when he felt stress on his lungs, he broke the surface, drawing in a deep breath. It was a rebirth of sorts, essential to get him through the day.

He swam and floated for a bit, allowing himself to relax. When he looked toward the bank, he saw the sun penetrating the leaves and brush. In his side view, Black, Elbert, and Luke were walking upriver. He quickly swam to shore and dressed.

"I been shoveling horseshit most of yesterday. I stink." Black said, as he stripped himself.

James laughed. "Yeah, ya do."

Elbert and Luke followed Black into the water; James kept watch from the bank. By ten, they were all bathed, dressed and ready to mount their horses. Black discussed some last-minute details to make certain everyone was clear.

"James, you are to set up a shoeshine stand on the corner near the president's home. The woman Elizabeth should be visible this afternoon," Black instructed.

"Done," James answered.

"Elbert, you are to set up a shoeshine stand by the hotel. We need to watch Tim's, Shultz's and the ambassador's backs. Luke will be your partner."

"Yeah," Elbert said.

"Frank, Lou, Jake, and Gilbert will be with me at the public stable. We will watch the dry-goods store and keep Tim and the others covered. At nightfall, Jesse, Emmett, Anthony, Josiah, and Ralph will take their positions in the park across from the store. Herman, Horace, John and Ephraim will watch the camp," Black concluded.

The men broke camp, headed toward their goals for the day.

❋ ❋ ❋

The Willard Hotel, for all its grandness, lacked something to Tim's way of thinking. It was wartime and life was expensive, but the ambassador had money for creature comforts. They stayed in a large room that boasted of a huge, four-poster bed with satin sheets and lots of pillows. At the front of the room was a settee that wasn't comfortable to sleep on, but it was better than the floor. Next to the couch was a matching, straight back upholstered chair. The three took turns shifting among the furnishings. The ambassador could sleep standing if need be, he wasn't picky. They kept the window closed to keep out the smell of manure from the street below.

As Tim, Shultz, and Bainesworth stepped from the grand

staircase into the busy lobby, the crowd was moving toward the dining room. The furnishings were simple, but the color scheme riotous. The walls were dressed in floral wallpaper, the carpet was burgundy, and the chairs placed strategically around the common area were varnished wood. The front desk was against the left wall and its counter was polished with great care. Two young men dressed in burgundy uniforms with shiny brass buttons stood behind the counter. On the opposite side of the lobby was an eatery with small tables covered with white tablecloths.

The three did not stop at the eatery, but continued out the main entrance onto 14th Street. When they stepped into the afternoon sun, the sidewalks were congested, and the roadways were hectic with horse and buggy traffic. Concerned about the pending meeting at the dry-goods store, Tim's goal was to walk about the city, learning the best routes. He needed to be prepared in case of an emergency.

At the left of the hotel entrance, on the corner of 14th Street, was a newly erected shoe shine stand. Tim recognized Elbert and Luke and moved in their direction. The closer he drew to the stand, the more he smiled.

Tim climbed into the chair and the ambassador climbed into the chair next to him. Elbert stood before them dressed in brown trousers, a white shirt that wasn't tucked in and black boots. The sleeves of his shirt were rolled up, revealing several, long-since healed scars. At his right hip, just under his shirt was a slight bulge. Tim was sure it was his gun. His appearance coupled with those lifeless eyes, ensured they were getting no customers. Luke looked more the part of a shoe shine boy than Elbert, but even he did not look subservient. Luke was dressed like Elbert, on down to the weapon. They were not shoe shine boys, and it was evident.

"Have you gotten many customers?" The doctor asked in a low voice.

Elbert glared at him before answering, "No, Nicholas, we haven't."

"I should say not. You look like you'll murder your patrons rather than shine their shoes," Bainesworth added, as he propped his booted foot up on the metal pedestal.

Tim put his head down and looked away to keep from laughing. Luke moved in and began shining the ambassador's boots, but Elbert just stared at Tim.

Tim cleared his throat. "Should I shine your boots instead?"

Elbert sighed in exasperation and seated himself before Tim.

Shultz caught everyone off guard when he asked, "Is James set up to make contact with Mrs. Lincoln's dressmaker?"

"He is," Elbert replied.

"Now I see Black's reasoning for setting you up here. The dressmaker wouldn't have talked to you," Shultz reasoned aloud.

"Mean looking bloke, that one. Why if I were a lady, I'd run screaming into the hills if I were to encounter him on the street," the ambassador added for good measure.

"Careful, Laverne, careful," Elbert said as he polished Tim's boot.

The ambassador smiled at Luke. "You missed a spot, my good man."

Luke rolled his eyes skyward, and the men had a private laugh before getting down to business.

"I'm scouting out the place. I'll make contact with James to make certain he's covered," Tim said.

"The rest of the men will be in place. Me and Luke will follow ya when night falls," Elbert added.

"If we don't kill this Herbert fellow soon," Bainesworth said, "the two in the bakery will be next."

Tim had not said as much, but his thoughts were the same. There was just something about the man in the dry-goods store that did not sit well with him. It was just one more matter that needed controlling. Black had been right, they did not have the manpower. Herbert was now on their list of victims.

❊ ❊ ❊

The Executive Mansion looked to James to be more like the main house of a plantation. The home of the president was set back from the street on a retaining wall. At the front of the mansion was a long, cobblestone horseshoe drive. The imposing home was white with several great pillars in the front. It also boasted of a well-manicured, rolling green lawn that further added to the plantation effect. Several colored gardeners worked tirelessly to maintain the refined appearance. Lastly, a black wrought iron fence separated the mansion from the street, though it looked more decorative than security based. James was unimpressed.

There was plenty of activity in front of the mansion and along Pennsylvania Avenue. Union soldiers moved about, setting up new camps and dismantling others. The energy was high, and from what James could see, dangerous. Colored men and women moved about selling food and helping the soldiers carry their gear. These efforts were sometimes met with violence; James watched as an older colored man was pushed to the ground as he attempted to shovel horseshit from the roadway.

Several of the soldiers had come to get their boots shined. But after services were rendered, they would walk off without paying. The day was shaping up to be a scorcher, and James' attitude was becoming just as hot. He had been called "nigger" more times in that day than in his entire life. He felt defeated, but rather than get himself killed, he was about to leave.

"I'm needing my boots shined, boy," a man's voice called out when his back was turned.

James was about to decline when he saw Tim approaching. Thankful to see a friend, he resumed his position, and Tim climbed into the chair. The ambassador and the doctor followed close behind, taking in the activity going on around them.

"Been like this since I got here. Some of the soldiers has orders and they movin' out," James said.

"Have you seen the dressmaker?" Shultz asked.

"Mable say she comes this way between two and two-thirty."

"It's getting close to two now. How are you going to get her to speak to you?" Shultz inquired.

Ain't sure. I'm shinin' shoes, honest work, but she workin' in the mansion. I'm gon try, but I don't see her giving me the time a day," James replied.

"You have a better chance than Elbert," the ambassador remarked.

James laughed. "Still don't make it no damn easier on me."

"I got a plan," Tim said.

"We ain't got days for me to get her to talk. I need help. What you thinkin' on?" James asked.

Tim hopped down from the chair and paid James. "You'll see...be ready."

The three walked away, leaving James to his shoe-shining. It was a quarter past two when James noticed a colored woman strolling toward him. She wore a plain, dark blue, long-sleeved dress with a white lace collar. Over the dress was a cream-colored shawl. Black curls peeked from under her bonnet, which was the same shade as her dress. She had light brown skin, small eyes, and a very large nose. Her lips were tiny and dwarfed by her nose, but there was no mistaking she was handsome.

She was almost upon him when Tim came out of nowhere and brushed past her, knocking her off her feet. As she fumbled with her skirts trying to stand, Tim stopped abruptly and glared at her.

"Why don't you watch where the hell ya going?" Tim said, offering her no gentlemanly assistance.

Shultz stood at his right side, the ambassador at his left, and they too glared at her. She stopped trying to get up and whispered, "I apologize to you, sir, it won't happen again. I beg your forgiveness."

Ignoring her apology, Tim took a threatening step forward. James intervened. "Is ya all right, Miss?"

The dressmaker feared Tim and did not look away from him. James hated the deception, but he stepped into his role, his voice deadly calm when he said, "Gentlemen, I ain't wantin' no trouble, but I manages trouble well if'n I needs to."

Tim turned his attention on James and fisted his hands at his sides. James allowed the homespun shirt he wore to move slightly to the left, revealing the gun jammed in his waist band.

"I'm outnumbered here for sho'," James said, "but one of ya won't live. On that I can promise."

Tim looked around as if weighing his chances before he backed away and stormed off. Shultz and Bainesworth followed, leaving James to focus his attention on the woman. He helped her up and brushed the dirt from her skirts, again feeling guilty over the sham. When she was more collected, he introduced himself.

"I'm James, and you is?"

"My name is Elizabeth. Thank you, Mister James," she replied, still glancing fearfully in Tim's direction.

"Is ya all right?" he asked.

"I am, just clumsy is all," she looked down in embarrassment.

"Where ya headed? I be happy to escort ya."

"No...no, I'm fine."

James smiled. "Miss Elizabeth, ya 'fraid to be seen wit' me?"

Her eyes watered, and he could see she was fighting the urge to cry. "I was told not to go walking today, but I—"

"Ya what?"

"I didn't want to be told what to do. Now I'm sorry I didn't listen."

She looked as though she were about to leave. James couldn't afford to wait until next Wednesday to see her again. He was trying to think fast on his feet, when he heard a crashing sound behind him. Tim, Bainesworth, and Shultz had knocked over his shoe-shine stand, dislocating the chair from the wood frame. A small crowd of Union soldiers had gathered in support of Tim. The soldiers were laughing, and Shultz looked anxious. James lunged forward, as if he were about to engage the men, but Elizabeth reached out and touched his arm.

"I'd like to walk this way," she said softly.

He looked down at her hand on his arm. Elizabeth gave it a firm squeeze. She was afraid. James nodded before turning and walking in the opposite direction. She looped her arm through his, and he could feel her trembling. The word "nigger" echoed at their backs. On the opposite side of the street, James spied Black and Gilbert watching them as they walked away. Black gave a slight nod and then disappeared into the crowd.

The sun was just starting to go down when the men regrouped at the campsite. Everyone was present except Tim, Bainesworth, and Shultz. It had been a rough and humbling day. It was quarter to eight when the men changed into all black clothes. There was no conversation as they broke camp to take their positions. It was the first step in the rest of a well thought out plan.

Tim, Shultz, and Bainesworth sat in the dining area of the Willard Hotel. The three were still shaken from the events of earlier that day. Two Union soldiers wanted to follow James and the woman to rape her. Tim thought they would have to kill them. Thankfully, the men were redirected by their commanding officer before it could escalate. He was happy when he noticed Black on the opposite side of the roadway.

Dinner consisted of roast duck, potatoes and carrots. Tim couldn't eat and neither could Shultz; Bainesworth, however, ate like a man condemned. They said nothing about the mission, as there were too many diners within earshot. High-ranking soldiers and their families filled the tables of the great room. Through a bank of windows to the left, Tim saw the shadows growing long. The time was near.

"Would you gentlemen like dessert?" A waiter asked them.

Tim looked at the ambassador, who checked his pocket watch. Bainesworth grinned and said, "I'd love a slice of chocolate cake."

The waiter, rushed off to do Bainesworth's bidding. Moments later, he returned with a mountainous wedge of cake. The ambassador ate without talking. His annoying humming and the clink of his fork against the plate grated on Tim's nerves. The waiter maneuvered between the tables and returned to remove their used dishes. When the table was cleared, the waiter offered coffee, to which they declined. They could delay no further.

Tim was grateful for the mild, balmy evening. Fall in Washington had not been what he had expected. They were about to walk toward 10th Street when a hansom cab pulled up on the street alongside them. Elbert was driving, and Luke hopped down to set the steps. The three men climbed in to find Black seated inside.

"It will be a long night. The goal is always to maintain life and freedom first," Black said.

"Yeah," Tim answered.

Inside the carriage was hot. The sound of people milling about, and the clip-clopping of horse hooves was the backdrop to an intense evening. It was a short ride to the dry-goods store. When the carriage reached 10th Street, Elbert made a left onto a side road. Before Tim opened the door, Black offered final instructions.

"Once you all step inside, we will lose contact—for that reason, anything you do will be considered a signal to move in. You will have fifteen minutes. If you don't want us to move in, step outside the back door to light a cigar. This will be your message for us to let the meeting continue. If you don't come out, we *will* come in. We have men in the park; they will create a distraction to cover the gunshots. Are we clear?"

"Yeah," Tim and Shultz echoed.

"Absolutely," the ambassador said.

Black reached out and handed Tim a cigar. Bainesworth opened the door, and the men jumped down from the carriage. Behind them the horse and buggy rolled up the block and turned the corner. The buildings on the side street were separated by a narrow alley. They had done this walk in the daylight hours, so Tim knew what to expect. The tight walkway let out to a small courtyard. The rear of the haberdashery, bakery and the dry-goods store faced them as they stepped into the clearing. To the left of the courtyard was a small grove of trees, and on the other side, another street. The back half of the block had not yet been developed.

It was pitch dark, save for the one lamppost that had been placed advantageously by the bakery's back door. The men's clothing store and the bakery were dark, with no signs of life. A bright light shone from beneath the door leading to the dry-goods store. Their boots made crunching sounds on the dry earth as they approached. They could still smell the sweet aroma of the bakery. Once at the back door, Tim looked at Bainesworth and Shultz one last time before he raised his hand to knock.

The door was abruptly yanked open before Tim could bang. Maynard stood in the doorway, flushed with anger. Behind him stood Kirk and Howard, but the sight of them did not put Tim at ease. Maynard spoke first, and his voice carried an authority that didn't sit well with Tim.

"Herbert said you all came by, but you didn't send a message as instructed. We thought you all weren't coming," he stepped back from the door to allow them entry.

Shultz entered first, followed by Bainesworth. Tim hung back, entering the store last. The doctor engaged Maynard, leaving Tim to evaluate the situation. "We would have left a message, but Herbert wasn't interested in speaking with us."

"No matter, we are here now," the ambassador said.

When the door closed behind them, Tim remained with his back to the door. As he stared around the room, he realized the situation was far worse than he thought. The back room of the dry-goods store was spacious, and it looked like someone's living space. On the right side of the room, against the wall, was a bed big enough for only one person. Next to the unmade bed was a pile of dirty clothes. There were several matching chairs in the center of the room, but there was no table. Directly in front of them was a closed door that Tim was sure led to the actual store.

A lantern sat on one of the chairs and a second lantern sat on the floor. Both were brightly lit. The place wasn't clean, but neither was it considered unclean. Kirk spoke up, directing his words at Tim.

"Will, glad to see you. Booth and Samuel have declined to move forward in our venture," he said, looking disappointed.

"I say we's betta off if they wasn't serious," Howard said as he stared around the room. "Welcome, gentlemen."

"Good evening," Shultz and Bainesworth responded. Tim just nodded.

Kirk was dressed in brown trousers and a white shirt. Tim noticed a small blood stain on his right shoulder. Howard was dressed the same, minus the blood stain. Herbert gave Tim pause, as he stood facing them. The storekeeper wore black trousers, a white shirt and black boots. He wore no bow tie and on the sleeve of his white shirt was a deep red blood stain. Each man wore a gun holstered to their upper left side, but Herbert wore his weapon holstered to his upper right side.

In the corner, behind Herbert was an unexpected confirmation of what Tim had already guessed about him. The heads of two spikes were visible in the floor and from both stakes, ran two chains. At the end of the four chains were two collars and two sets of cuffs. There was no sound coming from the corner, but Tim could see two naked women as they sat staring at him. One woman was colored, the other white, and both were badly bruised. Tim did not flinch when his eyes met Herbert's once more. The storekeeper smiled.

"Are we ready to get down to business?" Maynard asked.

The meeting had been underway for six minutes, and Tim would not be stepping outside to light the cigar. He spoke slowly when he addressed the room at large. "Two players have declined to show up, and still we held a meeting. We have no clue if they have gone to the authorities. I thought this mission called for ten men."

"We have three men on the inside; we will deal with Booth and Sam later. The men we have on the inside will not be able to step away. This is for their safety and ours," Kirk responded.

"We are here to discuss the plan. The presence of extra witnesses gives room for all of us to be damn hanged," Tim said, pointing at the women. "This situation speaks to failure when a man can't hold his strangeness in check."

"Now look here, Willie," Maynard replied, "the plan is your worry. Nothing else here is your concern."

Maynard was bold as brass now that he had Herbert backing him. Herbert smiled as he took a step forward. He addressed Tim in a flat, monotone voice. "Maynard here spoke on the fact that you think you in charge. But ya ain't in charge here, Willie–I am. My peculiarity *is* unquenchable, but that's for me to manage–not you, unless you are interested in addressing my needs. Ya might have manhandled Maynard, but that won't happen with me."

Kirk held up his hands, trying to defuse the situation. "Gentlemen, we are sidetracking."

They had been at it for ten minutes; Tim stepped cautiously to the left of the door. His movement seemed to agitate Herbert, who took yet another step in his direction. Maynard, who was still angry that Tim never returned his gun, said to Kirk, "We don't need them."

Tim ignored Maynard and addressed Herbert. "It appears you have to hold women hostage to get what you need. I can say for certain a man that can't handle women can't handle a fisti-cuff with me. You ain't managing shit, or we wouldn't be seeing this foolishness."

Herbert reached for his gun, but Bainesworth beat him to the draw. Shultz followed the ambassador's lead, aiming his gun at Maynard. Tim pulled his gun, keeping both Kirk and Howard in check. Maynard, Howard and Kirk had their hands in the air. Herbert, slowly but surely, continued to reach for his gun.

"I can assure you, my good man, I will blow your head off," Bainesworth said.

Herbert did not heed the warning. Bainesworth, true to his word, let off a shot, dropping his target where he stood. When his gun recoiled, the ambassador took aim again and shot Maynard, who reached for his gun. Shultz had moved in next to Tim and was holding his gun on Howard and Kirk. Maynard wasn't dead, but he was down and moaning. In the corner, the two women were now huddled together in fear.

Tim jumped back and pulled the door open. Black and the others filed in and went straight for the door leading into the store. Once they were sure the store was empty, they turned their attention to the back room. Frank and Lou set about releasing the women from their restraints. Tim and Black lingered in the darkened storefront, watching the fire in the park across the street. The soldiers were rushing about, trying to contain the blaze set by their men.

When Tim re-entered the back room, Maynard yelled, "You nigger lover. You ain't no true southerner. You a nigger lover through and through!"

Tim walked over and finished the job the ambassador had begun. Maynard's tirade was stopped mid-sentence as his body went lifeless on the floor. Jesse and Ralph tied up Howard and Kirk. Anthony and Emmett checked the pockets of the two dead men. Elbert and Luke then removed Herbert's body, heading toward the carriage waiting at the end of the alley. James and Gilbert carried Maynard out.

"They left the fat ass for me and you, Gil," James cursed as they labored down the narrow pathway.

Tim and Black turned their attention to Howard and Kirk.

"We want the names of the three people you have watching Lincoln," Black said, his voice low and calm.

Howard stood with his hands tied behind his back, glaring at Tim. He did not acknowledge Black. "Old Maynard was right 'bout ya, you's a nigga lover. I ain't finna tell ya nothin'. The Preservers of Southern Life will win—ain't no other way of life."

Black did not allow himself to be pulled in. Tim returned Howard's defiant glare. Behind them, one of the women cried out in severe pain as Lou attempted to remove the metal collar from her tiny neck. Tim's temper got the better of him and he pulled his gun, shooting Howard between the eyes. Blood sprayed on Kirk's face and clothing as Howard fell dead.

Tim raged. "You *will* tell us what we want to know!"

The women continued to moan in agony as the men worked to free them. "You have stopped nothing here this evening," Kirk declared. "We were nothing more than a secondary plan. If

Maynard doesn't check in, your president will be killed just the same."

Tim grabbed Kirk by the collar and yanked him down to the floor. Placing the barrel of his gun to Kirk's temple, he yelled, "Who's on the inside?"

Kirk laughed, as Tim held him by the hair, while banging his face into the floor. Jake and Josiah began the cleanup of the back room. Black spoke to Tim. "Put him down. Let us move on and get the women to safety."

Tim shot Kirk point blank. The bodies of Kirk and Howard were transported to the hansom cab that was immediately moved away from the scene. When the back room was set to rights, Tim removed all literature regarding Lincoln and the Preservers of Southern Life. Lastly, the women were wrapped in old blankets. According to Shultz, they were in bad shape.

Tim lifted the colored woman into his arms. She looked to be about eighteen summers and one of her eyes was swollen shut. His heart ached as she recoiled from him in fear. Her bottom lip was busted, and her face was swollen on the left side. She cried as she tried to push him away.

"*Shhh*, I'm not going to hurt you. I promise," Tim whispered.

"I hurts all over. I wants my mama," she cried, allowing him to lift her.

Bainesworth took the white woman into his arms. She too, was beaten badly and her face was black and blue. It appeared her arm was broken, and it looked to Tim like she had passed out as the ambassador moved with purpose toward the back door. Black turned down both lanterns and shut the door quietly behind them. At the end of the alley, another carriage driven by Frank and Lou waited for them. Black and the doctor climbed in first, helping Tim and the ambassador get the women into the cab. Behind them on 10th Street, the blaze was dying out. Frank drove away from the park, circling around to end up back on 10th Street. They began putting distance between themselves and the melee.

They rode in silence, and from the window, Tim could see soldiers running about, trying to out the last of the flames. The hospital on 7th Street came into view, and the carriage slowed then stopped. Black's voice drifted through the darkness.

"Drop her off and keep moving. Don't stay to answer questions. I'll take the colored girl back to the camp—the hospital won't take her."

"Yeah," Tim responded.

"I will come and look in on her in the morning," Shultz said, unable to hide his disgust.

"We need to execute the plan. With Maynard gone, the clock is ticking," Black said, using discretion in the presence of the women.

"I couldn't agree more," said Bainesworth.

Tim pushed the door open and hopped down from the carriage. The ambassador handed down the woman before he and Shultz jumped from the cab. Just before the doctor closed the door behind them, he addressed Black. "I can't help but feel they are one step ahead of us. If what Kirk said is true, *his* won't be the only death we have to worry about."

"James is in—we need to clean up and get out," Black replied.

The carriage rolled away, leaving the doctor, Tim, and Bainesworth standing in front of the hospital. It was a two-story brick building with several horse and buggies parked out front. The street was quiet. Tim carried the woman up the five steps and entered a well-lit hall. Bainesworth and Shultz followed close behind. A nurse was seated at the main desk. When she saw them, she came rushing forward.

"Lay her here," she instructed, motioning to a stretcher nearby. "I'll be just a moment. I'm going to get the doctor."

As she raced away to find the doctor, the three men disappeared into the night.

❊ ❊ ❊

Black rode with the colored girl in his lap. Unlike the white woman, the girl experienced longer bouts of awareness. He adjusted her in his lap as she wept from the pain. When she finally quieted, Black took a moment to think. He examined the problems at hand and the path was clear. They needed to get to Lincoln before he was abducted, or worse–murdered. He and the men also needed to figure out who was watching the Union president and possibly them. Black missed his wife and his daughter– he missed his family. But he couldn't go home without stepping properly through the plan while maintaining life and freedom.

Frank did some fancy driving to get the carriage to the edge of the camp. The women were in place and ready to help. Black carried the girl to a tent where the women would tend her. She had finally passed out from the pain, and he was thankful. Leaving her in the capable hands of the women folk–he left to tie off all the loose ends of the evening.

16

Hunter Plantation
October 1861

E.J. WAS SEATED behind his desk ordering supplies, when his mother in-law walked into his study. He instantly regretted that he had not closed the door, but he was attempting not to appear off limits to his wife. Suzanne was starting to show signs of life, though she was still skittish since the incident with the deserters. Julia spoke with him more often on his wife's behalf. He was becoming irked by the presence of his wife's family, though Maryam never gave him any trouble.

They had received word that Adrian Wells was finally on his way to fetch his wife and younger daughter. E.J. was grateful for the news. Julia had asked if Suzanne could come home for a visit and he had emphatically declined. It was unclear where his mother in-law had gotten the notion that she could run him. But she would have to be relieved of such an idea. He would also have to deal with Adrian Wells, for he had not given permission for him to marry Suzanne. Still, she was his now and for what it was worth, he loved her.

It was about eleven in the morning, and the curtains were pulled back from the open windows, allowing in the beauty of a crisp autumn day. Julia wore a dark blue taffeta dress and her hair was pulled back in a severe bun. When she spoke, she was demanding and condescending. E.J. was tired.

"Edward, I have decided to go riding this morning."

He was about to tell her that he did not think it safe, when she added, "I want Jeremiah to take me riding. I have ordered him to do so, but he refused. He has no right to defy an order."

E.J. put his pen down, leaned back in his chair and stared at her. He would have loved to have seen Jeremiah's reaction to being ordered about for sex. It was everything he could do not to laugh. He had not been this entertained in years.

When he trusted himself to speak, he replied, "You cannot go riding, Julia. It is too dangerous since the war started. Furthermore, Jeremiah would not be who I would choose to take you…ahhh…riding. Go walk the gardens; it's a lovely day."

Julia did not take kindly to being dismissed. "You will make Jeremiah do as I say. Perhaps my husband is right about you. Do you have a problem controlling your slaves?"

Though he tried to appear unfazed by her words, E.J. was boiling with anger. He chose his next words carefully, as if to drive home the point that he was in charge. "Once your husband has rested, you and Maryam are to make arrangements to leave Hunter Manor. I don't have trouble controlling my slaves. It's my unwanted guests I can't seem to regulate. As to my making Jeremiah service you–you might find your throat slit after your skirts come down. He is no longer a slave on this plantation. He is a free man who works as an overseer. You will not order about my help."

Julia gasped, but before she could add anything to the conversation, Jeremiah stepped into the study. E.J. decided to add insult to injury by stating the rules for all to hear. "It's perfect that you would wander in here at this particular moment. I was just informing my mother in-law that you are a free man and your job as an overseer does not include servicing my guests."

Jeremiah's eyebrows popped up. E.J. then proceeded to dismiss her. "We are about to discuss business. Please excuse us."

Julia turned in a flurry of blue skirts and stormed from his study. She slammed the door so hard, it caused the walls to shake, and the newly added portrait of his beloved mother swayed askew. Jeremiah grinned.

"I apologize for being desirable. I have tried–ain't no turning off my appeal."

E.J. was thankful for his brother's interruption and its redirection of his own anger. He was yet laughing at Julia's indignation when Jeremiah offered him a dose of reality.

"You just made an enemy. She needs to be gone from here."

"Agreed," E.J. responded.

❋ ❋ ❋

E.J. and Jeremiah met with the men to go over safety procedures. It had been a busy day, and though he was hungry, E.J. couldn't bring himself to sit at the table with his mother in-law. He lingered in his study, pacing and thinking, his anger mounting. When the hour had grown late, he stood stretched and headed for the back door. The evening was cool, and the air felt good against his skin. The moon was brighter and larger now that the trees had begun to lose their leaves.

He was going to Nettie's cabin. E.J. needed peace, and he needed sleep. He was about halfway in his journey when he sensed someone was following him. He looked back, but saw no one. Jeremiah moved about the plantation at night to make certain all was well. But his brother wouldn't stop him to converse when it was obvious he was going to Nettie. Unless there was an emergency, Jeremiah would remain invisible.

Once at Nettie's home, he saw the lantern light in the window. She was still awake. When he stepped up on the makeshift porch, the wood creaked under his boot. E.J. pushed the door open and found Nettie seated at the table, sewing. She smiled at the sight of him, and his heart squeezed at how welcomed she made him feel.

"Is ya hungry?" she asked.

"I am," he answered as he stepped over the threshold.

"I made yo' favorite—chicken stew and cornbread." She set aside her mending and stood to serve him.

Nettie was barefoot and wore a brown serviceable dress. He was attempting to dress her better and make certain that she knew he loved her. She still called him master, and to his shame, he had ceased correcting her. Each time she said it, he became aroused. E.J. found Nettie to be intelligent and a good listener. She eased his stress and though he worried about the future, he enjoyed the *now* with her.

He had not been seated at the table long when they heard footsteps on the porch. They were not booted and heavy—it was not his brother. There was a light knock on the door. E.J. stood with no shirt and strapped on his weapon. When his gun was in place, he approached and opened the door to find his wife standing on the porch. Suzanne's eyes were big as saucers, and there was no mistaking her hurt. His mother in-law was a bitch.

E.J. was nonchalant. "Come in."

Suzanne stepped into the cabin and stared from him to Nettie. She swallowed hard, and he patiently waited for her to speak. Behind him, he could feel Nettie's distress. Finally, his sweet wife found her voice, and he felt her pain.

"I had not believed you would treat me this way," she said, her voice cracking.

E.J. wanted to explain, but he didn't understand it himself. Suzanne had treated him as if he didn't exist and she had not come back to his bed. Assessing her, he now understood something he had not before. Julia was controlling the circumstance of his marriage. Still, he had fallen in love with Nettie, and it could not be denied. The fact that Suzanne had followed him to her cabin meant she loved him. E.J. did not know how to proceed. He was afraid to speak, for he wanted them both.

He cleared his throat. "It is not my goal to hurt you, Suzanne."

"I don't think it matters what you intended. The fact is you have hurt me, Edward."

Behind him, Nettie spoke up, "Masta, Imma step out sos'n you can speak freely."

"No, Nettie, that won't be necessary," he replied.

When Nettie spoke, it was as if Suzanne just realized she was still in the room. She stared at the slave girl as she addressed E.J.

"I want her sold from here, Edward. I want her gone by morning."

E.J. could feel Nettie holding her breath. He also understood that in order to get his life under control, he would have to be candid. There was no other way. He would set the expectation, so they could all move forward.

"No," he said. "I won't sell her."

"She is a slave, and I am your wife. If she is not gone by morning, when my papa comes, I will leave here!"

"You are my wife, Suzanne, and you will not leave me. I will not allow it," he asserted calmly, without raising his voice.

His wife was young, but this moment had aged her. He saw her eyes well up, and he too felt like crying. Taking her by the arm, he directed her away from the door. She looked as though she would bolt, and he didn't need the added stress of trying to find her. Reluctantly, she moved to stand in the center of the room, but away from Nettie. He moved a chair in front of the door and seated himself, while staring from woman to woman. They each refused him eye contact. E.J. sighed, as he leaned forward placing both elbows on his knees.

He gathered his thoughts and spoke carefully. "I love you, Suzanne. I have since the first day I laid eyes on you. But I will not sell Nettie. I love her, too."

Suzanne's entire body was shaking. "So, you are asking me to accept sharing my husband's affections with a slave?"

"I am asking you to see my attempt at being truthful, because I love you both. You are my wife; your status will not be diminished by this circumstance in our marriage. Slave owners have done this for years, and their wives have turned a blind eye. Surely, you are not so naïve. I am offering honesty because I refuse to treat Nettie poorly. There will be no one else; I can promise you that. The children I have with you will be my heirs, and the children I have with Nettie will be taken care of upon my death. I want to live in peace with both of you."

Suzanne was incredulous. "And if I refuse this madness?"

"Then you will join the ranks of women who have a marriage based on lies. If you grant me this, I will move heaven and earth to make you both happy. But, I will not sell her," he replied softly.

E.J. could see that she was overwhelmed. She sidestepped his request and asked, "May I leave?"

He was blocking the door. Nettie was anxious, and Suzanne was trembling. E.J. stood and walked over to Nettie. Cupping her face, he whispered. "I'll be back."

E.J. kissed Nettie softly, and soundlessly, she cried. Stepping back from her, he took Suzanne by the hand and led her from the cabin. Shirtless, the chill of the night air invigorated him. Suzanne had to run to keep up with him as he dragged her back to the main house. He wanted to wring Julia's neck, but that would have to wait. When they entered the back of the house, Suzanne pulled away from him.

"Where do you think you are going?" He asked.

Suzanne choked on her tears. "I am going to bed. I don't wish to see you anymore."

"You will share my bed. You will not sleep with your mother and sister another night," he said, realizing he missed her desperately.

"You would force me?" she asked, her nastiness apparent.

"I would force you to act as my wife–you have ignored me long enough."

"I don't want you to touch me. You have Nettie! She'll have to be enough," she hissed.

He ran his fingers through his hair and sighed. He backed away from his ire. This would get him nowhere, so he tried compromise. "It's not all about coupling, Suzanne. I miss you. Can you try to be my friend?"

"I wish I could be your friend Edward, but..." Her words trailed off as she sobbed. He wanted to comfort her, but she did not want his touch.

"But what?" he whispered.

"I was afraid after those men accosted us while riding. I slept with my mother and sister, because I was terrified. I came to our room several times because I missed you, but you weren't there. I know my father behaved worse to my mother with the female slaves. I just believed you loved me more and would be different. I am naïve, because I thought you a better man than my father. You are the same. I followed you because I wanted to believe I wasn't my mother. You have ignored me too, Edward. I guess we are even," she said, the fight gone from her.

"I am trying to tell you the truth because I don't want to lose you."

"There is no comfort in the truth, Edward. Maybe my papa does love my mama more because he lies to her to protect her feelings."

"I got involved with her while we were separated. I didn't think we would find ourselves married, the way things were going. I fell in love with her. Then we got married, and I found that I wanted you both.

"Would you have told me, if I had not followed you?"

"Yes, but later rather than sooner. I don't comprehend it myself, and it's hard to explain. I am scared to lose you," he said again.

"But not afraid enough to sell her?" she asked sarcastically.

"Don't do that."

She turned her back on him. "I am going to bed."

"You followed me and brought this thing to a head. You will sleep in my bed from here on out."

"So, you want me in your bed even when you're not there?"

"Yes."

"Are you always brutally honest?"

"With you–yes," he responded, and then he asked the question weighing most on him. "Did your mother encourage you to follow me?"

She did not answer. Instead, she asked another question that he never anticipated. "Would it be all right if I took a lover?"

Her words enflamed, and his father came to mind. In order to maintain communication, he did not answer. Stepping over her statement, E.J. held out his hand, and she took it. They went to his room, where he removed his gun and his boots. He kept on his trousers. Suzanne removed her dress with his help, but kept on her shift and pantaloons. He turned down the lantern that was left burning on a low wick for him, casting his bedroom in complete darkness.

E.J. allowed her in their bed first and climbed in after her. The balcony doors were open, and the moon shone down on them. He lay on his back with his hands behind his head. Suzanne lay with her back to him. She began to cry.

He rolled onto his side and whispered against her ear, "Can I hold you, please?"

"Yes," she whimpered.

He was thankful she was accepting his touch. She turned in the bed, and he pulled her close. Suzanne laid her head on his chest and wept. She was devastated and in truth, so was he. As he consoled his young wife, he worried about Nettie. They needed to find a way to coexist. And though his request was selfish, he needed to figure out how to be generous and loving. Above all else, he needed to be patient with both his women.

❀ ❀ ❀

Suzanne finally found sleep, but E.J. lay awake until dawn. He was concerned for Nettie and the anxiety he was sure she was feeling. He needed to get this matter under control. Suzanne did not confirm it, but he was certain his mother in-law incited the situation. It would change nothing. Nettie was with him to stay.

E.J. climbed from their bed, washed his face and pulled on a clean shirt. Seating himself in a chair at the French doors of the balcony, he watched the sun come up. The new day eased in with a blend of pink, orange and blue hues. He didn't want Suzanne to open her eyes and find him gone. Slighting her in any way after last night would not be good.

He heard her stirring, behind him. "Edward, I'm up, and I don't feel any damn better."

He smiled. "Come sit on my lap and watch as the new day comes."

E.J. thought she would refuse, but she scrabbled from the bed and came to him. She was still in her shift and pantaloons as she climbed into his lap and curled up against his chest. Suzanne was lovely.

They sat quietly for a few minutes until she asked, "Are you going to her? Is that why you're up, early?"

E.J. shifted in the chair. "I am up because I have work to do.

Yes, I will go to her. I know she is beside herself with hurt and fear. But I will not couple with her until you and I work through this."

"I want you to love only me," she whispered, bringing her eyes to his.

He understood her feelings, because he wanted her to love only him. As a man, he could demand that Suzanne and Nettie obey him, but he wanted to feel love from them—not resentment. He would not order—he would negotiate and beg. E.J. would not attempt to overpower.

"I love you, Suzanne," E.J. replied. "Nothing will change that fact. My love for her will not take away from your status in my life. I want you to try to get along with her. Nettie is not a threat to you."

"I don't want to get along with her."

"You will not have to worry about me fathering children with different slave women. There will only be Nettie, and you will be part of my life on all levels. You will be left out of nothing. I do not want to lie to you about anything. You will be different from your mother and women like her because you will be my true mate in all things. Please try. We will go at your pace."

"I don't wish to think right now," she said.

E.J. pushed no further.

❀ ❀ ❀

It was midday, when E.J. headed for Nettie's cabin. Off in the distance, he saw his brother speaking with Norman. When Jeremiah noticed him, he ended the conversation and moved toward him. E.J. was exhausted, and his brother looked worn out too.

"Why are you up?" E.J. asked.

Jeremiah gave a wry grin. "I'm up because I thought your wife or Nettie would kill you."

"So, you were nearby last night when Suzanne followed me. You could have offered some assistance."

"I did offer some assistance. I continued in minding my own matters."

E.J. glared at him.

"Ya need to get yo' women matters under control, so you can tend the important shit."

"You have Callie, so I know you understand that there is no such thing as getting women under control. I am ready for whatever comes our way, but I will live my life. I no longer give a damn what happened to *your* father. I am prepared to protect what we have built; don't nag me. I don't need an extra pussy."

E.J. stormed off to Nettie's with his brother's laughter at his back.

Nettie had opened both the front and the back doors of her cabin. Edward had not come back to her, and she had not slept. Though he had done more than she expected of him, she was still a slave and no match for his ivory-skinned wife. Life would become harder now that his wife knew of her. She had not made friends on the Hunter plantation because attachments only bred pain when it came time to be sold. She was twenty-five and had already been sold twice.

Nettie was a quiet person. As a slave, you lived longer if you listened rather than spoke. She had come from the Banks plantation in southern Mississippi. Her mother was a vague memory and her father a mystery. There had been a field hand named Joseph for whom she had felt some affection. The last time she saw him was at the old slave mart. Joseph had been dragged away in irons, and she had been purchased by Edward.

She had known immediately, she would warm his bed. Edward had not been able to take his eyes from her. She feared he would be unkind and certainly never expected to fall in love with him.

When he didn't come back, she suspected he would rather not

face her again. Nettie was sure he would send one of the overseers to collect her and take her to the auction block. She paced the back porch as waves of abandonment washed over her. She was dressed in the slave attire befitting her station and not one of the nicer dresses he had given her. Even the location of her cabin, set away from the slave quarters, indicated her status with the master. She gazed out into the grove of trees behind her house, watching their branches sway in the breeze. Their leaves were changing color. She breathed in trying to lose herself in the peace of the autumn afternoon.

When she turned to go back into the cabin, Edward was stepping through the front door. He did not advance into the room. Instead, he remained at the threshold, unsure of himself. His face was unshaven and his black hair an unruly mass of windblown curls. He did not look away from her, and she feared his rejection. He looked tired.

"I am sorry you have been left to worry," he said after a moment's pause.

"Imma slave here, ain't nothin' for you to 'pologize 'bout."

"So, you are angry with me for leaving with Suzanne?"

"I wants you to love only me. I wants you to set her aside, but I am a slave and colored ta boot. Yo' white and privileged woman ain't wantin me here. I's clear 'bout where dis is going."

"She understands that she does not have the power to send you away. I will not give her power over you. Suzanne is not a threat to you; I want you to try at friendship with her."

Nettie shook her head. "I don't like her."

E.J. grinned. "You don't know her."

She turned away from him. Her jealousy was getting the best of her. "I know when ya started comin' to my bed, ya ain't had no wife."

Nettie couldn't take the jealousy she was feeling. She heard his footsteps behind her. He placed his hand gently on her shoulder and turned her to face him. She started to cry, and he pulled her to him. His voice was deep and anguished when he spoke.

"It would make me happy if you both learned to love and support one another. Please try, Nettie."

"My taste don't run that way," she said, stepping away from him.

He raised his eyebrows and laughed. She tried to maintain her scowl, but his humor caught her, and she started giggling.

"You's nasty, Edward," she admonished him.

"First things first," he replied, wiggling his eyebrows.

❀ ❀ ❀

E.J. was up early; it had been a rough couple of days. Suzanne had arranged for breakfast to be served in his study–part of her ongoing effort to keep him separated from Julia. She had also begun assisting Ella with the meal planning. This morning she had elected to share a meal with him, and he was pleased. It was a sign of progress.

Suzanne looked as though she wanted to ask him a question, but she turned red and backed away from her words.

"What is it?"

"My mother doesn't like Jeremiah," she said, hesitantly.

"I know."

"It occurred to me, in light of what we are going through…" She blushed as her voice trailed off.

E.J. swallowed a mouthful of eggs and looked directly at her. "What occurred to you?"

"Well, my papa is old and Jeremiah–is not." She glanced over her shoulder to make sure none of the servants were within earshot. Then she leaned across the desk and whispered, "I think my mother wants to couple with him, and she's angry because he shows no interest."

E.J. sat straight faced, but he wanted to slide under the desk with laughter. She was incredulous that her mother wanted to be pleasured. He was, however, completely unprepared for her next words.

"It's amazing any farming gets done," she said over the rim of her teacup.

E.J. laughed, and it was straight from the soul. He didn't comment because he wouldn't discuss his brother, but he was thoroughly amused. Suzanne, ever prim and proper in her rose-colored dress and slippers, observed him without blinking. He was about to tell her how lucky he was to have her, when two gunshots rang out from somewhere in the distance.

Jeremiah appeared in the doorway of the study, his voice calm when he said, "I need to speak with you."

E.J. looked at his wife's fearful expression. "Suzanne, please fetch your mother and sister from the gardens and wait in the dining room for me."

She nodded and rose from her chair to do his bidding. When she was gone, E.J. addressed Jeremiah. "What has happened? Are we under attack?"

"Jeb rode out to a carriage rolling up on the property. Your father in-law was robbed and shot coming from the train station. It don't look good."

"How far out is he?"

"About half a mile."

"Shit!" E.J. hissed, as he went for the door.

"Another rogue group out and about." Jeremiah stated.

"I see it the same," E.J. replied.

They moved into the hall and headed for the front door. It was about eight in the morning and the sun was just sliding into position, when they stepped onto the porch. He could see the carriage as it neared. Jeb was standing at the bottom of the steps next to his horse.

"What are his injuries?" E.J. asked.

"He got him a gut wound," Jeb responded, "The coach driver says when they attempted to take his wedding ring Wells put up a fight. They got the ring anyway."

"Tell the men to bring a stretcher and a cot," E.J. ordered.

"Yessir," Jeb responded.

"Gut wound–ya might as well have his ass set up in the sitting room. He gonna be stretched out there tomorrow anyhow," Jeremiah said.

"You *are* an insensitive bastard," E.J. said, as he shook his head.

"Anything else would be setting yo' wife up to believe he gonna make it, and he ain't," Jeremiah replied.

E.J. stared at his brother, nodding slowly. Jeremiah was right. "Set him up in the sitting room. I'll go talk to the women."

He went back into the house and headed to the informal dining room. The women were seated at the table, wringing their hands as they waited. His sweet wife stood, moving toward him, and he hated having to hurt her again. Suzanne linked her fingers with his, as he stared at his mother in-law. His words were to the point.

"Your husband has arrived, but there has been a robbery. He was shot, and it doesn't look good."

Julia and Maryam collapsed into each other's arms and began to weep. Suzanne looked at him with tears in her eyes. "Is there a doctor around here?" she asked.

"Eva is the closest thing we got. She has some medical understanding. The nearest doctor is ten miles out, and he is elderly. Honestly, Dr. Murdock didn't seem all that efficient. I called on him for my mama," E.J. replied.

Suzanne, E.J. noticed, was thinking on her feet, while the other women were quietly hysterical. He was about to explain the next logical step, when Jeb and Jeremiah came down the hall carrying a cot. They helped set up in the sitting room, just off the dining room. Eva appeared, and Ella hovered in the background. E.J. nodded toward them.

"Come, Misses, so's we can get him settled," Ella said to Julia and Maryam.

Sonny rolled a cart containing the medical supplies into the sitting room. Suzanne pulled back the draperies for the best possible light. When she did so, E.J. saw the carriage as it approached the house.

"I'll go help the men." E.J. said.

Suzanne nodded, as he turned and headed back outside. Jeremiah climbed into the carriage, while Jeb and Gerry helped him from the exterior. Wells was a short fat man, and it took much to maneuver him from the cab. E.J. didn't think jostling him around like they were would be good for him. They finally got him on the awaiting stretcher. It took all four of them to get Wells up the steps and into the sitting room where Eva waited. The patient was not conscious.

Eva instructed Suzanne to remove his boots while Sonny cut the clothes from his body. Adrian Wells had been shot three times, twice in the stomach and once in the shoulder. E.J. stood for a few moments taking in the scene. His father in-law looked pale as he lay with his black suit tattered about him. Wells had aged since the last time E.J. saw him. As the women set to work, he backed out of the dining room. He would begin to process *what happened* because he knew that would be the next thing his wife and her family would want to know.

When E.J. walked back onto the porch, Jeremiah stood at the top of the steps. Jeb and his brother were at the bottom, standing on either side of the driver. His brother looked to him and shook his head before turning to address the driver of the carriage. E.J. had seen the man during his travels. But he couldn't recall his name.

The driver worked for the railroad carrying travelers to the nearby plantations. The service made traveling easy. The man before him was a white fellow with brown hair and dark eyes. The rail worker looked nervous. It was also evident that the man hadn't bathed in a great while.

"So, you are saying some men robbed you and your passenger. Your passenger was shot, and you weren't?" Jeremiah was too calm.

"What I's sayin' is they come outta nowheres. They told the old man, ain't nobody gon get hurt if we do's as they say," the driver replied uneasily.

Jeremiah addressed Jeb. "Unhitch the horses and search the carriage small by small."

"What is we looking for?" Gerry asked.

"We'll know when we see it," Jeremiah replied.

The driver all at once found his nerve. "You's a nigga; ya got no right treatin' me this way."

"Search him as well," Jeremiah instructed, ignoring the insult. Turning to E.J., he continued in a low voice. "The driver is in on this malice. He probably robbed the old man himself."

"Do you think he acted alone?" E.J. asked.

"I think we can't afford to misunderstand the facts," Jeremiah replied.

"Why would he bring the old man home if he were in on it?" E.J. asked, thinking out loud.

Jeremiah's eyes narrowed. "I say he come to gauge us. I think he got friends. If he worked alone, he would have disposed of the old man and went on about his business. Some of the surrounding plantations are being run by women–easy victims. The war has made this a fact. If we honest wit' one another, people ain't afraid of the Hunter plantation like they were when Hunter Sr. lived. We gon' have to dig a few graves for people to see ain't a damn thing changed."

Jeb interrupted their conversation. "His pockets is empty."

"Remove yo' boots," Jeremiah called out to the driver.

The man was indignant. "Ain't no nigger telling me what to do,"

Jeb and Gerry tossed the man to the ground and removed his boots. In the right boot, they found two dollars and a few coins; in the left boot, a wedding ring and a gold money clip. The initials on the money clip were "A.W."

E.J. looked at his brother and started to speak, but Jeremiah cut him off. "Tend to your wife; we got this."

Jeremiah shouted to Jeb. "Take him to the shed."

❊ ❊ ❊

It was around eleven in the morning when Jeremiah made it to his cabin. He stripped on the back porch and went to the pump to rinse the blood from his person. The events of the day had him riled up, and he could not calm down. The chilled air filled his lungs, and he exhaled as he stuck his head under the spout.

There was more to this posse of robbers than his victim had admitted. It was clear the driver didn't work alone. They would not chase leads and lessen their manpower. Instead, they would remain vigilant.

Jeremiah heard the back door open as he wiped the water from his eyes. Callie stood on the porch holding a towel for him. She was radiant, and he could not love her more than he did at this moment. Yet, he was angry with her. They argued and had not been speaking to one another. After the events of the morning, his temper was out of control. He disengaged from her to keep her safe from his rage. But Callie didn't care that he was cross, and it scared him. She appeared vexed herself, and he knew it could become volatile. Callie sought to engage him, but he refused.

"I heard the gunshots," she said softly. "I was worried about you."

Jeremiah did not respond, and she went on. "I have warm

water over the fire. Pour the hot water into the tub for me. I'll help you bathe."

He did as she asked, mixing the hot water with the cool water in the tub. He refilled the pot and placed it back over the fire before he climbed into the water. Once settled, he laid back and closed his eyes. Callie came forward and slowly lowered her awkward frame next to the tub. She went right to the heart of the matter and based on her words, he found that he weighed her incorrectly.

"I can't live without you," she whispered.

Jeremiah sat up and stared at her. She had taken the fight right out of him. "I can't live if something happens to you or the child. I want to send you away with Sonny, Eva and Ella so you will be safe. But you disobey me at every turn and refuse to do as I say."

"Sonny and the women should still go. I will not leave you."

"They worry for you and the child. They will not leave until you do. You hold them up from freedom."

"I won't leave your side," she answered, emotionally.

He sighed before Callie leaned in and cupped his face. She kissed him deeply–totally. She would not see reason. He had gone to Ella for help, and she had sided with Callie, refusing to leave. He was angry with Ella too, but the old woman didn't give a damn. Sonny and Eva had avoided him until he cornered Sonny. The key man told him he would look after Callie, but would not leave without the women.

No one listened to him anymore–and it was all her damn fault.

17
Washington D.C.
October 1861

JAMES STOOD BEHIND the stables of the executive home tending the horses. Lizzie, the dressmaker, had helped him secure work since she felt responsible for him losing his shoeshine stand. The land was vast, and it had the largest stables he had ever seen. It was a mild day and the trees about the property were dressed in fall leaves. The servants, James noted, were divided into three groups. There was the outside help of gardeners, drivers, and stable workers. Inside the home were the maids, butlers, and kitchen help. The third group of servants worked closely with the President and his family.

He also came to understand that the servant positions were coveted and most of the staff was white. James couldn't help but sense some resentment between the white and colored help. Though there were only a handful of colored servants, all were free.

James had managed to get Anthony a job in the kitchen with the help of Miss Lizzie. Neither of them had been back to the campsite since they started working on the executive premises two days prior. James had not seen Anthony for over a day.

The man who ran the stables was an older white gentleman with bushy eyebrows and sad, dark eyes. When he spoke, his small, pebble-like teeth came into view. His huge red nose made James think the man might be fond of his drink. His name was Louis, and he was by no means friendly. He took his business of running the busy stables with utmost seriousness. James rarely had a moment to rest.

Three stand-alone buildings housed the horses, the carriages and the blacksmith. The large, white-washed structures were weather-beaten. Over the front and back doors of the buildings were two, massive windows, promoting cross ventilation. Down the middle of the stable was a dirt path of well-packed earth. On either side of the path were the stalls that housed the horses individually. Behind the smithy was the corral, where the horses were exercised and treated for medical issues.

A wide, dirt path traversed the property and connected with the driveway in front of the mansion. The stables were pushed back on the acreage because of the smell. Between the stables and the back of the mansion were three smaller buildings. These small white dorms, with green paint around the windows, housed the outside workers. Inside each of the two buildings were ten small rooms. Each room had two beds, a nightstand and a chest at the foot of every bed. The third building was where the outside servants ate and bathed. Laundry for the entire mansion was also handled from this building.

James had no roommate because none of the white servants wanted to share lodgings with a colored person. And to his way of thinking, the situation worked to his benefit. Farther out on the land was a thick, wooded area with a stream that ran across the property. James was casing the joint. It was well after noon and the sun was shining brightly. There were overcast moments, when the clouds would engulf the sun, then suddenly release it giving way to a perfect day.

James had used his given name for fear he wouldn't answer when someone called him. He had just moved back inside the stables and was mucking a stall when Louis called down the aisle.

"James, you got company!"

James looked up to find Lizzie waiting for him at the front door of the stables. He leaned the rake against the wall and started toward her. She stood just outside the door, wearing a brown dress with long sleeves and black boots. Her black hair was pulled back in a bun, with curls about her temples. When he reached her, she smiled warmly, and again he felt a pang over his deception.

"Mr. James, Cook is short a server. I wondered if you might wish to fill this position for about a week. Richard has taken ill," Lizzie said.

James was taken aback and though he needed a way in, he wasn't polished like Black. He worried that he couldn't pull it off. "Miss Lizzie, I ain't proper like some."

Lizzie stepped closer and whispered for his ears only. "It ain't but nine colored workers inside and outside the mansion. If Cook fills this position with a white person, it won't be long before all the posts turn white. When Richard comes back, they won't give him back his job. If ya too proper, you'll be thought of as an uppity nigger. You just right, intelligent and unassuming–you'll do fine."

James nodded. He looked about for Louis in order to inform him of his temporary reassignment.

"Mrs. Lincoln already sent word."

He stared at her. *Mrs. Lincoln had sent word?*

Lizzie took him by the arm. "Come, let me help you get ready. George will show you what's needed."

James followed Lizzie across the dirt path into the back of the mansion. A narrow door leading to a dark stairwell was left open.

At the bottom of the steps, they made a left into the kitchen. The room was stuffy, but clean. There were several long, white counters used to prepare food. At James' right was a long, white table with eight matching chairs; on the left was a massive, black, pot-bellied stove.

The house servants lived in the dim, dank basement. Across from the kitchen, James could see another dining area for the help. A long, polished wood table with matching chairs filled the room. At the far end of the dining room was another stove. The windows near the ceiling opened inward. There were water stains streaming down the walls from wet weather. James was finally inside—but he wasn't loving it.

A thin, older colored woman wearing a brown dress with a white apron tied neatly about her waist came up to them. She was dark-skinned with a flat nose and thick lips. Her two thick braids were pinned neatly at her crown. She gave James a look that told him she was no-nonsense.

"Cook, this is James," Lizzie said, making introductions. "He come to help until Richie gets back."

The older woman looked him up and down. James anticipated her flat-out refusal. Instead, when she spoke, her words were refined and to the point. "Do you think you can manage?"

"Yes, Ma'am, I do," he answered.

"You don't have to do the serving; Diane will take care of all that. You have to be the brawn, as the trays are heavy. The days are long and its hard work."

"Yes, Ma'am," he said.

Cook turned to Lizzie. "Help him get ready."

When they turned to leave, James spied Anthony entering through a door opposite him. He had been introduced as James' nephew, using his own name as well. It appeared Anthony had made out quite comfortably. He was dressed in butler livery and wore a crisp white shirt and black bowtie. Anthony's eyes lit up when he saw James.

"Uncle!" Anthony rushed over to greet him. "I hear you gonna partner with Diane."

"Yeah," James replied with uncertainty in his voice.

"You'll be fine," Anthony assured him. "You can share a room wit' me."

James nodded as he followed Lizzie down the dark corridor in the opposite direction.

✾ ✾ ✾

Black was seated on a wooden crate, leaning back against a tree. He was reading the Washington Times. Tim, Bainesworth, Gilbert and Elbert stood in a circle to his left, talking. The doctor strolled up and his voice was strained as he directed his words to Black.

"The girl is awake. Her name is Molly. She is eighteen summers as Tim suspected. The young miss has been forced repeatedly. It appears objects were used," he said in disgust.

The men grew quiet and Shultz went on, "It will take some time, but she will mend. She is asking for the man who brought her here."

They all turned looking to Black who stood, silently folding the newspaper before placing it on the crate. He followed Shultz back to the tent where the young woman was being nursed back to health. The day was overcast and with the river at their backs, the temperature was cool. The camp was busy with the women cooking and washing clothes. The men did the hunting, and with Black's direction, they had begun closing ranks to keep the women safe. There was a clearing among the trees, and tents were erected within the lines of timber to create privacy. A small city had sprung up and there were shelters of all sizes and colors.

It was obvious that Black ran the camp, though he did so with few words. He offered direction and worked through his own men to establish control. The fact remained that they were on a mission, and he did not want the people to become dependent on him. An older woman moved her tent a few feet from his and began tending him. She shaved him, washed his clothes and fed him. She looked to be older than forty summers and though he allowed her to take care of his basic needs, Black did not converse with her unless it was necessary. She was small in stature with deep brown skin and keen features that, in his opinion, held up well through the years.

The camp had grown to about sixty people and Black considered this advantageous. It allowed him and his men to blend. While the men had paired off with the camp women, only their basic needs were being addressed. They remained focused—they would seek comfort later. Delayed satisfaction ensured life. Black's boots made crunching sounds, as he stepped on the leaves that covered the ground. He walked up to the blue, army-issued tent looking about before he pushed back the flap and went inside.

When his eyes adjusted to the dimness, he saw a cot in the corner with many blankets piled high. Next to the cot sat a woman who looked up when he entered. She quickly exited the tent, and he took her seat.

Molly lay with her eyes closed. He did not try to wake her. Instead, he thought of his own wife and daughter once more. A state of melancholy overtook him. The mission was beginning to weigh on him. He was staring at the adjacent side of the tent, lost in dreams of home, when Molly's soft voice broke into his reverie.

"What's yo' name?"

He smiled down at her. "My name is Black."

She turned her head as if to get a better look at him, wincing and moaning with the effort. "I ain't thank I would live."

Black nodded. "How did you come to be there?"

"I come wit' a group of slaves, tryin' fo' freedom. We was gon' press on from here to get away from Virginia. I's from the

Marshall plantation. We moved 'round at night. We was 'fraid. One night, trouble happened wit' the soldiers, and I got parted from my group. The man from the store clubbed me over the head and dragged me away. Some soldiers seen it, but he told dem I's his slave. I been wit' him a long time, 'bout two months."

Black leaned forward, but he could find no words. She began to weep. "The white woman—she were there when I come."

Black had just read on page two of the Washington Times that a white woman left at the hospital by two unidentified men had died. The article went on to say the woman had never regained consciousness and the authorities were investigating the matter. He offered up none of this information. Silence stretched out between them, and Black thought she had fallen asleep when she suddenly volunteered some unexpected information.

"Two white men come to the store the day fo' you come. They's dress in fine clothes. They come from the mansion. I only 'members one name cause'n he talked strange. He name Sheffield. I cain't 'member the others. They was wantin' me and the white woman killed. But soon they's wantin' us to give dem pleasure. The white woman cried, so they beat us both and took what they wanted," she whispered, averting her eyes in shame.

Black stared at her; he did not want to push. He needed her to hold on to her memory, and given her state, he considered her fragile. "Can you tell me what they look like?"

"I could sho' try." And then, as if it were an afterthought, she asked, "Will ya kill dem fo' me?"

"I will," he promised.

At his words, she found sleep. He would come again in the morning with his tablet and charcoal. The lighting would be better, and she would be more alert. When Black stepped from the tent into the fading light of day, his men were standing about, speaking softly with one another. Shultz, Elbert, and Lou approached him.

"Is she well?" Lou asked.

"It's slow going. She has fallen asleep," Black replied.

Elbert nodded. "Are we ready for the next step?"

Black looked at Elbert for a second, before he moved past him. The three men followed, and once they were back among their own men, Black spoke in a low tone.

"The young miss says two men from the mansion came the day before we did. They beat her and the other woman, then forced them into unwanted acts. She says one of the men spoke with a strange accent. His name was Sheffield. I will draw them in the morning. We need to get this name to James and Anthony."

They all looked at Tim, who put his hands up in surrender. "Remember, I pushed the dressmaker. If she sees me speaking with James, it will ruin all his hard work."

Black nodded, as Bainesworth said, "I don't know anyone by the name of Sheffield who is a peer of the realm."

"He may not be using his real name," Black responded. "I say we go to the mansion after dark. We will seek out James and Anthony. As for the Union president, we will take him tomorrow night."

"I agree," said Shultz. "We need to take heed from Kirk. He seemed to understand the issues better than Maynard."

"Yeah, I see it the same," Tim said.

Black issued orders. "Tim, Shultz and the ambassador will suit up like soldiers. You all will keep watch on the streets surrounding the mansion. The rest of us will test the security of the executive home."

❊ ❊ ❊

James stood at the back of the Green Room, next to the rolling cart. They had him dressed like a damn fop in black trousers, a white shirt, a black bowtie and black vest. Lizzie had cut his hair and shaved him. She was beaming when she presented him to Cook—he, on the other hand, was not pleased. He heard the dumbwaiter begin to move. When it landed, he began transferring the food to the rolling tray. Diane, his partner, had come to help him. She was about twenty-five summers and stunningly beautiful. She was a slender girl, standing almost six feet tall. She had slanted, brown eyes and lips that wanted kissing. Her hair was pulled into a tight bun, making her eyes dance when she smiled. James thought she looked far better in her uniform.

Her voice was throaty when she spoke. "Mista James, is ya ready?"

"Yeah," he replied.

"You just has to keep the tray rolling. I'll take care of the rest. Mrs. Lincoln has some lady friends visitin'. Mr. Lincoln will come to smile and be nice to the ladies. Unless we's spoken to, we ain't gotta say nothin'. Just serve and clean up," Diana said, staring down at him in mild amusement.

"I got it," he replied.

"We will come back to the Green Room and wait."

James looked around the room, it was definitely green. The wallpaper was a pea green and the couches that lined the far walls were a forest green. Over the fireplace hung an enormous mirror; on the table in the center of the room was a sculpture: a rendition of a colored man, with grotesque, monkey-like features. The Green Room reminded him of the pussy parlor—only there was no fun to be had.

Diane turned and started for the East Room. He followed close behind, pushing the tray of food. When they entered the room, six white women were seated on one side of a large table. They were all speaking at once and took no notice of them as they went about their duties. At the head of the table, sat a woman with dark hair piled high on her head. She wore a blue dress with a white decorative collar, and her hands were folded demurely before her.

James was certain she was Mrs. Lincoln. She had delicate features with dark eyes and a tiny mouth that appeared unhappy.

James kept his head down as Diane moved around the table, serving the women. They had just served the last woman when the president himself strode into the room. Mr. Lincoln was unusually tall, with thick dark hair, high cheekbones, a prominent nose, and a coarse beard that outlined his jaw. His eyes were deep-set in the shadows of his bushy brows, and when he smiled crows' feet fanned out from the recesses of the sockets. Hanging over his left arm was his black suit jacket and he bowed before speaking to the room at large.

"Good evening, ladies. I apologize for my tardiness."

James quickly sized him up and then went back to the task at hand careful not to stare. The women echoed polite greetings. Diane served the president from the left side of the table, next to a woman wearing pale yellow.

"Thank you, Diane," the president said.

"You welcome, Mr. President, sir," she responded. "This here is James," she added, nodding toward him.

James bowed slightly while looking low and to the left. "Mr. President, sir."

"James...you are new. I hope you don't scare easy. This place never sleeps." Lincoln chuckled.

James smiled, while offering minimal eye contact. When Diane signaled, James followed her from the East Room. Once back in the Green Room, they waited while the Lincolns and their guests finished dinner.

James waited in the doorway, taking note of numerous people wandering about who did not appear to be part of the staff. He saw two men enter the hall from the front. One of them picked up a vase from a dropleaf table against the wall and walked away with it.

Behind him, he heard Diane speak. "The public is 'llowed to

come and go. We sees what happens, and for the colored help we's worried we gon' get blamed. Sometimes we finds 'em on the second flo', even though they ain't posed to be up there. They ain't posed to come after three o'clock, but they do."

James was appalled at how nonexistent the security was in the mansion. He was hit with an ominous revelation. They would warn Abraham Lincoln of the plot on his life, but it would do no good—he would be slain anyway. There was no regard for the safety of the President or his family. He and the men had spent all this time devising a plan to warn him, when anyone and everyone had access to the house. He needed to see Black, and they needed to move swiftly.

❈ ❈ ❈

Music stood at the dumbwaiter in the basement near the kitchen. Cook had partnered her with the young man, Anthony, and it had made her uncomfortable. He wasn't unkind, but there was something about him that didn't sit well with her. At first, she couldn't put her finger on it; then, she met his uncle. They looked like ruffians and did not have the polish of people who had been in a servile situation for any length of time. She could not afford to get entangled in a circumstance that would cost her job.

Anthony stood at the other end of the rolling cart as she loaded the dirty dishes coming from Diane on the first floor. When she finished, he rolled the cart away and came back with dessert and coffee. She was about to begin loading the food onto the lift when Anthony spoke.

"Here, let me help you."

Music stopped and stared at him. She gauged him to be a bit older than her twenty summers but no more than twenty-three. His tall frame was muscular, like he was accustomed to doing manual labor. Anthony had flawless, dark skin that seemed to glow when he smiled. His front tooth was chipped, but the imperfection didn't diminish his appeal. She had been a quiet person from her days on the Hicks plantation in Georgia, but today she couldn't hold back.

"Who is you—really?"

Anthony looked away from her, as if he didn't hear her question. She put her hands on her plump hips and repeated the question.

"I say, who *is* you?"

Anthony searched her face. "No matter what you thinkin', I would never do anything to hurt you."

She looked deeply into his eyes and saw pure sincerity, though it was unsettling. She went back to loading the dumbwaiter, and he stepped in closer to help her. When the task was done, she turned to head to the kitchen.

"I could help you wash dishes," he said.

"Thank you," she whispered.

Music felt the tension of being near him, but Anthony had not been unkind. She would give it about two days and then see if Bonnie wanted to switch. She was sure Bonnie would agree–she hated old George.

It was well after dark when Black and the men took their positions. Tim, Bainesworth, and Shultz were suited up like Union soldiers, patrolling the front and side streets leading to the mansion. Black, Frank, and Lou were standing in the shadows behind the stables. Elbert, Gilbert, and Jake were positioned at the front of the mansion, watching the activity of the soldiers camped across the roadway. Jesse, Ralph, Josiah, and Emmett were at the public stables guarding the horses. Herman, Horace, John, Luke, and Ephraim were tending their supplies at the camp.

There was one lamppost between the smaller buildings and the back of the main house. The flame inside flickered with the wind, offering little light on the pathway. The hour was late, and Black knew James would be on the move soon. There was a door left ajar. Black was sure it was a servant entrance, but without knowing where it led, he didn't dare venture inside. All was quiet, until the door Black had been watching, creaked on its hinges.

Anthony and James emerged. Black smiled before letting out a bird call to get their attention. James immediately moved toward the sound as Frank and Lou wandered off to scout the terrain around the mansion. When James was close enough, Black reached out and touched his shoulder.

"Shit! You 'bout to get yo' head blown off," James hissed.

"Easy. It's just me," Black replied.

"Glad you here—we needs to talk," James said.

"Same here," Black responded, "Let us move into the trees."

"I'll watch the door," Anthony said.

"Frank and Lou is about," Black informed him.

Black and James walked across the back of the property into the trees. The weather held a damp chill, and Black could smell the rain to come. The odor of manure wafted from the stables. Under the full moon, the two men paused in the grove. The fluttering of autumn leaves in the wind drowned out their conversation.

"I seen Lincoln," an anxious James blurted out.

"The colored girl we took from the store says two men came from the mansion the day before we came," Black added.

"Did she have a name?"

"She could only remember one name, Sheffield. She remembered him because he had a strange accent."

"A Brit?" James asked.

"She didn't confirm," Black replied, "but I'm thinking he was. I will try to sketch them in the morning."

"They allows the public to come and go from the mansion. It's a damn free-for-all. Ain't no security, I tell you. Why would he live like that, and he got a wife and children in the house?"

John Brown came to Black's mind. He remembered John telling him that this was his calling, and it could not be altered. If what James said was true, then their actions would change nothing for the president. Still, he hoped their efforts would benefit colored folks. Black wanted to see slavery ended. He understood he wasn't truly free as long as colored children continued to be born into bondage. They would stay the course.

"I say we steal him tomorrow night," Black said.

"I would say the sooner the better. Them damn soldiers 'cross the street ain't making no nevermind. Send Shultz at midday in case something changes. I'll look for this Sheffield."

"We'll be out here for a while. You can go on back. Where does that back door lead?"

"The door leads to the basement and the servant quarters. The kitchen is to the left. On the right, three doors down and to the left is me and Anthony's room."

"Yeah," Black said, before fading into the night.

✾ ✾ ✾

James followed Diane up the stairwell to the right of the wine cellar into the main hall of the first floor. The thick burgundy carpet ran the length of the hall. Throne-like burgundy chairs, trimmed in white brocade, sat against the wall beneath a large mirror. Across from the sitting area was a white marble vestibule. Two white pillars stood opposite each other in the entrance way, and between the pillars stood two white men. Both were dressed in brown trousers and white shirts, and both of them were armed.

As James and Diane made their way to the grand staircase, one of the men—a dark-haired, beady-eyed fellow—eyed them with a look of disgust. His partner, a blond man with a fat nose, snickered at his partner's reaction. They were halfway up the marble steps leading to the second floor when James whispered to Diane.

"What they names?"

"They's Mista Sheffy and Mista Berkley; thems the President's bodyguards. They ain't so fond of coloreds."

James looked at her out of the corner of his eye. "His name is Sheffy or Sheffield?"

Diane shrugged her shoulders, and before he knew it they were in the second-floor corridor. The color scheme was the same as the downstairs hall only there were no chairs. The doors on either side of the hall were closed, and James suspected they were the bedrooms of the First Family. It was eight in the morning and all was quiet as they walked to the small reception room at the end of the hallway. When they entered, James could hear men talking in agitated voices.

"Mr. President, you don't listen to those who mean you well," an irritated voice said.

"I don't listen to anyone, so don't take it personally," Lincoln responded.

The rest of the conversation was muffled by the noise from the dumbwaiter. James was anxious to serve the food. Diane transferred breakfast onto the rolling tray and James followed her to the president's office. Lincoln was seated at a large, oak desk; behind him were two great windows with burgundy drapes pulled back to reveal the rainy day. The president wore a white shirt with a black vest. A man in a blue wool suit was seated opposite him. He was gray haired with a hook nose and huge ears that stuck out on the sides of his head. His mouth was clamped down firmly in a straight line.

James thought they would stop talking when he and Diane entered. But servants weren't really people to some, and colored servants were considered unintelligent.

"You wander off alone making it difficult for your staff to protect you," the man continued.

"These men are risking their lives in service to this great

country. I can't be too busy to visit the hospital," Lincoln sounded cross.

"You don't take the bodyguards," the gray-haired man said.

"I don't need them; besides, my wife and children need them instead of me."

Diane moved in and began serving coffee. "Thank you for the coffee, Diane. I think old Seward needs it more than I. He's a bear when he hasn't had that first cup," Lincoln addressed her.

Diane giggled. "Good morning, Mr. President, sir. Morning to you too, Mr. Secretary."

"'Morning, Diane," Seward grumbled.

Neither man acknowledged James, and Diane continued serving breakfast. They were about to go wait in the reception room until it was time to collect the dishes. At that moment, Seward leaned in and said, none too gently, "Berkley has let me know that you have refused to take him and Sheffy with you tomorrow night. You will take them to the town hall meeting and the hospital visit or...or I will involve Mrs. Lincoln."

Lincoln sighed. "You play dirty, John. As a compromise, you will read some of these requests for pardons. I am behind."

"I will help, but it seems we can get no real work done answering the request of overwrought mothers and worried wives," Seward replied.

James and Diane moved on to the reception room, but he remained near the doorway to listen. When the president and Secretary Seward finished eating, they cleared away the dishes and went back downstairs. They entered the kitchen, and Anthony was there removing dishes from the dumbwaiter. Diane went to find Cook, and when they were alone, James told Anthony what he had heard.

"Lincoln is goin' out tomorrow night."

"Will that change how we move?" Anthony asked.

"Shultz will be here at noon. We'll get word to Black and go from there," James replied.

"Music asked me who I really was," Anthony whispered.

"It's almost done," James said.

Anthony halfheartedly smiled, and James clapped him on the shoulder. He knew the look. Anthony wanted the girl. James was about to advise him to stay focused, but Music appeared. She ignored James' presence, causing him to shrug and move on to the kitchen.

❊ ❊ ❊

It was almost midday, and James and Anthony were waiting for Shultz. Cook had been correct, working in the executive mansion was indeed exhausting. James, Diane, Anthony, and Music had cleaned the first floor from one end to the other, yet the guards had allowed the public in unsupervised. Drinks were spilled and furniture previously polished was smudged. Miss Lizzie made an appearance to see if James needed anything.

"Sleep," he replied, and Lizzie laughed.

Anthony and Music were cleaning the East Room. Diane was polishing the banister of the grand staircase, and James was picking up litter from the main floor carpet. At precisely noon, Shultz, dressed as a Union soldier, walked into the main hall. The doctor had on a different pair of glasses and his hair was slicked back. He looked about and began to browse. The guards, who paid no attention to security, were joking with one another and laughing.

Music and Anthony exited the East Room. They would handle lunch, Bonnie and George would handle dinner. The doctor entered the East Room and began looking about. James appeared with his cart full of cleaning supplies. Several visitors stood nearby, admiring the artwork, as he began to polish the furniture. The doctor moved nonchalantly to a window near James and looked out onto the grounds.

"We need to take him tomorrow night," James said in a whisper.

"What happened?" Shultz asked as he slipped him Black's sketches.

"The president has a meetin' at City Hall and then some hospital between 7th and 8th Street," James whispered, making sure he did not look at Shultz when he spoke.

"Do you know times?" Shultz asked.

"No, I ain't clear on the times, but these events is open to the public."

The doctor nodded slightly, keeping his gaze fixed out the window.

"I found out that Sheffield is the dark-haired man at the entrance. The two at the door are supposed to take the president to these events. I ain't seen a third man."

"I'm sure Black will be out back tonight to speak with you, even if we don't take him. Be ready either way," Shultz said, and then he was gone.

At ten that evening, Black and the men assumed their positions around the mansion. The stable men could be heard talking loudly from the window above Black's head. They were playing cards and drinking. Keeping his eyes on the back door, Black waited patiently for James to appear. About an hour passed, before the door creaked on its hinges and James stepped into the dim light cast by the flickering lamppost. The men moved into the trees, leaving Anthony to keep watch.

"The president has two engagements tomorrow night. I have only just figured out who two of the men is."

"So, you would rather take them tomorrow night?" Black asked.

"I think it be better to take Lincoln wit' the bodyguards, so he can see the danger," James replied.

"The men tracked the events; the president is to be at City Hall from eight to nine tomorrow night and then at Campbell General Hospital from nine-thirty to ten-thirty. You and Anthony should leave the mansion at six tomorrow night to meet up with us. I believe they will strike on the way to the hospital around 5th Street. The area just after the hospital is wooded. This would provide the right setting for such dealings, although we will be ready should they strike sooner," Black said.

"I'm bothered that we don't see the third man," James said.

"You worry for nothing; whoever is driving is their third man. But, you focus on the small of it. The Kirk fellow told Tim that they needed ten men for this mission. He then confirmed that they were a backup group. This tells me there will be more than three men in place tomorrow night. Widen your thoughts, brother," Black replied.

When James said nothing, Black continued. "Me and the men will break camp before dawn and separate from the people by the river. We will regroup at an old cabin on the edge of town. Elbert will leave two horses at the stables by the dry-goods store for you and Anthony. Meet us on Indiana Avenue and 4th Street at six-thirty tomorrow evening. It will be crowded because Lincoln is expected to show."

"We will be there," James replied.

"We will work the plan as discussed. When we have completed this mission, we will leave Washington on its ear before we press on to the Hunter plantation," Black added.

The men parted, moving toward their assignments.

❊ ❊ ❊

After James and Anthony disappeared back through the servant's entrance, Black and the men remained on the premises. Black observed the routines of the outside staff and noted the drivers drank to excess. Elbert reported that the soldiers were "too comfortable," and Black saw it the same. The men moved in the quiet of the night, back to the camp. Elbert and Black made one detour going to the vacant dry-goods store. Once there, Black sent two messages—one to the fort and one to his men on Beacon Hill.

Black and Elbert arrived back at the camp around three in the morning. The people were restless as they observed the men packing. Black heard a small commotion and in the flickering light of the camp fire, he saw Shultz and Lou rushing toward him. He stopped gathering his belongings and offered his undivided attention.

"The young Miss is beside herself because you are leaving," the doctor said.

"I will speak with her. She is to be packed up and taken with us," Black replied.

Shultz nodded, obviously relieved at his answer. The doctor scurried off to handle the matter. Lou, however, continued to stare at him, his face full of emotion.

"Is something wrong, Lou?"

Lou was clean shaven, but his hair had grown out into thick locks that he wore wrapped about the crown of his head. He was dressed in all black down to the boots, and he stood just less than six feet. Like his twin, Lou was extremely dark of skin with a menacing appearance. Black and Lou stood facing each other until Lou finally broke eye contact. His voice was expressive when he addressed Black.

"I wants the girl, but she leanin' on you."

Black gave him a thoughtful smile. "I think she is afraid and remembers only that I brought her here."

Lou shifted his weight from one leg to another. He seemed to be searching for his words.

"I sent word to Beacon Hill," Black added. "The men will come to take her to the fort as we move south. The girl has been through much. Can you handle it?"

"Shit, I don't know nobody that been through a little," Lou countered.

Black chuckled. "I will let you take it from here then."

Lou nodded and walked off. As Black watched him go, Bainesworth appeared from the shadows, looking more anxious than either Shultz or Lou.

"Ambassador, is there something I can do for you?"

Bainesworth cleared his throat, but hesitated a moment. "It would seem you're almost done with me."

Black laughed slightly. "Yes, Ambassador, you will be free to leave us after tomorrow night."

Bainesworth looked troubled, and Black frowned. "We held up our part of the bargain. What issue do you still have?"

"I have no pressing engagements after this. If you still needed an extra gun hand, I would be happy to lend my assistance," the ambassador replied, holding his breath.

Black assessed Bainesworth, who stood before him dressed in all black. The exchange caught Black off guard. "You wish to stay with us until we head back to Canada?"

"Certainly, my good man," the ambassador responded with eagerness.

"It will be dangerous," Black cautioned.

"I'm up for it."

Black studied him thoughtfully. "James will partner with you, then."

The ambassador bowed and quickly turned to go, as if lingering might give Black a chance to change his mind. Next in line was the woman who had been caring for him. Black stared down at her and smiled.

"Mavis," Black said, "I appreciate all you have done for me."

"You welcome, Mista Black. We gon miss you 'round here,"

"Take care of yourself and please be safe."

"You do the same, hear? Yo' peoples need you," Mavis answered softly.

Before he knew what she was about, Mavis stepped forward

and hugged him. Black smiled and hugged her back. In keeping with their usual behavior, she stepped back from him and then blended in with the camp folk.

Black went back to packing; they would break camp one hour before dawn. He and the men would then head for the abandoned cabin. Later, they would rendezvous with Lincoln on the edge of town before tying off all loose ends.

Lou was accompanied by Frank, as he walked to Molly's tent. He was nervous. Neither brother spoke as they made their way. When they arrived, Shultz emerged from the tent with a look of concern on his face.

"Molly is still healing; she can't even ride a horse sidesaddle. I haven't told her she is coming with us. I thought to let Black handle that part. I found her some trousers and a shirt—thought they would be warmer than a dress."

"Black ain't comin'. It be me handlin' what she needin'," Lou replied.

Shultz looked from Lou to Frank and smiled. "I see."

Frank and Shultz posted up at the front of the tent, and Lou ventured inside. He adjusted his eyes to the lighting of the lone lantern. Molly was seated on the small cot wrapped in a blanket. She looked up as he approached, then craned her neck to look past him. Lou knew she looked for Black. His voice was gentle, but firm, when he redirected her back to him.

"I'll be takin' care of ya. Only me."

Molly's expression became fearful, and he thought she might ask for Black outright. Instead, she leaned forward and tried to focus the eye that wasn't swollen. She was brown skinned, and to Lou's way of thinking–lovely. She just needed time. Molly shocked him when she spoke.

"It hurt somethin' awful when you was removin' the collar."

"If ya trust me, I won't never hurt ya again," Lou promised.

She looked to the ground, and he sensed she was done talking. Calmly he asked, "Can I help ya dress? I wants to take ya wit' me."

"I cain't barely stand. The doctor says I'll heal, but up inside me is painin' me so bad," she whispered.

"I'll carry you," he said.

When she didn't refuse him, Lou stepped back to the opening of the tent. He whispered to his brother, causing both Frank and Shultz to walk away. After about five minutes, his brother called his name.

"Come in," Lou said.

Frank entered holding a bucket of warm water. Molly looked up and stared from man-to-man. Lou smiled as she leaned in to focus on them. Frank's hair had just started growing and he had the scar, but there was no mistaking they were twins.

"He the ugly one," Lou whispered.

Frank smiled. "Miss Molly," he said softly.

Lou was hopeful, as he watched her struggle to smile. In that moment, he saw her potential. Frank sat the bucket down near the cot and returned to his post outside. Lou fished a cloth out of the bucket and, after wringing it out, carefully sponged her face. He then bathed her neck and shoulders. Molly relaxed and let the blanket slip away.

When he finished bathing her, he helped her into the shirt and trousers. He located some thick woolen socks among the things given to her and put them on her feet. He then lifted her, blanket and all, into his arms and called out to Frank. His brother pulled the flap aside and Lou stepped out to where the other nineteen men were gathered. As he stepped into view carrying Molly, the plan shifted back on track.

Black came forward. "Me and Frank will do the driving. You ride with Molly. Inside the seat closest to the driver are the guns."

"Yeah," Lou replied.

Frank loaded their belongings into the carriage. Molly kept her head against Lou's shoulder. She was shaking, but they were making progress.

Black's words lit a fire. "Gentlemen, it's time to step through the plan."

❀ ❀ ❀

Around eleven the next morning, James pretended to dust in the main hall. From the corner of his eye, he saw movement. President Lincoln was descending the grand staircase. A stout, chubby white man followed him. He reminded James of a turtle. His mouth kept opening and snapping shut, but he was saying nothing as Lincoln was doing all the talking.

"I have two engagements tonight. I plan to spend the day at the War Department," Lincoln said.

A white butler stepped forward, handing both men their suit jackets. The shorter man, who was dressed in a blue suit, finally said, "We will walk over to the War Department together, sir."

"Hannibal," the president said, "I suspect this war is going to be a bad one, and I don't know what to do about it."

The man's agitated look softened. "We have to see it through, sir."

The two men exited the house through the front. James walked to the window to watch them as they crossed the street. The sun was shining and the temperature mild. It was as good a day as any to steal Lincoln.

❀ ❀ ❀

Black and his entourage set up shop at the cabin, a location recommended by Andy and Mable. True to his word, Andy had left supplies for him and the men. The place was clean. Mable had even left flowers on the small table. There was just one room, with a small bed and colorful quilt. The men hung a blanket, dividing the room for Molly, who was exhausted. Lou fed her some salted meat and beans. Afterward, she drank some whiskey and fell asleep.

They divided into several groups. Lou, Horace, Herman, and John remained inside the cabin to watch over the girl and their supplies. Ralph, Jesse, Emmett, and Josiah patrolled the property to make certain they were not being watched. At five-thirty that afternoon, Black and his men went to meet James and Anthony on the corner of 4th and Indiana. They rode slowly, allowing darkness to fall. Frank drove the carriage, and Black rode shotgun. Behind them, Elbert drove another carriage with Gilbert riding shotgun. The rest of the men moved into position on horseback.

When they reached Indiana Avenue, Frank and Elbert parked the carriages. Black and Gilbert moved in on foot toward 4th Street. Off in the distance, they could see the crowd that had gathered at City Hall. Fifteen minutes later, Anthony and James appeared on horseback. By seven o'clock, the men on horseback had disappeared down the side streets. As the eight o'clock hour neared, Black could feel the energy of the men at his back—they were ready.

Black and Gilbert stood on opposite sides of the roadway. They had moved up closer to City Hall to watch for the president's carriage. Black would have the men close in on the hospital while Lincoln was on stage delivering his speech. The streets were brightly lit. Washington could rise to the occasion of being modern when needed. The air smelled of rain. A yellow, waning moon hung low in the sky. Black felt as though he could reach out and touch it. On the streets behind him, the men had extinguished every other lantern.

Gilbert let out a bird call, signifying the time had come. Black could see a large carriage, with a team of four horses moving in his direction. He could hear the dull roar of the crowd and music. Two blocks before City Hall, the great carriage made a sharp right, driving away from the expected destination. The vehicle also picked up speed as it moved toward 3rd Street. Black whistled and several men on horseback closed in on the carriage, forcing the driver toward Indiana Avenue and 2nd Street. Elbert moved in with the carriage, blocking off 2nd and Frank sealed their getaway, by blocking 3rd Street.

Shots were fired from the presidential carriage into the night. The men didn't return fire for fear of killing Lincoln. Black, James, Gilbert and Tim approached on either side of the carriage. When the driver tried to reload his gun, James shot him causing him to fall from the vehicle. Gilbert hit him with the butt of his gun and dragged him away. There was a grim silence while guns were being reloaded. Black and James moved in with the quickness, yanking both doors open. Behind James, Gilbert pointed his .44 into the cab; behind Black, Tim pointed a Sharps rifle. Time stood still, as Luke and Anthony came with the torches adding light to the situation.

Inside the carriage, Lincoln was flanked by two men. The president looked dazed as torchlight lit up his gaunt features. He held his top hat in his lap. Looking about with perceptive eyes, Lincoln simply nodded when Black spoke.

"Mr. President, this way to safety."

18

The Blueprint

LINCOLN LOOKED ABOUT with apprehension as he stepped from the carriage. Black continued issuing orders. "Tie these two up and collect the driver."

Tim and Bainesworth took over driving the presidential carriage. James and Gilbert rode with the prisoners. Lincoln, himself, was led to the carriage driven by Frank. Black climbed in after the president and Elbert got in from the opposite door. Ephraim took over the vehicle that Elbert drove. The remaining men moved out on horseback, leading the horses with no riders back to the cabin.

They rode in silence, until Lincoln spoke. "My bodyguards were going to kill me–then you all appeared. I must admit my tension level has not changed."

The carriage was submerged in complete darkness, yet there was no mistaking Lincoln's fear. Black, sensing his unease, attempted to offer peace. "You are safe with us, Mr. President."

"May I ask your names?" Lincoln pressed.

"My name is Black."

Elbert remained quiet, allowing Black to handle the matter.

Black thought that Lincoln would say no more. Instead, the president surprised him. "I have heard of you."

Black chuckled. "We don't run in the same circles, so I'm sure you heard my name in conjunction with the Fugitive Slave Act."

"I'm afraid you're correct," Lincoln replied.

The conversation stopped as they rode the remaining distance. When the conveyance rolled to a halt, the door on Black's side of the carriage was yanked open by Luke. Behind Luke, Ralph and Jesse stood, holding torches. Black stepped down from the cab, followed by the president and Elbert. It seemed the moon had followed them to the cabin and though the wind had picked up, the weather was comfortable.

The men closed in around the president even though he was taller. They remained in a protective formation until Lincoln stepped up on the makeshift porch and entered the cabin. He had to bend his head to get through the door. Inside the cabin stood a white man with brown hair and dark eyes, and next to him was a blond-haired man with blue eyes. Both men had their hands tied behind their backs. The other men filed out of the cabin to watch the night. Black's men moved about in a disorderly fashion, so as not to be counted.

The president was taller than most and the ceiling in the little cabin was low. Lincoln's shoulders remained stooped, so he wouldn't bang his head. His black suit was wrinkled, and his hair was wild upon his head. The situation brought a type of realness that could not be disputed.

Black stared up at Lincoln and, noticing his distress, motioned toward a chair. "Please sit, Mr. President."

Lincoln sat down with a sigh. Lou was standing at the rear of the cabin in front of the blanket that hid Molly, a look of agitation on his face. Also crowding the small space were James, Elbert, and Bainesworth. The president's bushy eyebrows popped up when his gaze fell to James.

"Aren't you a butler at the executive mansion?" Lincoln asked.

Bainesworth stepped in, chest puffed out and gestured towards the bodyguards. "Mr. President, I am from London town. My name is Ambassador Bainesworth, and I report to her majesty, Queen Victoria. These men are part of a group called the Preservers of Southern Life. This organization has plotted against your very existence, and the queen sent me to make certain you were aware. I, along with Black and his men are an extension of the queen's hand."

Lincoln nodded and though he spoke softly, his anger was visible. "These two men were already part of the staff when I acquired the job of president."

"This plot originated in Canada, and the queen would not have your blood on her hands. There are those in Parliament who have their own agenda and attempt to work around her majesty. The queen is smarter than most men and will not have things done in her name," Bainesworth responded.

"Yet England continues to sell weapons to the South," Lincoln commented with disdain.

"One matter at a time," Bainesworth replied.

"What next?" Lincoln asked.

Black jumped in. "We find out where they were going to take you and shut the place down."

Lincoln crossed his legs. Leaning forward, he stared at Black before surveying the eager faces in the room. "I'm ready."

Black nodded to Lou, who pulled the makeshift curtain back to reveal a frightened Molly. She was seated in a chair beside the bed. At the sight of the men standing around the small room, she reached out for Lou's hand. The two prisoners' eyes bulged when they saw the girl. The dark-haired man, whom Black guessed to be Sheffield, looked up with a sneer.

Black began the interrogation. "Where was the president to be transported?"

Sheffield's British accent was abrupt and snide. He ignored Black, addressing Lincoln when he spoke. "Look what you have created! This slave thinks he is my equal—niggers toting weapons! Do understand, sir; it wasn't personal."

Bainesworth took offense and stepped forward, but Black stayed him before crossing the room and opening the front door. He whispered something to Frank and Gilbert. Both men nodded and walked away. A breeze flowed into the stuffy cabin, and moments later there was a scream from somewhere outside, followed by two gunshots. Seconds later, Frank and Gilbert appeared, tossing the driver's lifeless body onto the floor for all to see.

Lincoln spoke up. "So the man in charge of the stables was in on this as well. I would not have suspected Louis."

Black stepped to Sheffield and slapped him like a bitch. It was the type of blow to make a man's head ring. Reining himself in, Black realized this kill belonged to Lou. When Sheffield staggered, Black asked heatedly. "Do you remember her?"

Sheffield held his ear as he ignored the question and looked away.

"He come to the dry-goods store!" Molly cried out. "They both come, and they used us against our will."

Black turned to Lou. "You can have him."

Frank stepped into the doorway and smiled at Lou.

"Cut 'em loose," Lou said to his brother. "Won't be no fun if'n he tied up. We gon' see what he made of."

Frank cut Sheffield's hands loose and grabbed him by the hair. Sheffield screamed, "No! No! Don't touch me! No!"

The twins pounced on Sheffield and dragged him screaming into the night. Gilbert dragged the dead driver from the cabin, leaving a trail of blood as he pulled him over the threshold. No one spoke as Black turned to the other prisoner.

"What is your name? If I have to ask Mr. Lincoln, this will not go well for you."

"Berkley," the prisoner responded.

"Berkley," Black said, pausing for effect. "Where was the president being taken?"

The prisoner was visibly shaken. Perspiration dripped from his pasty forehead. "There is an old farmhouse about five miles out. We were to meet our men there."

"How many men?" Black pressed.

"Seven."

It was just as Black had assumed. He was about to speak when Elbert broke in. "I will handle this. Frank and Gilbert will come with me. When we finish, we'll meet you at the dry-goods store. I will bring the carriage."

"Yeah," Black responded.

Elbert drew his gun and shoved the barrel in Berkley's face. He nodded toward the door and the prisoner moved along quietly. Still inside the cabin were Black, Lincoln, James, Bainesworth and Molly. Lincoln severed the peace when he asked, "What now?"

Black smiled. "We take you home, sir."

Lincoln looked up at Black from where he sat. His usual austerity changed to a look of confusion. "Why would you take me back there? It's dangerous."

Black and the others threw back their heads and laughed.

"Mr. President, sir," James said, "you doesn't take the warnings being put to ya. Yo' house ain't secure."

The president wore an expression of incredulity. "The executive mansion belongs to the people. I can't just shut them out."

Black more than understood Lincoln's position on this matter; his own house was the center of the fort's activity and was always overrun with those who lived around it.

"You have to cut the public off from the personal space you share with your family. Select an elite group of soldiers and have them stand guard in the mansion. Limit the public to certain hours and one room," Black suggested.

Lincoln sighed. "I can't do this job in fear—I wouldn't be effective. But I will make the changes you suggest for the safety of my wife and children. The country has broken in half under my rule, and if I were speaking truthfully, it is a humiliation I can't stomach."

Bainesworth, James, and Black were solemn as they stood before the president.

"I do not believe in slavery," the president went on, "but it was not my goal to stop it. Still, I spend my days pardoning sixteen-year-old boys whose only offense is fear. I, of course, mean no slight as I speak here with you all."

Black gathered his thoughts. "This war represents the hate within this nation, though cotton and economics have their place in this conflict. When one race enslaves another, humanity is lost. Bondage is violent for both the slaver and the enslaved—the slaver must disengage from morality in order to carry out such atrocities. Such actions cause mankind to feed on itself. As I said, while cotton and money have their place, they are frivolous in the face of a mother being sold from her child. This war would have happened regardless. You just happened to be president at the time. Your humiliation cannot equal that of an enslaved man who can do nothing in defense of his woman and children."

Lincoln nodded in agreement, remaining quiet and thoughtful as Black continued.

"This war will not be won until you address the issue of slavery. Until the people who truly have something to gain from this war are allowed to fight, you will continue to pardon children for a war they didn't create. Let's hope you will address the real problem before there are no more sixteen-year-old white boys left."

"If I were to address the issue of slavery, the country would have to be whole. Releasing slaves in a country where I am not the president will not free anyone. Offering medical attention after death is useless," Lincoln remarked.

"Ignoring what is causing the death of this country will not make it whole again either," Black countered.

At that moment, Tim stepped into the doorway. "We are ready for you, Black."

Black stared at Lincoln for a moment before turning on his heels and heading for the door. He stepped into the night to speak with his men.

"I will drive the carriage; Bainesworth will ride shotgun," Tim said.

"I will stay and check on Molly," Shultz added.

The men were standing between the shed and the back of the cabin when two shots cracked the night. Lou stepped from the shed into the torchlight held by Jesse. As the flames flickered, Black could see he was covered in blood. Ephraim held the other torch on the situation. Black nodded curtly, and Ephraim pushed Lou towards the pump.

Black assigned duties and when the tasks were complete, he fetched the president. When he re-entered the cabin, he was followed by Lou, who had cleaned up. The curtain was again drawn separating Molly from the room and Lou went to her. Black offered instructions to Lincoln so they could move to the next step in the plan.

"Mr. President, sir," Black said, "it's time to travel. But before you leave here I would like to speak freely with you about what to expect. Of course, you are under no obligation to do as I say. Still, it's important you understand that what I say will prolong your life."

Lincoln looked at Black with a mildly amused expression but said nothing. Black took that as a signal to continue. "There is a dry-goods store on 10th Street. The Preservers of Southern Life used this place as a base of operations. We have shut the place down and will send a message to all of Washington that you are no easy mark. You will also find members of your staff missing—never to be seen again as we remedy the situation thoroughly. Remember, there is strength in silence."

"I understand," Lincoln said.

Black searched his face, trying to gauge the president's sincerity. Finally, he said, "This way, Mr. President. We will keep you safe—follow me."

Black, James, Anthony, and Lincoln rode under the cover of darkness as they headed back toward the mansion. The only sound was the clip-clopping of horse hooves against the cobblestone roadway once they were back within the city limits. The hour had grown late, and Black was certain people were looking for the president. They did not need to be hanged after saving Lincoln. The carriage they rode in was not the presidential vehicle. Lincoln must have been thinking about their security as well.

"I think we should enter the mansion through the servant's door."

"I agree," Black said. "We will park the carriage on a side street and make for the mansion on foot."

They rode for about fifteen minutes more before Tim brought the carriage to a stop a few blocks from the mansion. Lincoln, who was somewhat ungainly, moved as though he understood his safety was in question. The men surrounded him, moving as one unit until the executive mansion came into view. They approached from the back of the home, walking through the trees and swiftly moving through the building behind the great house. It had grown colder and the wind carried a small bite. Still, Black was sweating.

The lamppost by the back door was lit, but Anthony snuffed it out to maintain security. James pushed at the door and led the way. Lincoln went in next, followed by Anthony and Black. There were several lamps lit in the kitchen, and all the colored servants were lined up, being questioned by two older white men.

Lincoln strode into the room to gasps and shouts of relief. The president addressed the room calmly. "There was a change in plans. I am well, and there is no cause for alarm."

Everyone stared, but no one moved. Lincoln continued, "Will, Hannibal, I have decided to make some changes. We will discuss them in the morning. Go home and get some rest."

The Vice President and Secretary of State gawked at Lincoln and his entourage. They made no effort to leave, nor did they question him. Black leaned in and spoke for the president's ears only. "Because they are already here, I would rather take no chances. Why don't you have them take a seat in the kitchen, while we wrap up in the dining room?"

Lincoln nodded, and to Cook he said, "Please make us some coffee. Gentlemen, have a seat in the kitchen. I will be with you shortly."

The room came to life as Lincoln, Black and James got comfortable at the table in the servants' dining room. Anthony stood guarding the door. Black noticed Anthony refused eye contact when the young lady he suspected to be Music stared up at him. Lizzie stepped in to serve the coffee and James, like Anthony, looked away. Lizzie didn't speak to James, and when she finished serving them, Lincoln got down to business.

"Black, why don't you stay and work directly for me?" Lincoln asked.

Black smiled and formed his answer with care. "Mr. President, I am a farmer by trade. I appreciate the offer, but I must decline."

"You and your men are not farmers," the president declared with a chuckle. "I will pay you well."

"I work for Queen Victoria, and I don't think she would take kindly to my working for you," Black countered.

The president laughed, and then became serious once more. "Will I be able to call on you and your men?"

"I will check on you in the near future." Black was noncommittal.

Lincoln nodded but seemed bothered.

"Sir, are there any among the staff whom you can think of that we need to address?"

"I knew you would ask that question. Louis has a brother who works as a driver."

"What is his name, sir?"

James piped up. "Floyd."

"Yes, Floyd," Lincoln confirmed.

"Anyone else?" Black inquired.

The president shook his head. "No."

Tim and Bainesworth appeared in the doorway. It was the signal that this part of the plan was over. Black pushed back from the table. He stood, extending his right hand, and the president gave him a firm handshake.

"Mr. President, the pleasure was all mine."

Lincoln rose from his chair, eyeballing Black. In a low voice, he said, "I have a job I would like you to consider."

Black grinned. "I'm afraid I can't murder Jeff Davis, sir."

Lincoln reared back, stunned by Black's insightfulness.

"If I killed Davis, another who believes in bondage would rise up in his place. I agreed to warn you because having a man in office who doesn't agree with slavery is a start. If you would have been killed tonight, my people would have to wait another lifetime to see freedom. I am hopeful to be part of the first free black generation."

Tim stepped in reiterating, "It's time."

Black offered the president some final advice. "The back door needs a lock. The windows need locks, and you should interview the staff yourself. There shouldn't be any new hires who do not get your personal approval. And sir, limit the public to specific times and one room."

Lincoln emitted a long sigh. "Surely you understand the duties of a war president."

"I do understand, sir. Your duty is to stay alive."

Black and his men exited the dining room and went into the kitchen. Lizzie was standing just inside the doorway, looking panicked and confused. Tim approached her quietly.

"I apologize for my behavior, Miss Elizabeth. I hope you can forgive me and James. It wasn't his idea; it was all me."

"I wanted to tell ya," James added. "I apologize, too. I was wantin' to keep ya safe. I hope ya can forgive me."

Black hung back watching the exchange, and he too felt bad about the deception. Miss Lizzie smiled when she leaned in to whisper, "Mable said you were all great men. Though she never said what you were working on, she did say I could trust you all."

They all were shocked. Lizzie went back to acting nervous and disoriented, and Black chuckled as she climbed the stairs and disappeared. Anthony was speaking with Music, and Black could see it wasn't going well. She appeared genuinely perplexed. Finally, she nodded and then abruptly walked away.

"Do you need a moment?" Black asked.

"Naw, I'm gon' let it go here. I want to steal her, but now ain't the time," Anthony said.

They filed out the back door. Their last act at the executive mansion was to abduct Floyd, the head stableman's brother. James strangled the life from him with piano wire he acquired from the mansion.

❃ ❃ ❃

Bainesworth did the driving, and Tim rode shotgun. Inside the carriage, Black, James, and Anthony rode along with Floyd propped up in the corner next to James. The ambassador brought the carriage to a stop on the corner of 10th Street and New York Avenue. Black and the men hopped down from the vehicle and closed in on the dry-goods store. Across the roadway from the establishment, a small campfire burned as a group of soldiers settled in for the night. Along the street in front of the store, every lamppost was extinguished—a sign that Elbert, Frank, and Gilbert were nearby.

The air was heavy with the smell of rotted flesh, and the cool evening offered no relief from the rancid atmosphere. When Black and the others approached the store, Elbert struck a match off the bottom of his boot and lit a cigar. The tiny flame illuminated the scene just enough for Black to see Frank and Gilbert standing behind him. He could hear Elbert's breath as he blew the smoke about them. When Elbert spoke, it was to give an accounting.

"We found the farmhouse and closed it down."

"How many were there?" Black asked.

"There were eight, including the Berkley fellow. We dug a mass grave," Elbert replied.

"The carriage?"

"Everything is as it should be," Elbert said.

Black nodded. "Let's move out."

Anthony chuckled. "We can all fit in the carriage, but James got him a friend ridin' wit' us."

The men back tracked to the corner of 10th and New York Avenue. They climbed into the awaiting carriage, and it lurched forward. Inside the vehicle Black, Elbert and Gilbert sat to one side. Opposite them sat James, Anthony, Frank and the dead man Floyd, their destination the old cabin. There they would regroup and tie off all loose ends before pressing on to the Hunter plantation.

❊ ❊ ❊

Two days after his "abduction," Lincoln sat in his office having breakfast with his wife. Mary was going on about decorating the East Room. He couldn't concentrate as there was much on his mind. Diane handed him the Washington Times, and his hands shook as he read the headline: **FOUR FOUND DEAD IN A CARRIAGE ON 10ᵀᴴ STREET.**

The article went on to say that four Southern sympathizers were found dead in a carriage in front of the dry-goods store. The bodies appeared to be in varying degrees of decay, indicating the men had been dead for some time. One of the men was identified as the clerk from the store. The real owner could not be located for questioning and authorities suspected foul play. Literature supporting the Southern cause was found in the vehicle along with the deceased. It was unclear who was responsible, and the matter was still under investigation.

When the president finished reading the article, he stood abruptly and excused himself. Lincoln was just at the grand staircase when his secretary of state appeared at the bottom. William too had the newspaper folded under his arm. The two men gaped at each other as the president reached the bottom of the steps.

"Washington has been turned upside down," Seward said.

"Better Washington turned upside down than me stretched out in the East Room in a new suit," the president countered.

"Indeed," said the Secretary.

❋ ❋ ❋

Black and the men doubled back over the state line into Maryland. They set up camp and rested in shifts. On day three, the men from Beacon Hill rode into the campsite. They were headed to the fort and had detoured to pick up Molly and take her to safety. But, after all she had been through, she was too shaken to ride out with men she didn't know.

Black and the twins stood off to the side to speak privately.

Lou spoke up first, directing his words to his brother. He was emotionally torn.

"I cain't send her wit' dem. She ain't walking, neither."

Frank gave his brother a look of understanding, but said nothing.

Lou went on. "We ain't been apart, I know. It ain't that she mo' important. Shit just happens."

"I ain't seeing another answer. Go wit' the girl. It's right," Frank responded.

Lou turned to Black. "I ain't meanin' to let ya down."

Black looked from brother to brother before he spoke. "I am glad you are seeing this through. We can't not stop the mission, and this is a variable we could not foresee. You have not let me down—you saved the mission. Women and children always come first. We will watch Frank's back and do our best to keep each other safe."

Both men nodded, and Black stepped away to give them some privacy. Frank reassuringly clapped Lou on the back as they walked to the awaiting carriage. Molly was already inside. They spoke for a moment more, and then Lou disappeared into the cab. As the carriage rolled slowly away, Frank stood staring until it was out of sight.

Nineteen men then turned their attention to the Hunter plantation. They would leave at nightfall moving slowly toward the final steps of a well thought out strategy. Black had only one regret—they did not have the time to chase John Booth and his friend Samuel.

Hunter Plantation

October 1861

As E.J. gazed out the window of his study, he had come to a stark realization. He was now responsible for Julia and Maryam. While he was attempting to understand the meaning of such responsibility, he heard wailing from deep in the corridor. E.J. knew what had transpired. Adrian Wells had finally succumbed to his injuries. The man had languished for days between life and death. Now, he felt sorrow for his sweet wife.

He heard soft footsteps, just as he turned to face the door. Suzanne stood just inside the study wearing a dark blue dress with matching slippers. Her eyes were glassy, and her face tear-stained. Remembering how he felt when his mama died, E.J. reached out a hand to her. She came to him without hesitation, and he held her.

Against his chest, she whispered, "My papa is gone."

"I felt just like you when my mama passed on. It doesn't go away, but it gets better," he said, trying his best to console her.

"My mama and sister are distraught. What do I do?"

"I think it's important your mother understand we can't travel to take him home. It's too dangerous. The slaves will handle his body, and we will bury him day after tomorrow."

She nodded, wiping her nose with her handkerchief. "I will go and tend to my mama and sister."

He followed her from his study and watched as she helped her weeping mother upstairs to lie down. Maryam followed them, and when they were out of sight, he turned and went out the front door. The day was cloudy and cool. He descended the steps and headed in the direction of the barn. As he got closer to the weather-beaten structure, he saw that the large door was slid back into the open position. When he stepped inside, all conversation stopped.

Jeb, along with another overseer named Jeff—a rough-looking fellow with a mean stare and missing teeth—were standing guard while three male slaves cleaned the barn. E.J. waited by the great door as Jeb approached.

My father in-law has died," E.J. told him. "I need a pine box and a hole dug in the family cemetery."

"Me and Gerry will bring the box directly. While you all is stuffin' him in, we'll go on and dig the hole," Jeb replied.

"Walk with me," E.J. said.

While they strolled along the path leading to the slave quarters, E.J. instructed Jeb on the security measures he wanted in place during the funeral. They arrived at the rear of Jeremiah's cabin, to find Callie seated on the back porch. She frowned when she caught sight of him. Callie still feared him. Jeremiah had also informed him that she thought he would take her baby. In the past, his father had made good money in such ventures. He too would have endeavored to turn a coin. Now he felt shame. E.J. had been about to turn away when his brother appeared.

Jeremiah walked out onto the porch shirtless, his gun holster strapped to his bare chest.

"Wells died," E.J. said.

"He hung on longer than I thought," Jeremiah replied.

"I was speaking with Jeb here about the changes in security we discussed."

Jeremiah moved to the edge of the top step, blocking their view of Callie. Jeb pulled out his flask and took a deep swallow before passing it. E.J. drank deeply and then passed the flask back to Jeb, who held it out in offering to Jeremiah.

"I ain't one to partake in spirits, and if I did, it wouldn't be wit' white men," Jeremiah said, looking from E.J. to Jeb.

"Belligerent bastard," E.J. chuckled. "Will you come to my study later?"

Jeremiah nodded. E.J. turned and walked away. Jeb followed.

❈ ❈ ❈

Callie went back to her sewing as the master the overseer walked off. She was thankful Jeremiah had come outside when he did.

He had not spoken to her in days, but she did not push him. In her condition, she had no energy to fight. Miss Suzanne's father being shot—and now dead, apparently—made her all the more nervous. Jeremiah had not slept since the incident.

She thought he would go back into the cabin to avoid her. Instead, he leaned on the rail in front of where she sat. Folding his arms over his chest, Jeremiah gazed at her. When she looked up, his eyes were explosive. She couldn't look away, so intense was the moment between them. He reached out a hand to her. She put her sewing aside and slowly stood. Motherhood weighed her down as she waddled into his embrace.

He wrapped his arms around her and whispered against her ear. "I love you, Callie."

She began to cry, out of relief and fatigue. He led her into the cabin just as the sky opened up and a downpour ensued. Thunder rolled in the distance.

"Come lay wit' me," Jeremiah said once they were inside.

They undressed and climbed into bed. When she was settled, he pulled her close.

"Will you sleep?" she asked.

"No. I just want to watch you."

She felt safe, in the moment, with her head against his chest and her belly pressed against his side. Callie understood that he was angry, but the tenderness between them meant he was acknowledging that she could not live without him.

❈ ❈ ❈

The next afternoon, Adrian Wells was laid out in the front sitting room. Jeb and his brother Gerry had brought the pine box to the main house. Eva, Ella, and Sonny had prepared the body to receive the family. When Julia saw the coffin being carried in, she fainted, and E.J. had to carry her to her room. Despite his conflict with his mother-in-law, he did feel sorry for her. In the meantime, Suzanne and Maryam were bearing up as well as could be expected. They both rushed to comfort their mother.

Suzanne and her sister decided to keep their father's body on display until the next morning. In the absence of a preacher, his daughters would pray for his soul. The overseers came to pay their respects, gripping their hats. Some had the audacity to leer at the widow with looks of interest. Julia made one appearance in the front parlor, but when she saw her late husband lying in state in his dark suit, she became overwrought and retreated to her room, refusing to return.

That evening, E.J. worked late. Jeremiah, doing a walkthrough of the house, stopped in the door of his study.

"I added more men at night," E.J. said.

"When ya burying the old man?"

"We'll take him to the cemetery in the morning. Do you want to move north and set up in the city?"

Jeremiah looked baffled. "What will we do with the land?"

"We can shut the plantation down until after the war."

"The slaves?"

E.J. moved his ledger off to the side. "We could liquidate. I don't think my wife can take much more."

"I can't leave Ella, Eva, and Sonny," Jeremiah said.

E.J. nodded in understanding. Jeremiah continued, "What will you do with your mother-in-law and sister-in-law?"

"I will have to take them with me. I now have the added burden of Adrian Wells' holdings. Maryam will marry, I suspect. But unless Julia remarries, my wife will expect me to look after her. I would like her to remarry, but for now..." E.J. sighed.

"So, I would take three people, plus Callie. I worry to travel with her condition, but I worry as much to stay here," Jeremiah replied.

"We could take Jeb and Gerry for extra gun hands until we get settled. They seem the sharpest. We could travel by train to New

York. I need to finish helping my wife through the death of her papa and get him buried. Then, we could move forward."

"There will be eleven of us traveling. Ain't that costly?" Jeremiah asked.

"There will be twelve of us."

Jeremiah furrowed his brow. "Twelve?"

"I will not leave Nettie behind," E.J. reminded him. "Suzanne and I are working through the three of us being able to live peaceably together. If something should happen to me, you are to protect Nettie and any children we have together." He paused and looked at his brother in earnest. "I love her."

Hesitant, Jeremiah considered his brother.

"I will do the same for Callie and your children," E.J. promised.

Jeremiah's eyes searched the room for some sort of reply. "I'll be back in the mornin' to help wit' the body," he said before he disappeared down the hall.

❊ ❊ ❊

As James and the men moved along the outskirts of Virginia, he discovered it was much like Washington. The only exception, slavery was the platform in this capital city. The men continued on to North Carolina, traveling mostly during the night hours. The nineteen planned to set up camp on Jeb and Gerry's property so the men could rest and regroup before pressing on to the Hunter plantation.

It was almost dawn when they arrived on the edge of Jeb's land. The men watched under the cover of darkness as a group of confederate soldiers made camp at their intended location. Backing away quietly, the nineteen pressed on to a safer location. They would not engage in a fight they couldn't win. Most importantly, they would not linger in the South for health's sake.

The men rode to the border between North and South

Carolina and arrived at nightfall. Black and the others ensconced themselves in some bushes in a clearing near Myrtle's place. It had grown hotter as they traveled south, but the droopy vegetation indicated winter was approaching. In the distance, James could see a light burning in the front window.

"I don't member shit 'bout this place," James commented.

"The husband ain't like you," Elbert chuckled.

"Miss Myrtle loved her some James," Black added with a laugh, "and the men need rest."

"What I see's is you two keep lendin' me out like a cheap whore," James countered.

Elbert's chest convulsed with contained humor. "Well, ya prettier than me and Black."

"You are," Black agreed.

"Hell wit' both of ya," James replied, dismissing his brothers with mild annoyance.

The three brothers stepped from the bushes and headed toward Miss Myrtle's house.

19

The Loose Ends

AFTER THEY SETTLED in at Myrtle's, the men broke down into two groups; ten men roamed the property while the other nine rested. James, Black, Elbert and Tim gathered in a circle in the well-lit barn, along with Charles, Myrtle's husband. As the men conversed, James studied Charles by the light of the lanterns placed favorably around the loft. He did not remember this man. But the last time he was at Myrtle's, he had been shot in the face. Everything from that time was fuzzy in his mind. Charles, however, appeared happy to see Black.

"I ain't been sleeping much. We had deserters and soldiers come—they think we s'pose to give 'em whateva they wantin'. I don't have slaves and ain't never had 'em. This ain't my damn war," Charles said with a scowl.

"You enlisting?" Black asked.

If'n I enlist, my woman and sons would be alone," Charles responded.

Black nodded, and Charles went on. "You know, they's trying to make a law what says if a man got twenty slaves, he ain't gotta fight. This a rich man's war."

Elbert chimed in. "Head to Canada. The land will be here when this war is over."

Charles looked to Elbert and nodded. "I been givin' it thought."

"You can't think too long," Tim added.

The man was about to say more when a middle-aged white woman with dark brown hair appeared at the barn entrance. She was on the plain side; her hair was pulled back, accentuating her large dark eyes and her heart-shaped mouth. She wore a brown cotton dress and a black shawl draped about her shoulders. Charles reached out to her.

"Charles," Myrtle whispered, as she moved in to take her husband's hand.

She did not take her eyes from James, who smiled down at her. His greeting was deep with appreciation.

"Miss Myrtle, glad to see you is well."

"James," she said shyly. "You look well."

James grinned. "I feels well. Glad to be able to say thank you in person—thank you."

Myrtle stepped forward and reached up to touch his scar. She caressed James' face with her right hand, while holding on to her husband with her left. James allowed her soft touch. "The skin feels tight in the cold, but I promise I feels good."

As Myrtle smiled at him, her husband's eyes rolled to the ceiling. "I could consider Canada," Charles said looking at Black, "if'n *he* ain't living there. She flirtin' wit' me standing right here."

Black chuckled.

"Oh, you are awful, Charles," Myrtle said, not taking her eyes off James.

The men did a shift change and when the action was complete, James stood at the barn door staring into the darkness. As dawn approached, he found that he could not sleep. His thoughts were calm. He had set all emotion aside, seeing this mission as a spectator rather than an angry nigger. Amidst his internal peace, he realized something about his brother, Black. Taking this journey, in this way, was Black's way of allowing him time to weigh life. The pieces of his existence now fell into place like a puzzle. He could see it all clearly and in its order of importance.

Though his sorrow about Fannie was still keen, the situation seemed different now. It was a tragic accident that would always hover in the background of his life, but he could live. Fannie would forever represent the moment he realized shit happens. He still felt anger about being shot in the face. His life had flashed before him, and he felt real fear for his brothers and himself. But he now saw being shot as a predicted variable. It was part of the dangers by which they lived their lives as men of color. He didn't have it all figured out, but he did feel emotionally emancipated from all that held him back.

Black and Elbert walked up as he stood alone.

"We will leave here after nightfall tomorrow," Black said.

"Are we going to approach in the daylight?" James asked.

"They expect us at night," Black replied. "Did you have something different in mind?"

"No."

"You ready?" Elbert asked.

"I am," James replied.

"The plan is the same, and we will step through it as discussed and rehearsed," Black directed.

They stood in the doorway of the barn. Behind them, all the lanterns had been snuffed out except one. In front of them was complete darkness. There was a chill in the air that was warmed by the whiskey Elbert passed around. Though they did not say, the brothers were thankful for one another. They took these few moments to recuperate and silently offer strength to each other. After a time, James' words got their blood moving.

"I prefer the daylight; I wants to see him take his last breath."

"If all goes well, we should be moving away from the Hunter plantation by the time night falls again," Black estimated.

Elbert took another swig. "We need to get in and get out," he said with an air of resolution.

The men fell quiet again, each thinking on the outcome of the matter. James added one last thought and it was to be respected, "I brought me some extra piano wire, for dem intimate moments."

E.J. stood at the balcony door looking out into the morning rain. To take his father-in-law's body out into the downpour and dump it into a hole would assail his wife's and daughters' sensitivities. He was at once thankful for the cool season. In summer, the odor of rotting flesh would be intolerable. He would put off the burial until after the storm passed.

It was dawn, and his wife had just awakened. He could hear her moving about behind him. She was coming to his bed and allowing him to comfort her. His wife pleased him. They had not made love, and he had not pushed for it. She needed room and he understood based on his experience with loss. He had not dressed or left the room because he wanted to be sensitive to her feelings. E.J. was also hiding from the smell.

He leaned his shoulder against the doorjamb and crossed his bare feet at the ankle. A small fire burned in the hearth, warming his room. The weather outside was cool but not cold enough to offer the right mixture. She came to stand next to him in the doorway, leaning her slender shoulder against the frame, almost imitating him. He smiled down at her as she stood with her brown hair flowing about her.

"Papa is starting to smell of death. Are you hiding from the odor?"

E.J. chuckled and gave his wife a wry smile. "I am hiding, but I hadn't planned on saying such a thing to you."

"It's raining, and my mother will be hurt if we bury him in bad weather."

"I thought that as well. In situations like this, it's the small things that are remembered."

Suzanne sighed. "Well, I can't bear much more and neither can Maryam. If the weather clears, then we will bury him today. Should it keep raining, we will bury him in the morning before mother is up and about." She looked at him and paused. "I know you are not pleased about being stuck with my family."

He faced her straight on. "I will see this through with you."

"Because you want Nettie?"

"Because I love *you*," he countered.

"You have not gone to her?"

"You wish to discuss this now?" he asked.

"I wish to know when you will resume your nightly visits."

E.J. sighed in exasperation. "Will you ever allow the three of us to exist in the same space?"

"You wish for me to turn a blind eye?"

"I wish for both of your eyes to be open," he asserted.

"You have not pushed for intimacy with me. Do you not want me anymore? Is it because you only want her?"

"I want you, Suzanne. I am trying not to be a brute. As a man—as your husband—I could force you. But I want you to want and need me, the way I want and need you."

"And Nettie?"

He looked away from her, out into the rain that was falling in thick, heavy drops. "She *was* my slave. I am trying to back away from a relationship where she feels forced. As a man–as her master–I could impose my will. But I want her to want me, the way I want her. For the reasons I have given, I have not pushed for intimacy with either of you. I am choosing to work with you, Suzanne, on the pace of this matter."

Her voice broke and a tear ran down her cheek. "I want to hate you, but I still love you," she whispered.

He looked at her with gentle consideration. "I am humbled by you both," he said softly.

❀ ❀ ❀

The day dragged on slowly, and the rain did not let up. Around four in the afternoon, E.J. arrived at Nettie's. He took off his black slicker and shook it before he went inside. Nettie was seated in front of the fire, sewing. She looked up and smiled at him; she shocked him by speaking first.

"I's sorry for yo' wife. Sonny tell me what happened when he come to get the laundry."

E.J. nodded. Nettie did not acknowledge the fact that he, himself, had sent Sonny to keep her informed of events at the main house. He had also sent along some gifts: a set of decorative hair combs and a pair of gold earrings shaped like roses. They had belonged to his mother, who had inherited them from her own mother. He hung his dripping coat on a hook and pushed the door closed.

"Thank you for understanding. The weather is bad; we have not yet buried him."

She nodded and turned her attention back toward the fire. Needing her to welcome him, he did not move from the door.

After a minute or so, Nettie set aside her handiwork and rose to greet him. She was wearing her slave clothes and that bothered E.J. somehow. The shirt she wore was too large, and it draped off one of her smooth, chocolate shoulders. She had picked out her hair into a thick cloud and used the combs to shove it to one side. The gold earrings dangled from her ears.

"Is ya hungry?"

E.J. didn't answer. Instead, he bent and softly kissed her lips. Taking her by the hand, he led her back to the fire. He sat and pulled her into his lap. Pressing his face in her hair, he inhaled. She smelled of peaches.

"Hmmm, I missed you," he said, his voice thick.

She smiled. "Ya looks tired, Edward."

"I am," he admitted.

Nettie caressed his cheek. "I been missin' you too, Masta."

E.J. pulled back and looked at her. "Are you still upset with me?"

"I ain't upset. Just don't wanna believe ya ain't finna sell me and then I ends up on the block. I cain't take it if that happen." Her voice cracked.

He had been avoiding the conversation for fear of losing her, but he could no longer delay. He addressed her with ardor. "You are free, Nettie. We are no longer slave and master. What I want from you can't work if we continue in such a relationship."

Nettie leaned back in his lap and returned his gaze. She trembled as she searched his eyes, until finally, he looked away.

"I's free?" she whispered.

"Living here at Hunter Manor has become dangerous for us all. I plan to settle you and Suzanne someplace safe. I am ashamed to say, but I postponed telling you because I was afraid to lose you. We will all settle in a free state, and if you don't wish to stay with me," he looked into the fire, "I'll let you go."

Nettie cupped his face, bringing it back toward hers. Her eyes were full of doubt as they darted back and forth. "You's sho' what you is saying to me?"

"Yes."

E.J. didn't ask her if she intended to stay; he didn't want to pressure her. The words "free state" had shaken her, and he didn't think he wanted to hear her immediate thoughts. When she leaned in and kissed him, it tasted of "goodbye." They sat quietly by the fire and listened to the rain on the roof.

Three hours later, as E.J. prepared to leave, he heard Jeremiah's unmistakable heavy footsteps on the front porch. They would walk the property together. He donned his hat and coat. Nettie stood on tiptoes to kiss him once more. He reached for the door, but she stopped him.

"Will ya give me ma papers tonight?"

E.J. stared at her, his hand on the doorknob. His heart was in his stomach. He was losing her, and the pain was acute.

"I have drawn up three sets of papers. Sonny will bring two sets to you tonight."

She smiled. "Thank you, Masta."

He nodded and walked out, joining his brother for the night patrol.

❁ ❁ ❁

James and the others were on the move. The rain had let up and their target was now in sight. They had left Myrtle's after dark per the plan. It was midnight when they found themselves standing in the bushes, quietly observing the Hunter plantation. Everything appeared tranquil, but everyone knew looks could be deceiving. They would wait for daybreak. The next few hours would be organized chaos, and when night fell again, they would press on to the Mickerson plantation.

The weather was now warm and though the rain appeared to have stopped for good, it was wet and uncomfortable. The men broke down into groups of two in order to get a better handle on the problem. They witnessed a shift change, and Elbert counted at least fifty men, as they moved down through the overseer's quarters. James saw the matter as doable; his voice was low and deep as he gave orders.

"I say we deals wit' them what just came on duty—they's fresh and ain't expectin' nothin'. The others won't be rested 'nuff to deal wit' us."

"I'll look for Jeb," Black said, walking away with the ambassador in tow.

James knew Black had paired off with Bainesworth in order give him room to move about. Once Emmett and Josiah dug a deep hole in the underbrush, the plan was in motion. The lighting near the overseer's cabins was much improved compared to the moonlight. Candles and lanterns lit the intricate pathways from the cabin windows as the shift change continued. James and Shultz stood on the side of a cabin listening to the conversation between two white men as they stood on the porch.

"Norman," one male voice greeted.

"Been a miserable and wet night—getting too old for this shit." Norman grumbled.

"Look like the rain finna let us alone today," the other man stated.

"Watch yourself out there, Sam."

"Git ya some rest, Norman."

James and the doctor listened as one man exited the porch and the other went inside, closing the door with a bang. Standing on the side of the small structure, James watched as the man made a left, walking away from him and Shultz. His victim then turned walking along the opposite side of the cabin. Swiftly, he and the doctor rushed to the back of the cabin just as the man moved away from them onto the path. James closed in on the situation, and the whistle of piano wire cracked the air.

During the struggle, the overseer attempted to reach for his gun, but Shultz was on hand to help subdue the man as James strangled the life from him. When the fight was gone from his prey, James dragged the overseer into the bushes away from plain view. They took both of his guns and moved on.

Elbert and Gilbert moved quietly about the slave quarters. They watched as an overseer stepped from the cabin of a slave woman. He was obviously readying himself for his shift when he stopped to take a piss. Gilbert created the diversion.

"'Mawnin'," Gilbert said.

The man abruptly turned in Gilbert's direction, reaching for his gun with his fly still open. "Who the fuck is you?"

Elbert stepped in from behind and stabbed him in the jugular. The man gasped and collapsed as blood spurted everywhere.

"You always gittin blood ever damn where. Ya done got blood on me," Gilbert complained.

"I got piss on my boot. Yo' ass is alive, ain't you?" Elbert replied.

Gilbert chuckled, "Point taken."

The men dragged the dead overseer into the brush, took his gun and moved on.

Frank and Horace watched as two overseers left a cabin together. When they rounded the side of the crudely made cottage, Frank slammed the taller man in the face with a shovel. His friend attempted to intervene and, not seeing Horace, got his throat slit for his troubles. Frank jammed the felled man in the throat with the edge of the shovel, almost severing his head from his body. Blood splashed up at him.

The goal was to reduce the ratio of Hunter men to their men and do it quickly before anyone sounded the alarm. Herman and Ralph methodically dragged the bodies to the hole and rolled them in. The early morning hours would continue in this way until daybreak. Black lingered about with Bainesworth at his side, watching as the number of overseers dwindled. When he spied Jeb walking up to one of the cabins, Black made his presence known.

"Jeb," Black allowed his deep voice to float from the darkness.

Jeb turned in the direction of the voice and moved to the edge of the top step, trying to gauge the circumstances. Black stepped into the slice of light from the door, followed by the ambassador.

"'Bout damn time—thought ya forgot me," Jeb said when he recognized Black.

"I had other pressing matters. I apologize for the inconvenience. I will not forget this kindness." Black replied.

"Gerry is inside. They has 'bout sixty men," Jeb informed him.

"They *used* to have sixty men," Black corrected; his tone grim. "Go get your brother and come walk with me. Dawn is upon us, and I need some questions answered."

❀ ❀ ❀

James and Shultz met up with Black, Bainesworth, Jeb, and Gerry. They moved deep into the brush while Jeb and Gerry took turns explaining the dynamics of the plantation and how it was run. The chief focus was on Jeremiah and his movements about the property.

"The black cracker walks the property at night. He sleeps in the day hours," Jeb explained.

"Got him a woman too, and her belly full of his seed," Gerry added.

"Shit, the woman got him. She done mastered the black cracker fo' sho'," Jeb said, chuckling.

"Heard tell he kilt a overseer for her," Gerry said.

James closed his mind to Jeb and Gerry's revelation. It would not stop him from handling Jeremiah accordingly. *Nothing* would change the course of the next few hours. Jeb led James, Black, and Elbert to Jeremiah's cabin. The men watched both the front and back of the place from a safe distance.

Jeremiah had changed cabins. The men knew this was a move to conceal his resting place. James saw this as confirmation that Jeremiah was expecting them. He smiled to himself as he watched the cabin for signs of movement.

As the early morning hours pressed on, Frank happened along, and Black left with him to rally the men, leaving James to stand watch behind Jeremiah's cabin. Elbert and Jeb were posted up in the shadows at the front. Gerry had confirmed that the black overseer accessed his home from the back door. It was around four when James heard footfalls on the path and knew it was Jeremiah.

Droplets of water fell from the leaves in the cool dawn air. James waited patiently; his time measured in the erratic *drip-drips*. Though dawn was coming, it had grown darker with clouds and deep overcast. The wind picked up, as if more bad weather was moving in. Jeremiah emerged from the darkened path and stepped up onto the back porch. He paused to listen to the night. James was a few feet away in the shadows, contemplating the man's death. He sensed Jeremiah knew he was there, crouched and waiting like a panther in the night.

Finally, after what seemed an eternity, Jeremiah turned and opened the door. A small amount of light flashed from a lantern lit within the cabin, and the door closed as suddenly as it opened. Then there was nothing but the sound of James' pulse beating in his ears. He would wait for daylight. He wanted Jeremiah to be clear about who he was and why he had come.

❄ ❄ ❄

As the colorful shades of dawn appeared in the east, James, Black, and Elbert regrouped at the back of Jeremiah's home. Their hands went for their guns when the door suddenly opened. A woman stepped from the cabin; her belly was indeed full. She walked along the path toward the main house until she rounded the bend and disappeared. The three men did not move for a time, giving the man inside time to doze off.

James looked up and saw Frank standing at the side of the cabin. He lifted his hand, wiggling his fingers. James nodded—it was the signal to start the next phase of their scheme. Elbert walked off to follow Frank around to the front. James motioned to Black, and both men ran for the back porch. They kicked in the back door with a thunderous crash, and it swung from one hinge. A second later, Elbert and Frank exploded through the front door.

The plan was simple; the complicated part was trying not to get shot. They all knew from experience that the black cracker was an excellent shot. The element of surprise was only so good for an opponent that was expecting trouble. Inside the cabin, seated in a chair with his back to the wall sat Jeremiah. He held a gun in each hand with the hammer cocked back on both. His voice was smooth when he spoke. "Welcome."

"Drop yo' guns and get yo' damn hands in the air!" James yelled as he stepped through the door with a sawed-off shotgun taken from a dead overseer.

James felt the blood thrumming through his being. But the black cracker did not drop his guns, and he did not put his hands in the air. Instead, he rose from his chair, kicked it aside and pressed his back to the wall.

"Ain't no mistakin', two of you is going wit' me." Jeremiah's voice was laced with malice.

Before James could answer, Black backed out of the doorway. Behind him, James heard the screams and cries of a woman, "No! No! Please don't hurt him. Jeremiah! Jeremiah! Please, no!"

James smirked when he saw the dread that crossed Jeremiah's face. Black attempted to stop the woman, but she yanked away and ran into the cabin. The brown shawl she wore fell to the ground. The food in her hands splashed up the wall and chair as the wooden plate came in contact with the floor. James assessed the caramel skinned woman. As her fear pierced him, he almost looked away–almost.

Jeremiah moved from the wall and stepped in front of his woman. He looked squarely at James. "She ain't got nothing to do with this."

"Stand down!" James shouted.

Elbert cocked his gun, causing Black to step all the way into the cabin. He stood in front of the bed opposite Jeremiah. Black's voice was tight, "Their well-being is on you. We will not stand down."

Jeremiah's hands shook. It was clear he was afraid for his woman. He slowly uncocked his guns and placed them on the floor. He kicked them to Black and then unholstered the weapon at his upper left. When he placed his last gun on the floor, he remained standing in front of the woman.

"She ain't got nothing to do with this," he repeated.

Once the black cracker surrendered his weapons, James stepped forward outing his light with the butt of the shotgun. Jeremiah fell forward with blood spurting from his person. As James closed in on the situation, the woman began screaming.

"No! No! Please don't do this! Mercy! Please, mercy!"

She dropped to her knees on the floor next to Jeremiah and wept. The black overseer was out cold; she tried to shake him awake, but to no avail. James turned to Black, and he could see that his brother was agitated. The woman was a variable none of them had foreseen. Turning to Elbert and Frank, James nodded curtly. They would have taken Jeremiah away, but the woman continued to scream.

"Don't touch him! Please, let him be!"

The men stared at the woman on her knees at Jeremiah's side. They were all high-strung, and James wanted to finish what he started. He wanted to stick to the plan of killing the black cracker and shutting down the Hunter plantation. If it hadn't rained, he would have struck the match to set the place a blaze. Now here they all stood with their goal in sight, yet unattainable.

The woman wept softly as she pleaded with her man to wake up. James looked away as she begged. "Jeremiah, my love, please wake up! We can't make it without you."

Black stepped forward. "Miss Callie, you will need to come with me."

James was impressed Black remembered the woman's name. He couldn't remember a damn thing Jeb or Gerry had said because his emotions were so high. The woman calmed, though she remained visibly upset. She never let Jeremiah's hand go, but focused on Black. "Who are you?"

"My name is Black."

"*Black*," she sneered. "There was a time when I prayed you and your men would come and help me to freedom. Now you are nothing but a calamity that has befallen me and my child."

James did not know what calamity meant, but it didn't sound good. Black didn't show an outward reaction to her words, but James knew his brother was bothered.

The Callie woman, it appeared, wasn't finished. "Haven't I suffered enough as a slave and a woman?"

Black started to reply, but a brown-skinned, older woman with a scar above her left eye suddenly appeared in the front doorway. Shultz stood behind her, much to James' relief.

"Eva," Callie sobbed. "Look what they did."

The woman Eva looked to James and Black, silently asking for permission to enter the cabin. Black curtly nodded, and Eva turned her attention toward Callie, who was leaned over Jeremiah's lifeless form.

"Won't chu' come wit' me, honey?" Eva crooned.

"Stand aside," Shultz ordered.

Eva helped Callie to her feet, as the doctor dumped a bucket of cold water on Jeremiah's head. He sputtered awake. Callie broke down and cried seeing him move. Shultz dragged Jeremiah to the wall and helped him to an upright position. James could see that the left side of his face was swollen. The black cracker's eyes were alert, and James did not misread the threat coming from the felled man. James wanted to kill Jeremiah, but his woman had them all shaken.

❄ ❄ ❄

Jeremiah's vision was blurred. He was uncertain how long he had been out. Instinctively, he reached for his gun, but his upper left holster was empty. He surveyed the room, taking in the faces of the four men dressed in all black, holding their weapons on him. To his right, a white man looked at him strangely. On his left were Eva and Callie, their faces full of fear and concern. Callie's face struck him to his core; he was reminded of his inadequacies. He attempted to stand for her sake, but he couldn't do it without the assistance of the white man.

Disoriented, he shook his head for clarity, but lucidity did not happen. Still, he reached out his hand to Callie, and she pressed herself against his side. She wept softly, and he held her as he glared about the cabin. Jeremiah leaned heavily against the wall; he refused to sit and appear weak. His voice was stronger than he felt, directing his words to the man with the scar.

"Let us be done with this matter, so she can move on."

Callie looked up at him through her tears. "Don't say such things! Me and the baby can't make it without you."

Jeremiah smiled down at her and whispered, "We talked about this, woman. You ain't never listened to me. I told you not to come back to the cabin."

Callie had been about to plead for his life, but he cut her off. "Eva, take her away from here."

Callie screamed. "No! Jeremiah, please! Please!"

He was careful to show no emotion as Eva and the white man

dragged Callie from the cabin. He saw the morning sun spilling into the cabin from the back door as his woman—and child— were led away with Callie shrieking his name over and over. *Today is as good as any to die.* He looked at the men who remained.

"You make it worse on her by not finishing what ya started. Let's be done with one another," he said.

The man with the scar gave the order. "Tie his ass up."

Two of the men came forward and yanked him about. They turned him to face the wall as they secured his hands behind his back. They were about to lead him away, when the tall bald man standing in the center of the room said, "You will hold off on killing him."

Jeremiah watched as the bald man turned and exited the cabin. He was followed by the man with the scarred face. The man with the lifeless eyes shoved him roughly into a chair before posting up at the back door. The dark-skinned man with him guarded the front.

20

Complications

THE SUN WAS starting to rise when Black stepped from Jeremiah's cabin followed by James. As they moved down through the slave quarters, he could see that word of his presence had spread. The people had not run for freedom, taking heed to the message delivered by his men. He had hoped to sneak up on the main house, but that wasn't possible given the Callie debacle. The number of overseers had diminished greatly; the men had done well. Black and James walked among the people to the last cabin just before the big oak tree.

When Black finally stood on the main path at the edge of the slave quarters, the people gathered from porch-to-porch. They piled onto the walkway in front of where he stood; all eyes were on him. The sun shone brightly down on the people as Black stared from face-to-face. His own men stood among the slaves creating unity, minus James and Gilbert who stood at his back.

Black addressed the people. "I understand you all wish to run for the free states. But war is happening, and travel will be even more treacherous. You will also find that in the free states, there are some who fight in this war who will not see you as their equal.

But if we labor together, you will realize freedom, and should we die fighting back-to-back then we will have died practicing liberty."

The men began cheering, and Black held up his hand to silence them. When the crowd hushed, he went on. "I have but two requests. First, as men, look about you and assign yourselves to the women and children. This will help us keep them accounted for and safe. Second, you are all my men and will answer to me until we are in a free state. Any man who fails to take orders will be put down. Is there any among you that has a problem with my requests? Identify yourself so Gilbert and James can solve your issue with finality."

No man spoke up, and Black continued, his voice measured and calm. "Please look to your left and see the five white men who stand on the porch. They are *my* men, and they are essential in my plan to lead us from here. You will watch their backs as you would your own. Are there any questions?"

"Ain't dem two overseers?" A woman near the front asked, pointing to Jeb and Gerry.

Black looked at the woman, who looked to be about thirty-five summers and had a swollen bottom lip. It pained him to deal with abused women.

"Jeb and his brother took work at this plantation at my request. They are abolitionists by trade and an asset to our cause."

The woman nodded. When it appeared there were no more questions, Black turned his attention to the main house. It was time to move on to the next phase of the plan–capture the new Hunter. They would take over the plantation and shut it down by helping everyone to freedom. The people started moving about, doing as his men instructed. Gilbert addressed Black just before he walked away.

"Imma take Luke. Gimme ten minutes to get ready."

"Send Anthony to me and Black," James ordered.

When Gilbert walked away, he and James faced each other. There was no misreading his brother. James was angry. But Black also saw that he held it in check and did not question his authority. The respect was priceless and for that reason, Black explained himself.

"We don't add misery to the lives of our women," Black said to him. "I didn't take control from you to undermine your position. I took control because the woman's words bothered us all."

James exhaled loudly. "The bastard kills little Otis' mama and shoots me in the face. Why she gotta ask for mercy for him? I ain't got it."

"She's asking for mercy for herself," Black replied.

"How could this be? Afta all what he did—I should show mercy? I hear Fannie rollin' 'round in my head. I'm workin' on forgivin' myself. I ain't carin' 'bout his ass. I wouldn't set out to cause a woman heavy wit' child grief, but I gotta woman and child. I don't wanna be lookin' over my shoulder neither," James added.

"All good points," Black replied. "We are in control. Let's see to Callie and move on with the plan."

❊ ❊ ❊

E.J. had just sat down at his desk when Norman walked into the study. He had a look of panic, and E.J. bolted up from his chair.

"What is it?"

"Some of the men are missing, and the slaves have not started work for the day," Norman said. "The slaves are gathered between the cabins and our men can't get in. They are carrying guns. Jeremiah ain't anywhere to be found. There is blood in the bushes and on the ground."

E.J. paced. Jeremiah had been correct in his concerns. This was not the work of deserters. This was Black displaying his authority.

"How many men we have left?"

"Last count was twenty-eight," Norman answered.

He stopped in his tracks and stared at Norman, unable to believe what he heard. His thoughts turned to Suzanne, Nettie, and Callie. He strode for the hall, shouting orders to Norman in his wake.

"Have our men guard both the front and back of the house! It's only going to get worse from here."

"The men are already in position. They're afraid—they ain't never seen the like," Norman responded.

E.J. spied Sonny and Ella at the end of the hall. Callie was nowhere to be seen. At the opposite end, his wife stood with her mother and sister. They were all dressed in mourning clothes. Even in the dim corridor, he could see the terror on their faces. He moved toward them, his final intent to secure the French doors in the sitting and dining rooms.

"Go back up to your mother's room and don't come out until I call for you!" He directed them.

Suzanne opened her mouth to speak, but thought better of it. Instead, she took her mother by the arm and helped her up the stairs. Maryam followed. Thankfully, she didn't push because he had too much to do. As he rushed through the sitting room, he was assailed by the smell of death. Adrian Wells had not yet been buried, and it was just one more dilemma Black now controlled.

Once the main house was locked down, E.J. threw the front door open and stepped into the morning sun.

❊ ❊ ❊

Black, followed by James, Anthony, Bainesworth and Jeb stepped into the clearing just beyond the last trees and cabins. Out in front of them, the overseers stood about with their weapons drawn. The grass was turning brown, yet it was well kept. The mansion was white with a high porch and large windows. At the edge of the top step, stood the new estate owner, and even from this distance, he did not look pleased.

Black and the men approached the front of the house from an angle. The slave quarters and fields spread around the right side and back of the plantation. There was a large patch of grass before the long driveway, and farther to the right were the fields, barn, and corral. Several sheds and lean-tos sat about the property. Behind the new Hunter, standing slightly to the left of him, was an older, white man. Both men wore the slave attire of tan shirts and tan trousers. The overseers were in varying degrees of this dress.

The new Hunter held eye contact with Black, but the older man stared just past them into the trees. In Black's mind there was nothing as grand as a stand-off, and he breathed in sharply the air of control. They stopped a few feet away from the porch and, with the sun at their backs, waited patiently for Hunter Jr. to speak. The slaver did not disappoint.

"Gentlemen, welcome to Hunter Manor."

When he and his men made no reply, Hunter directed his attention to Black. "I am hoping to negotiate a peaceable end to this day."

"There *is* a peaceable end to this day," Black responded. "Stand down."

Hunter stepped over his request. "We could talk in my study."

Black was about to respond, when Hunter shifted toward them. Narrowing his eyes against the bright morning sun, he said snidely, "Morning, Jeb."

He didn't give Jeb the chance to respond, but to Black, Hunter went on in disgust, "You have covered all the possibilities, it seems."

"Not all," Black replied as Callie popped into his head.

"What have you done with my brother?" Hunter asked.

Black's tone was relaxed and casual. "I will ask the questions; you will do the answering."

Hunter looked past him to the slave quarters, and Black could see his pain. A squeaking sound got Hunter's attention, but Black did not acknowledge the noise. Twenty male slaves came forward led by Emmett. One slave pushed a wheelbarrow. When they stood opposite the overseers, Anthony and the ambassador moved in to assist Emmett. Anthony yelled the commands loud and clear.

"You will stand down. Place yo' weapons in the wheelbarrow slowly and you will live. Any sudden movement and we'll kill yo' ass!"

Bainesworth stood next to Anthony, facing an overseer who nervously wiped sweat from his brow. "My good man," the ambassador said, "I bid you, don't move. I am not like the rest of the men present. I am frightened beyond belief, and I will blow your bloody head off should you move again."

The overseers had not relinquished their weapons; they waited for direction from Hunter. Black moved forward taking the steps two at a time. When he stood facing Hunter, he spoke with authority. "I am in charge, and you will stand down or there *will* be bloodshed."

James and Jeb stood with their weapons drawn. Black waited patiently to give the other man time to weigh his situation. The older man looked to the floor of the porch to avoid eye contact. Hunter finally nodded, conceding without words his defeat.

"You will need to call it," Black spoke, his words composed. "The lives of your men are in your hands."

"Stand down!" Hunter called out to his men.

"Your weapons—" Black said to both men standing before him.

Just as they were about to remove their guns, a warning shot sounded. In the distance, Black could see Tim and Gerry riding toward them at breakneck speed. Black turned to Hunter. "Don't move."

Tim rode up to the house and swung down from his horse.

"We have company," Tim announced, "and they look like

trouble. There are about seventy of them, and they're headed this way—deserters, I think."

Black did not flinch. "Time?"

"Thirty minutes, maybe less," Tim replied.

Black gave a quick nod and turned back to Hunter. "Who's inside?"

Hunter hesitated. "My wife, mother in-law and sister in-law are inside, along with two servants."

What Black did not want, were more frightened women on his hands. Crossing his arms, he stared off in the distance. He was deep in thought; while all around him, the men waited. "Tie them up and move them down into the slave quarters," he said to Emmett.

In front of the house, the slaves continued to confiscate the weapons of the overseers. They went behind the main house to deal with the overseers posted up in back. Black turned to James and Jeb. "Go through the house and bring everyone outside."

Tim remained with Black on the porch. The front door was slightly ajar, and when James pushed it open, the smell of death saturated the air. Black turned to Hunter offering no reaction to the odor as he waited for accounting of the main house. After a few moments, an older male slave emerged. He had dark eyes with skin so black he appeared purple in the sunlight. His thick wooly hair was cut low, and his brows were pressed together denoting a frown. Black gauged him to be about fifty summers. He was dressed like a butler with many keys hanging from his waist. Black nodded and curtly signaled for him to step away from the door.

Three white women followed, walking out onto the portico with looks of trepidation. They were all dressed in mourning, coinciding with the malodorous air wafting from somewhere inside the house. A young woman with brown hair and bright, blue eyes stepped closer to Hunter. Her face was flushed while the other younger woman, presumably her sister by her looks, had a face almost anemic with fear. She clung to the older woman who was clearly their mother.

Lastly, an elderly, heavy-set, dark-skinned woman stepped from the house. She wore a brown dress with a clean white apron tied about her thick waist. On her head she wore a white kerchief. The old woman held eye contact with Black, and he saw no fear. Boldly, she asked, "Do ya has ma grandson? Is he still live?"

Black studied her a moment. "Who is your grandson?"

The old woman's eyes watered. "Jeremiah is ma grand."

"May I ask your name?" Black replied.

The old woman offered him a weak smile. "My name Ella, Mista Black. "I's happy and sad ya come 'gain. I loves him. He some of mine; I ain't wantin' 'im hurt."

Black did not want to answer, but he would not leave her twisting emotionally. He glared at Hunter before speaking. "Jeremiah is alive, Miss Ella."

Tears of gratitude spilled down her cheeks, as the male slave came forward. "May I ask 'bout Eva, Mista Black?"

"And you are?"

"I be Sonny, Mista Black. Eva is ma woman."

"Eva is fine. I have left Callie in her care," Black replied.

Hunter, Black noticed, looked relieved. James, who was standing in the doorway, did not. Miss Ella was yet another obstacle between him and the black cracker. Directing his words to Sonny, Black said, "Escort the women down to Eva's cabin."

"Yes sah, Mista Black," Sonny replied with a smile full of white teeth.

Sonny directed the other women to follow him as he took Ella by the hand to help her down the stairs. The young woman holding Hunter's hand turned to him and whispered, "Edward, what is happening?"

"Follow Sonny, darling. I will be along later," Hunter reassured her.

"I don't want to go without you," she said, sobbing and clinging to his arm.

Hunter looked in Black's direction as if to ask for assistance. The woman at his side trembled and averted her eyes. Black was annoyed, but to Sonny he said, "Miss Suzanne will be along directly. Escort the other ladies."

Sonny nodded and helped the other women from the porch. The sister appeared utterly petrified as she looked toward Suzanne, but followed Sonny anyway.

James, Tim and Jeb moved to stand behind Black while Hunter, his wife and the old man looked on. Hunter still wore his weapon, yet Black turned his back on him and began addressing the problem at hand.

"We will step though the emergency plan; ready the men."

James, Tim, and Jeb nodded in unison as they walked away to do Black's bidding. Turning back to Hunter, Black said, "I know you are not used to such, but you also will answer to me."

The two men stared at each other, and the shift in power was complete when Hunter asked, "What next?"

"You no longer have slaves," Black replied.

❄ ❄ ❄

The overseers had been moved down to the slave quarters. Black crossed the lawn, followed by Hunter, his wife and the older fellow. Once they entered the trees, the older fellow was relieved of his gun, tied up and taken to where the overseers were being held hostage. Black moved toward Eva's cabin, as it was now their base of operations. Elbert, Frank and Shultz stood on the porch, while James and the others gathered on the path in front of the cabin.

Tim spoke first. "There are a total of one hundred eight men, and thirteen is elderly. Ninety-five of the men are between fifteen and fifty summers. Only about twenty of them been hunting and can shoot a gun."

Black nodded as Shultz offered his findings. "There is a total of seventy-five women, ten are elderly and ten are with child, though not near birthing. Sixty-five of the women are between the ages of fifteen and fifty summers. There are five that can handle a gun."

Elbert's speech was flat. "Horace and Emmett watch the black cracker. Me and Frank will set up to cover you."

"Me and Luke is set up, and we's ready for whateva," Gilbert added.

James, whose agitation simmered, said, "I will stand at yo' back."

When the men finished speaking, Black turned to Hunter's wife. He could see her distress had not subsided. He knew he needed to step in because she was overriding her husband. He understood what was frustrating James—the women were controlling the matter. Directing his words to the woman at Hunter's side, Black engaged her.

"Miss Suzanne," he said, "you will need to go inside with the women."

She looked up at him with her glassy blue irises. "I don't want you to kill my husband."

Black was candid in his response. "I cannot promise that the situation between me and your husband will end well. He is a slaver, and I am an abolitionist. Still, I give you my word. Your husband is safe for now."

Tears spilled from her eyes, but she nodded. Hunter took his wife by the hand and led her to Eva's cabin. Black could see that Hunter was struggling with his manhood, but he did so silently. It appeared the slaver understood that managing his attitude was best for his woman. Elbert, Tim and James approached. James offered his thoughts, and Black saw it the same.

"Tim gave a count of seventy deserters. We ain't finna leave cause of the women and children. The overseers, we cain't use cause we cain't trust 'em. Just cause the male slaves can hold a gun don't mean they shoots well. I ain't wantin' to use the women unless we got to. I say we cut Jeremiah loose. We got his woman. Holding the girl will give him some act right."

"Same for his brother," Elbert added.

"Seventy was my guess," Tim said, "but I could be off. There could be more men that I didn't see."

"We will work under the assumption there are more than seventy," Black said.

Black looked up when Hunter appeared on Eva's porch. He stood between Gilbert and Frank. Hunter seemed defeated as he stood amongst his slaves, while holding no power. Nevertheless, Black would use his ass to maintain freedom for the people he exploited for personal gain. It took some doing, but Black would look beyond his individual feelings to get this job done. Riding off and leaving the women and children at the hands of the deserters was not an option.

"Hunter, you will follow me," Black said.

Hunter winced as he stepped from the porch. "My name is E.J. or Edward."

Black considered him for an uncomfortable moment. "Today, you will help keep colored women and children safe. You will step away from your slaver mentality or it will not go well for you."

E.J. looked at the ground, as Black waited patiently. Finally, he spoke. "When this is over, will you grant me an audience with you?"

"You are not in a position to negotiate, Hunter," Black stated bluntly. "We will talk, but make no mistake, slaver—your life is not spared."

Hunter swallowed, and Elbert jumped in. "I will slit yo' damn throat myself, if yo' ass steps outta line. We offer your woman a respect ya don't offer ours–careful, Hunter."

Black walked away, followed by James, Elbert and Hunter. They headed for Jeremiah's cabin to free up Horace and Emmett. All their manpower was needed for this endeavor. They could not waste men on nanny duty, and time was running out. When they got to the cabin, Emmett stepped aside from his post at the front door to allow them entry.

Jeremiah looked up from where he sat. A look of relief illuminated his face at the sight of E.J. in the doorway. When James followed, Jeremiah frowned, giving him a confused look. Black spoke, but Jeremiah never took his eyes off James.

"We have your woman. How she is handled will depend on you. You will help defend your people, this day, against the deserters. It is an attempt at redemption before death for a man that has lived disconnected from his true self."

Jeremiah looked away, and like his brother, it was obvious he was beaten. Black continued, "I am in charge. Any sign of hostility against the order that I have established will be handled with finality. You and your brother still breathe out of concern for the women. But should you show yourselves problematic, you will be put down without hesitation. Either you are with us or against us—there is no between."

Black stared from man to man; neither brother spoke. Horace stepped forward and cut the black cracker loose. Jeremiah did not stand right away, and Hunter moved forward to assist him. When he got to his feet, he was wobbly. The black cracker staggered out the back door to the pump. Once outside, he threw up twice before he removed his shirt.

E.J. played nursemaid, finding Jeremiah a towel and clean shirt. Black and James stood on the back porch watching as Jeremiah pulled himself together with his brother's help.

James gave Black a look of warning. "The women is controlling us."

"I know," Black said with a sigh.

"How could this be?" James asked, angrily.

"They are smarter than us," Black chuckled.

❋ ❋ ❋

Black stood on the porch of the main house staring off in the distance. The thunder of horse hooves could be heard as the gang of deserters neared. The women and children were heavily guarded; the overseers were on lockdown; the time had come to stand and deliver. Black could feel the blood pounding in his head as the posse appeared in the clearing. Jeremiah stood to his left, and James on his right. Hunter stood next to James and neither of them so much as breathed.

Some of the deserters hung back and began breaking off into groups. Tim had been correct; there were more than seventy of them in various stages of military dress. The deserters looked to be a rough bunch and from what Black had observed, they were slightly organized. One thing was for certain to the men on the porch, it was well before noon, but all hell was about to break loose.

Seven white men broke from the group and rode up to the front of the house. The leader was a black-haired, dark-eyed man with a clean-shaven face. The man next to him was also clean-shaven. Both men looked to be about thirty summers.

As the seven men fanned out in front of them, Black looked to the clearing. He was offering insult to the men before him by lending his focus elsewhere. When he turned his attention back to the men at the bottom of the stairs, the man who looked to be the leader appeared confused. The leader's eyes bounced between Black and Hunter. It was clear that even though his intent was malice, the leader had a preference. He wanted to do business with Hunter, who was clearly not in charge.

The sun was bright, the air about them mild, as Black gave the men before him a moment to recognize his authority. In an effort to flex his power, Black remained silent. He understood that to speak first would show weakness, so he waited. The man he thought to be the leader spoke up, causing Black to smile.

"We come looking for hospitality from the owner of this here fine plantation."

The man directed his words to Hunter, as he was the only white man standing on the porch. Black waited patiently, while around them a breeze blew. Finally, when Hunter offered nothing verbal, the leader turned and directed his next words to Black.

"You, boy! Get me the man in charge of this place."

"I am afraid you have come to the wrong place to rest your bones. You will get no hospitality here," Black responded in a loud, clear voice.

The man became wide-eyed. "Ain't no damn slave gonna refuse me rest," he countered.

"For your own safety," Black calmly replied, "you and your men best be on your way."

"We will be on our way after we get what we come for," the leader chuckled, looking to the man in the saddle next to him.

The other man called up to Black. "We will take this place over. We has a man we lookin' for and last we knowed he come here."

Jeremiah stepped up and whispered in Black's ear. A moment later, Black addressed the leader once more. "Your man is dead."

The leader cursed under his breath. When he looked as though he would say more, Black cut him off and added. "Me and my men have already taken this place and its people hostage. We will not be taking anymore prisoners."

The leader of the group reached for his gun. A shot rang out and he fell from his horse, bleeding from his temple. The others swung down from their saddles to take cover. Gilbert took the next shot and the bullet found its mark as the second man fell to the ground. The other five deserters ran for cover and from his side view, Black saw Jeremiah pull both his hip weapons. The black cracker took two shots, one from each gun and both his targets fell.

Black and the men moved swiftly down the steps to join the fray. Out in front of them the posse had begun taking cover and the shootout was well under way. Elbert, Frank, Gilbert and Luke controlled the clearing from the hidden places in the brush. The deserters couldn't return fire. It was the advantage they needed, turning the situation in their favor. James and Jeremiah put the men down who rode confidently up to the house. Hunter and Black moved back to back taking down any man that was not their own.

The quiet of the morning became flooded with the sounds of gunfire as Black and Hunter took cover. James and Jeremiah fought back to back and took cover to reload. Down in the slave quarters, the shooting had not let up and Black worried.

When James and Jeremiah got closer, Black ordered, "You two go check on the women and children."

Jeremiah shouted to James as he ran. "Come this way! It's easier to stay covered."

Shultz took cover alongside Black and Hunter. The doctor's hand shook as he reloaded. Yet, when it came time to take a shot, Shultz did so with precision. All at once, as suddenly as the shooting started, it stopped. The quiet was even louder.

The doctor and Black remained low, when Hunter whispered, "Imma move around and check the area."

Hunter stood and was immediately struck in the chest by a bullet. "Shit, they shot me," he gasped. The doctor went to his aid.

The shots were coming steadily once more when Emmett and Horace appeared. They helped Black take down the men who were at close range before dragging a bleeding Hunter farther into the brush. Horace ran off to get help. He returned with Jeremiah, carrying a makeshift stretcher. Shultz kept applying pressure to the wound as they carried him off.

Jeremiah, along with James, soon reappeared with extra guns

to finish what they had started. Jeremiah spoke up. "Let's move outside of the working part of the land. We need to keep 'em from running off."

Bainesworth appeared, and at his back were five slaves with guns. The men moved to secure the perimeter, and the gunfire continued.

❊ ❊ ❊

In the brush, Elbert and Luke continued shooting and reloading. They had taken down several of the deserters, when three men appeared, ambushing them before they could move on from their position. From his place on the ground, Elbert couldn't get his .44 out fast enough. James and Jeremiah stepped from the undergrowth guns blazing, giving Elbert the time he needed to get to his feet.

When the smoke cleared, Elbert turned to check on Luke and found him covered in blood. "Shit!" Elbert yelled, as he and James ran to Luke's aid.

"He been shot in the neck," James assessed.

"Dammit, kid! Hold on!" Elbert shouted, as he applied pressure to Luke's throat. "Go get Shultz!"

Luke exhaled a complicated and rough sound. James looked away as Luke's sightless eyes gazed toward the sky.

"Shit," Elbert hissed under his breath.

In shock, both men continued to stare at Luke in disbelief. Behind them, Jeremiah spoke up offering the voice of reason. "We need to keep moving or we'll be next."

Elbert nodded and stood, wiping blood on his pants. The men moved on, leaving Luke behind.

❊ ❊ ❊

Twenty-one men regrouped on the outskirts of the slave quarters. Jeremiah, James and Black led their men to the perimeter of the plantation to close the deserters in. The newly freed slaves rallied about the women and children, continuing in their duty to keep them safe.

They had crippled the deserters, but it was uncertain how many were left. The gunfire continued, but it was becoming increasingly sporadic. An indication that the deserter's numbers had diminished. Black and James were sure the remaining members of the posse would run, and they couldn't allow that to happen. The horses belonging to the deserters tottered about aimlessly adding to the chaos.

Black moved through the brush alone and came upon a man hunkered down in the bushes. The man was blond with ice blue eyes. He was quicker on the draw than Black. When the deserter pulled the trigger, his gun clicked–no bullets. Black popped him between the eyes and moved on, but not before kicking the man– hard. It was his only outward sign of emotion. The man had him beat, though Black was still standing.

James and Jeremiah moved about together. Jeremiah took aim, shooting a man in the side of the head when he stepped from behind a tree. James thought the black cracker was going to shoot him. The ball whizzed by his head so close, he could hear the wind part. Just behind him, he heard a thud and the deserter fell unceremoniously to ground.

"Shit," James said under his breath.

Jeremiah chuckled. "Our issue is separate from this matter. You ain't needin' to worry. I am a man of my word."

The two men stared at each other for a moment before moving on.

Elbert and Gilbert found a man hiding behind the barn. He had two guns and no bullets. Elbert assessed the man before him. He looked to be about thirty-five summers with brown hair and dark eyes. Their new hostage wore the gray trousers of a Confederate soldier with a homespun brown shirt. Elbert pulled his weapon and shot the man in the leg. He and Gilbert then dragged him down into the slave quarters.

Frank, Anthony and Emmett came upon a deserter hiding in the bushes. There was blood on the leaves and grass about the area. Anthony stepped into the foliage and finished him. This continued to be the pattern until all gunfire ceased. With the fighting over, the men would have to face the pain of loss.

21

Organized Chaos

JAMES STOOD ON the back porch of the empty cabin next to Jeremiah's. In the background, he could hear Shultz yelling orders as he attempted to stop Hunter from bleeding to death. He heard Black confirm that Hunter had passed out. His mind wandered to Luke, and his grief was beyond words. One of their men had fallen in the conflict. It was just one more issue to manage, and he didn't think he could. He wanted to go home and hold little Otis. James wanted to lie between Abby's legs and feel alive. He was drowning in sorrow.

Luke had been an amiable young man–full of life. James was caught off guard as he thought of Luke's interest in Anna, Elbert's wife. He chuckled at the hilarity of the comical memory, and then his eyes watered involuntarily. Now, all he could see was Luke lying lifeless on the ground, his eyes seeing nothing. He was back to feeling uncomfortable in his own skin. The sun was still shining brightly, the breeze was mild, and the female slaves had begun cooking. Life was happening, though Luke was gone. He needed to pull himself together; he still had the long trek home.

Black stepped onto the back porch, wiping his hands free from blood. James looked up when the floor board creaked. The brothers stared at each other for a moment.

"If we gonna kill Hunter, ain't no sense in saving him," James said.

Hunter's wife appeared on the back path before Black had a chance to respond. She was escorted by the slave Sonny and visibly panic-stricken. The young woman seemed both afraid of them and worried for her husband. As she stood before them dressed in all black, Suzanne spoke, and James thought her voice stronger than she looked.

"They tell me my husband is here, and he has been shot. I wish to be with him."

"He is passed out from blood loss. The doctor is with him and believes he will make it," Black replied.

She looked relieved, and James watched as Black nodded curtly, allowing her passage. He also saw Black's surprise when Hunter's wife stepped onto the porch and touched his arm. She then looked between Black and himself, "I believe these men killed my father. Thank you."

Hunter's wife did not wait for a response. Instead, she stepped into the cabin to be with her husband. James looked to Black, but before he could make clear his thoughts, Jeremiah's woman appeared next on the path. Callie did not look well, and James felt great shame. He wanted to look away, but he would not be a coward twice. The slave Sonny had moved to stand behind her. She was dressed in slave attire, with one of Jeremiah's shirts draped over her full belly. Gazing from him to Black, Callie flexed her power by remaining quiet. She waited patiently for an accounting of Jeremiah's well-being.

James was thankful when Jeremiah appeared between him and Black. Callie looked as though she would faint upon seeing him. The black cracker continued onto the path and when he stood facing her, she stepped into his embrace. James could hear her weeping and Jeremiah's words.

"Shhh, woman, it's all right."

"I don't want to be with Eva. I want to be with you," she whimpered.

"E.J. been shot. I'm trying to help the doctor tend him," Jeremiah said.

Callie looked up at Jeremiah, nodding and pouting at the same time.

"Did you eat, woman? Ya don't look well; I don't want ya to be sick."

"I can't think of eating; my belly is churning," she whispered, giving both James and Black the side eye.

Jeremiah looked at James. "Imma let her go back to our cabin."

James, along with Black, nodded their assent. Jeremiah walked Callie next door and returned shortly, filling two buckets at the pump.

"The old woman," Jeremiah inquired, "is she all right?"

"She worried for ya," Sonny responded.

"Will you bring me some food for Callie?" Jeremiah asked.

"Sho' thang," Sonny answered.

Sonny started to walk away when Jeremiah added, "Bring the old woman too."

Sonny stopped and looked at Jeremiah before continuing on his way. James allowed his eyes to follow Jeremiah's movements as he took the buckets of water back to his cabin. When he stepped from his back door after five minutes, he shut it quietly behind him. The black cracker then walked back over to the porch where he and Black stood quietly. Jeremiah did not continue into the house, instead he stood between James and his brother. There were no words between the men, and James begrudgingly felt the first pangs of respect for the black cracker.

Shultz stepped outside. "Looks like E.J. will be out for a while.

He lost a lot of blood, but it could have been worse. He'll be weak, but he will recover. The shot was clean through."

Jeremiah nodded at the doctor's words, showing no other reaction. James turned his attention to Elbert and Gilbert as they walked up the path toward them. When they were close enough, Gilbert spoke, directing his words to Jeremiah.

"Is it still a shed near the slave graveyard?"

"Yeah," Jeremiah responded.

Elbert chimed in. "The hostage we took gave us a count of eighty-five deserters. I think we got them all."

"The hostage?" Black asked.

"Dead," Gilbert replied.

"We have men digging graves," Elbert added.

James asked the question no one wanted to touch. "Is we burying Luke here or taking him home?"

"We will bury him here," Black affirmed. "Our goal is to move the people looking to freedom."

Shultz looked from man to man, his hurt obvious. "What are you all saying? Where is Luke?"

"The kid was shot in the neck," Elbert replied. "James and Jeremiah showed up at the right moment or I would be dead too."

Overwhelmed and speechless, Shultz turned and walked back inside the cabin.

Gilbert looked at Jeremiah. "The overseer McFadden, is him still here? I ain't see him."

"No," Jeremiah replied, before looking away.

"Where he at?" Gilbert pressed.

Jeremiah looked straight at Gilbert. "He was found wit' his throat slit."

Gilbert frowned in confusion. "Who cut 'is throat?"

"Someone meaner than him," Jeremiah answered.

Sonny and Ella came walking down the path, carrying baskets of food. The old woman smiled tearfully as Jeremiah walked up to her. She caressed his face and gave him a kiss, and he directed her to his cabin. James somehow sensed that Jeremiah wasn't used to such demonstrative affection.

James refocused as Black stepped to the edge of the top step and offered instruction. Though he attempted to cover his feelings, James could see that Black was grief-stricken. "Let's clean this shit up so we can move out. Elbert, come help me with Luke."

Black and Elbert walked away, leaving James, Gilbert, and Jeremiah alone. An uncomfortable silence ensued. Gil cleared his throat, sensing the tension. "I'll be in the clearin' helpin' wit' the cleanup," he excused himself, leaving James to glare at Jeremiah.

"I still wanna kill yo' ass," James said.

Jeremiah's nonchalant demeanor bothered James the most.

"Where is the boy?" Jeremiah asked. "He was not among the children left. Did you all take him?"

They took many children that fateful day, still James knew exactly which child Jeremiah spoke of. James stared down at him as he stood on the path. There was blood on his shirt and his blue-black hair was wild. The left side of his face was still swollen from being slammed with the butt of the gun.

"You ain't finna question me. I'm the one askin' the damn questions," James asserted.

Jeremiah nodded, conceding to his temper.

"You worry for the boy, but ya kill his mama. What sense that make?" James grew irritated.

Jeremiah said nothing. "Ya shot me in the damn face!" James added.

Jeremiah cocked his head. "The day ya came to take the children, would you have shot me if the chance showed itself?"

James was about to reiterate the rules on questioning him, when Jeremiah said, "So ya would have shot me."

"I wouldn't have missed killin' yo' ass, neither," James shot back.

"I'm an excellent shot. I wasn't tryna kill you," Jeremiah looked agitated as well.

"So ya meant to kill the woman?"

Jeremiah looked away, but not before James saw his regret. Interestingly, he saw no damn regret when they discussed his getting shot. "Why did you kill the woman?"

"It was the first and only time I allowed my anger to get the better of me."

James saw the same emotions in Jeremiah's face. It appeared to be worse for the black cracker because he meant to kill the woman. The two men glared at each other.

"Callie told me I was lost as a man. She ain't like me—said I was a slave that ain't know I was a slave. She ain't allow me the comfort of my ignorance," Jeremiah sighed, and then continued, "If we could find peace between me and you—I would offer you my loyalty and my gun hand whenever you called for it."

James couldn't help his own pettiness. "Is you beggin' for yo' life?"

"I could leave you to deal wit' Callie and my grandma," Jeremiah's face held no expression.

James scowled at him. There was too much truth to his statement. He stepped from the porch and spoke as he moved past Jeremiah. "I see you's a humble bastard."

He headed for the clearing with Jeremiah in tow.

❊ ❊ ❊

As the afternoon pressed on, the men collected the bodies of the deserters. Several mass graves were dug, and the dead were transported by wagon to the slave graveyard. Luke was placed in a coffin that Black himself nailed shut. They brought his body down to the edge of the slave quarters where the other men gathered. Jeremiah was fascinated by their behavior. He had never seen colored men like Black and his men. They were somber in their grief as they spoke quietly among themselves. Jeremiah stood a small distance away so as not to intrude on their sorrow.

Jeremiah noticed they offered the same respect for him when dealing with E.J., who had not yet awakened. He was cautious about keeping his emotions to himself, so he did not question the doctor, but he was worried for his brother. E.J. had been his only family for a very long time, and he did not want to lose him. Shultz had been cautious about people coming and going from the cabin where E.J. was being cared for. His wife had been by his side, and Suzanne had not left him.

He had gone to check on Callie several times, so she could see that all was well. She asked him to come eat something, and he had been truthful. Moving dead bodies did not make him want to eat. Callie had asked after E.J. and he told her there had been no change. Ella had gone back to Eva's cabin. He had been about to walk out the back door when Callie threw her arms around him. The last hours had been stressful, and he needed all the love she was giving him.

He had just stepped out onto his own back porch when he looked farther up the path and saw Suzanne speaking with Black. When she spied him, she moved toward him; Black remained where he stood, with his arms folded. Jeremiah moved to the edge of the top step and waited for her to get close enough to speak.

"I asked Mister Black if you and he could take care of burying my father. He is still in the house."

Jeremiah nodded and followed her back to where Black stood.

"We could use the men from here to move the coffin through the gardens to the wagon," Black said.

Jeremiah had been about to walk away when Suzanne added, "My mother and sister won't want to come, I'm sure. I will ride with you to take my father to his final resting place."

Jeremiah waited. He could see she had something else on her

mind. "I don't want to leave Edward alone. Please have Nettie brought to this cabin so she can be with him in my absence."

When Suzanne walked away, Jeremiah turned to Black. "I'll fetch Nettie."

❊ ❊ ❊

Black, Jeremiah, and the male slaves hung back as Suzanne stood at her father's graveside. When she finished praying, she turned and walked back to the wagon. Jeremiah helped her up into the front seat. The sun was just starting to go down and with it the temperature. They returned to the slave quarters, where the people had hot water boiling on the main path and food cooking. One path over, on the end of the dirt road, Shultz had insisted that tubs were set up for the men to bathe in order to keep down infection after dealing with death all day.

A woman was sent to handle Black's washing and see to his needs. The young woman reminded him of his wife, though she might have been closer to his own age. She told him her name was Teensy, which was ironic as she was nearly six feet tall, Black guessed. She had a scar across the bridge of her small nose. Her hair was braided in several cornrows, and she had a tan cloth wrapped decoratively around her forehead. She was gorgeous.

Black missed his wife, and he was grieving for Luke. He was distant with Teensy; nevertheless, he thanked her for the food and clothing she brought him. All his men were dressed like slaves, as the women laundered their clothes. When night fell, they would not rest. They would walk the perimeter of the property and make certain all was safe. As the men stood about speaking in low tones, Black could feel their pain. They too could think of nothing but Luke.

It was dark and chilly when Jeremiah reported for duty. The men moved up the path and stood in front of Black's cabin. James was about to assign partners when Shultz rushed toward them.

Jeremiah's eyes widened, and it was clear to Black, he thought his brother had died. When the doctor neared, he spoke specifically to Jeremiah.

"E.J. has awakened, and he is asking for you. I can't get him to calm down—he thinks I am untruthful when I say you are well."

Jeremiah turned to Black, who in turn looked to the others and said, "I will partner with Jeremiah tonight."

"Yeah," Elbert responded.

Black stepped from the porch and followed Shultz and Jeremiah. When they reached the cabin where Hunter was being cared for, Shultz made them wash up again at the pump. After drying their faces and hands, Black allowed Jeremiah to enter first. The cabin was basic with a wooden table and one chair. Shultz had a small fire going to ward off the chill, but the cabin wasn't stifling. Hunter was propped up with several pillows under him to keep his torso elevated. The bed he lay in was pulled away from the wall to allow a chair to fit.

On the right side of the bed sat Suzanne, who had changed into slave attire. It was an indication that Shultz thought Hunter would live. She smiled weakly at him when he entered. On the other side of the bed sat a brown-skinned woman, who looked to be about twenty-five summers. She had slanted dark eyes, a button nose and plump lips. Nettie looked up at him, but she did not speak.

The look on her face was strained.

Hunter was pale as death, and his eyes bounced frantically about the room. When he saw Jeremiah, his eyes watered. Jeremiah walked over to the bed. "You look like shit."

Hunter attempted to smile. He tried to follow Jeremiah's lead and back away from the emotion, but fell short. "Brother, I am glad you are well."

Jeremiah gave in. "I thought you wouldn't wake."

The patient lay with a colorful quilt pulled over him; the right side of his chest was heavily bandaged. He did not take his eyes from Jeremiah. When he noticed that Jeremiah still had his weapons, he looked to Black. Jeremiah caught his brother's silent plea.

"Imma be out walkin' the property. Ain't no need to be worrying; get some rest," Jeremiah said.

"Callie?" E.J. inquired.

"She is restin'," Jeremiah replied.

Hunter held eye contact as if searching Jeremiah's face. When he was satisfied that all was well, he reached for the hand of both women and intimately linked his fingers with theirs. Black interpreted this action for what it was—possessiveness. He understood such behavior for he felt the same about Sunday. Nettie reached up and ran the fingers of her free hand through his hair. Hunter's wife caressed his cheek, and he fell fast asleep.

Jeremiah turned to Shultz and nodded curtly before leaving the cabin. The doctor looked to Black and spoke softly. "I'll sleep for a few hours in a cabin just up the path."

"We will be moving to the next part of the plan at daybreak," Black stated.

The night had grown colder as he and Jeremiah began patrolling. Black wore a woolen brown cap on his bald head that matched his hip-length overcoat. Jeremiah was dressed the same, minus the hat. The two men trekked to the main house, and Black allowed him to enter first. The kitchen was dark, and Jeremiah lit two oil lamps.

Black observed the black and white color scheme of the kitchen. Standing with his back to the wall, he reached up and removed his hat. When he looked at Jeremiah, the black cracker stared intently at his boots.

"What should be done with a colored slaver?" Black went straight to the point

Jeremiah sidestepped Black's question. "I ain't know a colored man like you was real."

"This does not answer my question."

"A man can't be somethin' that ain't thinkable in his head." Jeremiah replied.

"So, you are saying you didn't understand enslaving your own people was wrong?"

Jeremiah stood to his full height and looked Black in the eyes. "Being an overseer allowed me enough room to let my blindness grow."

"What changed?" Black probed.

"Callie."

Black was unimpressed. The girl had shared her body, and the black cracker appeared to be controlled by it. This was not enough to change a man.

"Callie told me she wanted to live free wit' me. I reasoned later what she meant was in my head more than running from here. Everything I thought I had figured out she showed me I didn't. She is smarter than me. I ain't see myself as lost."

Black asked the question that troubled him most. "Why kill the woman?"

Jeremiah's eyes searched the ceiling. "I allowed my anger to get the better of me."

"You will have to do better than that," Black snapped.

"I don't have no good reason for killin' Betsy—nothin' sounds good to my own ears. I can't give somethin' I ain't got," Jeremiah shouted, his voice shaking.

He looked at the floor, and his voice dropped. "Old man Hunter ordered Betsy put down, but he became fixated with the Turner plantation. He ain't even notice that Betsy was still around. She had days when she spoke outta her head, and when the boy was born, she worsened. Betsy loved him, but some days she ain't know he was hers."

Black knew of the practice of putting down slaves that couldn't produce. He also knew of elderly slaves being starved to death when they could no longer work. Refusing to let Jeremiah hide in the conversation, he asked, "The old Hunter was dead. Why put her down? Why that day?"

"My patience with Betsy faltered in the chaos and confusion. It ain't no excuse, but the boy is better off without her," Jeremiah replied and then he added, "When other female slaves attempted to care for the child, she got violent. But she ain't know no better."

Black turned over what Jeremiah was saying. Still, when James came to mind, he became angry. Luke popped into his head, and Black realized he was ready to go home. After getting his feelings under control, Black asked, "What should I do with the man who tried to kill my brother?"

"My gun hand is excellent; I wasn't tryna kill him. I was trying for a hostage," Jeremiah responded.

Black glared at him.

"I'll ask you the same as I asked James. Would you have shot me that day if you had the chance?"

Black didn't answer.

"So, you would have shot me?"

"I may still shoot yo' ass," Black replied with agitation.

Jeremiah leaned against the counter behind him and crossed his arms. Black waited—Jeremiah had more to say.

"Will you help me with Callie?"

Black knew it was coming, especially since Hunter was hurt. "Help you how?"

"E.J. is weak and will move slower. I will move at his pace, but this won't be safe for Callie. Will you take her with you and allow me to come for her before our child comes?"

"Why would I invite you to my home?"

Jeremiah waved his hands with impatience. "I offer you my loyalty and my gun hand. I am trying to figure out how to keep Callie and my child safe. I want the same for Ella, Eva, and Sonny. Must I beg?"

Black gave him a stony stare. "Callie doesn't like us. She'll not accept our help."

Jeremiah chuckled. "She will come around because it's best for the child."

"Where do you plan to settle?"

"Canada—the States are too dangerous," Jeremiah replied.

Black nodded.

"I asked James, but he wouldn't answer. I must know. Betsy's boy—do you have him? Is he well?"

"We do, and he is well."

Jeremiah looked away. Black saw the pain in his eyes. There was regret over the woman, but none about James. It was, of course, the business of shooting intruders, but it still made Black angry. He then had another consideration.

"We renamed the boy," he said, "but I'm sure you can provide his real name."

Jeremiah gave him a curious look. "What do you call him?"

"Otis. What did Betsy name him?"

The black cracker gave him a thoughtful look. "Betsy named him Jeremiah."

Silence fell between the men before they turned and stepped back into the night.

❀ ❀ ❀

E.J. lay awake between Suzanne and Nettie, who were both fast asleep. He did not miss the fact that he was in bed with two women for whom he felt mad affection. But today, this hen house had three hens, and it galled him. He was inspired, but his manhood was not. He could hear activity going on outside the cabin. The doctor had come and checked on him several times, but his brother had not returned. He felt anxious, but he did remember seeing Jeremiah with all three of his guns—that had to be a good sign.

He was weak, but grateful to be alive. His mind tried to reconcile the last several hours, and he lay thinking of what was next for his life. The back door opened, and the doctor stepped in, along with a small amount of sunlight. He closed the door behind him and moved to the center of the cabin.

The doctor pushed his spectacles up on his bulbous nose. He seemed more of a ruffian than a man of medicine. He was young, no more than thirty-five.

"How are you this morning, E.J.?" he asked.

Feeling like he had a frog in his throat, E.J. coughed. "Where is Jeremiah?"

"Your brother came back last night, but I sent him away, so you could rest. I'm Dr. Shultz."

E.J. glared at him, and Shultz returned his gaze with a knowing look. "If we were going to kill Jeremiah, he would already be dead."

"Bastard."

"Yes, well, I've come to get you out of bed and moving on your own steam. Your insults will carry more weight if you didn't appear to be at death's door," Shultz retorted.

E.J. chuckled, and the doctor smiled. He felt Nettie stir and then Suzanne. The doctor excused himself, giving them a moment of privacy. When they were alone, Nettie helped him sit up, and Suzanne gave him a soothing glass of water. Now that he was awake, both women seemed shy with him and each other.

"How are you feeling, Edward?" Suzanne asked.

His wife looked worried for him and unsure of herself in Nettie's presence. "My body hurts, and I can't tell if it's from lying about or getting damn shot."

"Ya looks betta than when I first come," Nettie said.

"Dr. Shultz said you would be sore," Suzanne added.

He looked from Suzanne to Nettie. They were both so beautiful, even in the slave clothes. He closed his eyes to get his irritability under control. He hoped the women would not revert to old behaviors once he mended. After catching a glimpse of such intimacy, he didn't want to lose it.

Suzanne became concerned when he closed his eyes. "Edward, are you feeling pain?"

Before he could answer, Nettie piped up. "Look mo' like his pride is painin' 'im. Is ya upset 'cause we was in yo' bed, but you weak as a kitten?"

Suzanne looked at Nettie and breathed in sharply. Nettie stood with her hands on her hips and a smirk on her face.

E.J. chuckled. "I'm afraid she's correct."

Suzanne's expression turned impish. "We thought to give you something to live for," she quipped.

It was E.J.'s turn to breathe in sharply, and Nettie giggled. There was a sudden knock on the back door and Shultz walked in, followed by Jeremiah. His brother toted two buckets of water, one of which he hung over the fireplace. The doctor added wood to the fire and then turned to address the women.

"Ladies, I am here to give you both a moment to handle your own toilette. We will clean him up and come get you both later."

Suzanne was about to refuse when E.J. said, "It's all right, darling."

Turning to him, Suzanne whispered, "I'll go see about my mama and sister, then."

Nettie was silent, and E.J. reached out to squeeze her hand. Both women left the cabin, leaving him in Shultz's and his brother's care. Jeremiah got him to his feet so that he could take a piss in the bucket in the corner. Shultz checked his wounds. Jeremiah then filled the tub, handing him a cloth and towel.

"Allow the water to fall lightly over the wound," the doctor instructed.

His brother left and was gone for a time, before returning with clean clothes gathered by Suzanne. Shultz bandaged his wounds and placed his right arm in a sling to alleviate the pressure caused from leaving the limb dangling. Finally, he was placed in a chair at the table, and Nettie appeared with chicken stew. E.J. felt weak and ready for sleep, but he ate a little.

When Nettie left, he looked up to find Shultz and his brother staring at him. He placed his spoon back in the bowl. "What are you two looking at?"

"Black and his brothers would have a word with you and Jeremiah this morning," the doctor replied.

E.J. looked to Jeremiah who shrugged. He was exhausted, but he would not admit to such. The truth was he wanted to settle shit with Black so that he and his brother could move forward.

"We are ready," he replied.

Shultz nodded and left by way of the front door. When he and Jeremiah were alone, E.J. asked, "Are they still looking to kill us? What was the point in pulling the bullet out my ass if they are going to kill me?"

Jeremiah chuckled. "I think the women are controlling the matter. If not for them, we would both be dead."

E.J nodded just as the front door swung open. Black entered first, followed by the man Jeremiah had shot in the face. The man with the lifeless eyes stepped through the door next, followed by a white fellow who was slightly shorter than Black. They were all dressed in black with their weapons holstered to their upper left sides. The door closed with a bang behind them.

He had wanted this meeting because he wanted peace for himself and his brother. He wasn't in great physical condition, but Black was tactical in his every move. It wasn't lost on E.J. that Black was exerting his power over the situation.

The white man spoke first. "I was at the Turner plantation when your father came with the other plantation heads. They were hunting Black. I shot and killed him."

E.J. had not expected to care, but he did. He was finally

standing face to face with the man who killed his papa. As he looked at the man, he felt beaten on so many levels. He hated his father for his treatment of Jeremiah's mother, but the boldness of these men, he could not stomach. E.J. wasn't unwise—Black was doing this on purpose to get a rise out of him—and it was working.

"And your name is? It would seem only right to know the name of my poor papa's killer." E.J.'s voice was tight to his own ears.

"Tim," the man replied with cold candor.

Black chuckled, and E.J. was dumbfounded. "I am failing to see the humor in Tim's words. What exactly do you find so funny?"

Black stood with his feet spread apart and his hands clasped behind his back, unmoved. "We all knew the cruel and ruthless acts of the old Hunter. Gentlemen, your father was a cold bastard. Let us move forward in reality or peace will not be achieved. Concern for your women is why we are here, but do not be misled—we can kill you both and comfort your women."

Jeremiah placed his left hand to his jaw, thinking. The three men with Black all drew their guns, and the black cracker laughed out loud.

"Easy," Black cautioned.

"Black, I gave you and James my word. I will not lift my gun hand against you; be reassured that my word is my bond," Jeremiah said.

Black nodded. The three at his back holstered their weapons and the charged energy in the room lessened, but did not go away.

"Ain't no sense in us gettin' off track," Jeremiah said. "The issue here, accordin' to James, is my killing Betsy and shooting him in the face. Let me answer as I have already done. I don't have a good answer for killing Betsy—my regret rides me daily. As for shooting you, James, I feel no regret. You were an intruder, and I handled the situation as expected. As of late, our positions with each other have changed."

It was E.J.'s turn to laugh. "It would seem we all have to move past a slight perpetrated by the other."

James flashed him an angry look. "I has a question for ya, Hunter. Did you threaten Rose Wilkerson?"

E.J. didn't hesitate. "I did threaten the Wilkerson woman. I went to the Turner plantation to speak with Will Turner, but his sister was in residence. Mrs. Wilkerson was not forthcoming, and I thought to intimidate her. I can assure you she was not cowed."

"So, you set the man with the ponytail on her and her husband?" James asked.

"Simpson was hired when I was still under the illusion that our papa was a saint. I discovered later that nothing could be farther from the truth. As for Simpson, when I got the telegram, I knew he had been killed. There was no need to call him off," E.J. explained.

"How did you know he was dead?" Black asked. "We used the code."

E.J. waved him off. "There was no code. When the message referred to Rose sending her love, I knew he was dead."

Black smiled. "We have confirmed what happened to your papa, and we are not regretful in our actions. The question now— is peace your goal?"

E.J. felt his temper flare. "Let me see if I have the right of it. Me and my brother are in the hot seat because you and your brothers came uninvited to molest me and steal my property. You are angry because Jeremiah shot your brother during an uprising you caused. Oh, and let us not forget that your man shot and killed my papa. I think the real question before us is—are me and my brother willing to accept responsibility for something you and your brothers caused?"

"What you said would be correct if not for one small fact," Black replied.

"What small fact?" E.J. mocked.

"Our women and children are not your property. As men, we cannot abide such atrocity. And though you are angry, you are clear on what I speak. Your love for your brother proves it. Do not be so contrary that you end up dead. Oh, and let us not forget several other facts. If me and my brothers had not come this day, you would not have fared well against the deserters. We settled the score of your father in-law while saving your wife, her mother and sister from rape–a brutality from which our women are never spared. Most importantly, we lost a man while protecting not only our women and children, but yo' ass. My man has nursed you back to health. Be careful, Hunter–be very careful," Black replied. It was evident to all in the room that his temper had indeed boiled out of control.

E.J. stared at Black for a moment. Finally, he conceded. "I want peace with you, Black."

"Peace does not come by words alone, Hunter. You and your conscience will no longer straddle the fence on slavery. You will help to move the people you exploited for personal gain to freedom. And you will do so minus the arrogance. You, Hunter, will recognize my authority and the benefit happening because of my presence," Black responded.

E.J. felt his brother place a hand on his shoulder. "You have my loyalty, Black, and my gun hand. I ask one thing of you."

"And that is?"

"My name is E.J., not Hunter."

Black looked around the room. "Fair enough, E.J."

Black turned and headed for the front door. When he pulled it open, E.J. could see Suzanne standing in the doorway with Nettie peering out from behind her. Black did not step through the door frame. Instead, Suzanne entered the cabin. E.J. thought she would be afraid, but he couldn't have been more wrong.

"Good morning, Mister Black," his wife said.

"Good morning, Miss Suzanne," Black replied, setting aside his anger.

When his wife saw him seated at the table, she turned to Black and patted his arm. E.J. wondered at their newfound friendship. Black gave him a rather smug smile. Suzanne's next words only hammered home what Black had just stated.

"My mama and sister wanted me to say thank you for getting my papa buried."

"You are welcome, Miss Suzanne, and I am sorry for your loss," Black replied.

Behind him, E.J. heard Jeremiah chuckle. Both women came to him. Nettie stood behind his chair, and Suzanne stood to his right. Black spoke directing his words to the brothers.

"I will address the people, and the two of you will stand at my back."

※ ※ ※

Black walked outside onto the porch. He had to better manage his anger. He still wanted to choke the life out of Hunter, but he had to acknowledge that, though they had lost Luke–thanks to Jeremiah Elbert was still alive. James had even confirmed that Jeremiah had saved him from an attack he did not see coming. It was as Jeb said, the black cracker was impressive. Black also begrudgingly conceded to the fact that when Hunter took the bullet to the chest, he or Shultz could have been in his place. Still, he would not allow disrespect in the form of wittiness to take hold in his dealings with the reformed slaver.

Black looked about while trying for calm; he spied Anthony and Bainesworth moving toward him. He could see the hurt on Anthony's face at the loss of Luke, but the younger man held it well. It was clear Anthony understood they would be free to grieve when they made it home and not before. When they neared, neither the ambassador nor Anthony spoke; still, they posted up in front of the cabin. Behind him, Black could hear his own brothers, along with Tim, Jeremiah and Hunter. As the people noticed him, they gathered before the two steps.

Callie, Eva, Ella and Sonny were among the people that began to gather. Jeremiah stepped from the porch to help his grandma and his woman up the stairs. Sonny helped Eva and when everyone was in place the crowd hushed. Black moved forward, but remained quiet for a time, allowing the people a moment to take in the sight before them.

The day was young and there was a chill in the air. Warmed by the heat of his emotions, Black did not feel it. He looked from one face to another, faces that were searching for hope. People filed into the pathways and between the cabins for as far as the eye could see. Women and children huddled together, wrapped in blankets to ward off the cold. Black was suddenly worried that he could not give the people the hope they needed.

"You are all waiting for me to tell you that you are free. But I am afraid I don't have such news. What I can tell you is when I became free–I became free the moment I thought it. The very second freedom entered my head, I was liberated. Leaving the plantation is only part of liberty, and if you can't reason what I say, then you will fail. Me and my men will lead you from this place, but seeing yourselves and loved ones as free is part of the journey. When I was able to understand my independence, I was then able to extend freedom to my brethren."

A buzz started in the crowd, and Black raised his hands. "We will move the elderly, the women, and the children first. You will break down into groups and move out to achieve physical freedom. As for you men, I am not special. I am the same as you, except I believe myself to be free. Your goal is to keep our women and children safe—they are what make you a man. It is not enough to break physical servitude, you must *stand* for freedom—and it will be a constant battle. We will labor together to make this thing work."

Black then quieted for a moment before he concluded, "I believe you all to be free."

The crowd cheered, and Black looked to Hunter who was red in the face. Yet to his surprise, Hunter stepped forward and removed his arm from the sling. He offered Black the handshake of peace, and Black accepted. Hunter leaned in and whispered for Black's ears only, "Shit, you gave me hope."

Black smiled, before disappearing into the crowd. He had a goal; he would mingle with his people and labor with his people.

22

The Hunter Plantation
November 1861

JAMES STOOD OUTSIDE the cabin they were using as base. The men were sleeping in shifts, but he could not rest. They had been on the Hunter plantation for two days, and it seemed a lifetime. Two waves of people had been moved out, with Jeb and Gerry leading the packs. Tim and Frank were Jeb's back up, while the ambassador and Anthony backed Gerry. Elbert would remain in charge of the Hunter plantation while he, Black, and Jeremiah handled some late-night business.

The sun was starting to go down when Black approached him. James did not know how to express what he felt, but he needed Black to understand his pain. His voice broke, when he addressed his brother.

"I ain't agreeing wit' leaving Luke here."

"Yeah, I knew you felt this way. Elbert has already come to me. Shultz will pack the body in salt, so we can take him home."

James could only nod.

"You rested?"

"Yeah, I'm ready," James answered.

The men stood about watching the activity around them, saying nothing. When darkness fell, Jeremiah appeared.

"It's time," Black said.

The three headed for their horses without a backward glance. They whipped their horses into a fast pace, and three hours later, they arrived at Myrtle's.

The hour wasn't late. Still, James remarked, "Can't see a damn thing."

"Good," Jeremiah replied.

"I'll knock—you two keep watch," Black instructed.

Black stepped into the clearing, and James moved out behind him, followed by Jeremiah. James listened as Black banged. Charles opened the door.

"I thought ya forgot us," Charles said in a low voice.

"You ready?" Black asked.

Charles grabbed his coat and stepped from the house. He and Black headed for the barn. James and Jeremiah closed in, posting up at the door. Inside, Charles lit a couple of lanterns.

"We gonna be travelin' light. I sold everythang I could," he told Black.

"Let's move out. I want to get where we'll have more backup," Black said.

"Yeah, I almost ran into a group of deserters when I went to market. They's close to here—had to take the long way home wit' my family. I worry for my wife mostly; menfolk can be dangerous," Charles replied.

"Let's get the horses hitched up so we can move out. Do you have a gun?" Black asked.

"I has a shotgun and a .44," Charles replied.

"Good."

The horses were hitched, and Charles pulled the carriage from the barn right up to the front of the house. Myrtle and the kids quietly appeared carrying small bundles. James and Jeremiah stood guard as Black and Charles helped them into the carriage. It was one in the morning.

The carriage slowed down their commute, adding an additional two hours. When dawn broke, Horace and Ephraim rode in the shadows to the left of the carriage. James rode to the right of the carriage with Gilbert as his partner. Black took the lead and Jeremiah brought up the rear. It was six in the morning when they rode onto the Hunter plantation. Charles, Myrtle, and their children were given a cabin down in the slave quarters to rest before they moved out with the next wave.

※ ※ ※

Jeremiah had not really slept since the uprising. When they made it back to the plantation, he took a bath and went to sleep. He was roused hours later by a small sound in the corner of his cabin. Opening his eyes, he turned on his side. Callie was seated at the table, reading a book. She looked up at him and beamed, then pushed back from the table and waddled over to him.

She was wearing one of his shirts and had a tan wool blanket about her waist. She let it fall to the floor and climbed into bed next to him. Words could not convey his happiness. If things went well, he would live to see his child come into this world. He would also see his other child, the boy he had with Betsy. He had never thought of the boy as his son until now. The problem he faced was how to tell Callie he had killed his son's mother while she carried his seed.

Jeremiah had admitted to Callie as much as he could stomach. It was why he had been calm when faced with the truth of his mama's demise. Yet, he felt hypocritical, for he wanted to dig Hunter up and kill him. Allowing his mind to wander, he thought back to when he found out about Callie's condition. For the life of him, he had not seen it coming. Becoming one with her had engulfed him so completely, he had not thought of the possibility of children. And when it came to past, he had not been pleased. Finding out that Callie carried his child represented what he thought he could never have, and it caused the boy to stop being just Betsy's son.

The afternoon sun shone through the window, illuminating his dishonesty. He had an ulterior motive, but in his head the end justified the means. He had asked—no begged for Black's help in keeping his woman and his child safe until he and E.J. could settle their lives. It would be best for her and the baby. The added reward would be seeing the boy. They had renamed him Otis and to his surprise, it bothered him.

Callie had wiggled next to him, breaking into his train of thought. As usual, she showed herself to be more intelligent than he.

"I'm not leaving with Black."

Callie lay on her back, staring at the ceiling with her hands folded over her belly. He leaned up on his elbow and smiled down at her. They would not fight. She would do as he requested, and he would put his foot down.

"You have saved my life, and against my will, I might add. Ain't no sense in us arguing—you will go with Black for the safety of the child. You will put the needs of this child before your own. Do you not care about the child?"

"Of course I care about our child. But, they wanted to kill you." Her voice broke.

He leaned down and kissed her lips. "I ain't dead woman."

Callie turned on her side, resting her belly against him. She closed her eyes, but the tears still came. He knew she was living under great stress. "I don't like Black," she whispered.

Jeremiah couldn't help it; he started laughing. "How could you not like Black? Even I, the black cracker, like him. I ain't think it possible, but you been corrupted by the company you been keeping."

"It's not funny."

Jeremiah sobered. "You know, if Black and his men had not come to kill me, we may not have survived that damn gang of deserters. I will forever like him because I am able to hold you and our child in my arms. You will do as I say, Callie, so that I can try and make a life for us. You said you wanted to live free wit' me. I am trying, and you are being stubborn."

"How long will I be stuck with them?"

"I will come to you before our child comes. I promise."

"What if they don't give me back to you? What if they try to kill you when you come?"

"Woman, they have not spared me because they fear me. They have spared my life because Black does not believe in harming women. You will do as I say, and then you will go back to controlling this thing we have after you are safe. If you do not do as I say, I will see that yo' words are contradicted by your actions."

"I don't contradict myself," Callie responded with indignation.

"You do. You say you want the child to be safe, and then you don't do the things it takes to keep the child and yourself safe."

She would not look at him. He, too, felt the pain of separating from her. But he would not straddle the fence as he had done in the past. He would send her away, as it was the right thing to do.

"You will come to me before the baby. You promise you will not miss the birth of our child?"

"Woman, you have my word," he whispered against her ear.

❈ ❈ ❈

Early evening was fast approaching as Callie listened to the activity going on just beyond their cabin doors. Jeremiah had dressed and gone out. She knew he was helping get the people moved out, and though she had not said as much, she was proud of the personal changes he made. The problem now–she did not want to be separate from him. She feared Black because he was larger than her understanding of freedom. Black represented all that Jeremiah was not.

As she sat thinking, Jeremiah returned from his labors. When he saw she was dressed properly, he held the door open and Black walked in. Behind him was the man Jeremiah shot in the face, next came the man with the cold eyes. They all three stood facing her across the small room. Callie left the burden of conversation to the men because in her mind, she had not yet agreed to anything.

Jeremiah stood to the left of them with his back against the front door. She knew he was trying to figure out how to control her responses, but she offered him nothing to go on. Her eyes fell to Black, and he held her gaze. Black was a large man with dark smooth skin. His name was fitting. Callie would have thought him handsome, if not for the threat he posed.

"I asked Black and his brothers to come meet you."

Callie briefly glanced at Jeremiah before turning back to Black. She clasped her hands together, placing them gently on top of her belly. After her last interaction with Black, she was sure he knew what she thought of him. The other men at his side were frightening and intimidating as they stood with their weapons holstered to their upper left sides. Though she fixated on Black, it was the man with the scarred face who spoke. Reluctantly, she gave him her attention.

"My name is James, Miss Callie. I come to say I'm sorry for upsettin' ya."

She could not find words to convey her pain, and to her shame, her eyes watered. Jeremiah swiftly crossed the room to her. He got down on his knees and whispered, "I love you."

Callie nodded, then brought her eyes back to the men before her. Jeremiah stood, but remained at her side. Black spoke up next. His voice dripped with authority, and there was no apology in him. He was attempting to control the matter.

"Can me and you make peace, Miss Callie?"

"We are not at war, Mister Black," she answered.

"But neither are we at peace."

She shook her head, conceding they were not at peace.

Black then tried a new angle. "I too apologize, Miss Callie."

"And what exactly do you apologize for, Mister Black? Are you sorry that I had to beg for mercy to save the man I love, while Miss Suzanne, the slaver's wife did not?" She refused to be handled.

"I am regretful about all of it," Black answered.

"When you say all of it, Mister Black, are you also speaking of the way you used me?"

"Used you?" Black questioned.

"Yes, Mister Black. I realized later that you didn't exactly try to stop me from entering the situation. You knew Jeremiah wouldn't have shot both of your brothers with me in the cabin. From where I stand, you used me to keep these two alive," Callie jutted her chin curtly in the direction of the men standing at Black's side.

The man with lifeless eyes shifted uncomfortably next to Black, and Callie turned her stare on him. He held her gaze, and Callie found him frightening, but she wouldn't show it. She had been living and dealing with Jeremiah. She could not be cowed. When the man said nothing, her gaze turned to a glare, and he responded accordingly, after clearing his throat.

"Miss Callie, my name is Elbert. I am sorry for what you been through."

Before she could acknowledge Elbert, Black spoke again. "A man in my position has to be able to weigh a circumstance for the benefit of everyone involved. I would have let the situation play out, but because you happened along on the path, I did not want bloodshed in your presence. My goal in the matter you speak of was to get all the men to stand down—not just Jeremiah. It was not pretty, but we are all still standing. Again, I express my regret to you, Miss Callie."

She assessed Black, weighing his words and his intelligence. What he explained made sense. As she continued in thought, Black repeated his request.

"Can we make peace, Miss Callie?"

She sighed. "I suppose."

"My brothers and I have made peace with Jeremiah. You have our word."

As Black spoke those words, a weight lifted from her shoulders, and she burst out crying. Jeremiah helped her up from the chair and hugged her. Against her ear, he said in a low voice. "Stop cryin', woman. It will be all right."

When she finally calmed, Black took a step closer. "Jeremiah has asked that I take you home with me to keep you and the child safe. I have agreed, if you are comfortable with this arrangement. He tells me you think we will kill him when he comes for you. This is not so, as you have our word. When he arrives at my home, we will take his guns for his own safety, and he has agreed."

Jeremiah kept his arm around her. "Are you taking his guns because you don't trust him?" she asked.

"Jeremiah has given his word, and we trust it. But the black cracker is known far and wide. We are attempting to help the people see him in a different light," Black explained.

She looked to Jeremiah for confirmation.

"I trust Black," he said, "and you can trust that I will come to you before our child's birth."

Callie turned to Black and whispered, "I thank you for taking me to safety, Mister Black."

Black chuckled. "I am clear that you do not like me, Miss Callie. But you will like my wife, so all is not lost."

❀ ❀ ❀

E.J. stood on the back porch, contemplating the last three days. He had first observed the activity going on about him with indifference, but as the hours slipped away, indifference turned to relief.

Hunter Manor had been his whole life; now he wanted change. They would travel light, taking only the necessary items to sustain life. He was annoyed for two reasons: first, he was still weak; second, he was fighting with Nettie, and he was not winning. She had informed him that she was carrying his child—and that she wanted to leave him.

When he re-entered the cabin, the women looked up from where they sat at the table. Nettie had cooked beef stew and neither of them had touched their food. E.J. never thought he would see the day when they all could coexist in the same space, but it was to be temporary. His wife looked hurt, and he was finding that it came with the territory. Nettie reached out and gave Suzanne's hand a reassuring squeeze before giving voice to her thoughts.

"Masta, I ain't wantin' to hurt ya, but I wants to try freedom."

He leaned against the back door, and it was cool in contrast to the warmth within the cabin. Their circumstance had changed, and he wanted to force her to stay with him. E.J. attempted to calm down before he spoke. He very much wanted her to see reason.

"Nettie, how will you make it with a child? I want to care for you and my child." His voice was raw.

"I wants to leave wit' the last peoples tomorrow. I ain't leave sooner causin' ya wasn't well. Ya cain't understand what's in me; ya always been free."

He was about to explode when Suzanne cut him off. "Edward, I too am with child."

E.J.'s eyes landed on Suzanne, and the words escaped him. He understood the facts, still he did not expect both women to be with child at the same time. Thinking back on his wedding night and the week that followed, their couplings had been intense; but the deserters happened, and Suzanne had backed away from the sex act. He was pleased that his wife was carrying his child; E.J. wanted intimacy with her again. He also couldn't let what was happening with Nettie ruin his reaction to his wife's news.

He walked over and pulled her to her feet, embracing her. "I am so pleased."

She looked unsure when he backed away from her. He was about to ask her not to doubt him when Suzanne spoke, directing her words to Nettie.

"Nettie, I was hoping since we found common ground when Edward was under the weather that we could be friends. I am nervous about being with child. I am also worried about my mother and sister. My papa's death has only complicated matters. Please let us take you to freedom. You and the child could settle with us. If you are unhappy, I will help you at whatever you wish to do."

Nettie looked at Suzanne and then at him. E.J. was holding his breath when Suzanne whispered rather loudly, "Please don't leave me to deal with Edward alone."

Nettie laughed. "If'n I wishes to leave later—"

"We will settle in Canada," E.J cut her off. "Colored people are free there. It will be what's best for you and my child."

"I thought you was wantin him for yoself," Nettie said to Suzanne.

"I love him, and I want him to be happy. He will not be happy without you. I can see now that I will not be happy without you, either," Suzanne replied.

He was shaken by his love for them.

"I ain't sho' where we gon end up, but Imma stay for now," Nettie agreed softly.

"Good," Suzanne replied. "We can help each other with the children."

E.J. was so overwhelmed that he turned on his heels and headed for the front door. Once on the porch, he leaned over placing his hands on his knees to brace himself. He took two cleansing breaths as he tried to calm down. The power in the triangle belonged to the women. Nettie was staying because Suzanne asked, not because he had begged.

When he could breathe again, he sat on the top step. Jeremiah appeared and stood quietly behind him. They did not speak. Still, it was comforting to have his brother near.

Shultz came to check on him and cautioned, "Don't stay out here too long; you still need your rest."

Long after his brother and the doctor left, E.J. remained on the porch. Two hours went by before he got up the nerve to finally venture back inside the cabin. The lanterns were turned down, and his women had gone to bed without him. He undressed quietly, removing only his shirt and boots.

When he pulled back the covers, his breath hitched at the lovely sight before him. Both women lay gloriously naked and huddled together for warmth. Suzanne looked up groggily and whispered, "Come to bed, Edward."

E.J. hastily shucked the remainder of his clothes, fearing the women would come to their senses. He settled between them and involuntarily groaned; their body heat was so stimulating. Suzanne moved in and pushed her tongue into his mouth; he was lost. Abruptly, his shy wife pulled away, allowing room for Nettie to lean in and kiss him just as deeply. When Nettie backed away, he closed his eyes attempting to control his emotions.

At the feel of fingers in his hair, his eyes blinked open to find both women smiling at him. Nettie's voice trembled, "I loves ya, Masta. My wantin' to be free ain't meaning I don't love ya."

E.J. grabbed her roughly by the back of her neck and pulled her mouth back to his. "I'm making change for you, Nettie. Please don't ever leave me," he pleaded against her lips.

Suzanne reached out and gently rubbed Nettie's back. The act of kindness caused E.J. to turn his attention to his wife. His very soul shook when he said, "I know this is not what you were looking for when you agreed to be my wife. I will spend the rest of my life trying to make you as happy as you make me. I love you so much, Suzanne."

Tears spilled from Suzanne's eyes as she whispered, "I love you too, Edward."

"We wants to feel ya body against ours. Is ya well enough, Masta?" Nettie asked concerned for him.

"Yes," he groaned. "Please."

Both women backed away, and he felt the absence of their touch, acutely. He was about to beg for more, but they leaned in, trailing hot kisses down his torso. When they came to his manhood, they each took turns licking and sucking him. They also kissed each other with his hardness at the center of their scorching mouths.

"Aaaahhhh shit," he ground out.

It had been too long since he had lain with the women he so desperately loved. He thought he would burst and spill his seed prematurely.

"Easy," E.J. hissed, his breathing labored, "Ladies you gonna take it from me before we can get started."

He pulled himself up, placing his back against the headboard trying to get away from the sweet torture of their lips and tongues. They stayed with him as he adjusted his position in the bed. He felt fingers massage his testicles, and his eyes rolled up in head. His stomach muscles clinched–he wasn't going to last.

"I'm right there," he warned thickly.

At his words, Suzanne licked her way back up his chest and lightly bit his right nipple. She took his mouth in a stormy kiss. "We want to please you. Let go, my love, and feel good."

As if on cue, Nettie took him deep in her throat, causing his body to stiffen and then explode. E.J. saw stars, as Suzanne continued to ravage his mouth. His body was still on an ecstasy high, when he felt his wife mount him and rub her wet folds along his soft shaft, as it lay against his belly. It was Nettie's turn to kiss him and tasting himself on her lips made him hard again. E.J. was ready for more, and he leaned forward, sucking Suzanne's nipple.

Suzanne moaned, "Ohhh, Edward, how I have missed you."

His wife reached down and positioned him at her core. When she slid down onto him, her head fell back, and her lips parted. This was the most beautiful moment of his life, feeling Suzanne clamping around him, while Nettie kissed and touch his burning skin. As Suzanne rode him, he pulled Nettie, who was on her knees facing him, close and bit down lightly on her erect nipples. He pressed two fingers into her wetness and groaned.

Nettie gasped in sheer delight, "Masta... Masta, ohhh."

He felt Suzanne's steady strides falter and then her walls constrict deliciously around him. She leaned in mingling her tongue with his and Nettie's. As she burst into an orgasm, he thought she would pull him along. E.J. gritted his teeth as he weathered the storm that was Suzanne. He gripped her hips to anchor himself through the sensations until she slumped forward spent. She slid to his left side breaking the connection and he held her not wanting to relinquish the tenderness.

E.J. was kissing Suzanne all over her face, when Nettie lined herself up with his rigid shaft and slid down onto him. Suzanne caught his cry of pleasure with the caress of her mouth. He held his wife in his left arm and gripped Nettie with his right hand. They were going to kill him, the stiffness in his shoulder forgotten.

"Damn," he choked out. "Damn."

Nettie took him from head to hilt–over and over, while Suzanne stroked his chest with her tongue. The edge of his vision darkened, as he approached euphoria. His fingers found Suzanne's wet folds and he inserted two fingers. E.J. wanted her to find pleasure with them. When Nettie began tightening and releasing, he was helpless as she snatched the orgasm from him. Suzanne followed.

E.J. lay flat on his back, heart pounding and breathing hard. Both women had snuggled close to him. He would never be the same–they would never be the same. It was the beginning of a deeper affection. He would move heaven and earth to keep it.

❄ ❄ ❄

Daybreak was upon them when Tim, Frank, Anthony and the ambassador rode back onto the Hunter plantation. The third wave of people left the night before, among them was Myrtle and her family. Three carriages and two wagons would meet Simon and his men in Ohio for the hand off. Slowly, but surely, the last of the plan was coming together.

Black stood in front of the cabin he and the men were using. His thoughts wandered to Callie and the level of intelligence she displayed. It was yet another facet that explained Jeremiah. Black could see that the colored overseer really had made change with the help of a woman. Still, he wondered how the situation with little Otis would play out. Black's line of thought was broken when the men came forward to give an accounting.

Tim and Frank came to him first, explaining that the people they moved connected with Moses. Jeb and Gerry remained with Moses, and they would continue to push the people to New York. Shultz reported that E.J. was on the mend. Elbert informed him that the men were still watching the perimeter of the plantation to ensure safety. Jeremiah and James came forward posting up on the porch, both men were silent. Finally, Black spoke, and the men around him listened.

"Tonight, we break camp. We will step through the remainder of the plan."

At Black's word, the men moved on to their respective duties.

As they walked away, the sun began to rise denoting a new day. Black was about to go inside and rest when he noted Hunter walking toward him. The morning held a chill, but for Black it was invigorating. He wore a roughly made black woolen cap, pulled down over his bald head. He assessed Hunter as he approached, the slaver did not seem broken. In fact, it appeared a weight had been lifted from his shoulders.

Good morning," E.J. greeted.

"Hunter."

E.J. winced at Black's reply. "I came to ask you about the overseers. What do you plan to do with them?"

"What do you have planned for them?" Black countered.

"I have Suzanne, Nettie, Julia and Maryam to move. They all will have personals to bring. I was hoping to use the overseers to help the women ready for our journey."

Black nodded. "The overseers will stay at the main house. If they venture back down into the slave quarters, we will kill them. They are not to wander off or we will kill them—and then we will kill you."

Hunter sighed, but he did not attempt to verbally spar. He was so quiet that Black turned to look at him. He didn't seem fazed by the threats being issued, and it was all too clear. The bastard E.J. had engaged in the sex act with both his women, so laid back was he. And from what Black could tell—his give a damn was broken. He smiled, as he watched E.J. stroll leisurely away.

❄ ❄ ❄

When night fell, Callie would leave him. Jeremiah almost called off her departure because the pain of being separated from her was great. Once Callie left the plantation, he knew time would pass loudly. He had much to do, and to start with, he would seek out Ella. Jeremiah wanted to speak with his grandma to make clear his thoughts.

As the final group of people readied themselves to move out, the Hunter plantation was the busiest Jeremiah had ever seen. He noticed the few male slaves left would not hold eye contact with him. Their fear of him was still prevalent, and he felt some regret. The morning was cold, and he was dressed accordingly, in tan slave attire with a brown woolen coat. The people milled about, packing their meager belongings. When he arrived at Ella's door, he found her doing the same. Eva and Sonny were with her.

"Mawning, Jeremiah," Eva greeted.

Ella stopped packing and came to him. Reaching for her shawl on the peg by the door, she stepped onto the porch. They both looked at one another as they gathered their thoughts on the changes that were taking place. Jeremiah found that he was worried for the old woman and something else he had not before noted. His mama looked like Ella, and now that his mind was opened to the truth, he couldn't help but see the resemblance.

He spoke first, because the power had shifted between them. She no longer feared him, and he supposed it was a good thing. "I have asked Black to take you, Eva, Callie, and Sonny home wit' him. You will remain wit' Black 'til I come for you. I plan on tryna make a life for myself and Callie. I also plan on keeping you wit' me."

Ella looked on him with raised brows. "Whats to come of ya uncle and Eva?"

"Sonny is his own man."

"Is ya not wantin' ya uncle 'round? I wants to be close to you and Sonny," she countered.

He did not want to speak with Sonny. They had managed peace, but he wanted Sonny to make his own choices. Ella stood with her hands on her hips, glaring at him. The power between them had definitely shifted. Stepping back through the door, Jeremiah cleared his throat before speaking to Sonny, who stood by the table with a smirk on his face.

"I'm leaving the women with you. When I come, we will try and set up close to one another, so Ella can go back and forth. Is this all right wit' you, Sonny?"

"That be fine," Sonny grinned.

When he went back onto the porch, Jeremiah could see Ella was pleased. She kissed his cheek before rushing back inside to finish her packing. Eva came to the door.

"I's glad it all worked out. I knows ya ain't wantin to send her away. How is ya holdin' up?"

Jeremiah looked down at her and smiled. The words wouldn't come, and she reached out, touching his cheek. "I'll see 'bout Callie—you ain't got to worry."

He nodded and headed for his own cabin and Callie. Along the way, he encountered Elbert and Gilbert. Of all the men, Jeremiah knew Gilbert and Simon; they had come from the Hunter plantation back when his papa was in charge. They had never been friends, but they had not been enemies. His papa had made him an overseer after they had run off. In fact, it was their escape that raised him to overseer. It was another lifetime.

"Black say he wants yo' people ready soon as night hits," Gilbert said. "They's to meet us on the side of the main house."

"They'll be ready," Jeremiah responded.

Just as he was about to move on, Elbert said, "I appreciate you saving my life and James' life. Your woman will be safe until ya come. You have my word on the matter."

Jeremiah stared at Elbert. Black's brother was a scary fellow. Still, Elbert had tapped into his greatest hurt. Sending Callie away only proved that he could not care for his woman or his child properly. It was more than he could bear.

"Callie is angry that I am sendin' her away," Jeremiah said.

"She will be fine; just get there before the child," Elbert said.

"Yeah," Jeremiah replied, before walking off to his cabin.

The sun was now shining brightly, and in contrast, the small one room cabin was dimly lit. There was fire in the hearth and one lantern burned on the table. The curtains were drawn, and Callie was seated in front of the fireplace. In the corner near the front door, everything they owned was packed up. On the table were two pair of trousers and four shirts for him. Next to his things were a smaller pair of trousers and one of his shirts; under the table were her sock and shoes.

Jeremiah did what he always did; he undressed and stepped into the bathwater that she had not long exited. The water wasn't hot causing him to wash quickly and get out. Callie, he noticed, didn't acknowledge him as she gazed at the flames. He knew she was hurt, but like him, she also knew this was the best choice. When he finished drying himself, he moved to stand close to the fire and her.

"You angry with me?" He asked.

"No."

Jeremiah sighed. "I miss you already."

"I am worried for you."

"You should be restin'. You have a long journey ahead."

"I don't want to leave you, Jeremiah."

He extended his hand. "Come and lay with me. We will talk about what we will do when I come for you."

Jeremiah helped her stand and led her to the bed. He pulled back the covers permitting her in first. When she was comfortable, he let his towel drop and climbed in next to her. Callie allowed him to spoon her and his hardness pressed against her bottom. She was so soft and warm.

"I wanna be inside you, Callie."

She turned her face back toward his, and he kissed her tenderly. He caressed her belly and felt his child move within her. She was his everything. He was nothing without her, and they both knew it. Reaching down between them, he placed his manhood at her opening and pressed forward. When he could go no further, he didn't move. Instead, he enjoyed the connection.

"Jeremiah… Jeremiah," she moaned.

He gripped her hips tightly and growled. "Tell me you love me, woman."

Slowly, he began to move within her. Callie's breath caught. "I love you, Jeremiah, oohhh."

He stroked her gently, though he wanted to be rough. Hearing her words of affection made him emotional, and he picked up the pace. He found a rhythm that filled the little cabin with sounds of pleasure.

"Damn, woman, I can't live without you," he said breathlessly.

His words caused her to shudder and when she found release, he followed. They splintered into tiny shards of delight, as the bed creaked and the headboard knocked the wall. Jeremiah's seed burst from him with such intensity, he cried out telling her over and over that there was no one for him but her.

❀ ❀ ❀

Early afternoon, a group of ten men dressed in black rode onto the Hunter plantation. Black was standing at the edge of the slave quarters as the extra men rode right up to him. Among them was Simon. He had come back with Emmett and the others, bringing with him four men from the hand off. There were three carriages and three covered wagons. The people immediately set to work loading the wagons.

Simon swung down from his horse and approached.

"Sunday?" Black asked.

"She well," Simon replied. "She missin' ya."

Black nodded. He was about to inquire after the rest of his family when Simon's facial expression suddenly changed. The men were bringing Luke's coffin forward.

"They tell me Luke ain't make it," Simon said.

"No," Black replied, "The men didn't want to leave him here."

"You, all right?"

"Tired," Black answered.

"Yeah," Simon countered.

Elbert and James walked up. They all watched as Luke was loaded onto one of the wagons. The people gathered, loading their belongings where directed. Jeremiah brought Callie's things while she rested. Black saw Hunter come out of the main house, guiding the overseers on how to load his possessions. Shultz appeared with his black bag, and upon seeing Simon, the doctor clapped him on the back.

"Mary?" Shultz asked.

"She well. Told me to tell ya she missin' ya."

Shultz looked at his boots as he blushed. James and Elbert asked after Abby and Anna. Simon offered the same words. "They's fine and missin' ya both."

The doctor excused himself, "Gentlemen."

"Shultz, where you off to?" Black asked.

"I'm headed to the main house. E.J. asked me to check on Miss Nettie and Miss Suzanne before I leave tonight. Both women are with child."

Black nodded and fell in step with the doctor. Jeremiah followed. The other men continued to get the posse ready to leave. When they reached the porch of the main house, Hunter greeted them.

"Doctor–Black."

"I'm here to check on the women," Shultz said.

"Yes, doctor, and thank you," E.J. replied.

Black followed Shultz up the stairs, with Jeremiah behind him. Once on the landing, the men stood facing each other. There was tension in the air.

Shultz cleared his throat before asking, "Where are Miss Suzanne and Miss Nettie?"

"They are in my study at the end of the hall on the left. Suzanne is also worried for her mother, who has not said much since her father was killed," E.J. said.

"I will check in on your mother in-law if she will allow me," the doctor assured.

Shultz turned to Black, who nodded curtly, giving the doctor the silent go ahead. Shultz disappeared down the hall.

"You haven't brought you and Callie's belongings to be loaded," E.J. said to Jeremiah.

"Callie, Ella, Eva, and Sonny will be leaving with Black tonight," Jeremiah replied.

"I see. And when were you going to tell me? I thought we agreed to move our families together."

Jeremiah looked at Black as if he wanted him to go away. It was clear he wanted to speak privately with his brother. Black, wanting to see how far this argument would go, crossed his arms over his chest and stared between the brothers.

The black cracker turned to E.J. "I made a decision about Callie's safety. She will leave with Black."

"She should not be separated from us," E.J. said, and then narrowed his eyes, as if something had just dawned on him. "Maybe you plan on separating from me as well. Are you ridding yourself of your enslaving brother?"

Jeremiah looked to Black before turning back to his brother. His anger was evident. The sharpness in Jeremiah's voice left no doubt this was the step before it would get physical. "We are brothers, ain't nothin' will change the fact. But you will not question my decision about my child and my woman. I will travel with you, and Callie will travel with Black."

Hunter opened his mouth as if to speak, but Jeremiah put up his hand. "You will stop here, E.J., or you will get the thrashing that goes with this circumstance. It was hard enough to make the decision to part with her. Push me no further, man."

Black was reminded of the quarrel between him and James. Brothers who loved hard also fought hard. Hunter's face was red, but he backed off.

Jeremiah turned to Black. "Callie will be ready."

Black nodded as he watched Jeremiah descend the stairs and walk away. He could feel Hunter vibrating from his anger. Hunter was about to walk away, when Black said, "Your brother is trying to understand life away from the plantation. He doesn't want Callie to see him trying to figure it out."

Hunter stood at the edge of the top step, staring off in the distance. He sighed. Black noticed he wore two guns at his hips, and his movements were slow. It was clear he was still on the mend.

"You may not understand this, but Jeremiah is not the only one who has to figure things out. This is the only life I have known. I too must retrain my thoughts; I too must learn to make a living in a different profession. I am struggling against what has been normal my whole life."

"I understand that slavery is a double-edged sword. But you will make your changes in white skin."

Hunter looked at him thoughtfully. "I have fallen in love with a colored woman and made her my wife's equal. I have jeopardized the safety of both women with my actions. I will also father colored children, and I worry for them already. I am not totally naïve. My brother has been my constant. It is a friendship I can't bear to lose. Callie does not like me, but I care for her and the child she carries. It has not been easy on me, either."

Black chuckled, and E.J. frowned in annoyance.

"You find what I say funny?"

"I do. You say Callie don't like you—she doesn't like me either," Black continued to laugh.

Hunter laughed too. "Even I like you, Black. There is no chance of her liking me, if she doesn't like you."

In Black's mind, Hunter had a point.

23

Going Home

THE HOUR HAD grown late and darkness couldn't have come fast enough for James. The people were all packed and ready to go; life had begun to progress once more. Standing off to the side, he watched as Jeremiah spoke with his grandma, Sonny and Eva. When the black cracker came to his woman, James turned away. Fannie came to mind, and he felt heavy with thoughts of the young life that had been snuffed out. He found that some days he could embrace Fannie and other days it was all too much.

James watched Jeremiah help a crying Callie into the carriage and shut the door. He tried to harness his anxiety, as Jeremiah and E.J. moved in to speak with Black. Simon, Anthony and Emmett carried torches, shedding light on the departing people. The night air was cold, yet it felt good against his face. Any physical discomfort he felt subsided with the promise of finishing the mission and going home.

Black stepped forward to address the group, and James felt the blood shift direction in his veins. It was time to step through the last part of the plan. The firelight danced against Black's face in hues of orange and blue. Simon handed his torch to Gilbert and stood next to Black.

"The man to my left," Black motioned toward Simon, "is here to help you to freedom. You will follow his words as if they came from my own mouth. Are there any questions?"

Black and Simon both waited for a response. There was only a low murmur from the crowd.

Simon raised his hand. "You is to watch the back of the man next to ya! Ain't no turnin' back, let's move out!"

James watched as the black cracker and his brother moved out in the opposite direction, with the remaining overseers watching their backs. Black and Elbert approached him.

"You ready?" Elbert asked.

"Yeah."

"It'll be just the three of us; Simon and the men will stay the course," Black said.

James nodded, before swinging into the saddle. He and his brothers brought up the rear as they rode away from Hunter Manor. Once on the move, the men made for the Mickerson plantation. They rode for about three hours, before he, Black and Elbert broke away from the caravan. When they finally made it to the plantation, James felt pain in his stomach.

The men stood for a time at the edge of the Mickerson plantation before leaving their horses in the brush and proceeding on foot. James recalled where they first encountered Fannie. Elbert must have read his mind. "I believe it's one of these cabins on the end," he said.

There was a half-moon and the skies were clear, but what helped the brothers most were the lit candles shining from the cabin windows. The chill was less severe, because they had moved away from the water. They finally came to Fannie's old cabin, and it was uninhabited. As they pushed the door open, it creaked on its hinges, and a cat darted past them.

Across the way, a colored man stood on his porch, observing them. The door to his cabin was open and a woman's silhouette drifted just beyond the entrance. Black and Elbert backed him up, as he crossed the path to speak with the man.

"My name James and yours is?"

"Ross be my name," the man responded.

"These two is my brothers, Black and Elbert."

Ross looked over his shoulder at the woman. "Dolly, ya hear dat? Black is here! Ain't that somethin'?"

Black stepped forward shaking the man's hand. Looking up at the woman, he said, "Hello, Miss Dolly."

"Hello, Mista Black. Won't ya come in outta the cold?"

"Yes sah, Mista Black, come on in," Ross echoed.

The men joined the couple inside. The one room was small but clean. There was no bed, but on the floor piled in front of the fireplace were several blankets. Furniture was sparse; there was a table and only one chair.

Ross was a small man with matted, gray hair. His left eye was lazy, and he had a wide nose, with full lips. Dolly looked to be around forty summers, but she had aged well, James thought. Her hair was cut short, she had high cheekbones, and a heart-shaped mouth.

"Either of you know Fannie?" Black asked.

Dolly smiled warmly. "Yes, we knows Fannie. She run from here a time ago. I told her you all would come back for her, but she ain't thank so."

Black nodded. "Who did she leave with?

"Some a da young folk got togetha and runned. Fannie say ya lit a fire in her, and she wanted to be free. It was 'bout seven what runned. When you all come last, Fannie mama died the mawnin' after ya left here. She was beside herself wit' grief for givin' up freedom to only be witout her mama," Dolly explained.

James could not believe Dolly's words. The woman confirmed what he had suspected all along. Deep down, he felt it was a mistake leaving Fannie behind, but he hadn't wanted to force her. He knew if he had pressured her to go with him, her mama would have lived longer in her head then for true. Elbert had been right. All this no longer mattered. He felt no better, and Fannie was still gone.

"Fannie was wanting to find you all. Even though she ain't here, she free," Dolly said.

Dolly's last statement knocked the wind out of him. James muttered his excuses and went out the front door. He had to pull himself together. He paced in the darkness, breathing deeply and trying not to pass out. His ears hummed, as he thought of Abby to calm himself. He heard Black speaking to Ross and Dolly before he emerged from the cabin.

"Yes, we will help you to freedom. You'll need a horse."

"I'll go wit' him to the stable and meet you by the horses," Elbert said.

"Yeah," Black responded, before turning to Dolly. "Get dressed, me and James will wait on the porch."

Elbert and Ross walked off into the darkness, and Dolly closed the door to dress herself in warmer clothing. Black stood quietly next to him. "She said what I already knew," James said.

"But had we not come, your head would have doubted what you knew," Black replied.

In that moment, James knew he was like Fannie, unaccepting of the obvious. He wanted to believe more had happened. The truth was that she had followed him because many knew of Black. It was no stretch that she had come to Canada hoping to be safe with him. Instead, he had killed her.

Black broke his train of thought. "It's time to put this burden down so you can enjoy Abby and your son. I had to do the same with Otis."

James didn't get a chance to answer, as Dolly appeared on the porch.

"I's ready, Mista Black."

※ ※ ※

The men rode hard, catching up with the group on the edge of North Carolina. At daybreak, they had crossed over the border of Virginia into West Virginia. They set up camp at a safe house, with the people seeking shelter between the stable, barn, and a small cabin. The men rested in shifts. In the middle of the afternoon, Jeb, Gerry, their mother Miss Esther and Moses arrived.

Black was relieved to see them. The weight of the situation was starting to ease. The sun made for a mild day, still one could feel winter setting in. The people broke down into two groups, Jeb and Moses formed one group. Gerry and their mother formed the other group. When night fell, they were all on the move. At the next safe house, the people moving toward Canada had thinned greatly. Callie, Ella, Eva and Sonny would be their guests. The remaining riders were the men that initially rode out on this undertaking, along with Simon and the men he brought with him.

Twenty men had ridden out to see this mission through. Lou had to leave to see to the safety of the woman they found in the dry-goods store. Luke had been killed in the fray at the Hunter plantation. Twenty-three men now crossed into Ohio. Each man was emotionally drained and beaten down. Still, they continued on, stopping only to offer rest to the women. When they crossed the border into Canada, they stopped once more. Each man was pressed to the limit, and they were ready to be home.

The day was dawning when the men rode through the gates of Fort Independence. The weather was bitingly cold, but they were so happy to be home they didn't even notice.

※ ※ ※

Just inside the gate, Black swung down from his horse. A stable boy came forward, relieving him of his load. Under normal circumstance, Black would have made for the bath house. But today, he couldn't. Luke had been killed, and he needed to be on hand to answer questions. He had ridden through the gate with Elbert and James. Tim drove the carriage; the ambassador drove the wagon with their belongings and equipment, and Shultz drove the wagon carrying Luke's body.

The people of Fort Independence came forward to help the men. Black was just about to ask that Callie and the others be shown to a cabin when he heard a commotion. It appeared Lou had wandered up from the barracks. He saw the coffin, but did not see Frank. The younger twin became frantic as he searched the crowd for his brother.

"Where my brother? Where Frank?" Lou's voice was rough and expressive.

Black, along with Elbert and James, moved toward him to try calming him down. Black realized their mistake. They shouldn't have approached Lou at once. He backed away in horror, still calling for his twin. Black shook his head. He was about to say Frank was well when Frank appeared.

"Lou!" Frank yelled.

Lou turned at the sound of his name. He stepped to his brother and hugged Frank tightly. Black, Elbert and James looked on understanding more than they cared to admit.

"I's glad you's home. I worried for ya every damn day," Lou's voice cracked with emotion.

"I ain't finna die on ya. How the girl is?" Frank asked.

Lou stared at his brother for a moment. "Molly good. Yo' Carrie is well too."

Frank nodded. Black could tell he was struggling to hide his feelings at seeing his brother. When he, Elbert and James walked away, Frank abruptly stepped forward and hugged Lou in return. As the twins walked away from the gate, Harry, Gilbert's brother appeared. The two men spoke for a few moments, before they walked away with Harry clapping Gil on the back.

Black looked again at Luke's coffin. It was a nightmare in

the middle of the daydream of their safe return. No one asked about the identity of the deceased, probably because many knew all too well that freedom required grim sacrifice. Black sighed as he remembered finding two young boys, half starved to death, on the Eaton plantation in Georgia. Luke and Anthony had been together ever since—and now Luke was no more.

The crowd dispersed, and Black offered instruction to Tim, Bainesworth, and Shultz. It was so cold, frost hung from his every word. "Tim, move the carriage to the front of my house. Mama and Sunday will help me sort this out. Ambassador, Elbert will take you to the barracks. You will stay with the men until you leave. Shultz, James will help you store the body until the weather breaks and we can give Luke a proper burial."

Stepping over to the carriage, Black pulled the door open. Sonny blinked into the sunlight. "Is we here?"

"Yes, you are at my home. You will first meet my wife and mama. They will help you get settled," Black replied.

Ella grinned with anticipation, but Callie did not look so well. Black was about to ask after her health when she threw up on the floor of the carriage. He reached in and helped her out of the cab. She sucked in the cool air too quickly.

"Easy, breathe slowly," he told her.

Callie wore a brown woolen coat with a blanket pulled about her shoulders. She had a tan woolen hat pulled down over her ears. She looked feeble, causing Black to decide to keep her at his house until the matter became more stable. Ella and Eva made short work of the mess on the carriage floor.

"My house is up the hill and you can rest," Black said, trying to reassure her.

"I'm ready, Mister Black," Callie replied weakly.

Black climbed onto the driver's bench with Tim, and the men began moving toward the final step in closing out the mission.

Tim brought the carriage to a stop in front of his home, and Black felt emotional enough to cry. The front door abruptly swung open.

"Glad you's home!" Paul shouted.

"Glad to be home. If I'm seeing you, I'm alive." Black joked.

Paul was dressed in all black with a shotgun in his hand. The bright sun was shining, and when Black set the steps to the carriage, Paul leaned his gun against the wall to assist. Sonny stepped down first and then helped Black with the women. They climbed the steps slowly and once in the house, Black directed everyone to the sitting room off the front hall.

"Please make yourselves comfortable. This is Paul. He will be helping you all," Black explained.

Big Mama appeared at the end of the hall, arms outstretched as she rushed to him. Her gray hair was braided in two plaits. "I been missin' my baby."

"Mama, you look well."

Black leaned down and kissed her cheek, then led her into the sitting room to make introductions. Sonny stood while the women rested on the orange sofa.

"Mama, this is Callie, Eva, Ella, and Sonny. They are from the Hunter plantation. Callie is not well, so I brought them home until we could get three cabins ready." Iris appeared as he spoke—but no Sunday.

Black was about to ask after his wife when Big Mama said, "Sunday is in bed this mornin'; she ain't been well. Anna at the barracks, and Cora got the chilren. Go on; rest yoself. Me, Paul, and Iris will see to our guests."

Black turned back to his visitors, "You are in good hands. I will see you all later."

When they all nodded, Black turned on his heels and strode away. Sunday was not well, and he was anxious. He would not back track to the bath house as he normally did when he returned from travel. He would see his woman now. Black's strides were quick; he stepped through the kitchen and into the back hall. At the door of their bedroom, he stood for a moment before twisting the knob.

A fire burned. The room he shared with his wife was warm and welcoming. Sunday was bathing and looked up when the door opened. Her eyes watered at the sight of him. Black had missed his wife terribly. Closing the door behind him, he assessed her. She looked well enough. Still, his mama wouldn't have said she was under the weather if she wasn't. He walked over to the tub. She was up to her shoulders in bubbles. He leaned in, kissing her forehead.

"Mama says you are not well."

"I's better now that you here," she replied.

"What ails you?" he pressed.

"Sour belly I believes."

Black gave her a final look of concern. When he was sure she was well, he began undressing.

"Come bathe wit' me, Nat."

"No, I'll wait for you to get out. I am plenty dirty and never made it to the bath house."

She pouted, and his heart squeezed. After removing his shirt, he knelt beside the tub and kissed her deeply. Sunday smiled. "I missed ya somethin' fierce."

He stood and walked to the window. Luke was on his mind.

"What troubles ya?"

Black needed a moment. "Natalie? How is my little Miss?"

"She well. She missin you too," Sunday chuckled. "Little Otis ain't been happy since Elbert left. He ain't done nothin' but cry and ask after his 'mama'."

Black turned to his wife and smiled. Little Otis was yet another matter he told no one about. Jeremiah had sent Callie to Canada because he wanted to see his son. The black cracker was attempting to get his woman and both of his children in the same place. Sending Callie was his way of making it clear that there was no hostility. It was a big gesture on Jeremiah's part, and Black did not miss the implications. Jeremiah wanted his son, and it meant more pain for everyone involved. Lastly, he did not think Callie was aware of the boy.

"Come help me from the tub, Nat."

"You don't need to rush. I can wait."

"No, cause ya won't let me touch ya til you has bathed."

Black took Sunday by the hand and helped her up. He reached for the towel on the chair behind him. When he turned back to wrap the towel about her, he saw that his wife's belly was full. He was so moved that he collapsed in a nearby chair.

Sunday wrapped the towel around her and moved to stand between his thighs. She kissed him. "Bathe yoself and come tell me what pains you. You ain't gotta be Black right now; you can just be Nat. You's home."

Black leaned his forehead against her belly, his wife's words broke him. Unable to help himself, he sobbed uncontrollably. Sunday rubbed his back, while telling him how much she loved and missed him. He cried for Luke and the pain he knew Anthony was feeling. Black cried for both the women they found in the dry-goods store. He was incredulous that men could mistreat women in such a manner. Finally, he cried for the pain he caused Callie. He had used her, and she had been aware. He knew without a doubt that Jeremiah would have shot and killed both his brothers. He could not allow such a thing. Black did not like Callie–her perception was too sharp. Worse, she knew he didn't like her and she didn't care, because Callie *did not* like him, either.

When he finally calmed, Black climbed into the tub, washing away the dirt and sins of the last few months.

❊ ❊ ❊

Elbert made it to the barracks with Bainesworth in tow. When they brought the wagon to a stop, the men came out to unload the flat bed. Among the barracks' men was Charles, Myrtle's husband, who came forward to shake his hand. Elbert was pleased to see that the family made it safely. The other men greeted him as well but were distant with the ambassador.

He looked to the front desk, hoping to see Philip. Elbert had decided to dump the ambassador on the older man. Instead, he found his wife standing behind the desk. His Anna was wearing a gun and handing out supplies. Her voice was loud and clear when she said to the room at large.

"You ladies need to move along faster so we can get all the supplies handed out!"

The men laughed. Sarah, Tim's woman stood next to Anna. She too was wearing a gun and shouting orders. Elbert couldn't believe his eyes. He moved down the aisle with the ambassador on his heels and stopped in front of the desk. Anna was looking down at a list while Sarah leaned over her shoulder.

"What are you needing?" Anna asked, as she looked up.

"I need you," Elbert replied.

Anna covered her mouth, and Sarah stepped back in surprise.

"You're home." Anna whispered.

"I missed you and the boys," Elbert's voice was thick.

Tim and Philip entered the barracks through the back door. Sarah moved from behind Anna, and Elbert noticed Tim's wife was in a family way. Tim's shock made everyone laugh. Sarah went to her husband and embraced him. The couple left through the back door.

Elbert turned to Bainesworth and smiled. "You are on your own, Ambassador."

"I understand, my good man. I can manage from here," Bainesworth replied.

Elbert nodded before taking Anna by the hand and exiting the barracks through the front door.

❋ ❋ ❋

Shultz helped James store Luke's coffin in the shed on the edge of the graveyard. The morning had progressed, and though it was great to be home, the weather was uncomfortably cold. The doctor knew he should head to the barracks and the bath house. But he needed to see Mary. He desperately wanted to be in her company, and he didn't want to speak about Luke. Black and the other men had become family. The loss was too great to bear.

As he walked along in the cold, Shultz thought of his younger life at the orphanage. Like Black, his mama had died in childbirth. It was what drove him to become a doctor. He remembered his father taking him to the church and leaving him. The nuns had been kind, still it hurt to be abandoned. If the truth were told, he was better off without his father, for he had not been a kind man. Shultz had been a loner after his schooling was complete. He had avoided connections for fear of rejection. Then, Sunday had abducted him, and his life was forever changed.

It seemed now that he was home, he could no longer hold mind over matter. He was shaking from the freezing temperatures as he briskly walked the frozen dirt paths to Mary's door. Once he arrived, he banged on the door a little more forcefully than he intended. Herschel answered and broke into a smile.

"Shultz, it's good to see you!"

"Good to see you, too, Herschel. We just got back. I was hoping to let Mary know I'm home," the doctor responded, as he peered past Herschel in search of his love.

"Son, Mary ain't here. Try the cabin on the left," Herschel directed, still smiling.

Shultz stood in the doorway, confused. He adjusted his glasses and pushed his hair back from his face. He had been about to ask another question when Herschel pointed abruptly to the left and shut the door in his face.

The doctor walked up the path to the next cabin. He banged, and the door suddenly opened. Mary stood, peeping out at him.

"Nicholas, come in, my love."

Shultz stepped into the warm and cozy cabin. There was a table next to the fireplace with two chairs. A brown sofa sat in the small living space, and at the back of the cabin was a door. Mary's space smelled of freshly baked bread.

She closed the door quietly behind him. Shultz turned his gaze upon her, and his breath caught. Her beautiful golden hair was hanging about her shoulders. Mary was wrapped in a colorful quilt, and it was evident he had gotten her out of bed. He had been about to apologize when the circumstance hit him.

"Why are you here instead of at your house?"

She didn't answer his question. "Are you hungry?"

Shultz was tired and heartbroken. He needed answers. "Please, Mary, don't ignore my question. Why are you here in this cabin?"

She fidgeted with the quilt wrapped about her. "I moved out so we could live together. Do you still want to live with me?"

Her response was completely unexpected, but he answered immediately. "Yes, Mary, I desperately want to live with you. I have not changed from wanting you."

He was about to hug her when Mary let the quilt fall to the floor. She stood before him unsure, dressed in a pink night gown. His Mary was heavy with child, and he was faint from the realization. The doctor seated himself to the table unable to look away from her. He reached out his hand to her, and she came to him, climbing into his lap. They remained that way for a time, until he leaned back to stare in her face.

"I love you so much, Mary."

"I love you more," she whispered back.

It was Luke's death, and Mary's words that pushed him beyond his emotional limit. The good doctor wept, while Mary held him.

❀ ❀ ❀

As James made for Abby's cabin, he decided he would move out of Black's house. He would first help Elbert build Anna a bigger house, and then he would build Abby a home. His heart was broken in two places with thoughts of Fannie and now Luke. It was time to step back into his life, understanding that some days would be better than others.

He reached Abby's and stood for a moment to collect his emotions. He had been gone since July and it was now November. The sun shone brightly down on the little cabin, and James found he was happy to be home. The freezing cold made him feel uncomfortably alive, and he welcomed the sensation. Taking out his flask, he drank deeply before finding the nerve to step onto the porch.

He knew when he entered the cabin Fannie would have to become part of his background. James was accepting forgiveness of himself while sustaining life. He would work at being a whole man to Abby.

Sighing, he placed his flask in his back pocket and approached the cabin. When he pushed open the door, Abby was seated at the table folding clothes. She wore a yellow nightgown. She looked up and began to cry when she saw him. He felt the same, and her beauty struck him once again. It was her large expressive eyes and lovely dark skin that called to him. The very sight of his woman was soothing to his soul.

"Abigail, I missed you."

She wiped her eyes with the backs of her hands, but she did not move to come to him. James waited patiently.

"Don't I deserve a hug?"

He smirked at her hesitation. She was still shy. Finally, she whispered, "Yes, you deserves a hug."

Yet, she still didn't move. James became concerned that she no longer loved him. It was a thought he couldn't bear. He moved toward the table, slowly, carrying his insecurity with him. He stopped opposite her and began to remove his road-weary clothes. The pot of water on the stove was boiling and steam rose in billowing clouds. This was home.

"Will you shave me?"

"Yes of course," Abby replied.

James took off his shirt and folded his arms over his chest. "Is ya mad at me for being gone so long?"

"No."

She looked away, refusing him eye contact. James' voice broke, "Come hug me, Abby. Please."

Abby looked as though she were about to refuse him. Instead, she placed the shirt she was folding back into the basket at her feet and pushed her chair back from the table. She did not stand.

"I has somethin' to say, but I ain't sure how to go about the words."

He searched her face. Anxiety and apprehension grew before his eyes.

"Later," he said. "Not now."

She nodded, exhaling as she stood. At the sight of her full belly, James plopped down in the chair behind him. Abby walked right between his thighs and leaning in, she kissed him. James had no words. He reached his arms around her and placed his face against her belly, then broke down and cried. It was a soul shaking cry - for Fannie, for Luke and for his newfound love. Abby was offering him yet another aspect of family and manhood.

She rubbed his back and whispered reassuringly, "I love you, James."

※ ※ ※

Gilbert stood in front of his cabin in the icy breeze, facing his brother. Harry looked emotional, and Gil was sorry his brother had worried for him. His brother was dressed in all black, and the hat he wore almost covered the ache in his eyes. Gilbert hugged Harry—he was about to go inside, but when they stepped back from each other, Harry spoke his mind.

"I ain't wantin to lose ya again."

Gilbert nodded. "Same here."

"Ya saved me and Margie."

Gilbert could think of nothing to say.

"Go on; get ya some rest," Harry said.

Harry turned and walked away, leaving Gilbert staring at his front door. He thought of Luke, and his belly started churning. He missed Hazel and needed her closeness. It had been a long mission, coupled with the fact that he never thought to love again after Peaches. But he *had* fallen in love with Hazel, and there was no turning back. He just wanted the hurt about Luke to recede. Gilbert wanted to lie between her welcoming thighs and feel alive.

He opened the door and stepped into the cabin to find Hazel kneeling before the fire. The one room was warm and welcoming; he was excited to be in her company. She looked up and whispered, "Oh, Gilly, you's home."

He pushed the door closed against the chill and opened his arms to her. Hazel struggled to her feet. His emotions threatened to unman him, as he looked upon his woman ripe with his seed. She stepped into his embrace, and he whispered, "The past few months been hard. I just wanna lay wit' you, woman. I wants to hold you and my child."

"Come let me help ya undress."

Hazel moved around the cabin, and Gilbert realized that he had never been so damn pleased in his life.

❊ ❊ ❊

Callie had been at Black's house for three days. In that time, Sonny and Eva had transitioned off to their own cabin. She started off sharing a room with Ella, who had also moved off to her own cabin. They had not moved her because she had not been eating. She was drained, and her belly wouldn't cooperate. The room she was in had a tub and fireplace along with a large four poster bed. She had not left the room since she arrived.

Eva came every day, as did Ella. Sonny emptied her chamber pot daily, and she was thankful to him, because he did so while leaving her dignity intact. They had not stayed long in visiting with her, because she was under the weather. She noticed that even with the cold, Eva, Sonny and Ella were thrilled to be at Fort Independence. It appeared they had all made new friends. Eva spoke highly of a woman named Iris. Ella made friends with Big Mama, and Sonny found a new friend in Paul. She was happy for them, but she only wanted Jeremiah.

Her body was tired from travel, but the fogginess of exhaustion was lifting from her mind. As clarity began happening for her, so too did heartache. Callie found solace in reading the journals, learning about life on the Hunter plantation and him. She was on her third journal. Reading was all that kept her from sinking into insanity.

She sat near the window, reading where the light was good. She read every day until the natural light faded. Callie didn't want to mingle. She wished to move to one of the cabins and be left to herself. While she was in thought, there came a knock at the door. The very idea of privacy was a new concept. She just stared at the door and when the knock sounded a second time, Callie engaged.

"Come in."

The door opened and in walked a brown skinned, young woman. She wore a long sleeved, blue dress with black shoes that peeked from under her hem. The woman before her smiled, and it was clear she was with child. Callie closed the book.

"Good mornin', Callie. My name Sunday."

"Good morning, Sunday."

496 | Joan Vassar

"I tried to give ya some time, but they says ya ain't feelin' well. I has asked the doctor to look in on ya," Sunday said.

"My belly is unsettled is all."

"Well, ya cain't go witout eatin' and ya cain't stay in this room all day. Ya has to come out, so you can get some strength."

Callie narrowed her eyes. "Did Black send you?"

The woman chuckled. "He is concerned, but that ain't why I's here."

"Then why are you here? Are you moving me to a cabin?"

"I done told ya why I's here. You ain't eatin and ya cain't stay in this room all day. It ain't good for ya," Sunday explained again.

"So, Black did send you?" Callie repeated.

Sunday smiled. "Ya really ain't likin' my husband, is ya?"

"Is Black your husband? I am sorry for being rude," Callie said, as she dropped her gaze.

Sunday laughed out loud. "Ya ain't sorry for being bad-mannered. Black don't like you neither, ya know. So, I guess you's both even."

"Yes, I know." Callie returned Sunday's smile.

"Out in the world, my husband is the man in charge, but here in this house, I's the boss. You will eat somethin' and ya gonna come outta this room. It's best for yo' baby. The doctor will be along directly. He will show ya to the kitchen after."

"Are you angry because I don't like your husband?"

"Naw. Women folk like my husband too damn much. Meetin' a woman what don't like my husband is refreshin'," Sunday said, before exiting the room.

❋ ❋ ❋

November gave way to December, and the days seemed to be moving too quickly for Black. It had snowed twice, and the ground would remain frozen until spring. The people of the fort went about life without incident. The day was overcast as Black stood at the window contemplating a problem that could not be ignored. Several packages were delivered to him after the men went to town to get supplies. The contents of the packages said much, causing him to send for James and Elbert.

Black turned, just as his brothers entered the study. James saw his expression and paused. "Ya looks like we 'bout to ride out."

Black smiled. *Riding out would be easier than this conversation,* he thought.

"What's all this?" Elbert asked, looking around.

Eight packages of various sizes cluttered the study. Black couldn't back away from what needed to be done. He took a deep breath. "The night Jeremiah and I patrolled the Hunter plantation together, we had a discussion that I need share with both of you."

James stepped back and closed the study door before he gave his undivided attention. Black went on. "Jeremiah told me Otis' mama was named Betsy."

"I asked why he shot the damn woman; he ain't give no good reason," James interrupted.

Black stared at Elbert, who stood with his arms folded over his chest. Clearing his throat, he continued. "Yes, well, I asked the same question, and he basically said the same thing to me."

"Why don't you get on with it?" Elbert said, growing impatient.

"I have had time to think on the matter. And while I don't agree with his killing the woman, I see things I didn't before." Black exhaled and walked to the window. Over his shoulder, he said, "Jeremiah was ordered by his father to kill Otis' mama. He did not carry out the request as ordered."

Elbert reared back in confusion. "Old Hunter was dead, why kill her then?"

"It seems Betsy's mind was broken, and she could not be sold. I gathered she was unable to care for the boy. Yet, when other slave women tried to care for him, she became violent. At times,

Jeremiah said, the woman didn't know the boy was her own. But he did believe she loved him as best she could."

"What ain't you saying?" James asked.

"Jeremiah told me the woman's mind got worse after Otis' birth," Black said. "I asked if he knew the boy's real name, and he did."

"And what *is* his real name?" Elbert asked.

"Little Otis' real name is Jeremiah," Black replied, and they all fell silent for strained moments.

Elbert whistled. "Are you saying Jeremiah is the boy's papa?"

"The packages you see are from Jeremiah, for Callie and both his children. He has also sent money for the upkeep of his woman and children. I believe he sent Callie with us to get his woman and children in the same place."

"Is ya asking us to give up our child?" James asked.

"I am not asking anything. What I am saying is we have children, and we wouldn't want them taken from us. I believe Jeremiah has guilt because he wasn't strong enough to protect the boy from his mama. I also believe he feared selling her and think-ing of her being abused. I think the uprising gave him the nerve to do what he needed to do—for both Betsy and the boy. I think the woman was kind to him, and when her mind worsened, he couldn't get away from what needed to be done," Black said.

"Me and Elbert love the boy, the women love the boy—and he loves us," James said. There was panic in his voice.

"Yeah," Black responded. Shit, he loved the boy too.

"It seems like Jeremiah is trying to work wit' us. Does his woman know?" Elbert asked.

"How you figure he tryna work wit' us? He shoulda told us the truth," James said angrily.

"Jeremiah said he tried speaking with you about the boy, but you refused," Black stated calmly.

"Cause I ain't wanna discuss my child wit' a man that shot me in the damn face," James was almost yelling.

Black moved from the window and got right up on James. "I think you wanna calm yo' ass down."

Elbert stepped in between them. "Ain't no sense in us fighting. We need to see how Otis is wit' Jeremiah. I think he is working wit' us and that says he loves the boy, too. If the boy is afraid, the black cracker will not take him from here. I am willing to end the peace to keep the boy. We will kill him if need be—we are in the position of power, not him."

"Callie is smart. This conversation alone shows why she don't like us," Black said.

"We will strive to keep our word to her, but the boy will not be forced to go if he is afraid," Elbert repeated.

"Agreed," Black said.

"Agreed," James snapped. The tension in the study was still very high.

❁ ❁ ❁

It was now January, and Callie had come to like the fort. Most of all, she loved Sunday. Black had been right. All was not lost, because he had a wonderful wife. Since Callie had moved to her own cabin, Sunday looked in on her daily. They would walk down to the school together and help Mary with the children. She loved being in a place where learning was happening all around her.

Callie found that she was better at helping with reading and writing. Sunday was better at helping the children with arithmetic. She also found Sunday to be highly clever with a very quick wit. After what she had seen of Black, she thought Sunday to be his best possible partner.

She met and made several new friends in Sarah, Anna, Mary and Morgan. Callie enjoyed the other women as well. Abby, however, remained reserved in her company. She and Sunday had discussed the situation, and it was clear. Jeremiah shooting James in the face didn't helped matters. Callie understood and didn't push. The women gathered at times, lunching and discussing all manner of things. Several were expecting like her; each had a May due date. She felt sorry for poor Dr. Shultz.

The ache troubling her heart now was Jeremiah's absence. January was ending, and their baby was due in the beginning of February. She worried he wouldn't make it on time for the birth. Callie also feared he wouldn't come at all. She often thought of E.J. keeping both his women with him. This only promoted thoughts of abandonment. She dreaded that Jeremiah would find life easier without her. Though he purchased new clothing for her and their baby, she still worried she would never see him again. When she told herself she was being silly, her mind would start the process over.

At night, when being with child weighed her down, Callie read the journals. She was in the fourth and last book when she came across something that gave clarity to many of Jeremiah's actions. Callie did not know whether to feel betrayed, jealous, or insignificant in his life. But she knew one thing for certain, Jeremiah would come. She need not concern herself with thoughts of being left by him. In the wee hours of the morning, her jealousy got the better of her, and she cried.

The next afternoon, Callie dressed and went to see Sunday. She would not discuss the matter of the journals with anyone, but she needed to see for herself. Jeremiah had purchased a brown cowhide overcoat stuffed with fur, along with matching boots and hat for her. Callie walked the path to Black's house. The day was cloudy and brisk as she moved along. Men were chopping wood and carrying water. She was almost to Black's home when she met up with Dr. Shultz.

"Miss Callie," the doctor called to her.

"Dr. Shultz, how is Mary?"

"Mary is wonderful," he replied. "Shall we continue?"

When they reached the house, Black was standing in the doorway. "Shultz—Miss Callie."

The doctor helped her up the stairs, as they reached the landing, Black said, "The women are in the dining room. They can't fit in the kitchen anymore."

Shultz chuckled, and Black led the way. In the dining room, the women chatted while drinking tea and swapping baby clothes. When Sunday saw her, she came forward. "Callie! I thought you was tired. I's glad ya here."

"Thank you, I feel better when I move around," Callie replied.

"Come on, ya knows everyone," Sunday said, welcoming her.

Morgan and Anna were at the table with their babies. Sunday's daughter was on the floor, playing with little Otis. Myrtle, Abby, Hazel, and Sarah were also gathered around. Abby averted her eyes when she entered. Eva and Ella waved from the other side of the room.

Big Mama called out to her. "Callie, ya lookin' well. Come sit 'tween me and Cora."

On the left of Big Mama sat a young woman Callie didn't recognize. Sunday made the introductions. "Callie, dis here is Molly. Molly—Callie."

"Nice to meet you," Callie said.

"Nice meetin' you, too," Molly replied.

When she was finally seated, Callie focused in on the children. Specifically, she watched little Otis as he danced and ran about. She was offered tea and cake while engaging in small talk. Otis ran to Big Mama and climbed on her lap. He turned around and looked straight at her. There was no mistaking; he looked like Jeremiah.

"Tell Miss Callie 'hello', chile," Big Mama instructed.

"Hello, Mith Caddie," little Otis said between swallows of cake.

"Hello, sweetheart." Callie choked back her pain. The boy was adorable.

"I not thweethot—I Otith." Callie couldn't help but laugh.

Little Otis hopped down and took off running with Natalie in hot pursuit. In her head, Callie knew she had pieced together the puzzle. She and Sunday had spoken in passing about the plantations from which the children were rescued. All the other children were older than the boy. Otis came from the Hunter plantation. It was clear why Sunday had changed the subject. Callie didn't want to speak about Jeremiah killing the boy's mother. What she wasn't sure about was if Sunday knew Jeremiah was the child's papa. As Callie observed Ella and Eva with the boy, she could clearly see they recognized him. How could they keep such a secret?

When Elbert and James entered the dining room, Otis ran to Elbert. "Up Mama—up!"

Elbert picked him up, and Otis kissed him on the cheek. Sunday had told her about Elbert and the child, but she had not seen it for herself. Callie did not like, nor did she trust Black and his brothers, so she steered clear of them. But tonight, she observed that the child called Elbert 'Mama' and James 'Papa'. It was all too much. She did not know who to ask about the matter. When her gaze collided with Elbert's, he glared at her as if he read her thoughts.

Dr. Shultz took her home by carriage and helped her to her door. When Callie was settled in bed for the night, she cried once again. She had been looking forward to naming their son Jeremiah—now that wasn't possible.

24

Fort Independence
January 1862

IT WAS THREE in the morning when Jeremiah made it to the gates of Black's home. He could delay no further. It was time to deal with the matter of his son and be present for the birth of his youngest child. As for Callie, no words could describe how much he had missed her. It was as he feared, he could not live without her.

E.J. had rented a home on the other side of the closest town. They had purchased a piece of land not too far from Black's home, and when the weather broke, they would build on it. The goal was to raise horses and feed themselves off the land. The War Between the States had caused everything to be overpriced, and they worried they wouldn't get a buyer for the plantation. They eventually got two offers and sold the Hunter estate to the highest bidder. E.J. was now working to sell his mother-in-law's land in Georgia. When February came upon them, Jeremiah left his brother. If Black was gracious, he would wait the cold weather out before moving Callie.

Jeremiah brought his horse to a complete stop and waited. He heard men yelling and finally the gates opened to him. Once inside, he swung down from his horse and was promptly relieved of his weapons. A man named Jake stepped forward and directed him to follow. A second man led his horse to the stable. Even his saddle bags were taken. He had been cold to the bone, but now his anger was ignited. They manhandled him, and all discomfort left his thoughts.

As he walked the path, it was dark save for the torch carried by Jake. Jeremiah was impressed with the lay of the land. They finally came to a large structure; inside were beds, men and weapons. An older fellow who identified himself as Philip spoke up.

"Black, Elbert, and James been told ya come."

Jeremiah nodded. He was directed to a chair in the corner of the dormitory but did not sit. Instead, he removed his cowhide leather coat and hat, placing them on the chair. He then stood, waiting patiently. The men around him went about a shift change as though he were invisible. He in turn ignored them. The goal was to not be killed before he saw Callie and his boy.

He had been standing in the same spot for two hours when Black and James finally entered the barracks. Black showed no emotion upon seeing him, but James looked a step above annoyed. Elbert walked in moments later, and his reception was cool, yet his dead eyes could not have been colder.

"Jeremiah…" Black greeted.

"Gentlemen," Jeremiah responded.

Both James and Elbert nodded.

"Callie?" He asked.

"She is well. You made it on time," Black replied.

Jeremiah exhaled, and the four of them stood in awkward silence for a few moments.

"We will take you to Callie. At noon, Sonny will come for

you and bring you to my study. The four of us will have a much-needed conversation," Black said.

Jeremiah nodded, retrieved his belongings and followed the brothers from the barracks.

❊ ❊ ❊

Callie sat at the table in a blue night gown. It was early morning, but still dark outside. As the freezing wind howled against the little cabin, all she could think about was birthing her baby. She was tired of her condition and anxious to meet her little one. It had been a trying few months.

Breakfast consisted of weak tea and warm bread. She had just lifted the cup to her lips when she heard a carriage stop in front of the house. The jingle of the harnesses and the groaning of the large wheels lurching forward signified the vehicle was now rattling away. Next came the sound of heavy booted feet on the porch. Jeremiah had arrived.

There was a quick knock before the door opened, and he burst into the room. He was dressed in thick dark trousers, a black sweater and black boots. After hanging his coat and hat on the wooden peg, he turned his gaze intently upon her. The black cracker was a sight to behold; his blue-black hair had grown to his shoulders and on his face, was a thin shadow of whiskers. He did not move from where he stood by the door.

"Callie," he said, his voice thick with emotion. "I was unhappy without you."

Placing her hands over her face, she wept. When finally, she spoke her thoughts, Jeremiah didn't flinch. An indication that he expected the conversation.

"I was hoping to name our son after you. I see now that it isn't possible because you already have a son—and he is beautiful."

He took a small step forward. "I ain't want to test the limits of your love for me by admittin' to being like my papa."

"You sent me here, where I did not want to be because you wanted the boy. This was not about my safety," she accused.

"I sent you here for your safety, *and* because I needed to see my son," he corrected her.

"I am jealous," she whispered–defeated.

Jeremiah smiled. "Woman, I have never been in love before you—you need never be jealous. I was fond of Betsy, and she was a sweet woman, but I was not in love with her. We were friends. I had not had a friend because of my position as overseer. It did not bother me that she was strange, but when the boy came, she got worse."

Callie looked at him, searching for sincerity.

"The compassionate thing to do would have been to put her down, but I could not. I was angry the day I shot her, and still, I regret it. I have guilt about all the boy went through at her hands. I love the boy; I will not lie to you about that fact."

"The last journal stopped abruptly in October of 1859," she said, changing the subject.

"The old Hunter was killed," Jeremiah explained.

Callie nodded and looked away.

"I want the boy to be part of our life."

"I know," she whispered.

"Will you help me?" he pleaded.

"Yes, because I love you."

He moved toward her and helped her up from the chair. Jeremiah held her, and she needed his closeness. "You ain't gonna be able to name the child after me no way," he whispered.

She leaned back and showed him her confusion.

Jeremiah's eyes twinkled. "We will have a girl. 'Jeremiah' won't work for her."

Callie smiled, thinking of how unhappy she had been without him.

❊ ❊ ❊

Jeremiah stood on the porch taking in his surroundings. The cold was piercing. He didn't know how he would get used to such severe weather after growing up in the South. More challenging than the Canadian climate was Black and his brothers. He was sure in his absence they had decided once again to kill him. Regardless, he would face the matter of his son as he had not done in the past.

Sonny showed up promptly at noon, and Jeremiah went back inside to get Callie. He helped her with her coat and hat before leading her out the door to the awaiting carriage. Sonny hopped down, setting the steps for her, and she thanked him. Before he could climb in after her, his uncle stopped him.

"Glad ya come."

"The old woman?" Jeremiah asked.

"She will be happy ya come too," Sonny replied.

"Eva?"

"She well. She done made a few friends. I cain't keep up wit' her now." Sonny chuckled.

Jeremiah nodded.

Sonny leaned in and whispered, "The boy look like ya mama."

It had been a year since he had seen his son. "He is well then?"

"Yeah," Sonny answered.

Jeremiah turned and climbed into the carriage. Sonny got in the driver's seat, and they were off. Once inside the vehicle, he and Callie did not speak. He stared out the window, watching the cabins go by. When they pulled in front of the house, the brothers were standing on the porch. They were armed and dressed in their usual black. Sonny set the steps and handed Callie down.

Jeremiah helped her up the stairs. "Miss Callie, you look well. My wife and the ladies are in the dining room," Black greeted.

"Thank you, Mister Black," she replied, refusing to look at Elbert or James.

They greeted her all the same, and Callie nodded.

"Come," Black said, "let me help you find Sunday. Gentlemen, I will meet you in my study."

Jeremiah kissed her cheek and whispered, "I'll see you in a little bit."

She smiled weakly before following Black in the opposite direction.

Elbert tapped his arm. "Come with us."

Jeremiah followed Elbert, and James brought up the rear. His eyes scanned the artwork on the walls and the high-quality furniture. This was colored folk living well, something he had never conceived. In the study, he seated himself on the gold couch. Elbert leaned his hip against the desk and James walked to the window. They did not converse as they waited for Black.

When Black finally appeared, he closed the study door and all three of the brothers turned to face him. Jeremiah sat with his right ankle crossed over his left knee and gave them a blank look. In the past, he had been worried for Callie and E.J.; he even thought he would never see his son again. But today, at this moment, he did not fear them, and they knew it.

"We care for the boy; our women care for the boy. We want what's best for him," Elbert said flatly.

Jeremiah made no response.

James piped up. "We ain't finna force him to go wit' you."

"I come in peace, but ya can't have my son," Jeremiah said, "You can have my loyalty and my gun hand, but not my damn son."

Elbert chuckled. "Shit, we may kill you after all."

Black looked at him with a matter-of-fact expression. "We had actually decided to kill you again."

Jeremiah laughed. "I understand."

"Our women have mothered the boy, and you will take

them into consideration, as we did for you and your brother," Elbert said.

"Yes," Jeremiah agreed.

Black went to the door and propped it open. The men waited for a time until the sound of laughter and little feet came storming down the hall. Jeremiah heard a little voice say, "Nattie, hur-up!"

A little boy dressed in all black ran into the room, stopping at the desk. He turned around to call out once more, "Nattie!"

A little girl then entered the study. She wore a pink dress with pink ruffles on her legs. She was giggling and trying to keep up. The children danced about, and the girl went to Black, who picked her up. His son went to Elbert and cried, "Up, Mama, up!"

When the little girl wiggled to get back down on the floor, his son cried, "Down, Mama!"

The children were just about to take off running again, when the boy finally noticed Jeremiah seated on the couch. The child stopped dead in his tracks and stared at him. He seemed genuinely confused as to how Jeremiah came to be there. He hid behind Elbert's leg, peering out at him from time to time. Callie had been right. His son was beautiful, and he had grown. He looked like Betsy and the thought caused pain.

Elbert picked the boy up, walked across the room and sat on the couch next to him. The boy moved to stand on the cushions between he and Elbert. His son gazed at him; his little eyebrows pressed together.

"You Miah and I Miah," he said in a small voice.

Jeremiah reached out his hands, and his son climbed onto his lap. "I'm Jeremiah and you Jeremiah."

The little girl came screeching over to them and climbed onto Jeremiah's lap too. Within seconds, they both wiggled down and raced off. The children screamed in glee all the way down the hall, leaving the men to ponder what they had just witnessed. A brown-skinned woman appeared in the doorway.

"Is you menfolk hungry? We has plenty."

Black reached out his hand to her, and she gracefully went to him. Jeremiah could see that she was with child. She smiled nervously at him. "Jeremiah, this is my wife, Sunday," Black said.

Jeremiah stood and greeted her. "Miss Sunday, thank you for looking after Callie."

"Mista Jeremiah," she replied.

"After you," Black said to his wife.

Jeremiah and the others followed Black and Sunday to the dining room. Ella was seated at the table next to three older women. She beamed when she saw him. There were also two younger women along with Callie. Sunday made introductions.

"Jeremiah, please meet Miss Cora, Big Mama and Miss Iris. Next to them is Anna, Elbert's woman, and that there is Abby, James' woman. Ladies, dis Jeremiah, Callie's man."

"Ladies," Jeremiah greeted.

He went to his grandma, kissing her cheek and she caressed his face. "I's glad ya come," she said.

Jeremiah smiled. "Me too."

As everyone took their seats, his son ran to James and climbed into his lap. The boy addressed James as "Papa" and the word felt like a physical blow to Jeremiah's stomach. He was seated next to Callie, who grabbed his hand under the table. The meal began, and everyone helped themselves. There was beef stew, roasted yard bird, sweet potatoes and greens. Jeremiah had not realized he was hungry until he reached for a piece of cornbread. He helped himself to a sweet potato and some collard greens and, as was his way, he avoided the meat.

Jeremiah looked up from his plate to find the woman seated next to James staring at him. She was afraid. He looked away, cutting the eye contact between him and the woman called "Abby". He did not wish to intimidate. Just as he turned his attention back to his plate, his son hopped down from James' lap and rushed around the table. He climbed up on his lap to sit with him.

"I do it. I help you," his son said.

Jeremiah waited patiently as his son took a spoonful of food into his own mouth before spooning some food to him. The room grew quiet as everyone watched father and son doing what had clearly been their norm. The conversation picked back up, and barring some spilled food, the meal was pleasant. By the time they finished eating, his son had fallen asleep in his arms.

The women began the cleaning, and the children had been moved for their naps. Callie attempted to stand and help.

"You ain't finna help; ya looks tired," Sunday chided.

"I am a little sleepy," Callie replied.

Jeremiah and Callie stayed till around four that afternoon. He was about to take Callie by the elbow when Elbert said, "Meet me at the barracks tomorrow."

"Time?" Jeremiah asked.

"Whenever Sunday comes to be with Callie," Elbert said.

Jeremiah nodded. Both Sunday and Anna came forward hugging Callie. When they stepped back, Anna looked at him.

"Will you take him from us right away?" Her voice was filled with dread.

Jeremiah ran his fingers through his hair, pushing the strands back from his eyes. Anna looked nervous and so did Sunday. He formed his words carefully.

"I think I need you two more than the boy does. I was hoping you both would continue to help me with him. I purchased a piece of land not far from here, and I thought to start out by visiting him. Eventually, I would like for him to spend time with me in my home. Callie was hoping both the children could get their schooling here. I thought we would continue to share him."

Anna reached out and touched his arm. Jeremiah smiled, as Callie gave his hand a reassuring squeeze.

❀ ❀ ❀

It had been a week since Jeremiah arrived at the fort, and James was in a predicament. Abby was terrified of the black cracker. She had not slept, nor had she eaten since he rode through the gates. James did not know how to proceed because she had not come to him with her feelings. The fear he witnessed in her eyes caused him to linger in his thoughts of murder. At times, he could do nothing but respect Jeremiah–other times he wanted to commit homicide.

James stood in the dark behind the barracks with Elbert and Jeremiah. The weather was mild compared to what they had been experiencing. Elbert smoked a cigar, and the three of them were quiet for a time until James spoke directing his words to Jeremiah.

"My woman ain't slept since ya come."

"Is ya askin' when I'm leavin'?" Jeremiah inquired.

"I am," James said, his attitude visible.

"I will be gone when the weather breaks. When it's safe to move Callie and my youngest child," Jeremiah replied. "Yo' woman will have to get used to me because I will be back and forth to see my son."

James felt his temper boiling over, but Jeremiah cut him off.

"Callie is afraid of you, Elbert, and Black. She does not like nor trust none of ya. I deal wit' it; maybe if yo' woman knew of yo' know-how with piano wire, she might fear you."

Elbert broke out in guffaws, but James just got hotter as he glared at Jeremiah. The tension was thick between the two men.

When Elbert stopped laughing, he addressed Jeremiah. "You don't like when the boy calls James 'Papa'."

"No, I don't like it," Jeremiah responded without hesitation.

James did not comment, as he considered Jeremiah's point. But, he would not stop Otis from calling him "Papa." He loved the boy.

"The three of us is gonna have to learn to get along for the boy and the women," Elbert said.

"Agreed," Jeremiah replied.

"Yeah," James offered begrudgingly.

"Ya have a problem wit' us calling him Otis?" Elbert asked.

Jeremiah sighed. "I did."

"And now ya don't?" James asked.

"Callie thinks his first name should stay Jeremiah and his middle name should be Otis. I'm fine wit' him being called Otis. Jeremiah seems to be a mouthful for him right now," the black cracker replied.

James said to Elbert, "I realize now he was telling me his name, but I couldn't understand him. He did say he was 'Miah'."

"Yeah," Elbert responded then looked to Jeremiah. "I notice ya don't laugh like everyone else when he calls me 'Mama'. I take it ya don't like that either."

Jeremiah was quiet for so long, James thought he was ignoring the question. It was dark, and because of the cold, the back door wasn't open. They couldn't see each other. The end of Elbert's cigar was the only thing discernable. After clearing his throat, Jeremiah said, "It troubles me that the boy calls ya 'Mama', but not for the reason ya think."

"What's yo' reason?" Elbert pressed.

"His mama was a sweet woman, but her mind had left with his birth. She loved him, but she was not good wit' him because of her condition. I ain't wanna face choosing between the boy and his mama. Betsy wasn't difficult wit' me about the boy, but when other slave women tried to help wit' his care, she became violent," Jeremiah replied.

As if gathering his thoughts, Jeremiah paused for a moment. "When she became mama to my child, she became my responsibility. She was my friend. At times, she was so confused and frightened, it hurt to watch. The boy callin' you 'Mama' only reminds me of my failure to have mercy on Betsy and him. His calling you 'Mama' shows I took too long to come to the decision to put her down. Ain't no other way to think on it—the boy suffered because I could not do what needed to be done. You being his 'Mama' means he needed mothering and tenderness. I reason he gets that from you."

"Shit, that's a tough spot to be in," Elbert conceded.

"If not for my anger during the uprising, I don't think I would have had the courage to shoot her. The boy would still be suffering—or dead—in her care," Jeremiah added.

James could now see the matter from all angles. He didn't think he would have been better in such a situation.

"Well, Jeremiah," Elbert said, "I like being yo' son's mama. The boy makes my life good."

Jeremiah chuckled. "James feels ya ain't been honest wit' him, and another man is the boy's papa."

They all burst out laughing.

James struggled to speak as he chuckled. "I think the women is mad 'cause Otis don't see one of them as 'Mama.'"

As their laughter wore on, the men moved toward friendship.

❊ ❊ ❊

February ushered in more cold weather, and Jeremiah could see that Callie was slowing down. Ella and Eva came by daily to help her get ready for the baby. When the women came to visit, Jeremiah went to the barracks to work and earn his keep. One afternoon, when he had been in the barracks for about an hour, Black appeared at the front of the dormitory. Sensing something was wrong, Jeremiah stood and moved toward him.

"Sunday and the women have gone to help Callie. They sent me to fetch you."

Jeremiah did not respond as he moved past Black headed for his cabin. When he stepped out the front door of the barracks,

Sonny was waiting for him. He climbed into the carriage, realizing he was afraid to lose her. He agonized and when the carriage stopped in front of his cabin, he had to take a moment to collect himself.

Sonny pulled the carriage door open and yelled, "Hurry, man! From the sounds of it, ya runnin' outta time."

Jeremiah jumped down from the vehicle. He heard screaming as his feet moved swiftly toward the cabin. He pushed the door open with a bang to find Callie standing by the fireplace. She was leaning against the wall, breathing rapidly. The crash of the door must have startled her because she looked up. A big splash of water hit the floor between her legs, and it was all a blur from that point.

Present in the cabin were Shultz, Ella, Eva, and Sunday. The women replaced Callie's gown with a fresh one and helped her lie down. Sunday cleaned up the floor, and Shultz directed Callie to breathe. Ella placed a chair by the bed and ordered him to sit. Jeremiah did as he was told. Callie reached for his hand, and he leaned in, kissing her cheek.

"I hurt," she whispered.

Jeremiah didn't know what to say, and his worry for her mounted. Callie began to bear down and scream. Shultz was on hand to tell her she was doing well. "I see the head," the doctor exclaimed.

Betsy popped into his head briefly, and he had a renewed appreciation for her. Jeremiah did not get up to see his child enter the world. Instead, he stuck to holding Callie's hand. Shultz directed her to push, and she did, until he heard the baby cry. He wept.

Jeremiah leaned in and whispered to an exhausted Callie, "Woman, I love you."

"Got us a fine baby girl," the doctor announced as he handed the baby to Ella.

Ella moved to the table next to the lantern. Shultz stayed with Callie a few moments more before Eva and Sunday stepped in to clean her up. Sunday spoke, offering him instruction. "Jeremiah, why don't cha' go see the baby while we help Callie."

He looked to Callie who whispered, "Go. I'm all right."

Jeremiah went over to the table. His daughter was crying as Ella wrapped her up and handed her to him. He was moved beyond words at the sight of his beautiful baby girl. The baby's skin was brown, and she had lots of blue–black hair. When they had tended Callie, Eva called for him to come sit.

He handed the baby to Callie, and she whispered, "Oh, look at you. Look how wonderful you are."

"What ya gonna name her?" Eva asked.

Callie smiled down at their new baby. "I want to name her 'Miah'."

Jeremiah grinned with pride. "I like it, woman."

❁ ❁ ❁

March brought with it the rain and the black cracker's brother. Black had instructed that Hunter be brought to the house instead of the barracks. He and his women would be arriving momentarily. Black exited the study and went to the porch. He waited patiently for the carriage to bring his guests.

When the carriage came to a stop, Sonny set the steps and Hunter emerged first. He handed down his women, followed by Maryam. Looking up the steps at Black, he called, "Black, good to see you."

"Hunter," Black replied.

When his guests reached the landing, Black greeted the women.

"Mister Black," Suzanne said, "it is good to see you. Have you been well?"

"I have, Miss Suzanne, and how about you, have you been well?"

"I have and thank you for asking," Suzanne responded. "You know Nettie and my sister Maryam, don't you?"

"I do. Good afternoon, ladies, welcome to my home." He looked to Suzanne. "How is your mama?"

"Mama is well. She has gone to stay with a cousin," Suzanne replied.

"Good aftanoon, Mista Black," Nettie said.

"Good afternoon, Mister Black," Maryam added.

"Follow me." Black turned and led them inside.

In the dining room, Sunday came to him and Black introduced Hunter. "Darling, this is E.J., Jeremiah's brother."

"Nice to meet you, Mista E.J.," Sunday said.

Black smiled, because he was leaving Hunter to make the rest of the introductions. E.J. did not falter. "Miss Sunday, what a lovely name."

"Thank you," Sunday responded.

"I would like you to meet my wives. This is Suzanne, and this is Nettie," Hunter said, before adding, "And last, but not least, please meet my sister-in-law, Maryam."

"Good aftanoon, ladies, won't you join us?" Sunday said.

Black took in the sight before him. Hunter was dressed in brown trousers, a black sweater and black boots. On his hips, hung a gun holster—with no guns. Hunter looked, for once, as if he worked for a living. Nettie wore a light blue dress with a matching purse. Her black wooly hair was held in place by two fancy combs, and from her ears dangled silver earrings. Suzanne's dress was black, and her brown hair was pulled away from her face. Gold earrings suspended from her ears. It was also obvious that both women were heavy with child. Maryam was dressed the same as Suzanne. Black understood the sisters were still in mourning for their father.

Once the women settled with Sunday, Black headed back to the porch. Elbert, Jeremiah, Simon and James were walking toward the house. He and Hunter descended the stairs. Jeremiah, Black noticed, was happy to see his brother. Hunter stepped up, clapping Jeremiah on the back.

Simon being about business directed his words to Black. "The weatha betta than it's been for months—time we put Luke away."

James sighed. "I'll dig the grave."

"I'll help you," E.J. said.

James nodded his appreciation, and all the men walked to the graveyard.

❊ ❊ ❊

It was just getting dark when Sunday heard the men enter the foyer. Abby was talking and holding Otis. Seated at the table beside Abby were Miss Cora, Big Mama, Iris, and Anna. Little Elbert was holding onto a chair as he tried to keep up with Natalie. The kids saw the men and ran to them. Little Elbert cried, and James picked him up. Once in James' arms, he reached for his papa and Elbert took him.

Otis wiggled from Abby's lap and ran to Jeremiah. "Up, Miah, up!"

Jeremiah picked him up and Otis kissed his cheek. Elbert sat down so he could manage holding both Natalie and Little Elbert.

"Good evening, Miss Abby," said Jeremiah. "You look well."

Abby looked up and smiled weakly. "Evenin', Mista Jeremiah."

The black cracker smiled before he addressed the other women in the room. Black came over and stood behind Sunday's chair, placing a hand on her shoulder. She noticed her husband looked upset.

"What is it?" Sunday asked.

"We dug Luke's grave. We will bury him tomorrow," Black replied.

"Me and the women will cook tonight," Sunday said as she patted his hand.

As Sunday looked around the room her eyes fell on E.J., who was speaking with Suzanne and Nettie. He was handsome, but she imagined he could also be very threatening. She could readily see the resemblance between him and Jeremiah. Otis favored both men.

When the evening ended, Maryam stayed upstairs in a room next to Miss Cora's. Suzanne and Nettie stayed with E.J. in a cabin. Little Otis asked if he could go home with Jeremiah to see the baby. Before Jeremiah left, Otis ran back and kissed his Papa James and his Mama Elbert goodnight.

❧ ❧ ❧

James had not slept all night. At four in the morning, he dressed and headed for the barracks. The men had just finished a shift change, and the back door was propped open. The weather was mild and there was no smell of rain in the air. As he made his way down the aisle, he saw Anthony, standing at the back door looking out into the darkness.

Anthony must have heard him approaching. When James was close enough, he said, "Shit different now."

"Yeah, it is. I felt the same wit' Otis," James replied.

"But ya still got Black and Elbert," Anthony's voice cracked.

"You still got me, Black, and Elbert," James offered.

"Yeah," Anthony said.

Black, Elbert, and Shultz appeared at the front of the barracks, and James smiled.

"You got Shultz, too," he reminded him.

Anthony nodded and just then Gilbert, Frank, Lou, and Simon appeared. The ambassador had left his shift to come be with the men. James turned to Anthony.

"Let's go take care of Luke."

James let Anthony lead the way. They exited the barracks, and all the men from the mission were patiently waiting outside. They formed a solemn procession to the cemetery with Horace and Jake carrying torches.

At the gravesite, they spoke among themselves about freedom, family, love—and brotherhood. The men watched the birth of a new day, as the people of Fort Independence gathered around to pay their respects. As Luke's body was lowered into the earth, Black's voice rang clear.

"Let us continue to live well, so when death comes, there is no regret."

COMING SOON

ANTHONY:
UNSHACKLED

The Hen House
New York, September 1862

THE BLUE ROOM had a canopy bed large enough for five people. There were pillows everywhere, and the satin sheets were a powder blue. Anthony had two drinks in his ass, enough to dull the pain, but not enough to put his dick to sleep. He was seated in a blue, velvet-upholstered chair that put him in the mind of a throne. Standing before him was a brown-skinned, curvy woman, he figured to be about twenty summers. He had been to Miss Cherry's House of Comfort once or twice. The woman before him was fresh, not hard in appearance like the women who worked the pussy parlor back home.

Anthony didn't want to talk; he just wanted to ease into her body and feel something other than pain. He didn't even want to know her name, but he *would* keep her all night. She stood about five-feet, six-inches. Her hair was braided in one thick French braid with a blue ribbon at the end. She had dark eyes that seemed void of emotion, a small nose and big juicy lips. She lingered by the door and he liked the illusion of her innocence. She wore a black, gauzy gown that clung to her beautiful body. Her nipples were visible, and he thought her striking.

"You gonna help me undress?"

"Yes," she responded, her voice throaty, but hesitant.

He watched the sway of her hips, as she moved toward him. When she was close enough, he reached out for her. She accepted his hand, and he pulled her onto his lap. The woman smelled of roses, but it wasn't overpowering. He kissed her, and she accepted his tongue. When she whimpered, he pulled back and gazed at her. He touched her lips with the pad of his thumb, and she smiled nervously. He leaned in, kissing her again, and she was even more receptive. He groaned.

Anthony stood to his full height of six feet and allowed her to slide down his body. He removed his guns and placed them on a small table next to the chair. She reached up and unbuttoned his white shirt. When it fell to the floor, he removed his own trousers and boots. He was already hard, but he would pace himself. She was his for the night.

His manhood jutted out between them, and he took her by the hand and showed her how he wanted to be touched. The action caused him to close his eyes and revel in the feel of her fingers wrapped about him. It had been a while since he had been with a woman for he had been immersed in grief. He was in danger of spilling his seed where they stood. Backing away, he lifted her night dress over her head and carried her naked body to the bed. He climbed right between her legs and kissed her deeply.

Leaning down, he allowed his tongue to play with a brown nipple. She cried out, and Anthony found that while he did not want to know her name, he wanted her to know his.

"My name is Anthony," he said against her ear.

When he took her other nipple into his mouth, she panted, "Anthony–Anthony."

Hearing her chant his name almost brought him to conclusion, but he had a plan. He would sink deep within her, take the edge off and then enjoy the rest of the night. Placing himself at her core, he could feel the promise of her heat, and he pressed forward. Taking her mouth in a stormy kiss, he plunged deep within her sweetness, until he was buried to the hilt.

"Shit," he hissed, as she pushed at his chest trying to dislodge him.

"Ohhh," she cried out. "Anthony, ya hurt me."

Backing out of her tightness caused him to ache. He had not expected to find a virgin at a damn whorehouse. Dazed, he rolled off her and tried to collect himself.

"What's yo' name?"

He lay facing her, as she looked up at the ceiling. "Emma," she answered.

Anthony allowed her to pull the covers over her, but not before he saw the blood on her thighs. She cried softly as they lay in silence. He started to rise from the bed, not feeling good about the situation.

"Please give me another chance," she whispered, "I'll do betta."

He sighed. "How you come to be here?"

Emma looked afraid, but she did not answer. He stood and walked over to the window, naked. Looking down onto the dark street, he knew he needed to leave this place. He also knew he couldn't leave the girl. His mind was going through the floor plan of the gentleman's club on the first floor. Turning away from the window, he grabbed his clothes from the floor and began dressing. Emma sat up in bed wrapped in a sheet, watching him.

"Please," she said. "Are you gonna complain?"

His eyes narrowed. "How old is you?"

"Twenty summers."

He was relieved. "Get dressed."

She went to reach for the night gown and he asked, "Do you has anything else to wear?"

"No."

He stopped moving and glared at her. She looked away.

"You will leave here wit' me. This ain't no place for you."

"I cain't leave. They owns me," she answered, anxiously.

"Who is 'they'?"

She didn't answer, but he wouldn't leave her. He went back to dressing himself and when his guns were in place, he moved to the bed and yanked the sheet from the mattress.

"Cover yoself," he ordered.

Emma did as he asked, and he took her by the hand, leading her to the door. She pulled away from him.

"I cain't leave here; they will kill you."

Even if she wanted to stay, he wasn't going to allow it, but he asked anyway, "Ya wanna stay here?

"No."

Anthony nodded, and then backed away from all emotion. Taking her by the hand once more, he pulled the door open and stepped into the dimly lit corridor. An oil lamp sat on a table to the left of the door and just beyond the light, he could hear the moans of a satisfied customer. On the opposite end of the hall, he heard giggling. He moved toward the stairs with the Emma in tow. The combination of piano playing, and plush carpet helped drown out the frenzy of his foot falls.

At the top of the landing, he looked about. The steps curved to the right at the bottom, giving way to a well-lit parlor. The Hen House was an upscale brothel, and colored women were the main attraction. His back was to the wall as he dragged Emma along in his wake. Her steps faltered twice, and he had to stand her back on her feet. Holding her with his left hand kept his right hand free for business. He moved into the curve of the staircase, and out in front of him was the saloon. A few tables dotted the area. Beyond the tables, male patrons sat on overstuffed couches while scantily clad women vied for their coin.

Left of the bar, an older colored fellow played the piano accompanied by a young, dark-skinned woman who sang. She was dressed in nothing but yellow feathers. If the situation had been less stressful, Anthony would have appreciated the scene before him. His eyes fell to Jeremiah, who stood with his back to the bar. E.J. sat at a table a few feet away speaking with a white man in a dark suit. When Jeremiah spied him on the stairs, he moved, ever so slightly, away from the bar.

Anthony stepped down into the saloon and moved toward the entrance. He could see Frank posted up at the door, but not Lou. Still, Anthony knew Lou wasn't far. A white man wearing a brown suit stood and stepped forward. He had blond hair, small eyes and lips that were proportionate to the rest of his face. The man looked to be about forty summers, and his speech was educated.

"Boy, where is it you think you're going with Moonbeam?"

Anthony did not answer the question, countering with his own question. "How much for the girl?"

"You can't afford her," the man replied. "You aren't the first patron who has fancied himself in love with one of our girls."

E.J. walked over. "I will pay for the girl. What is the price?"

The man in the brown suit never took his eyes from Anthony. "Moonbeam isn't for sale, gentlemen. Let's stop here and go back to having a good evening."

Anthony glanced at Jeremiah who had turned his back toward his brother. The black cracker spoke calmly to the bartender. "Get yo' damn hands on the bar."

The man in the brown suit looked at Emma. "Moonbeam, honey," he said in a patronizing tone, "look at the trouble you're causing. Get back upstairs until I come for you."

Anthony's grip tightened on her wrist as he made for the front door. The music and singing stopped. The woman dressed in the yellow feathers disappeared through a door behind the piano.

When the man in the brown suit reached for his gun, Anthony

drew his weapon and shot the older fellow twice in the chest. Emma screamed and began hopping up and down. Anthony stepped to his victim and shot him once more, making certain the job was done.

He dragged Emma toward the door as Jeremiah brought the bartender down with one shot between the eyes. E.J., in the meantime, shot a man seated on the couch with two women. Jeremiah went over to E.J.'s companion still seated at the table and knocked him unconscious.

"This way!" Frank called out.

They all made for the door, and Lou was out front with a carriage he had stolen. Frank drove, and Lou covered him. Anthony, Jeremiah and E.J. climbed into the carriage after tossing a shrieking Emma inside. The darkness engulfed them, still men pursued them on horseback. Stray bullets rang out, but Frank kept the carriage moving. They broke away, headed for upper New York, with the men inside the carriage taking turns shooting into the darkness from the windows.

The carriage continued at a break neck speed. When they thought they were in the clear, one of the horses collapsed from a gunshot. Frank yelled, "Oooh shit!"

The other horses stumbled over the fallen animal, causing the carriage to shift violently to the left. Suddenly the cab itself began rolling, and Black's first rule popped into Anthony's head. *Business and ass don't go together.*

The carriage came to an abrupt and brutal stop against a tree. Anthony heard the girl moan as he lay in the blackness of the cab, taking inventory of his own person. When he found he wasn't injured, he asked, "Emma, ya alright?"

"I think so," she whispered.

"Jeremiah–E.J.!" Anthony called out.

"I'm good," Jeremiah answered.

"Yeah," E.J. said.

Jeremiah climbed out of the carriage; Anthony followed and called out for Frank and Lou.

Both brothers answered to his relief. They needed to keep moving. Frank put two of the horses down. The other two animals were cut loose and taken along. They headed on foot to the nearest farm where an old white man sold E.J. a rickety carriage and two older horses. The price he paid was robbery, but he couldn't haggle. The old man's wife took mercy on Emma, giving her a dress and boots that were too tight.

Lou took over driving the new carriage, and Frank covered him. The small posse headed for Canada. They had been traveling for about thirty minutes, when E.J. asked the question everyone was thinking.

"Which one of us is going to explain this shit to Black?"

CPSIA information can be obtained
at www.ICGtesting.com
Printed in the USA
LVHW030857200322
713908LV00001B/23